FALL OF HEROES

BOOK THREE
OF
THE GALILEE FALLS TRILOGY

JENNIFER HARLOW

DEVIL ON THE LEFT BOOKS

COPYRIGHT

Devil on the Left Books
Copyright © 2015 by Jennifer Dowis
All Rights Reserved
First Edition

ISBN-10: 0989394492
ISBN-13: 978-0-9893944-9-9
Library of Congress Control Number: 2015916496
Devil on the Left Books, Peachtree City GA

ALSO BY JENNIFER HARLOW

THE GALILEE FALLS TRILOGY

Justice

Galilee Rising

Fall of Heroes

THE F.R.E.A.K.S. SQUAD SERIES

Mind Over Monsters

To Catch a Vampire

Death Takes A Holiday

High Moon

The Sin Eater (Out 2016)

THE MIDNIGHT MAGIC MYSTERY SERIES

What's A Witch To Do?

Werewolf Sings The Blues

Witch Upon A Star

A HART/MCQUEEN STEAMPUNK ADVENTURE

Verity Hart Vs The Vampyres

For Joe Conte, attorney extraordinaire

A true crusader for justice.

With my eternal gratitude.

"An old Cherokee told his grandson,
'My son there is a battle between two wolves inside us all.
'One is Evil. It is anger, jealousy, greed, resentment,
inferiority, lies, and ego.
'The other is Good. It is joy, peace, love, hope, humility,
kindness, empathy and truth.'
The boy thought about it, and asked,
'Grandfather, which wolf wins?'
The old man replied,
'The one you feed.'"

-Author Unknown

I'm alive. Goddamn it, I'm alive. No.

Staring up at the stars, every centimeter of my body is awash in agony, I attempt to wrap my brain around this disturbing fact. I'm alive. How did this happen? I was ready. More than ready. I wanted to die. I was prepared. I let go. I needed to die.

I curl into a ball on the sandy shore, my mangled, now non-existent hand tucked inside my torn shirt, and sob until my eyes and lungs scream in pain like the rest of my traitorous body. I haven't sobbed this hard since Jo told me about my family. Rebecca. Daisy. My sweet Daisy. Murdered because of me. Because of who I am. I was going home to them. To Mom and Dad. Gunshots, a beating, falling thirty stories into a river, and still I live. I failed. Again. Why? Why? *Why does God hate me? It was to save her. They know who I am now or soon will. She'll never be safe again. None of them will. Lucy. Dobbs. Shannon. Every villain will come after them. Lucy's still unable to leave the mansion without being sedated. And Jo...*

A flash of my best friend holding onto the fence, terrified, seconds away from death because of me, fills my mind. My every sense. A waking nightmare.. I've almost broken her so many times before without knowing it. She loved me, and I was too stupid to notice. I flaunted my girlfriends in front of her. I couldn't...return her love. I lied for years and still she stood by my side. She was ready to give her life for mine. She's suffered so much for me, and I couldn't even do this one thing for her. She'd be better off without me.

When there are no more tears, when I'm done cursing God and my own pathetic ineffectiveness, and I can finally breathe again, I fall onto my back and stare up at the clear, starry sky once more. This is my penance. Life is my penance.

For not saving them. For lying to her. For not having the strength to push them all away when I knew the moment I slipped on that mask, the path I chose would lead them all into ruin. To agony. To the arms of death for the simple crime of loving me.

Never again.

I know what I have to do. I will *have the strength to do it. She's told me she cannot live without me. She truly believes it. She's a fighter. A survivor. She's wrong. I...just don't know if* I *can live without* her. *So many times she's been my strength. My hope. She always thought I saved her the night we met, but she had it so wrong.* So *wrong. And now she'll see that.*

Protocol No Exit.

Justin Pendergast AKA Justice died tonight. He died saving his best friend. He died showing her what he could never put into words. That she was the most important person in the world to him. That he loved her more than himself. That she was worth the sacrifice.

That is my penance for my vanity. My weakness. My blindness. To exist in this dark, polluted world with only half my soul. Without hope. Without her.

God's justice. It finds us all.

CHAPTER ONE

WEDDING BELL BLUES

I swear to fucking Christ, if he's late for this wedding, a supervillain won't kill him, I will.

If your boyfriend is the premier superhero in the city with the highest concentration of the super-powered in the country, you get used to situations like this. Dinners where you find yourself sitting alone in a restaurant, cancelled vacations, missing birthdays. I've endured them with a smile and forgiveness, but not today. I've stressed to him a thousand times how important this day is to me. Just this morning, before my hair appointment, I told him three times. But no, when I got home to put on my dress, he was nowhere to be found. I had to start up the comms on Doris Jr. to track him down. Sure enough he was out in the field fighting Hexen and more of the villains damn zombies at a war reenactment. Still, he *swore* he'd be here on time. Trust me, he said. Damn superheroes. Guess it's partially my fault for falling in love with one. Again. I should have learned the first time around. Damn you for being so amazingly brilliant, Jem Ambrose. Damn you.

"What are you still doing out here?" my old partner Cam, Detective Terrence Cameron to you, says behind me. I spin around just as he reaches me on the bottom of the church steps. He looks damn fine today, the white shirt off-setting his dark skin, and he's even sporting the paisley blue silk tie I bought him two Christmases ago. "You should get inside. It's freezing."

"I'm not going inside without him."

"You catching pneumonia won't make him show up any sooner," Cam points out.

"If he shows up at all," I mutter. "Fucking Hexen."

"He'll be here," Cam insists.

Two stragglers hustle toward us from the overflowing parking lot. I recognize the man, former plainclothes now Detective Conover, who worked the Alkaline case with me. He and his date both smile and nod as they pass us up the church steps.

"Seriously, Jo, come on. The ceremony's supposed to start soon. And—"

"I *can't* go in there without him, okay? This shit's awkward enough for me already. Just…I'll give him a few more minutes then I'll come in. These things never start on time anyway."

"Fine. I'll just tell everyone…I'll figure something out." I nod at my friend who nods back before returning inside the warm church.

Dead. Jem is so fucking dead. And I get he's saving people's lives, I do. Most of the time I'm on the comms in our apartment, guiding him, literally watching his back on the surveillance feed. Hell, I'm the one who suggested he become the new Captain Moonlight. I should have kept my damn mouth shut.

It's not as if we had tons of free time on our hands before. I had to cancel my fair share of dinners too. Being the figurehead of an international billion dollar empire with the board meetings, charity events, and general boring day-to-day business bullshit leaves little time to sleep let alone spend quality time with the man I love. Add to that Jem's day job at the hospital, his research for his new virus project, and the city constantly being in peril from asshole villains, we're lucky to spend a few hours a week face to face just being a damn couple. At least we make those few precious hours count. And we do work damn well together. Just last week we stopped an eco-terrorist cell from releasing a toxin in the meat packing district that would poison anyone who consumed the meat. If this were any other day I'd be on Doris Jr. helping him bring down Hexen, but this isn't any other day. He needs to be here. He has to be here. He will be here. He *will*. Unless of course he's…no.

God, why does my mind always go there? I have personally seen him survive multiple gunshots, being impaled by a rod, being beaten to a pulp, and an explosion. He has super-healing, super-intelligence, has a black belt in Judo and Karate, knows Krav Maga, not to mention the suit I commissioned for him is bullet, knife, and flame resistant. But every time I lose contact or he's a minute late, that is my first damn thought.

I should be used to this by now. I knew what he was before I fell in love with him. Hell, I had a front row seat to that side of his life. I ended up in the hospital twice because of it, well three times if you count the plastic surgery needed to fix the scar on my face left by his brother. Not to mention the horrible minute when I thought he'd died that day. I lost my soul mate, my best friend to a supervillain, I couldn't handle another man I loved dying for me.

We should have learned our lesson then. Jem killed Lord Nightingale right along with his psycho twin brother, and that should have been it. No more capes and cowls. No more kidnappings, attempted murders, and torture for either of us.

Yeah, that lasted all of three months. The crime rate skyrocketed again, there was a supervillain attack every week, and despite his assurances he was content fighting crime behind our supercomputer Doris, I knew he was lying. It was in the way he'd stay glued to the computer and news. The way he'd stare out the window down at the city when he couldn't sleep. How he spent more and more time in his dojo beating up the punching bag and dummy. He couldn't help it. He'd fought the good fight for almost a decade. Before me, it was all he had. It was what got him out of bed. Something else we had in common. He couldn't deny that part of himself, it was literally in his blood, and I know the longer he repressed that for me, the more he'd resent me down the road. So one night I shoved his new black and yellow costume at him, and told him I wanted him back before dawn. That was three months ago. Crime's gone down twenty-two percent, two new villains are now rotting in Xavier Maximum Security Prison, they've just released the new Captain Moonlight action figure, and I'm freezing my ass off worrying about the man I love. Doing the right thing sucks balls.

Shit. He's not coming. He's not. I'm going to have to go in there and face all those people alone. All their whispering, their looks, their stares. How am I going to explain his absence? Fuck. Damn it. I need to get in there. Me being out here just looks worse. With a sigh, I start up the steps. Jem Ambrose you are—

"Joanna!"

Here. Thank Christ. Never had a doubt.

I spin back around and just like that, with one look at him, all my anger vanishes, replaced with pure love. I even smile. Oh, he must have worn his suit under the costume it's so creased and wrinkled. His curly dark brown hair isn't much better with three cowlicks in back and tendrils plastered to his forehead. Looking at this skinny, pale, disheveled man no one would ever believe he could fend off an army of zombies or take down a supervillain. I didn't either at first. Of course now I regularly get to see him with those clothes off. There's nothing stringy or weak about him, just firmly defined muscles as sharp as his cheekbones. And a *great* ass. I've literally bounced a quarter off it. And it's all mine.

"I'm sorry," Jem says, rushing up to me. "I'm *so* sorry. Am I late? I—"

I silence his words with a sweet kiss. "You're just in time. As always." A huge grin stretches across his face bright enough to blind lesser humans. I smile back and straighten his tie. "Bad guy caught?"

"Down with one punch. Zombies took some doing, though. And the costume's a goner. It reeks."

"You're a little ripe yourself. Here." I open my purse and remove my perfume, squirting him. "It'll have to do. If anyone asks, we'll say you were in the cadaver lab."

"You think of everything, my love," he says, smile growing.

I reach inside my purse again and retrieve his spare pair of horn-rimmed glasses. "Yes, I do. You are damn lucky to have me, Jem Ambrose."

"Don't I know it." He slides the glasses on, sadly hiding those breathtaking sapphire blue eyes of his. "So, how do I look? Am I presentable?"

"Good enough."

"Gee, thanks."

"No time for ego stroking," I say, grabbing his hand. "The ceremony's about to start. Come on."

I drag him through the church doors and down the aisle to the third pew where Cam and his wife Tawney are saving our seats. A few people do stare and whisper, but I don't give a shit anymore. Mirabelle and his wife both nod as we sit. Oh thank Christ, it hasn't started yet. Harry O'Hara, my old boss and ex-boyfriend, stands at the front of the church as his best man fixes the groom's tie. I must catch his eye because when Harry faces forward, he smiles at me. I smile back. Yes, the woman who faced down two supervillains was afraid to walk into her ex-boyfriend's wedding alone. I'm a damn mystery to me too.

I'm forgotten seconds later when the music swells and Bella Harding begins walking down the aisle. Definitely an upgrade from yours truly. She isn't in love with another man like I was when I dated Harry. And if she ever cheats on him like I did, I will make her pay. But she won't. She's good people just like him. I even heard she's four months pregnant. Alls well and all that jazz.

And as my hard won friend pledges his eternal love to his blushing bride, I slip my hand into the man I love's hand and hold on. Not that he's going anywhere. For better or worse, he's all mine. And I don't have a doubt we'll live happily ever after too.

Me and my hero.

*

"No, it was seven," Jem says on the ride home. "Tawney asked twice."

"All I know is if one more person asked us 'When's the wedding?' I was gonna scream," I reply.

"It wasn't *that* bad."

"Well we were spared the biological clock countdown lecture at least," I say. "Why is it so hard for people to believe not every couple wants kids? That there's no need for us to rush down the aisle too? Hell, why get married at all nowadays?"

"I don't know. Standing before those closest to you pledging your fidelity and love to the person you treasure most in his world? That's a good reason, no?"

He's trying to keep his face neutral, but I can sense his discomfort prickling my skin. Can't have that. I wrap my arm in his and rest my head on his shoulder. "How on earth did I end up with a true romantic?"

"Just lucky I guess."

"Damn straight."

The taxi pulls up to our apartment building, and Jem supports me as I hobble—damn heels—to the elevator. Not to be rude, and because my romantic boyfriend loves to dance, we stayed until the end of the reception. My feet are punishing me for it now. Oh, all I want is a shower and to crawl into bed. One stop to make first. Jem rides all the way up to the penthouse floor, but I make a pit-stop two floors down. Dobbs opens his front door with a smile.

After I got out of the hospital six months ago, Jem brought me back to his apartment to take care of me, and I just never left. I never felt comfortable in Pendergast Manor. Too many ghosts, too many memories. It was really only mine in name only. Besides my clothes and a few DVDs and superhero goodies, I only brought one thing with me: Dobbs, the butler. There was no way in hell I was leaving him alone in that mausoleum, so I bought him an apartment in our building. It took a week to convince him to actually move in, but he's flourished since. He still insists on cleaning our apartment, once a butler always a butler I guess, but he's actually ventured out into the world. Going to movies, attending the symphony, I even think he had a coffee date with one of the ladies from his pottery class. Even his trips to the manor have grown further apart number.

I haven't decided what I'll do with the manor yet. Jem and I still use the "Chamber of Justice" as Jem calls it, when we need to do analysis on evidence, but we can semi-easily move all the equipment to a new location. And it's not like I haven't had offers to buy it, including one from the city to turn it into a historical landmark, I just…can't. Not yet. Like Pendergast Industries, and Dobbs, Justin entrusted me with its curation. With his family's legacy. The man gave his life for me, not letting a developer tear down his ancestral home to build condos is the least I can do. And in a way it was my home too. My sanctuary growing up. Where some of my happiest memories occurred. Some of the worst too. But that's the past. Justin's dead, and Justice has been replaced. But I'll be damned if they're forgotten.

"Hello, Miss Joanna," says Dobbs.

"Hi. I brought you some wedding cake."

"Oh, you sweet girl. You didn't have to do that," he says, taking the plate.

I shrug. "No biggie."

"Was the wedding lovely?"

"It was. A good time was had by all. And I've never seen Harry happier."

"He's a good man. He deserves it."

"That he does."

"And Dr. Ambrose? I saw on the news—"

"He's fine," I assure him. "Not a scratch."

"Thank God. And the preparations for his birthday celebration have been confirmed. They'll set-up the dinner table inside the labyrinth. There may be rain, so I added a tent to the order."

"Thank you."

"Of course."

My phone begins ringing inside my purse. Probably Lane, Pendergast's CEO, again. He's called three times in the last hour. Sure enough the phone's display confirms my suspicion. "I have to get this," I tell Dobbs.

"Of course. Tell Dr. Ambrose good night for me."

"I will. Sleep tight."

Not to be ruder, I wait until his door shuts before I answer. "Hello, Lane. What's up?"

"Where have you been? I've been trying to reach you all day."

"I was at a wedding. *And* it's Sunday. What the hell can't wait twelve hours?"

"I received a call from Bennett Stone earlier today. The deal might be in trouble."

I roll my eyes. "What? Why? We've been working on that deal for over six months. The government even rubber stamped it. It's a go."

"Stone personally called me, Joanna, to express his displeasure. I got the sense he somehow feels disrespected, like we haven't been taking this buy-out seriously."

"It's got to be a play. He's bluffing. He wants us to lower the price or something. In truth, after I reviewed the numbers, I was shocked Goliath offered as much as they did. Blackwater Pharmaceuticals sure as shit isn't worth five hundred million bucks. They have only produced one viable drug in fifteen years, and besides their gene therapy division, they're not exactly cutting edge."

"Exactly. And we've already allocated the money for other ventures in the pipeline. Without this deal we'll have to withdraw our bid for Telefirma Media with penalties."

"So what do we do?"

"You and I need to be there."

"No," I state emphatically.

"We *have* to be there, Joanna," he replies with equal force.

"I-I can't. Lane, no. It's Jem's birthday. I have a big thing planned. I can't—"

"And I'll be missing my daughter's cello recital. *Again.* It's five hundred million, Joanna. We don't have a choice."

Damn it. Fuck, fuckity, fuck fuck fuck. "Fine. Whatever. We'll work out the details tomorrow, okay? Just…fuck."

"Well put. I'll see you tomorrow. We'll phone Stone together once you've calmed down."

"And fuck you too. Bye." I end the call.

And the award for the world's shittiest girlfriend goes to…ugh. Now I wish Jem *had* missed the wedding. I wouldn't feel as damn guilty about missing his birthday. Thousands of dollars, weeks of planning, all down the crapper. I planned to kidnap him for the day. Wake him with a blow job, serve him breakfast in bed, spend the day on our boat *The Athena*, then his favorite dinner in the labyrinth at Austen Castle where we had our first non-date. I even bought new lingerie for desert. Bennett Fucking Stone throws a hissy fit, and it's all for nothing. Asshole.

The shower's running when I step into the penthouse. It hasn't changed much since I moved in, mostly because I didn't have much to contribute in the way of furniture. Nothing at Pendergast Manor was mine, and a year before a supervillain blew up my apartment, so besides the couch, lounge chair, and shelf filled with DVDs beside the TV, it's the same as when I first walked in. Gleaming hardwood floors, bookcases with a million books, telescope pointed out the panoramic window that overlooks Stan Lee Park, cathedral ceilings with skylights, all the same. I didn't feel the need to mess with something working already.

Without even kicking off my shoes, I fall face first onto our bed. With the worry, the wedding, putting what I believed were the final touches on the Goliath deal, and planning his birthday, I am exhausted. Jem and I haven't had more than a day off in five months and that was to recover from surgery. That's it. I'm calling it. As soon as possible, we're taking a damn vacation. Our last vacation was a rousing success. A week alone on *The Athena*. No phones, no e-mails, no people, no clothes most of the day. Just the open water, the sun, mind blowing sex, pillow talk, and plans for the future. Heaven on damn earth. Time to visit again. We've damn well earned a break.

The shower shuts off a few minutes later, and a minute after that, the scent of shampoo and soap wafts past me. "Are you asleep?" Jem whispers.

"Almost," I mutter. I sense him moving down the bed and gently removing my shoes. "Thank you, love."

"My pleasure, darling." I open my eyes and watch as he lets the towel slip off—yum—and changes into his purple silk pajamas. "Enjoying yourself there?" he asks before turning around with a mischievous grin.

"Of course. You know I love objectifying you."

"Any chance of returning the favor tonight?"

"Only if you don't mind the corpse pose. It's all I can muster tonight."

"I've had more than my fair share of corpses this day, thank you very much." Jem climbs onto our bed beside me and scoots down so we're eye level. God, he is a sexy beast. Not classically handsome like Justin was, very few men are, but with those sharp cheekbones, full lips, and long eyelashes, you wouldn't kick him out of bed for eating crackers as Pop liked to say. My father would have loved Jem.

"Did you enjoy yourself tonight?" I ask.

"Immensely. You? It wasn't too awkward? No…old stirrings? Regret?"

I pretend to consider the possibility. "Well…" I say sarcastically. His eyes narrow playfully before I chuckle. "Of course not, you idiot." I run my finger across his cheek. "You know, *I'm* the one who should be insecure here. You're the practically perfect one with legions of women writing you love notes pledging their undying love, oh captain my captain."

"You're right. I must go to them. Now." He sits up, but I yank him back, both of us laughing the entire time. I scooch up and over to rest my head on his chest as he wraps his arm around my torso. He kisses my forehead.

"You may actually want to take one of them up on their offers," I say. "I'm going to have to miss your birthday."

"What?"

"Lane called. The Goliath deal hit a snag. We have to fly to Independence to smooth it out. I'm sorry."

"It's okay," he assures me.

"No," I wince, "it's not. You rented a helicopter for my birthday. I had this whole day planned and…" I sigh. "I suck."

"I don't care. *Really*. I'd rather simply forget the whole day like I have for well over a decade."

"You wanted to forget it because to you it wasn't a big deal. The day you were born is a big deal to me. It's important. You've done a lot of good for countless people, none more so than me. You should get a damn parade, and instead I'll be hundreds of miles away, and you'll work all day then get your ass beat by junkies and goons. I'd invite you to come, but I'll be working the whole time. I'll be lucky if I see the inside of my hotel room."

"Joanna, don't torment yourself up about it. We can celebrate when you get home. I've missed a lot of your events too. All that matters is when it *is* important, we are there for one another. And in that, you have never failed me. Not once."

I run my finger across his lips, which brings a smile to them. "I don't deserve you. I really don't."

"You have it reversed there, my darling love," he says kissing my fingertips. "But you're stuck with me. Right?"

I lean over and kiss him. Deeply. God, can this man kiss. The toe curling, heat inducing, cat in heat writhing sensation he draws from me with just the touch of his lips, three times better than any drug or drink out there. Oh, how I love this man. I break apart first and smile. "For a million nights, then a million more."

"Promise?" he asks, insecurity painting each syllable.

I stare into those sapphire eyes and see all the way down to his battered soul. Into the darkness life's infected inside him. For so long it was all he had. It fueled him. I know because I was the same. Angry, hopeless, dead in all but body.

Sometimes I look at him and can't believe he's real. That he's beside me. That this brilliant, astonishing man loves *me*. I don't trust it. I don't trust it won't be snatched away from me like everything else I ever loved. But I trust *him*. I love him and trust him with every fiber of my being. He's my best friend, my partner, my savior. And I'll be damned if *I* cause him a millisecond of pain or doubt.

"Marry me."

His eyes narrow in disbelief as at the same time a smile forms on those magical lips. "What?"

"You heard me. Marry me."

The smile dissipates a little. "Really?"

"Hell yes." I press my hand to his cheek, grinning like an idiot. "*Marry me.*"

A hundred emotions pass across those eyes of his. Disbelief, confusion, fear, then bliss. Pure as if sent by the angels themselves bliss. Tears spring out, as does a laugh. "Thought you'd never ask."

After another guffaw, he grabs my neck and pulls my lips against his in a fierce kiss before breaking away again. I wipe his still streaming tears as mine threaten to fall too. "I love you," I whisper with a small smile.

"Nowhere near as much as I love you," Jem whispers back, serious as a tempest.

"Say it again," I order.

"I love you."

"And again."

"I love you."

"Once more with feeling."

He cradles my face in his long, soft hands, eyes boring into mine. "Joanna Fallon, you have blessed my life in ways you cannot fathom. You are my heart, my soul, you are...my hero. You have given me pure, true, once in a lifetime love, and I thank you for every moment of it. I love you tonight, tomorrow night, a million nights then a million more, Joanna Fallon. *I love you.*"

"Then I guess you better marry me, huh?"

Our grins grow in tandem before he kisses me again. And again. And again. He brings me back to life, and we celebrate the proper way.

All my life I believed I wasn't good enough. Not for my mother, not for Justin, not for anyone. How wrong I was. How wrong I will never be again. Because he'll set me right. He'll help me up when I fall, as I will him. And if there is any justice in the world, we'll get our million nights and a million more.

We've earned them.

CHAPTER TWO

THE VIOLET HOUR

It's too big. Gaudy almost. Of course by billionaire standards it's a crackerjack ring. Barely two carats with a platinum band. People might not even suspect it *is* an engagement ring. Though it is a diamond ring, they're colored diamonds, the exact same shade of blue as my beloved's eyes, in a multi-layered flower pattern that to me resembles more of a snowflake than blossom. I love it though. Found it at the first store we went to last night. My fiancée put up no fight when I suggested we shut off our phones, computers, and basically vanish for the day in celebration. In the end we just stayed in our penthouse, in bed, until he insisted it wouldn't be official until I had a ring. He's such a traditionalist. In my mind we're already together in every way that matters. A piece of jewelry, a piece of paper and a few words from a priest won't change a damn thing. But it means the world to him, which is why I asked in the first place. I do almost have him agreeing to a quick justice of the peace ceremony when I return from this trip. Just him and me. All I need.

"Will you please pay attention?" Lane snaps beside me in the limo.

"Why? We spent hours going over this on the plane."

"Because you missed all the meetings, all the preparation sessions yesterday, and there are a million tiny details you need to know."

"Oh, please. We all know I'm little more than window dressing. As always I'll say all of twenty words, smile, and make Stone feel important because the infamous Joanna Fallon took time between supervillain kidnappings to meet him. If he's lucky, I may even remove my cardigan so he can see the acid burn scar. Hell, maybe he'll just ask to see it like those Tamagotchi men did."

"You make it sound like you're a mascot," Lane says.

"You do more than that," my assistant Shannon insists.

"No, *you* just make it seem like I do," I say truthfully.

I'm the first to admit I have no idea what I'm doing. I barely passed high school, and there are precious few transferable skills between police officer and figurehead of an international conglomerate. Dividends, gross versus net profit, tax shelters, it goes way over my head. Don't know what the hell Justin was thinking leaving his shares to me. I'm not good at it, I don't particularly like any of it, but Justin trusted me with his legacy and I owe him far more than I can ever repay in twelve lifetimes. So I'll be their dancing monkey for as long as they need me to be.

Today my monkey moves are all for Bennett Stone, CEO of Goliath Industries. I did do my homework on him. Thirty-five, never married, spent the last fifteen years at the top of Independence's Top Ten Bachelor's List. Loves fast cars, fine honeys, and even climbed Mt. Kilimanjaro. Twice. Took control of Goliath after earning his MBA at age twenty-three, the same age Justin was when he took the reins. Also like Justin he inherited the business as a tender teen when his parents died in a super related incident. Stone's parents and seven-year-old sister were crushed by debris while inside their limo during a battle between Bruiser and Hippomatus when the boy was just fifteen. He was inside the car too. Trapped for almost four hours with the bodies of his parents, who were killed instantly. His sister Molly wasn't so lucky. She died around hour three, reportedly as her brother cradled and comforted her. Justin had to watch his father die too but on the television. To be right there? Covered in their blood? Being unable to save his sister? Fuck me. But what from the clippings in the dossier it appears he managed to overcome whatever demons the incident spawned to become a well-rounded, shallow, billionaire playboy. We're in my wheelhouse now.

The Goliath Tower lives up to its name. The tallest building in our country's capital is fifty stories tall, ten more than any other building or monument. The builders are hard at work on about the fifth floor repairing the gray masonry and windows on three levels as we pull up. Collateral damage from the brawl between White Knight and The Nothing Man last week. Saw a clip on the news. Hell, every other building on this street is getting repaired. I know their pain. At least every other year some part of the Pendergast building gets demolished in one of these battles. Last year the whole building almost went up when my future brother-in-law planted a bomb in the boiler room. Jem defused it but five percent of our workforce quit within a week. Places like this might as well have targets literally painted on them. I know Jem does his best to keep his damage to a minimum, but it's hard to do when one is literally fighting for their life.

We're escorted through the lobby to the elevator by Stone's assistant Lena, who takes us up to the fiftieth floor while making small talk about the weather. Snow's expected tomorrow. I swear if we get snowed in, I'm going to be pissed. I only know two people in the city, and one is walking the catwalks in Milan. Alexia "Lexie" Darby, formally Lady

Liberty, and I have kept in contact after she moved back to Independence. Mostly phone calls and e-mails with the occasional lunch if we're in the same town. She's been keeping busy with work of the official variety, modeling non-stop all over the world. I was much the same after Justin died. Work, work, work as a Band-Aid for a broken heart. Blowing up her husband's murderer hopefully helped too. I did eventually tell Jem what she did. I didn't want any secrets between us. He took it well. "She did what she felt was necessary. What I couldn't," were his exact words. I just wish she would reach out to Jem. They were teammates for years. Friends. She says the wound is still too raw. He says he understands, but I can tell her rebuff stings. Maybe a wedding will bring her round.

Besides Dobbs, Lexie, my cousins, and aunt and uncle, the only other person I'd really want at the courthouse with us is Lucy Helms, Justin's aunt. Like Lexie, she fled Galilee for Independence after a loved one died. Don't blame either of them. I wouldn't call Lucy and me close. In fact, for years, I thought she hated me, the guttersnipe her nephew literally picked up from the side of the road. But when push comes to shove, when it really matters, she's always been there. Kicking my ass. Making me see sense. She was more of a mother to me than my own ever was. I'm going to surprise her after the meeting. She hates surprises.

The elevator doors finally open and once again we follow Lena to the conference room. It's a damn good thing I'm not afraid of heights because an entire wall is nothing but glass overlooking the city. In the distance I can even make out the arch of The National Monument near the President's Mansion. Not that there'll be much time to enjoy the view what with the binder the size of a novel we have to review before the deal gets finalized. I'm falling asleep already.

We're the first to arrive, but within minutes, others filter in. Our lawyer, Goliath's three lawyers, their CFO who starts reminiscing about business school with Lane, and other executives one right after the other. They outnumber us two to one. And even they begin growing restless when ten minutes pass and Stone doesn't show. At twenty all but the lawyers start texting and calling him. Thirty, I'm halfway through the binder and even understand twenty percent of it. The assistant Lena comes in every five minutes with apologies but no answers. Fifty minutes and I'm about to murder someone. Before that happens, I excuse myself to the restroom.

After the usual bathroom activity, I check myself in the mirror. Having to get up at three AM to make our flight does nothing for my pale skin. Even caked with concealer my blue eyes are rimmed with dark circles just a few shades lighter than my curly black hair. My friend Bitsy is always on me to straighten my unruly mop, but I don't have that kind of patience. I have taken her advice in other areas, namely clothes. It's damn hard for a jeans and t-shirt type of gal to fit into fashionista land, which is why I rely on Bitsy and my personal shopper Isolde to tell me what to wear. Today it's a simple black dress, knee high boots, white polka dot cardigan with black accents, and one strand of long pearls. I'm an elegant bitch. And I'm leaning more toward bitch every minute that prick doesn't show. I fluff my hair and reapply my red lipstick regardless.

Seriously, the fucking nerve of his asshole. Playboys. I much prefer working with professionals whose livelihood is actually tied to how well deals like this end. Stone's entire company can go belly up and he could still buy his own private island. I'll bet Justin never pulled shit like this, and he moonlighted as a superhero. Maybe Stone has an alter-ego too. If I remember my statistics correctly there are three superheroes in Independence since The Royal Triumvirate left: Bronco, Rayna, and White Knight. I guess Nemesis could be considered a hero as she only attacks pedophiles and rapists, but she's more vigilante than superhero. Keep up the good work though, babe. Anyway, right now I don't care if Stone's part of the cape and cowl brigade. He needs to get his ass here before *he* needs a hero to save him from *me*.

I meander back toward the conference room, my anger growing with each step. This is serious, unprofessional bullshit. I'm missing my fiancée's birthday for *this*? I would never—

The elevator dings behind me, and just as I spin around, the man of the hour steps out. In spite of the mussed chestnut brown hair and askew tie, Bennett Stone is a damn fine looking man in a Senatorial way. Big brown eyes, flawless nose, awe shucks half smile directed straight at me. His boyish good looks probably diffuse many an uncomfortable situation, but right now I want to bruise the bastard. "Ms. Fallon. Hello, I—"

"An hour," I snap.

"I beg your pardon?" he asks.

"We have been waiting for you for a goddamn hour, asshole. I woke up at three in the fucking morning, flew hundreds of miles, and *I* managed to get here on time. At your behest. I should be at home with my fiancée celebrating his birthday. Had a whole day planned. Reservations, vendors, weeks of planning and thousands down the fucking drain because you felt disrespected. You don't even know the meaning of the word. If you demand respect, you damn well better be willing to return the gesture." The man stares at me, that smile actually growing as I continue my tirade. It damn well better be a defense mechanism because if he thinks this is a joke, I will rip those lips right off. "I'm sorry, do you think this is funny?"

"No, I don't," he assures me, "I'm sorry. I just…you certainly live up to your reputation, Ms. Fallon," he chuckles. "I can see why supervillains cower in your presence."

"Well, if you wanted your ass kissed instead of kicked, you should have been here when you said you would be."

"And I would have been except my fourteen-year-old goddaughter overdosed late last night and I've been with her mother and father, who also happens to be my cousin and best friends, at the hospital. I didn't want to leave until she was out of the woods."

Oh, fuck.

My face boils red from the mortification properly due. My mouth flops open and closed like a dying fish for several seconds. "I-I-I'm sorry. I had no idea."

"Nathalie's been fodder for the local tabloids so we've been keeping things quiet otherwise I would have had Lena inform you all. Even she doesn't know."

"Well, she won't, uh, hear it from me. I'm truly sorry for my outburst and your troubles."

"Thank you. Nathalie will be fine, at least physically. They're researching rehab facilities now."

"Well, I can personally recommend Whitegate Center in Norwalk. They helped *me* tremendously."

"I will pass that on. Thank you," he says sincerely.

"Welcome. And here…" I straighten his tie, trying to ignore the full force of that panty dropping smile of his. "Now you're respectable."

"Wouldn't go that far, Ms. Fallon," he quips. I do smile back. "Best not keep the others waiting any longer."

"After you."

Goddamn, I am an asshole. I can't look at him as we walk into the conference room or as we take our places across the conference table. Bennett has no such qualms. Out of the corner of my eye, I notice him alternating between smiling and staring to catch my attention. I throw a few smiles and reverent nods back between reviews of the fine print. Yeah, I would so rather be on a boat with my fiancée than fake flirting with a billionaire to quell my guilt and embarrassment.

Around one in the afternoon we break for the day, well everyone but the lawyers. All terms and provisos have been hammered out with minimal fuss and bloodshed. I contributed exactly one suggestion during the whole process. I absolutely didn't need to be here, but then again I never do. At least it's just Independence not Tokyo or Berlin. Twenty-four hours and I'll be home. I cannot fucking wait. I rise from the table along with everyone else. Of course not everyone else gets cornered by our host. Stone rounds the table as we all pack up. "So, what are your plans for the rest of the day?" he asks.

"Room service and porn?" I quip.

"A woman after my own heart," he hits back with that puppy adorable grin. "Do you mind if I ask you to postpone the festivities for an hour or so? Let me take you out to lunch. There's a fantastic restaurant in your hotel. Well, *my* hotel. You can check in, freshen up, and meet me down there. What do you say?"

"I-I don't think—"

"Just lunch," he says, holding up his hands. "I only want to pick your brain. I know you've been through something similar to what Nathalie has. I was hoping you could give me some insight. We're all more than out of our depths here. Please?"

Goddamn it, there go the puppy dog eyes. Ugh, I'm such a softie. "Okay. Give me half an hour."

"You are a goddess among men, Joanna Fallon."

"Okay, just…lay off the charm, playboy. I'm immune."

Without hesitation he takes my hand, kissing the top like a courting gentleman. The audacity makes me chuckle and even blush. "We'll see," he says, peering up through his long lashes. He drops my hand and nods. "See you in half an hour, gorgeous." With one final smirk, Stone strides out of the conference room. I just shake my head and sigh.

Okay, if this were a year ago my panties would already be on the floor. He was exactly my type: handsome, cocky, and a total asshole. We can spot our own kind. Another bad habit I somehow cured myself of with a little help from AA and Jem Ambrose. It's still flattering. I stare down at my engagement ring, which I didn't know I'd been playing with all this time. Yeah, those days are over with. Thank God. Why settle for fast food when you have prime rib at home? And I am full.

*

After checking into my five star accommodations, compliments of Goliath, I change into my civvies: black slacks and dark green sweater with my Justice Trench coat. The moment my good deed's done, I'm off to surprise Lucy. She'll so hate that. I can hardly wait to see her face when I tell her I'm getting hitched. I think we both thought I'd end up one of those old spinsters who spit on children and had an apartment full of newspapers stacked to the ceiling. She'll be happy for me. The three of us had dinner a while ago, and she pulled me aside to give her approval, something not easily earned from that woman. I'm not even sure *I* have it.

But first things first. Lunch with the panty dropper. He's already waiting at our table, texting on his phone as the hostess escorts me there. Cue that smile of his. He even rises to pull out my chair. "Thank you," I say as I sit.

"No, thank you," he responds. "I just got a text from my cousin. They're releasing Nathalie tomorrow. Graham and CeCe have already contacted Whitegate Center. They just have to convince her to go."

"Well, since she's a minor, they can legally force her to. But I wouldn't recommend that. She has to *want* to go. She has to want to get better."

"What made you want to get better?" he asks. "If that's not too personal."

"No, it's okay. I don't know. A lot of reasons. I cheated on my boyfriend? I was hurting the people I cared about? I was becoming my mother? Mostly, I think, it was Justin."

The waiter pops by to fill our water goblets. "Justin?"

I wait until he's gone. "Yeah. I mean, he *died* for me. He literally threw his life away for mine. And how was I honoring him? Drinking, screwing around, hurting people? I owed him more than that. A hell of a lot more."

"So you got sober for him?"

I shrug. "I got sober for a lot of reasons that was just the biggie. I'm not going to lie and claim on occasion I don't crave booze like air, especially when life gets nuts, but I don't give in because I know I'm a better person sober. And I've never been happier. So whatever her reason, family, friends, seeing her favorite band in concert, you need to help her find it and support her on every step of her new path. But *she* has to want to take those steps to sobriety."

"Thank you," Bennett says sincerely.

I pick up the menu. "You can thank me by being there for her. She can't do it alone."

"Who can?" he asks, picking up his menu as well.

The waiter promptly returns and we place our orders, burger and fries for us both. I raise my eyebrow when he orders that. "What?"

"Nothing, I just…you don't strike me as a burger and fry kind of guy."

"What sort of guy do I strike you as?" he asks, amused already.

"You know. Fine food, fine wine, fine honeys. You are part of the Silver Spoon Brigade."

"What, Pendergast and Ambrose never ate with just tin silverware?"

"Not until I broadened their horizons and brought them into the muck with us mere mortals."

"And if I want to wrestle in the mud with you too?"

I hold up my engagement ring. "Sorry, playboy, my ring's closed."

"Not necessarily. I've found there are many degrees of engagement."

"Well, I am as engaged as one can be. So like I said, save the charm."

"Can't blame a guy for trying, especially with someone so fun to play with. There's nothing I admire more than a quick wit. Keeps things interesting."

"My fiancée would agree with you," I say.

"And I assume this fiancée is Dr. Jonathan Ambrose?"

"The one and only."

Bennett shakes his head. "The fierce, infamous, scourge of supervillains everywhere marrying a man who actually wears a pocket protector? Really?"

"Excuse me?"

"I'm sorry but he's so…dull. I've met him a dozen times at events. Brilliant without question. He earned the hospital a lot of money with his patents, but the man's a wallflower. A nerd."

"Can you please stop insulting my fiancée?"

"Sorry. I just cannot for the life of me see the woman who took down two supervillains sitting at home every night talking about dragons in Klingon or whatever he's into."

I sip my water. "Not a lot of talking goes on. Mostly we just fuck. The man's a stallion in bed."

To his credit, Bennett actually laughs and shakes his head. "It's always the quiet ones." Still shaking his head, he sips his water too. "You never can tell with people. Not really. Take Justin. We went to college together, you know? I was a year ahead of him, but we were in the same Frat. Think we even dated the same girl at the same time. Never had a damn clue he was a super. None."

"That makes two of us," I say.

"He really didn't tell you? Even when that psychopath was after you? Not to speak ill of the dead, but who does that?"

"He had his reasons," I say. "I wasn't exactly his alter ego's biggest fan. Or a fan of supers in general. I was basically a bigot."

"Why?"

"Stupid bullshit reasons like every other bigot. Justice didn't save my Pop. Too much collateral damage to people and the city. Heroes breed villains. Like I said, bullshit. I was just angry at life, and it came out that way."

"I wouldn't call your reasons bullshit. I mean, billions of dollars in property damage a year? Hundreds of citizens killed a year caught in the crossfire? *That* is definitely not bullshit."

Crap. I forgot his family was said collateral damage. Me and my damn mouth. "No, you're right. I mean, hello, aren't we the poster children for super collateral damage? I still have nightmares about that rooftop. That boat."

"Me too," he says. "Yet, I sense a 'but' coming on."

"*But* having known them, having worked with them, I discovered supers are exactly like us. Just doing the best they can with what life's given them. They worry about money, about love, about if they left the oven on at home. Even those who put on the mask. They don't *have* to go out there and risk their lives for perfect strangers, but they do. They didn't ask to be born with their powers. Most don't even like having them."

"I just don't think they should be held to a lower standard than us mere mortals," Bennett says. "Their actions should have consequences. And they sure as hell shouldn't be worshiped as gods. I just read about a new cult in town. The Fellowship of the Triumvirate. It's just so fucking pathetic." Jem and Lexie will get a kick out of that, being worshiped as gods. "Sorry," Bennett continues. "I know you worked with them. Of course they also almost got you killed so..." He shrugs. "But regardless, as a citizen of Independence, I personally thank you for bringing down that psycho Cain. I was at two events he decided to crash. My ex-girlfriend still has respiratory problems from the gas he released. She actually had to have a lung transplant."

"Jesus."

"Well, I'm sure you have worse super war stories than even I. If you're unlucky maybe you can add another one before you leave town. I hear The Nothing Man is still gunning for White Knight. They took a chunk of out my building last week."

"I actually had an encounter with the Knight a few months ago. I helped him stop a bank robber."

"Maybe you should put on a costume and mask yourself. Make it official."

"Hell no. No one wants to see me in spandex."

"I wouldn't mind," he says with that boyish smile. "I'd prefer you in nothing at all though."

I just hold up my ring again. "Still engaged."

"Still gonna try."

We chuckle in unison. "Well, you best be careful there. Mr. Stone. You keep making me laugh, I might begin to think of you as a friend. And considering what's happened to a lot of my old ones, that is a dangerous thing to be, even for a thrill seeker such as yourself."

"Think you might be worth it, Ms. Fallon," he says with a seductive smile. It brings one to my own lips. "You might be worth it."

*

Bennett was kind enough to arrange a town car to take me to Lucy's house. I'm still enjoying the buzz from lunch, so there's really no better time to see her. I'd forgotten how much fun a little harmless flirting, the playful back and forth of a mental tennis match, could be. Jem, for his billions of excellent qualities, never learned the fine art of flirting. He's gotten better under my tutelage, but going up against a master like Bennett Stone is damn invigorating. And I'm now completely confident the deal will go through without a hitch. Guess me coming here did serve a purpose after all.

The car turns down Lucy's idyllic street, lined on both sides with tall, skinny townhouses literally right next to each other with trees popping out of planters inside the cobblestone sidewalks. Children dressed in school uniforms play in their small patches of grass as foreign nannies watch. My driver finds a spot between a Mercedes and Porsche across from Lucy's red brick abode. The curtains to her living room are open so I can see the woman herself talking on the phone. I've known Lucy Helms since I was twelve, over twenty years, and I cannot say for sure she's aged a day in all that time. Her short hair is more gray than black now, and I think she has crow's feet, but beyond that she's still the same Lucy. Slim, graceful, severe and on extremely rare occasions, almost pretty at least when she smiles. Not happening now. She sets down the phone and shouts something to a person inside the house.

Bad mood or not, I'm here. I'll make the bitch smile if it kills me. I climb out of the car, with instructions to wait in case she's having a *real* bad day, and cross the street. Two muffled voices reverberate from the house, a man and a woman's, on the other side of the front door I knock on.

"About damn time," the woman, I think Lucy, shouts. "Don't give him a tip, Joe!"

"It's not his fault," the man replies.

That voice. I know…

"Sorry about—"

The door opens, and my life cracks apart all over again.

That smile, the one that could effortlessly banish my blues, falters the moment he sets his Caribbean blue eyes on me. And in that moment I know I'm not crazy. I'm not hallucinating. I'm not having an out of body experience, and I haven't dropped dead and finally found him waiting for me behind the pearly gates. That behind the brown goatee, the unkempt dark brown hair reaching his neck, the jeans, the baggy gray sweater stands the man who talked me off a bridge twenty years ago. Who was my best friend, my confidante, the man I loved with everything I possessed. My soul mate. The same man who lied to me. Who never made me feel good enough. Who destroyed my life.

And he's just done it again.

"Joe, make sure they're—" Lucy says as she walks toward us. She stops dead, mouth gaping open when she realizes who's here. "Joanna."

"Surprise," I say, not taking my eyes off *him.*

They're both lucky, damn lucky I didn't bring my gun today because all the confusion, the humiliation, the agony, and above all the rage swirling through me needs an outlet. I can't breathe. I can't think. All I know is I want them to hurt as intensely as I hurt now. I want to turn back the clock thirty seconds before I found myself consigned to hell again. It's not fair. I just crawled out from the pit. It took everything I had, every ounce of my strength to claw my way out, and I'm right back there again because of him. It's *always* because of him.

"Hello, Justin."

And I throw up all over his bare feet. At least it's not a bullet.

CHAPTER THREE

CASTLE OF GLASS

Once upon a time, in a land filled with gods and monsters, there was a little peasant girl with the deck stacked against her. Alcoholic mother, dirt poor, the only bright spot in her otherwise dismal life was her father. His unconditional love helped her flower in the muck, helped her grow into a strong, take charge girl able to survive the fates' game. But they had another card to play. One night, a monster crawled out of the darkness and snatched the kindly father from his little girl, leaving her alone in the ever expanding darkness overtaking the land. With such little light remaining, and no guide, the twelve-year-old girl found herself standing on a bridge, willing herself to jump.

Until the brave prince arrived to save her.

Like the girl, the prince had lost his father to the monsters. Lost his mother. Lost his direction in the world. He had no reason to stop and help the peasant girl. He didn't know her. He owed her nothing. But he stopped his steed on that frigid night and spent an hour convincing the girl there was light if she searched for it. But she didn't have to look long. The moment she set eyes on the handsome prince, she had found the light in him. She had fallen madly in love with the prince before he even opened his mouth. And after he did she knew she would do anything for him. Lay down her life if he needed her to. So the peasant girl and the prince became the best of friends. They went on many adventures together. They saved one another and walked out of the darkness together. For a time.

So the prince and peasant grew into adults in the land of gods and monsters. He went on to rule the land, becoming beloved by all, and she decided to become a knight of the realm. To stop the monsters from destroying more lives. To make the world better alongside the man she loved. Because the knight's love for the prince never wavered, never waned. She never lost the hope that one day her love would be returned. That the prince would open his eyes and see the knight for who she was: his heart and soul. Never to be. Because one day the prince met a princess who was everything the knight was not: gentle, kind, graceful, beautiful. As perfect as the prince. The man she loved was happy, so the knight did her best to accept the princess, to truly be happy for her friend. The person she trusted above all others.

But the prince had a secret.

For the prince was not only a prince. He was born one of the gods. The one worshiped above all others in the land. But unknown to all there was a monster lurking, waiting for the perfect moment to destroy the God Prince. The monster slithered out of the abyss to eat the princess and maim the knight. It was then the knight learned of the prince's true nature. That he'd betrayed her from the moment they met. So the knight turned her back on him, walking away and snuffing out the light they shared with her. The God Prince, having lost everything, found himself on that fateful bridge searching for hope in the seemingly hopeless world.

It was the knight who carried it back.

For despite the lies, the unreturned affection, the anger she still harbored, the God Prince was her soul mate. The one person who knew her. Understood her. Loved her unconditionally as she still did him. And that love saved him from the fate's bridge as it had her. And together they trapped the monster. They fought until they bled and burned, but it wasn't enough. The monster got the upper hand, the knight literally hung on the precipice of death. So the God Prince stared into her eyes and said the words she'd longed to hear. "I love you." And the prince flung himself into death's embrace to save the knight. He made the ultimate sacrifice for the nothing peasant girl.

But it seems he didn't.

He merely pretended to. He ran off to another kingdom, leaving the girl with her guilt. Her misery. Her self-loathing. She lost everything because of his sacrifice: her knighthood, her strength, her sanity. And just when she'd regained it all, with the opening of a door, he snatched it away from her again.

I would have sold my soul to have him back. If the devil had popped into my bedroom with a contract, I would have signed in blood without hesitation. I *should* be happy. I should have leapt into his arms and hugged him until my arms went numb. Instead I threw up, ran away, and haven't left my bed since I returned to the hotel. I've just been staring into space for hours, trembling with rage and willing myself not to raid the mini-bar. At least my phone stopped incessantly ringing. Lucy or even Justin calling with apologies and explanations. It was for my own good. They wanted to protect me. They didn't mean to hurt me. I've heard them all already when I discovered Justin was Justice. That he'd lied to me all through our supposed friendship. That he'd kept a large part of his life, a large part of himself, hidden from me. Bullshit and more bullshit. Fool me once, shame on you. Fool me twice, shame on me.

Justin's alive. He's alive. *Alive.*

And I want him dead.

There's a knock on the hotel door. It must be the concierge coming to check on me again. The driver must have called Bennett about my breakdown because that damn concierge comes up to check on me every hour. One would think, "Fuck off," would be self-explanatory.

"Joanna?"

Oh, thank God.

I climb out of bed and literally fall into Jem's arms. The love of my life hugs me back almost as tightly as I do him. Fresh tears spill down my cheeks as I inhale his scent. Enjoy the sensation of his body pressed against mine. My lifeline. He came. Of course he came.

"I'm here," he whispers. I squeeze tighter. "I'm here."

"Thank you," I whisper back.

"Of course. Of course."

He waits until I let go first. It's almost impossible to release him. I never feel as safe, as content as I do pressed against him. But somehow I force myself to take a step back and wipe the tears away. I wait until he's shut the door to say, "Justin's alive."

My fiancée just blinks. That's his only reaction. "He...what?"

"Justin's alive," I say again.

Another blink. "How-How do you know?"

"Because I saw him. I spoke to him. I went to surprise Lucy, and *he* answered the door."

Jem's face tenses and his eyes grow wide. But not from shock. If I didn't know better I'd swear he was scared. "Are-Are you sure it was him?" he asks, beginning to pace around the room. "I-I-I mean just-just because it-it *looked* like

- 47 -

him doesn't mean it was him." He finally looks at me but won't meet my eyes. "It-It could have been a cousin or-or you-you've said it yourself, you-you thought you saw him and it turned out to be someone else."

"Are you calling me crazy?" I snap.

"Of-Of course not! I simply…you-you didn't sleep well, and-and per-perhaps you-you saw Joe and-and there was some con-confusion."

A boulder drops into my stomach, causing the bile to rise up my throat. "How did you know his name was Joe?"

Jem stops pacing, but still won't look at me. "I-I'm sorry?"

"That's what Lucy called him. 'Joe.' How did you know his alias, Jem?" I ask, my voice as hard as my clenched stomach. I try to meet his eyes. I walk over and grab his face. Even now he refuses to catch my gaze.

And I know. At least I don't puke on him.

It's too much. I grow numb. It's like I leave my body. I'm outside myself staring down. I watch as I drop my hand from his face as if it were caked in shit. As I take a step back from the man I love, the one who stares at my shell with guilty terror beaming from his eyes. As they plead for forgiveness. The same exact expression Justin had a few hours ago. "Joanna…"

"Of course. Of course you knew," my shell says in a monotone. "Of course."

"I'm sorry," he whispers desperately.

"Of course you are. You didn't mean to hurt me."

"I wanted to tell you."

"Of course you did. You wanted to protect me. It was for my own good."

"Joanna…" He steps toward me. My body calls me back inside to stop this affront. I pull my arms toward my chest with my hands up as if he were about to physically assault me. It's not me I'm worried will end up bloody. Jem stops mid-stride, face falling from shock. "I-I—"

"You need to leave now," I say, my voice cracking along with the rest of me. Along with the rest of my life.

"I-I couldn't tell you," he whispers. "I made a promise before I even met you. I vowed—"

"You vowed? You *vowed*?" I shriek. "To me! You made a vow to me! To-To be honest. To put me above everyone else on the planet! You knew, you saw firsthand what I went through because of him. You held me when I cried because I felt so guilty. You let me torture myself to the brink of madness over a lie. You're supposed to love *me*."

"I do love you." He takes another step, but I move back. He has the audacity to grimace in pain at my rebuff. "I-I love you with all my heart, all my soul."

"Just not enough to tell me the truth," I counter. "I trusted you. I almost died for you. I wanted to build a life with you. And you were going to let me build that life on a foundation with a sinkhole beneath it. Consider us swallowed." I rip off my engagement ring and throw it in his face. "Get the hell out of here, Jem. We're over. This is done. *Done.* Get the hell out of my sight before I claw your fucking eyes out."

"Joanna…please…" he says breathlessly.

"GET OUT!" I roar at the top of my lungs.

Every muscle in his body strains in fright. He takes a step backwards. "I-I'm sorry." He holds up his hands in surrender. "I'm sorry. I love you."

"Just words. Get the fuck out."

Jem, realizing I mean it, backs toward the door. "I'm sorry."

"More words. Meaningless. Leave."

He opens the door. "I'm sorry."

And he finally does as I ask. He shuts the door behind himself. The moment he's out of my sight, I slump onto the bed and stare at the empty spot the love of my life used to inhabit. The man I thought I knew. Who I trusted. My partner. My silver lining in this black, shitheap we call a world. I should have known better. There are no happy endings. There are no princes, and gods and monsters are often one and the same. And us brave knights more often than not are swallowed whole by the dragons we're trying to slay. Love does not conquer all. Because this isn't a fairy tale.

This is hell.

*

442 days. I have not had a drop of alcohol for 442 days. I was proud of my sobriety. Damn proud. I worked hard at it. I went to rehab. I attended meetings. I found a sponsor. It was important to me. But all that's important right now is that I don't give into the strong impulse to murder myself or other people. It's important I don't *feel*. So fuck sobriety. Tonight, I drink. A lot.

Thank God there's a bar in the hotel. It was so hard to pick my poison. Vodka, Bourbon, Rum, I've craved them all in those 442 days. I finally settled on Jack Daniels whiskey. Oh, sweet mystery of life at last I've found you. One glass, it's as if Justin's back in the grave. Two, I never set eyes on Jem Ambrose. Three that guy at the end of the bar sure is cute. Hell of a lot cuter than my ex-fiancée. Even in the haze of love I was aware he wasn't classically handsome, not like Justin. But to me there was no one fairer in the land. He was beautiful despite his angular, thin face, his awkward personality, his know-it-all speeches. He was beautiful down to his soul. Or that's what I told myself. Perhaps the masses are correct. Physical beauty is the be all and end all. Screw the brain, the intellect, the soul. Surface trumps all. At least tonight.

I should have known better. In thirty-four years of experience when has a single, solitary soul ever lived up to my meager expectations? Trustworthy. Kind when it earns the person nothing but the satisfaction of improving the world. Accepting others without judgment. If I, a mere mortal with a boulder on her shoulder the size of Jupiter and a mean streak a mile wide, can accomplish those, why the hell can't others? I've never been accused of being an optimist, far fucking from it, but I do know a person can't survive without a tiny sliver of hope, be it in people or God giving them the tools to make the best out of their lot in life. That something or someone is right around the corner to make all the shit worthwhile. That must be why God invented booze. For when we realize we're morons for believing life is anything but us shoveling shit with no end in sight. And that momentary reprieve we're occasionally bestowed just makes picking up that shovel again infinitely harder.

What the hell was I thinking? Seriously, what the *hell* was I thinking getting involved with Jem Ambrose/Lord Nightingale/Captain Moonlight/Fucking Asshole? Did I learn nothing from the Justin/Justice/Other Fucking Asshole debacle? Supers lie to everyone about who they are day in and day out. As if that wouldn't extend to every facet of their lives. But no, I thought I was special. That *we* were special. I'm a moron. Worse, I'm a fool. A moron can't help their stupidity, it's just how they were born. A fool has no one to blame but themselves. They have all the tools at their disposal to diffuse the situation, to realize they're being a fool, but go on anyway. I should have known better. I sip my whiskey. Well, I'm paying for it now. Though not as much as I'll be paying for it tomorrow.

"Hello, Ms. Fallon," a familiar voice croons behind me.

Sure enough when I swivel around, Bennett Stone strolls through the hotel bar toward me. Be it the low lighting, the whisky goggles, or just him in white slacks and V-neck black cashmere sweater, there has never been a finer looking man to ever say my name. Jem's a circus freak by comparison. With that smile of his affixed, he sits beside me at the bar. He's not the first in that seat tonight, a lone woman in a bar is a damn magnet for men, but he is the first I don't tell to fuck off. I'll blame the third drink. Later.

"Fancy meeting you here, Mr. Stone," I purr.

He glances at my almost empty glass. "I believe that's my line, Ms. Fallon."

"You come here to lecture me?"

"Would it do any good?"

I finish my drink. "Hell no." I nod at the bartender. "Another Jack please." The bartender looks at Bennett, who shrugs. Good man. I'm liking him more and more by the second. The bartender pours then walks away. I take a sip. "Took your spies long enough."

"Took my spies long enough to what?"

"Let you know I was here. I was beginning to think you didn't care," I say with a fake pout.

"Nothing could be further from the truth," he says in a way I almost believe him. "I got here as soon as I could."

"I'm honored." Another sip. "So, how much do you know? How good are your spies?"

"Just that you became ill and upset, then returned to the hotel. Now you're here, drinking, minus your engagement ring."

"You would notice that last one."

"So, what did he do, the seemingly perfect yet dull Jem Ambrose?"

Crap, I forgot to work out a cover story. I could just tell him the truth. I sure as shit don't owe either of those motherfuckers a damn thing, certainly not loyalty. But as I open my mouth what comes out is, "Let's just say he turned out to not be the man I'd hoped he was. That he betrayed me, lied to me, and just one of those is a deal breaker."

"Good to know." Bennett smiles empathetically. I better start getting used to that again. The pity. "For what it's worth, I'm sorry. I'm sorry you're in pain. Is there anything I can do to help?"

"Yeah. You can take me upstairs to my hotel room and fuck my brains out." I down the rest of my Jack Daniels. "That'd help."

Bennett's eyes narrow as he chuckles. "Oh, my." He shakes his head. "You don't beat around the bush do you?"

"Nope. So, what do you say? Are you all bark or do you want to bite, playboy?"

He blinks wildly. Adorable. "No, I, it's an enticing offer. I just…think Jack Daniels is making it."

I touch my nose with both fingers before reciting the alphabet backwards. My reluctant Romeo chuckles at the whole performance. "Want me to walk in a straight line too?" I slip off my stool. "Watch me do it all the way to my bed."

I turn on my heel and like a forties femme fatale, I sway my hips as I walk away. Five steps later he's at my side. On the walk, on the ride in the elevator, we don't say a word. Don't even look directly at one another, until the door to my hotel room closes and I ask, "Do you have a condom?" He removes his wallet and holds up the packet. "Then take off your pants and lie on the bed."

Though he raises an eyebrow, he complies without a word. Nice. Tanned, toned legs of an athlete, perfect sized cock growing bigger by the second. He'll do. As I drink the smirking playboy in, I remove my own pants and panties with the same quick efficiency. Like his, my shirt remains on. If he minds, he doesn't say. He doesn't utter a word the entire time. Not when I straddle him, not when I force his hands down onto the bed when he attempts to touch me, not while I ride him. Roughly. Cruelly. Until it hurts. I barely look at my toy. What's attached to his cock doesn't matter. I just take what I want. And when my toy's spent, when he cries out in pleasure, I feel nothing. Only the ever present numbness since Jem left. Now he's gone forever.

As I climb off Bennett, he laughs, "Holy fuck! That was amazing!" I flop beside him, staring at the ceiling as he continues to laugh and pant. "Really. Amazing. You're a damn hellcat, Fallon."

His chuckles begin to make my skin crawl. "Glad you liked it." I pause. "You can leave now."

"I'm sorry?"

"You got what you wanted. So did I. So you can leave now. Bye."

Out of the corner of my eye, I watch as he sits up to study my face. I continue staring up. "What? Seriously?" he chuckles nervously.

"Seriously. I'm tired. I want to go to sleep. We have a meeting tomorrow morning. So…bye."

My boy toy stares for several seconds then shakes his head. "O-kay…" The man stands, tosses the condom in the trash, and retrieves his pants from the floor, treating me to a great view of his ass. Good but nowhere as fine as Jem's. *Jem.* My heart physically wrenches at the mere thought of him. "You are something else, you know that, right?" Bennett asks.

"What? You want to stay and cuddle? Maybe braid each other's hair?" I scoff. "Please."

"Did I say it was a bad thing?" He zips his fly and turns around. "I can stay, you know. If you need someone to talk to. I am also an amazing hair braider."

"Bye," I say in sing-song. Shaking his head, he moves to the door. "Thanks for the sex!" I call as he walks out.

The moment the door shuts, the show's over. Alone once more. Just me and the pain. I still feel him. Jem. Inside me. On my skin. In my soul. I thought that might cleanse him. That the booze, the sex would kill him like an antibiotic against an infection, or at least anesthetize me enough I could pretend it worked. It used to work. But now, if anything, I just feel worse. Physically ill. Disgusting.

Fuck it.

After grabbing a tiny Bourbon from the mini-bar, I stumble into the bathroom and turn on the shower. I don't even bother to take off my sweater. I just slump in a heap onto the tile and chug the bottle as the water burns me. Baptism by fire. I've fallen before. Like the phoenix, I shall rise from the ashes, blah blah blah. What other choice do I have? What other choice have they left me? The men I loved? Love. What bullshit. I won't make that mistake again. I'm nobody's fool. Not anymore. And never again.

*

One thing I didn't miss about drinking were the damn
hangovers. My tolerance has regressed to the neophyte stage. I
used to be able to consume an entire bottle and only get a
headache. I only had four drinks and one mini-bottle and have
thrown up twice, needed two showers to help with the body
aches, and not even four aspirin have quelled my headache.
It's our turn to be late today. Shannon had to break into my
room and shake me awake. After the second shower, I slapped
on lipstick, put my hair in a wet ponytail, slid on a black
pantsuit, and chugged the coffee Shannon made me as we
trekked to our limo. Lane and our lawyer Sherman have been
waiting in the lobby for over half an hour and seem none too
happy when I finally do drag my carcass downstairs.

"What—" Lane begins.

"I overslept," I snap as I put on my sunglasses. "It
happens. Let's go."

I lead the posse to the awaiting limo. Goddamn the sun
is bright today. Is it always this bright? Not even the
sunglasses help. Thank God for tinted windows. Darker but
not dark enough I can remove my sunglasses. Shannon gets in
beside me with Lane and Sherman to the left.

"I already told them we're running late," Lane says as
the door shuts.

"Good for you," I mutter.

"Are you okay?" he asks, more hostile than concerned.
"Are you—?"

"Shannon, does Pendergast have a spare corporate
apartment open? You know, the ones we have clients stay in?"

"Yes. Two."

"Then I'll take the nicer of the two. Have someone prepare it for tonight. Air it out, buy some food, usual shit. I'm also going to need you to arrange for a dozen boxes to be sent to the penthouse. I'll pack myself, but I'll need a moving company to pick them up and carry them to the new apartment. Then again when I find a permanent residence. Got all that?"

"Yes," she says, scribbling on her pad.

"You're moving? Again?" Lane asks. "Why?"

"Why do you think?"

"You and Ambrose split up?" Lane asks. "When did this happen? What—"

"None of your damn business."

"I'm sorry but it is my business," Lane counters. "You splashed around the tabloids and coming to meetings hung-over affects Pendergast."

"Then it's a damn good thing I'm quitting Pendergast," I say.

"You're what?" Lane asks. "You can't."

"The hell I can't. I never wanted to work for your damn company anyway. I hate it. I hate the boring meetings, the asshole executives who treat me like a sideshow freak, and I hate having to dress up and pretend I have any idea what I'm doing. I've given enough of my life to it, but I'm done. Fuck Pendergast."

"What the *hell* is going on?" Lane asks Shannon, who just shrugs.

"What's going on is I'm tired. I'm tired of giving, and giving, and getting fuck all in return but pain and heartache. I'm tired of living for other people. If other people don't give a shit, why should I? It's over. I'm *done*. Today's my last official day as your dancing monkey. Plus Shannon'll be much better in the position than me." I look over at my flummoxed assistant. "Congratulations, you've just been promoted."

"I—" Shannon begins.

"This is madness!" Lane proclaims. "Joanna, if this is another ruse like the one during the Cain incident, you need—"

"It's not. This is a hundred percent real." I look at Shannon. "Draft up whatever papers are needed for you to become my proxy. Convene the board, scream it from the rooftops, whatever. As of tomorrow, I quit."

I stare out the window at the passing shops and boutiques. I know the others exchange confused and worried glances, but I don't care. I made up my mind last night, even before the Jem bullshit. I only stuck it out this long for Justin. To preserve his legacy. Well, if he doesn't give a shit about it, why the fuck should I? Besides, he should have given his shares to Shannon in the first place. She knew all the players, all the plays, and actually has a business degree. The company's in better hands with her making my decisions. Falling in love with Jem, drinking my weight in whiskey, and fucking Bennett Stone show I clearly make wrong ones.

"Joanna, whatever happened with Ambrose—"

"This has nothing to do with him," I insist. "This has to do with clarity."

"No, this has to do with the alcohol you obviously consumed last night. If you're checking yourself into rehab, you need to let us know," Lane says. "It won't leave this—"

"Jesus Christ! I thought you'd be over the damn moon I'm quitting, not leading the Spanish Inquisition."

"Well, we need to tell people something," Shannon points out.

"I'm resigning to pursue other ventures. I'm resigning to focus on charity. I'm resigning to become a nun. I don't care what you tell them. And if they ask about the break-up give them the standard, 'No comment.'"

"Well, what did happen?" the lawyer asks.

"No comment."

Lane throws up his hands in frustration. "This is insanity. You have lost your mind."

"Maybe I have, maybe I haven't. Either way, you're well rid of me."

"But what *will* you do?" Shannon asks.

I haven't gotten that far in the plan. Not that there really is a plan. "I'll do whatever I want. The world's my oyster, right? Untethered and unencumbered, answering to nothing and no one. Aren't I the lucky girl?"

The trio smartly stop their inquiries and we ride in silence the two minutes to Goliath. As the glass behemoth comes into view, repairs still underway, it's so strange to think that when we arrived here not twenty-four hours ago my life was completely different. I just *had* to surprise Lucy. I just had to show up when he was visiting her. If I had chosen to arrive ten minutes earlier or later I'd still be living in blissful ignorance. Everyone's always harping about the goddamn truth, myself included. The truth is overrated. Seriously. The truth can suck my dick.

We're ushered back to the conference room where the Goliath team wait. I suppose I should feel a sense of shame or at least embarrassment when I set eyes on Bennett, but nope. My give a damn's busted. He smiles at me as he rises from the table. "Hello. All."

"Sorry for our tardiness," Lane says.

"Well, you know what they say about glass houses and stones," Bennett retorts as we sit.

I remove my sunglasses. "Doesn't stop most people from throwing the fuckers."

"Guess that makes me better than them," he says, not missing a beat. "Go me."

Even I manage a smile for that one. His grows larger. Just for me. I look away.

"Let's not waste any more time," Lane chimes in. "I understand we only have a few wrinkles to iron out. Shall we begin?"

As I sit for two hours listening to dull as hell negotiations about arbitration liability and tax write-offs, I realize without a shadow of a doubt I've made the right decision. For once. I've wasted over a year of my life in conference rooms bored out of my skull. No fucking more. Bennett keeps trying to catch my eye, but I stare straight ahead at the door. Thank Christ we did all the heavy lifting yesterday, so today's torture only lasts two hours. The novel size contract gets signed, notarized, and I'm finally free.

That's that.

After the last signature, I leap from my seat and rush for the bathroom, mostly to avoid Bennett, okay mostly due to the five cups of coffee I drank to stay awake. An empty bladder. The highlight of my day. I—

When I step out of the stall, I'm shocked to find the person—well, one of them—I was actively trying to avoid, leaning against the sink with that damn boyish grin of his affixed.

"Jesus Christ," I gasp.

"Not quite," Bennett quips, smile growing.

I roll my eyes. "So you're a pervert as well as an asshole. That your kink? Listening to women pee?"

"Maybe I was hoping for a quickie."

I roll my eyes again and move toward the sinks to wash my hands. "What? Were you doodling 'Mr. Joanna Fallon' surrounded by hearts in your notebook earlier?"

"You peeked," he says with a fake pout.

A wry chuckle escapes me. "Look last night was last night and this morning is this morning, and never the twain shall meet again. I like you. I do. You're funny, you're gorgeous, you're decent in bed, but my life is fucked right now. Not to mention you live hundreds of miles away and I have no intention of ever, *ever* setting foot in this shitty city again." I move around him to the paper towels. "But hey, if you ever find yourself in Galilee, given time, I may be up for a few laughs, who knows? Life can turn on a dime, right?"

He studies me, eyes narrowing. "He really did a number on you, huh?"

"Which he?" With an eyebrow raised, I turn my back on him and walk toward the door.

"Joanna?" Bennett calls. I spin around. "Take care of yourself."

"No one else will, huh?" I pucker my lips in a kiss and step out. "Bye, playboy. It's been memorable."

The Pendergast contingent wait for me by the elevators and don't say a word the ride down to the lobby. There's nothing they can say, and maybe they know me well enough to realize that. Or maybe they don't want me to change my mind. They'll be popping champagne when they return to Pendergast. Shannon will be ten times the dealmaker I'm supposed to have been.

We step off the elevator and through the foyer. I have so much shit to do now. Packing, selling the manor, I'm sure there'll be a ton of paperwork needed for my resig—

"Joanna?"

I cringe when I hear her voice. Of course. When I spin around, Lucy's already risen from her chair in the vast lobby. Just waiting to pounce. Lane and Shannon actually smile at Judas as she slowly begins her approach. Nope. I stride toward her to intercept. I am in no mood for this.

"He would send you," I hiss. "What, is he too much of a pussy to face me himself?"

"Don't be vulgar," Lucy admonishes.

"Don't tell me what to do. *Cunt.*" I step in close, getting right in her face. "You. Of all people…you saw. You were there from the beginning. You had a front row seat to my agony. My misery. My guilt. And you could have stopped it all with a few words. But you didn't. And I understand loyalty, and that he asked you to keep his secret. Again. But sometimes plain human kindness trumps loyalty. I always knew you were a cold bitch, but I never had you pegged as a cruel one." She opens her mouth, but I don't give her the chance. "I know, you had your reasons. I just don't care. I'm not gonna waste a second of my time listening to them because I've heard them all before. From you, from Justin, even from…Jem." My lip twitches when I say his name. "I'm done listening. I'm *done*. With all of you. Never speak, never contact me again. These are the last words I ever intend to speak to you, so *you* listen. Tell your nephew I wish I'd never met him. I wish he'd stayed dead. And if he ever comes near me, not only will I tell the world his secret, I'll put the bastard in the ground myself. Go to hell, Lucy, and take him with you."

If possible my scowl deepens, and I turn on my heel, stalking past my gawking colleagues outside into the sunny fucking day without looking back. Get me the fuck out of this town. Get me—

Halfway to the car I can't help but notice a tall man with a beard and the hood of his jacket up staring at me. I stop walking to stare right back at the coward for a second, the hope quickly draining from his gorgeous face in time to his slumping shoulders. My eyes, my scowl, hell my every pore radiates atomic fury at that man. He must sense it—how could he not—because he takes a step back. For a moment, just a moment, he's scared of me. The big damn hero afraid of little old me.

He should be.

I can't stand to gaze at him a second longer. I turn my back on the bastard and don't dare look back. For both our sakes. My rage could consume the city. My soul is being held together by glue and string. Perhaps I should let the bindings burn. Allow the pieces to shatter. Something that doesn't exist can't hurt, right? And right now mine's in agony. Having a soul's overrated. Hasn't done me one bit of good. It'd be a mercy, really.

But the world seems fresh out of that.

CHAPTER FOUR

FAITH FOR FOOLS

Home.

A place. A word. A feeling. A person. It's different for everyone. I've lived in many dwellings, had many roofs over my head, but only have had three true homes, all ripped from me by the evil men do. A thief's bullet. A supervillain's pride. The lies of a lover. I don't waste a moment disassembling what remains of the last one. The always efficient Shannon worked her phone and when we landed in Galilee, my temporary digs were aired out and stocked with food while boxes and a reservation for a van tomorrow were waiting at the old. I call up to the penthouse, but there's no answer. He'd pick up if he was there.

When the car pulls up to my building, and I get out with a sigh. Let's get this over with. Barry, the doorman, opens the entrance. "We, uh, put your boxes in the apartment, ma'am. Are you and Dr. Ambrose going—"

"Just me. And tomorrow I'll be back with the movers. Should only take an hour or so."

"Okay, ma'am."

I know he's dying to ask what happened, but I hustle to the elevator before he can say another word. Only one person gets the whole story. *He* deserves it.

"I'm sorry?" Dobbs asks.

"I said Justin's alive," I say as I step into his apartment.

Shaking his head, the old man shuts the door. "No. Miss Joanna, he—"

"I saw him. I talked to him. He faked his death. He's been living in Independence with Lucy this whole time."

"No," he chuckles. "No. He…" Dobbs stares at my stony face, his smile slowly dropping along with the rest of his wrinkled face. But after the disbelief fades, he does something odd. A giant, brilliant grin overtakes his face. "He's alive?" Dobbs begins laughing. "Oh my God, it's a miracle."

Not the response I'd anticipated. "Dobbs, he lied to us. We mourned him. Together. He allowed us to think he was dead."

"But he's not! He's alive and breathing and…nothing else matters but that, Miss Joanna. Nothing."

I remain silent.

"I-I want to see him," Dobbs continues. He turns his back on me to walk away. "I-I have to see him. He's with Miss Helms?" he calls from his bedroom.

My legs are suddenly made of rubber. "Yep," I call back.

Why the hell is my stomach churning? Because he's leaving too. And he may not know it yet, but I do. He's never coming back. Justin will welcome him with open arms and Dobbs will never leave them again. I've lost him too. Goddamn you, Justin. Godddamn you to hell. I slink away to my apartment without another word. I'm afraid of what I'll say if I open my mouth again.

Thank Christ there's no one in the penthouse when I enter. The boxes rest against the couch Jem and I picked out together. Our first act as an official couple. My stomach churns again, and I have to look away. If I take too many detours down Memory Lane I'll break down. Just get this done, Jo, and get the hell out of here.

I collect a few boxes and start on the living room. Neither of us is that sentimental, so I don't have tons of photos or knick knacks around. All I take are the photos of my cousins, uncle, and aunt before moving to the DVD collection. Fuck. When I come across the copy of *Excalibur* I snap the disk in two. I never should have invited him inside that night. I should have followed my first instinct and let him drive off. Fuck you, hindsight.

With the kitchen and living room, I barely fill two boxes. The Moonlight room fills three. All the files, the computer equipment, the maps, I take it all. Jem doesn't get to profit from his crimes. I did fine on my own before. Guardian lives on as a solo act. Captain Moonlight is a lone wolf from now on.

The exercise room gets raided too, especially the secret compartment filled with our toys. Guns, MACE, batons, handcuffs, everything a superhero needs to fight crime. I take all the stuff I brought from the Justice lair, about half the arsenal. I have no immediate plans to use any of it but may need it in the future. And I never want to set foot in this apartment again.

The bedroom takes the longest. I have so many damn clothes. Isolde, my personal shopper, insists I don a new outfit at every public appearance. That's ending for sure. I am so going to become the recluse I've always wanted to be. No need to maintain the pristine Pendergast legacy through charity and business events. I actually run out of boxes and have to throw my designer duds into black trash bags. Isolde would faint if she saw me do this to my Chanel suits. Sorry, CoCo.

I'm stuffing the last of my underwear into the bag when the front door shuts in the other room. I stand stone still like a burglar about to get caught by the home's owner. Goddamn it. Five minutes. I just needed five more minutes. You couldn't give me that?

"Jo-Joanna?" Jem calls.

He steps into our-*his* bedroom a few seconds later, dressed in his work clothes, black slacks, white buttoned up shirt, and black silk tie. He went to work. Life implodes and he goes to work. A small part of me expected, okay *wanted* him to burst into my hotel room or meeting demanding to see me. Begging for a chance to explain himself. To fight for me. I'll bet he called Justin on the elevator ride down then went straight to the airport. Came here, caught a few Zzzs, then was on time to his lab where he cured Ebola. Like it was just another day. Asshole.

"Good day at the office, dear?" I ask snidely.

"Wh-What are you doing?" he asks.

"Some great detective you are."

"You're moving out?"

"That is what happens when people who co-habitate break up. It was your place first, so…" I tie up the bag. "I'm almost done here."

He gazes around the room, mouth agape. "Joanna, this is…you-you were just going to leave without even talking to me?"

"We said everything we needed to last night." I snap open the next trash bag. "And if it were up to me, we'd never utter another word to each other ever again." I turn my back on him to start on the last drawer. "Let's start now."

He waits several seconds, several heavy, cringe worthy seconds, before working up the nerve to say, "He came to us broken beyond measure, Joanna. He'd lost the woman and child he loved. He lost his hand. The whole of the world knew who he was. His life was in danger. Worse, the lives of those he loved were in danger. He'd placed a target on your back for every criminal in the world to take a shot at. So the man left everything he loved behind. His family, his legacy, his home, his friends, *you*. He gave up everything for you, Jo. And-And-And he wanted to reach out, he did, but the world had you under a microscope. One slip and the planet would realize he was alive."

"So he let me implode because he didn't trust my acting skills?" I snap.

"He did it because he knew how strong you are. You're a survivor, Joanna. He knew you would come out the other end stronger than ever. And was he wrong?" I keep my mouth shut. "What he did, he did for you. To keep you safe. He knew if you ever found out he'd lied that there was a chance you would hate him forever, but at least you'd be alive."

"Fine. Cruel to be kind. Got it." I tie the bag and spin around, giving him the full force of my glare. "And what's *your* excuse for betraying me?"

"A promise to a friend. To a brother in arms. All of this was set in motion before I ever met you, Joanna."

"And after? After you met me? You told me you loved me? I almost died fighting your psycho brother? We got *engaged*? Your promise to him was more important than me?"

"No!" he gasps desperately. Jem bridges the gap between us, stopping a mere foot from me. "I love you. I would rather cut off my own arms than cause you an instant of pain. I love you more than life itself. You *are* my life. When I came to this city, I never anticipated…that you could love me as well. Not even in my wildest dreams could I have envisioned how happy you would make me. But...*he* was always there, Joanna. You still loved him. You still love him. And...I know I can't compete. I could barely compete with the memory let alone the man in the flesh. So the God's honest truth is I didn't tell you to protect him, not fully, I didn't tell you to protect myself. Because I feared the moment you realized he was alive, you'd go running back to him. Your soul mate. And I'd lose you."

"So it's worse than I thought," I say, doing my best to stop my voice from trembling. I will not fall apart. Not in front of him. I tap into the boiling anger beneath the sadness. "You lied to me day in and day out, you let me torture myself with guilt because...you didn't trust me."

"That's not—"

"You didn't trust in *us*. When I trusted you with everything. My heart, my soul, my life. Because yeah, Justin may have been my soul mate, but I thought you were the love of my life. You should have trusted in that. Because you didn't and look where it got you. You lost my trust, you lost my heart, you lost *me*." I lift up my two trash bags, scowl tightening. "The movers will be here tomorrow for the boxes." I side step him and start toward the door.

"No," he says behind me, "no!" Jem moves in front of me, eyes doubling in size, trying to catch mine. "It was never *you* I didn't trust. It was me. It was all me. I was selfish. I wanted you all to myself. All my life, everything I loved was ripped from me. Uma, Brendan, Lexie, Jordan. I was terrified I'd lose you as well. I'm only human, Joanna. I'm not perfect. I made one mistake for mostly the right reasons. Please do not throw everything we mean to each other, everything we will mean to each other in the future away because of one mistake.

This, *us* is too important. And you know it. You sense it even now. We clawed through hell to find one another. And until the day I draw my last breath, I will do everything in my power to make this up to you. To prove to you I am worthy of your love and trust."

Goddamn it. Be it his words, those pleading heartbroken eyes, or the pure belief dripping from each syllable, my resolve wavers. Because love cannot be switched off like a light. It can't. I still love him. I do. Just like Justin, a part of me will probably love him until the day I die.

Fuck love.

I finally meet his tear rimmed eyes with my cold as ice gaze. "I screwed Bennett Stone last night," I say matter-of-factly.

His face contorts in agony, like I've just physically stabbed him. "What...?" he asks breathlessly.

"Last night. After I kicked you out. We met in the bar, I brought him upstairs to my room, and fucked him."

He stares at me as if I were a stranger. "Why...why would you do that?"

"Besides the fact he's handsome, funny, and uncomplicated? *This*," I hiss. "To put a period at the end of our sentence. So there would be no going back. So don't waste your time or energy. We're done. *Done*." I turn my back on him again and start walking.

Just keep going. Just keep...

"Don't do this," he pleads, voice brittle. "Don't do this to me, and please don't do this to yourself. Do not punish yourself for my mistakes. You're better than that. You're stronger than that."

I scoff. "*Now* you have faith in me."

"I've always had faith in you. And I always will. Just as I'll always have faith in us."

"Like you had faith in your brother?" I stop walking and pause. "Faith is for fools. I should know." I look back at him with a cruel smile. "I put my faith in you." I stare straight ahead again, and I walk out the door with my head held high. Not a good actor my ass.

Not the doorman, not the cabbie, not the man at the liquor store ask me if I'm alright. If I need help. Not a one sees through my façade. But the moment me, my suitcase, trash bags, and bottle of booze hear the door of my bland, stale apartment shut, my legs suddenly give out and I cannot breathe. A panic attack. I haven't had a panic attack since that horrific minute when I thought Jem died. That I'd lost the love of my life. Because he is. He is the love of my life. He is and he's gone. We were supposed to get married today. We were supposed to get married and...

I'm beginning to see spots. I can't breathe. I can't breathe. Jem calmed me down the last two times. I place my hand over my racing heartbeat and try to concentrate on drawing in breath in time to it. *It'll be okay. It'll be okay. Just breathe. Breathe!*

I gasp, but the sobs make it just as difficult to draw breath as the panic. Because I have nothing left. Not hope, not faith, not even the memories. Tainted. They're all tainted. All that remains is me and the pain. I may as well be back on that damn bridge. No, it's worse. Because I've seen the light, and now I'm back in the darkness without a way to find my way back. There *is* no way back. Love has ruined more lives than hate ever could. I should have learned my lesson the first time.

Only a fool has hope in this hopeless world.

CHAPTER FIVE

THE LOST GIRL

Strong.

All my life, the one word always used to describe me is "strong." That or bitch, but if you're a woman those two words are synonymous. I do have a strong personality. I am who I am, and I make no bones about it. With few exceptions, I truly don't give a crap if someone doesn't like me. If a person says or does something I don't like, I'm damn well going to say or do something about it. I can take a punch and give as good as I get. Growing up in Diablo's Ward with the abusive alcoholic mother doesn't leave a little girl much choice but to be strong. To survive. But it's always been fake it 'til I made it. More often than not there wasn't an ounce of fight or strength in me, but I couldn't allow anyone to know that or I'd be dead. Literally. But the well is dry. Even the fumes have evaporated. The one good thing about losing everything and everyone is that when you implode, there's no collateral damage. Score one for freedom.

I don't leave my shit corporate apartment for a week. Not because I love the place. It doesn't have a lick of personality. Beige walls, factory produced artwork of flowers and cityscapes, cheap pots and pans, easy to assemble furniture as comfortable as granite. But it does have a television and a grocery/liquor store that delivers nearby. What more could a depressed alcoholic ask for?

Most of the past week is a blur, which means the booze did its job. I remember watching tons of reality television and true crime shows. I remember throwing up. A lot. And sleeping. All the slumber I've missed through the years due to stress and a mountain of other obligations has been made up for with change. With my cell phone off, the landline off the hook, and computer in one of the few unpacked boxes, I've been on my own little desolate island. Just me, Jack Daniels, and Captain Morgan. A threesome. A triumvirate. Trio of assholes is more like it. Fuck him. Fuck them all.

On day six, at least I think it's day six, my coma's interrupted by a woman calling my name, followed by a half dozen expletives. Oh God, my head. The bottle of aspirin is half empty, but I dry swallow four just as the interloper steps into my bedroom. "Jesus Fucking Christ, Jo. What the hell?"

My cousin Veronica stands in the doorway, pretty mouth agape at the sight of me. Okay, not just me. I was three drinks in when the maid arrived yesterday and I wouldn't let her in. No doubt V's seen all the take-away cartons, empty bottles, food stains, dirty clothes, and half full boxes with their former contents strewn around. I meant to hire someone to take the boxes to a storage unit but that never happened. Hell, using soap barely happened.

"How'd you get in here?" I ask.

"Shannon told me where you were and called the concierge to let me up. She was worried about you. Apparently with good reason. So back to the original question: what the hell, Jo? I'm away for a week and you fucking implode?"

"Yes, I timed the total collapse of my life for the one week you're away just to stick it to you. I'm an evil bitch.

Fuck off." I pull the covers over my head. Jesus, they reek of sweat and farts. Really should have used fucking soap.

V snatches the covers completely off the bed, leaving me exposed. "Get up."

"Bitch!" I snap.

"You're going to take a shower, shampoo your hair because you could cook French fries in all that grease, get dressed, and while you're doing that, I'll call your sponsor to meet us at AA."

"I'm not going to a fucking meeting, V. I'm not going to sit around the most miserable people on the planet as they bare their souls like anyone else gives a shit. Because they don't. Not really. Even the best humanity supposedly has to offer are just cruel, selfish, deluded monsters. And I want nothing to do with them. *Any* of them. Or you. So fuck off." I grab the other pillow, press it to the side of my face, and close my eyes. "I mean it. Leave or I'll call the police."

There's several seconds of silence before she says, "You do know who you just sounded like right then, right? Aunt Maeve redux."

"Well, maybe she had the right idea. Say what you want about her, but she looked out for number one. Her only mistake was having me. Luckily I didn't make the same one. I'm not hurting anyone else."

"You're hurting me. I love you, you stupid cow. My brothers love you. My parents love you. Jem still—"

I sit straight up. "V, Justin's alive. He's alive and well and Jem knew but didn't tell me. So fuck off and let me have my nervous breakdown in peace."

This information does its job. It shuts her the hell up. Her jaw literally drops as she stares at me to gage if I'm lying or just crazy. My stony face must convince her because she says, "Jesus."

"Yep. So I realize I'm a fucking mess right now, I do, but I kind of think I've earned the right to a little alone time as I figure out how the fuck I'm going to continue in this filthy, disgusting, nightmare of a world and come to terms with the fact that the two people I almost died for think so little of me."

"I'm so sorry, Jo. I truly am. What they did…is shitty beyond words. But drinking yourself to death isn't the solution."

"Then what is?" I snap. "Oh great, wise one, what the fuck am I supposed to do?"

"What you've always done. You pick yourself up, and put one foot in front of the other because though it might take some time, eventually you'll find yourself someplace else. Someplace better. And then you rub their noses in it. Living well is the best revenge, Jo. What you're doing is drinking poison and hoping they're the ones who die."

"You got that from a fortune cookie."

"Doesn't make it any less true," she counters. "So you've had your little pity party for one. Time to get up and join humanity again. And you can call the police, you can throw things at me, you can even call me names, but I'm not leaving. Because if the tables were turned, you wouldn't leave me. So get your ass out of bed and get in the shower or I'll call my brothers and parents and they'll invade this place like Vikings for an impromptu intervention. Won't that be fun?"

Fuck. Fuck! She'll do it too. Bitch. I do need a shower though. I also don't have the energy or brain cells to fight. I throw the pillow at her. "I hate you."

"I can live with that. I know you'll get over it. Now get up!"

Rolling my eyes, which wasn't wise with a headache, I pull my carcass out of bed and into the bathroom. I don't dare glance at myself in the mirror. Made that mistake two days ago. The shower does help with the headache and the shampoo with the rest of it. In the back of my mind, I knew this was coming. The day I'd have to face the world again. A not-so-tiny part of me kind of hoped I wouldn't wake up. Not exactly a death wish but more of a death acceptance. Maybe the hooch is the only factor keeping that acceptance crossing over into darker territory. Another reason not to stop. I just need to get V out of here. I'll cut down—I'm tired of physically feeling like shit—but not go cold turkey. Or to meetings. Being a functional alcoholic worked for me in the past, it'll be good enough for the future.

Judging from the noises in the other room, I assume V's cleaning. Better her than me. I slip on jeans, a white t-shirt, and braid my wet hair before joining her. Sensing I'm not up for talking, as we continue cleaning, V blabbers about her week in Jericho unearthing ties between the Andretti mob and our mayor. I've never been much of a housekeeper, but I let it get to a whole other level. Stains everywhere, food already molding, Jem would have a heart attack if he saw this. The man is anal and not in the fun way. If I left a sock on the floor he'd pitch a fit. That took some getting used to. Well, I hope he enjoys his spotless, empty, soulless apartment. I don't—

"Jo?" V asks, bringing me out of my head. "Did you hear me?"

"No. Sorry. I spaced out."

She ties up the full trash bag. "I asked if you still had access to the Justice computer."

"Of course. Why?"

"Because I think this story is bigger than I thought. The mayor, senators, even the governor may be involved."

"And you want me to do your job for you." And the true reason she came by has revealed itself. Concern for my welfare had nothing to do with it. She just wanted something from me. Why am I so surprised? I roll my eyes. "Fuck you."

"What now?"

"You actually had me thinking you came here out of the kindness of your heart. That you gave two shits about me."

"I-I do!" she snaps, mouth agape in disbelief.

"No, you just wanted an excuse to come over to get something from me."

"Fuck you! Don't you dare question my integrity and loyalty, not after all these years. I'm not stupid, Jo. I knew Jem was Lord Nightingale, and I know he's probably Captain Moonlight, and did I say anything? Print a damn word? No, because I wouldn't do that to *you.* Because I love you." She puts her hands on her hips. "I came here because no one had heard from you in a week. I came because we're all shit scared for you. And with good reason. You're losing it. I just thought taking down the mayor with me might be a good distraction. That's it. My only ulterior motive." Her cell phone begins ringing, and V rolls her eyes. "Fuck! Just…fuck. I have to take this." She removes her phone from her pants. "Veronica Lilley." She listens. "Now isn't a good time, sir. I—" Her mouth snaps shut for a few seconds. "Can't you send Mason? I'm—" She rolls her eyes again. "Fine. *Fine.* I'll get down there. I'm ten minutes away. Bye." She hangs up and groans. "Your ex is beating the shit out of Gearhead at the Tech Expo." My stomach clenches. Gearhead can control machines. Jem could be facing an entire army of super robots or something. "I have to get down there."

I keep my face neutral. "Whatever."

She picks up her purse from the floor. "But we're not done here. I'm coming back. At least once a day."

"Don't bother."

"Still doing it. Don't make me sic Mom on you." V frowns at me. "Go to a damn meeting, Jo. Get out of this place. Do *something*. Because this isn't you." She tries to smile, but only makes it half-mast. "I love you."

I don't reply. V shakes her head and hustles off to play girl reporter. I plop on the beige couch with a sigh. That was uncalled for. I've known V all my life. She's always been straight with me, always had my back. Like the big sister I never had. Damn my temper. Thankfully she doesn't hold a grudge like the rest of us Irish. I'll apologize. Find a way to make this up to her somehow. She has been sitting on the story of the year. For me.

She knew about Jem. Can't say I'm shocked. I'm actually surprised more people haven't put it together. Before he became Moonlight we talked about that eventuality. A hero with similar powers, similar build just appearing in Galilee months after Lord Nightingale "died?" Could happen. We saw the way people studied him. As if he would lift off the ground and fly around the room. Then he'd open his mouth or trip on his own feet, and that would be that. No one who meets him socially or professionally would ever think the gangly, unkempt, monosyllabic researcher is the man currently beating up a supervillain.

Gearhead. He hasn't been active in a while. Not since before the Triumvirate arrived. That time Olympia and Geronimo teamed up to stop him, and then Geronimo wasn't seen for two months after. He's right up there on the deadly scale with Bruiser and Giagantor. Dozens dead. Always gets away. And Jem's never faced him before, let alone whatever nasties he's recruited at the Expo. Who the hell knows what they're unveiling there. A robot army with nukes? One thought and Gearhead has them doing his biding. Maybe Olympia's there too. Maybe—

Shit.

Doris Jr is on the kitchen counter already booted up. In my more sober or drunk periods I combed the Independence news stories researching Lucy and anyone named Joe associated with her. Fuck all so far on a "Joe," but a ton on White Knight, the super-strong, super-healing, super-fast hero. I came face to mask with that fucker, even caught a bank robber for him. And what did he do? Chided me. I should have known then. Idiot me.

I flip on the TV too as the remote connection to Doris Senior boots up. As always the news has trumped regularly scheduled programming. A weekly occurrence in Galilee Falls. And–oh, fuck. The police have cordoned off a city block to keep the lookie loos from becoming further casualties. Smart because the white four-story convention center's already crumbling. The gaping hole in the roof, in the side of the building, and all the windows on the east side are blown out. Disintegrated. Shit. Fuck.

"…how many hostages remain inside," Rick Diaz says to the camera. "People have been slowly filtering out, but it is estimated three thousand people were attending the International Technology Expo. There are—"

There's a burst of red light inside at the same time another portion of the roof explodes out. A collective gasp, mine included, escapes all watching this nightmare. Shit.

"There-There appears to have been another explosion," Diaz says.

Fuck, fuck, fuck, fuck…

The program finally boots up as there's another explosion. Godddamn it. Two clicks and the video feed pops up. When I commissioned the Moonlight suit I had them install four pinpoint cameras: one in his forehead, one on each arm, and one on the back of his neck. A 360 degree view. And right now that view is chaotic. I don't know where to focus first. Thousands of terrified people run around, some bleeding and others crying, but all trying to find cover from the flying black drones firing beams of light I think are lasers. Tech displays are consumed in fire or blown to pieces when the light connects. The roof caves in in two locations, large chunks of burning masonry raining down like brimstone. Henchmen dressed in brown leather outfits with gears adorning their clothes guard doors with automatic weapons. They're nothing but window dressing with the drones and the ten foot tall bi-pedal metal man with lasers on its thick arms firing right at Jem. At least the Gatling guns on the monster's shoulders appear inactive. Lasers are deadly enough.

Jem lifts off the ground and veers right, barely clearing the latest laser shot. He can't see that right behind him one of the drones changes course. Jem zooms toward the metal machine, dodging left and right to avoid its laser blasts. The drone behind him mimics his every move. And gains. Shit.

I dash to the box and retrieve the headset and microphone. Jem's almost at the giant, as close as the drone is to him, when I plug in. "Drone, six o'clock, ten meters."

"Copy," Captain Moonlight says over the comms.

The hero continues as he was, winding mid-air toward the giant, but slows. The drone doesn't. Oh hell, not this again. It only works 2/3 of the time. "Eight meters," I say. With about five to the giant. Jem slows further. "Seven…six…" The drone fires its lasers as the giant does the same. Right, left, right, left like a leaf on the wind, Jem dodges them mid-air. "Two…" He flies down all of a foot off the floor, gliding straight. He has to time this perfectly. "One…"

Jem sails between the giant's legs without incident. The drone isn't so lucky. That's the problem with machines, no imagination. It locked onto Moonlight and forgot all else. In a burst of plastic and fire, the drone collides with the giant's legs. The giant fares better but not by much. The drone acts as a bomb, blowing off one of its legs at the joint. It's enough. As Moonlight changes course, the giant totters then collapses on its side with a loud thunk. Down but not out. Moonlight touches down beside the machine. He grabs hold of one of its arms, yanking it from the socket.

The henchmen finally spring to life.

The five closest dash from their posts, machine guns in hand, toward Moonlight. "Five incoming with M-16s."

"Have you spotted Gearhead?" Moonlight asks.

"He likes to hide in the crowd or as a henchmen," I inform him. "Nine o'clock."

Moonlight tosses the arm to his left. The henchmen raising his gun gets hit right in the face with the hunk of metal. Unconscious. Four left. Arm still outstretched, Jem fires the blaster on top of his wrist. A recent addition, one on each arm, emitting an energy blast that targets the inner ear, instantly rendering the target unconscious before they even hit the floor. Lasts about ten minutes. A prototype from Pendergast. I will miss having access to everything cutting edge from weapons to medical breakthroughs. Moonlight takes out the guard at eight o'clock, then raises this right hand to take out the third.

"Remind me," says Moonlight as the third hits the dirt.

"Early forties, shortish, brown hair, thin. Five o'clock."

Moonlight spins around and blasts number four, but not before the henchmen gets a shot off. The hero groans in pain as his body jerks from the impact to his shoulder. "I'm okay," he tells me without prompting.

My stomach still won't unknot. I've watched that man take more bullets than I can count, and it never gets easier. Even now. At least the fifth henchman wises up, suddenly sprinting toward the exits like the smarter civilians. They should all be running now. They—

"The second drone," I say.

"Where?"

"Don't see it. And they're retreating."

I glance up at the neglected TV screen as Diaz points up to the sky before the cameraman zooms in on a black speck growing smaller. "Shit! I think he flew the drone out."

"Which direction?" Jem asks, lifting off the ground.

"Toward the river, but he has a massive lead. And— ceiling!"

A huge chunk of concrete and metal the size of our bedroom falls right where panicked people flee. Off like a shot, Moonlight zooms toward the smoldering debris, stopping its descent like a strongman with a barbell, holding it above his head with shaking arms. "Move!" he bellows to the people below. They obey, giving him wide berth as he lands and gently places the debris on the floor. "Gearhead?"

"You probably wouldn't have caught him anyway," I offer.

Police officers, EMTs, and firemen finally rush inside the Expo center. The cavalry. On the TV screen I watch as more, practically a third of the police force, swarm the place.

A few stray henchmen get wrestled to the ground. What morons. The pay can't be that good.

"Any way to track him?" Moonlight asks over the comms.

"Maybe. The drone might have GPS or satellite feed. That'll take time though. The henchmen might be a better option."

"I'll take the latter, you the former?" he suggests.

Shit. This isn't what I wanted. I didn't consider this possibility. Further involvement. "I, uh…think you have it all well in hand. He's uh, all yours Moonlight. I have to go now."

"Guardian…thank you. It's good to hear your voice."

"I didn't do it for you," I lie. "Good hunting. Guardian out."

I cut the feed and yank off my headset. A week. I couldn't even go a damn week without talking to him. Without watching his back. But it felt good. For all of three minutes I forgot everything but stopping that supervillain fucker. But I didn't do it for the civilians, I did it for him. He was in danger, and I had to make sure he made it out alive. Maybe I can separate business and personal. Just because we're not a couple doesn't mean the work has to end. Babies and bathwater or whatever.

I stare at the TV screen as Jem carries out a crying woman caked in blood and dust. A familiar surge of pride and love spreads like warm tentacles through my body. Fuck. He sets the survivor on a gurney but she sobs unheard words and clutches onto his hand. He squeezes it to reassure her, I'm sure with a smile behind that mask. "Fuck!" I shut off the TV.

No. No half measures. Not with him, and not with alcohol. I can't trust him. Right now I can barely trust myself. Cold turkey. From them both. I grab my jacket from the chair, take a deep breath, and step out of my cave. Time to rejoin the human race. One foot in front of the other, Jo. Because quite frankly where I'm going can't be any worse than where I've just been.

*

"You look like hell."

"Oh Ryder, you always say the sweetest things to me. You always perks me right up."

Supervillain James Ryder aka Alkaline, the scourge of Galilee, sits in his cell on the other side of my computer screen, pale handsome face scrunched up in concern. Genuine concern or as much as a psychopath is capable of producing for someone other than himself. A year and a half ago he was trying to kill me, now the monster cares about my well-being. Probably more to do with the fact if something were to happen to me not only would his limited access to the woman he claims to love vanish, but so would the only human contact he receives in the form of our weekly chats. Life's pretty dull when you're stuck in a cell all but two hours a week. That's what he gets for breaking out of prison, raping, murdering, and generally being evil incarnate. I was happy to let the fucker rot but his inside knowledge of Galilee's underbelly has proven invaluable to our investigations. Plus the sight of him no longer makes my stomach churn. That's something.

"Would you rather I lie to you?" he asks.

For some reason this question makes me laugh. Chuckles become full guffaws as the ridiculousness of those words coming from his mouth hits me. "You know the most fucked up thing in the universe? You are the only person who has never lied to me. *Never.* Even when you were trying to kill me, you were upfront about the reasons. A psychopath who wanted me dead is the one person I can trust to respect me enough to always be honest. That is so…fucking…sad."

Ryder's mouth sets straight in displeasure not of me but *for* me. "I take it you and the doctor have hit a rough patch."

"We hit an atomic bomb." I pause. "We're done. We're over."

"Care to share what happened? Did you finally uncover the fact he was Lord Nightingale? I figured you'd already sussed that one out but I could have been wrong."

My mouth drops open in shock. He knew? Jesus, does everyone know? "How—"

"Don't worry, that secret is safe with me. There's no gain for me to harm him. I have no quarrel with him." He pauses. "Unless you *want* me to have one."

"Meaning?"

"He obviously hurt you. Perhaps it might make you feel better if you returned the favor. It always made *me* feel better."

"It also got you life in prison," I point out.

"Doesn't mean you will meet the same fate," he counters. "Come on, Joanna. I know the thought has crossed your mind. I always thought you were one step away from crossing into the dark side. Maybe this was the push you needed to join us. It's far more liberating on this side. No rules. No ties. No judgment. Beholden to nothing and no one. There's something to be said for pure, unadulterated chaos."

"Sounds more like being lost."

"You're been walking the straight and narrow all your life, and you're telling me you're not lost right now?"

I want to parry back but can't think of a single comeback. Because he's right. I haven't been this unmoored since Pop died. I almost threw myself off a damn bridge because I couldn't see a way out of the misery. Not only was there no light at the end of the tunnel, I'd fallen to the depths of hell so there wasn't even a damn tunnel anymore. Even when Justin "died" I had Harry. My job. Of course I lost them as well, but I had Justin's legacy, Pendergast, and Informant 794 to keep me sane. As long as I had a breath left in my lungs I would continue what he began. For him. For the man who sacrificed himself for me. Who loved me. Who I *thought* loved me. "I don't know what the hell I'm doing, Ryder," I whisper. Goddamn it here come the tears again. I will not cry in front of a supervillain. I *will not*. "You're right. I am...lost."

"No. What you are is Joanna Fucking Fallon," he says angrily, as if I've insulted him. "The girl who crawled out of the hellscape of Diablo's Ward using her wits and pure determination. Who held her head up high as the upper crust tried to tear her down. Who faced two of the most dangerous men ever to live and bested them both. *That* woman doesn't fall apart over a *man*. She kicks that bastard in the family jewels, smiles down at him, then walks into the sunset with her head up, never looking back."

"It's not just Jem. It's—"

I could tell him. There's even a part of me that wants to. The look on Ryder's face would be priceless. But even at my worst I'm not that vindictive. Or that stupid. I have no doubt, despite this whatever we have now, if he knew Justin were alive, this psycho would cut my head off and wear it like a hat just to spite his nemesis. He escaped from that prison once, and though I've taken every measure to ensure it doesn't happen again, I'm not willing to bet my life on it. I don't underestimate the man before me anymore than he does me.

"It's..." Ryder prompts.

"I quit my job. I lost my fiancée. I lost my faith in the world. Where the hell do I go from here?"

"Wherever you desire, Miss Fallon. What brings you pleasure, Joanna? *True* pleasure? What is your *raison d'etre*?" he asks as if he already knows the answer.

"Why don't you tell me?"

He raises an eyebrow. "Why do you still submit to these little video chats of ours? Every week like clockwork. I killed the man you loved. I raped your friend. Suffocated a child. Why would you subject yourself to my company week after week? Why?"

"Because you help me."

"I help you *what*?" he prompts.

"Stop people like you from turning others into people like me. Into victims. Into broken things that never truly get reassembled."

"If that's not a reason for living, I don't know what it," Ryder says with a smile. He slowly drops it. "So stop your pathetic whining and get on with it. I saw on TV that Gearhead got away today."

"Any thoughts to where he might be holed up?"

"One or two," he says with mirth. Then he grows silent. I raise an eyebrow and glare. He chuckles. "There she is. I was getting worried."

Me too. Me too.

*

Albert Ross, aka Gearhead, you have been a blight on my fair city far too long. Time to go down, asshole. I'm coming for you, or at present your fence. Seems Gearhead isn't in the random havoc game like so many others. He's nothing more than a common thief. He creates as much destruction as possible to conceal which gadgets he's stolen. The owners just assume their latest microchip/weapon/next big thing is amongst the rubble and write it off with the rest. Clever. I so prefer mayhem with a purpose as opposed to violence for its own sake or worse for a ridiculous principal. I like my motives concrete. Tangible. Makes them easier to thwart. Know what a person wants and you're three fourths there. It's the believers that scare the shit out of me. There's no reasoning with them.

Take Mr. Ross. He has a drone and God knows what else to sell. They're useless to him in their current state. Checks are just pieces of paper until you take them to the bank. Per my new therapist, Dr. Ryder, only one woman deals in that level of tech, Diamanda Roth. Need a ray gun or giant walking eye, she's your gal. And she must be damn good at her job because there is fuck all in the Justice or police databases about her. The only time her name appears in any state is on the lease for Diamond's Bar. She must have other aliases but Ryder only knew the one. I've heard of Diamond's Bar. It sits right on the outskirts of Diablo's Ward, which means a person probably won't get shot walking to their car but might come to find the car's been stolen.

My car, my old Accura from my old non-billionaire days, should be safe here. I actually kept the clunker for nights such as this. Since Jem handled the butt kicking and I mostly stayed behind the computer, save for a few nights where I joined him on surveillance duty, the neglected car barely started when I picked it up from the mansion's garage. I haven't been *there* in over a month. Jem went more often to use the lab and machines to analyze evidence he collected. I only go there now to get clothes or to update Doris Senior. Tonight I took not only the car but my Kevlar vest, untraceable gun, brass knuckles, blonde wig, fake glasses, and nose ring.

Say hello to Missy Royal. She does not fuck around.

It was so odd walking through Pendergast's halls tonight knowing what I do now. It's been legally mine for a year and a half but never felt *mine.* I was a false heir, a usurper, a trespasser. It's worse now. It really isn't mine in all but name. For all I know Justin's married and has a child or most likely will in the future. Shouldn't it go to his kid? Just because its father is a lying asshole doesn't mean the kid shouldn't get his or her rightful due. Jesus, thoughts like this make my head hurt, and the hangover is more than enough to complete that job. I pray the cure is tracking Gearhead down. A good start anyway.

I park on the street with only one hooker working the corner—it's below freezing tonight—and adjust my wig, glasses, and check I have all the essentials. My heart begins racing the moment I shut off the car but do my best to ignore the adrenaline rush. I'm so out of practice. I used to do this type of thing on a daily basis when I was a cop. Being behind the desk was torture. I went from alley to pampered housecat, tucked safely in my penthouse watching all the action instead of being in the thick of it. Well not anymore. Kitten's getting her claws back and intends to shred anyone bloody who gets in her way. Part of me hopes to see blood tonight.

Like the area, Diamond's Bar falls just shy of full blown ghetto. The reek of cigarettes is overpowering but patrons fall short of smoking anything stronger. The crowd is a mix of gangbangers and lower middle class worker bees with some prostitutes chatting up both sets. A few people clock me as I enter, but return to their billiard games or sexual negotiations a moment later. Still. My damn heart's about to pop through my fucking ribcage. This is just a fact finding mission, Jo. It'll be fine. I do wish I had back-up. *Never* go in without back-up.

The bartender comes over the moment my butt hits the stool. Unless Diamanda had a sex change to become a fifty something, potbellied, bald man I'm pretty sure this isn't who I'm hunting for. "What can I get ya?"

"Coffee if you have it," I answer. I will earn that one day chip. "Black."

"Haven't seen you in here before," he says as he pours my drink.

"I'm from New Urbana. Just here on business."

He returns with my coffee. "What business you in?"

"The buying kind." Oh, this coffee tastes like motor oil. "And I'm looking for someone in the selling trade. A friend of my employer said to come here."

"This friend got a name?"

"Two, just like my employer. But for the purposes *your* employer would know him as Alpha Omega. I understand Ms. Roth often supplied him with tech before his unfortunate demise."

"I don't know a Ms. Roth," he says, smooth as silk.

"Of course you don't, but I'm going to keep talking anyway. Big tip coming your way if you just listen," I say with a wink. "My employer with two names understands that today a Mr. Ross came into possession of a certain machine my employer wishes to acquire. Even us Urbanites are aware all deals should be brokered through Ms. Roth. So he sent me here to do just that. He even made sure to provide her introductory fee." I reach into my pocket for the little black baggie, handing it to the bartender. "Two karat diamonds, correct?" The man checks the bag. "My number's in there too. Untraceable cell of course. Only you and my employer have the number."

"And just out of curiosity, your boss is…"

"Not important. The woman you claim not to know will deal exclusively with me. Safer for all parties involved. If she needs more information or references, have her give me a call. I can *drone* on for hours." With a smile, I drop a twenty on the bar. "I'm Missy by the way. Missy Cassidy Royal," I say, giving him one of my old undercover names. "I can give you my Federal ID number too if it'll make it easier to check up on me."

"That won't be necessary."

"Good. And you are?"

"Darryl Paul."

"Well, Darryl Paul, thank you for the motor oil. Hope to see you again soon. *Ciao*."

With a wink, I climb off the stool and stroll out of the dive, smirk plain as day. Really I feel like bursting into laughter. That…was…amazing. Thrilling. Fucking brilliant. The mental chess. The fact he could have pulled a gun at any time. God I've missed this. Almost as good as sex. Okay it was better than quite a few times I've had sex. Thank you, James Ryder for the info and the pep talk. Couldn't have done it without you. Which is really fucking sad. But it worked.

Oh yes, the bitch is back.

CHAPTER SIX

A THIN LINE

Waiting is the hardest part. It can be actual agony when you used up what little patience God gave you in the womb. I'd forgotten how much I hate being idle. A job, a boyfriend, a hobby, friends, and multiple charities counting on you doesn't leave a lot of spare time. I'm used to juggling three things at once. The past few days I just had V's investigation, which took all of three hours to crack, and staring at my burner phone willing it to ring. Sadly the only person to call is Pendergast in-house council to inform me the resignation papers are drawn up. During my lost week I must have received three calls a day from various company men to verify I still intended to step down. In one of my drunker moments I drafted an e-mail to the other board members, Lane, Shannon, possibly even the janitors that read, "I resign. My reasons are none of your business. As my final act as Head of the Board, majority shareholder, and figurehead, I hereby appoint Shannon Abrams as my proxy and replacement, which as I've heard whispered by you assholes, should have happened a year and a half ago. You officially have your wish. Later bitches." I should never let Jack Daniels speak for me.

At least today there's a distraction. Instead of waiting by the phone in my borrowed apartment, I bring it with me to sign away my right to Pendergast Industries. Shannon, Lane, one of the lawyers and our CFO Leonard Pak wait around the conference table for me. They've taken care of everything. For five million a year, drawn from my shares, Shannon will represent me at all board meetings, make all my votes, and be privy to all major deals acting as advisor to the CEO and CFO. If she's daunted by her new windfall it doesn't show on her pretty face. The consummate professional. She'll do ten times the job I did.

Not a hell of a lot changes after I sign the papers. I'm still a billionaire. I still have my positions on the hospital board and other charities. At the end of the day all I've done is given up the right to stick my nose into business dealings I barely understood. Which must be why I don't feel a damn thing as I scrawl my name a dozen times on the mountain of documents.

"We'll send out an official press release today," Lane says. "There have been rumors of course, but the official story is you're resigning to focus more on your charitable work."

"An oldie but a goodie," I say.

"We may need you to do a press conference just to—"

"Nope," I say as I sign the final page. I slide the document across the table to the lawyer and rise from the table. "Just don't bankrupt the company, huh? Now if you'll excuse me, I have an office to clean out. Gentlemen. Shannon."

"I'll walk with you," says Shannon as she stands as well.

"Afraid I'm going to steal the silverware?" I ask with a wink. With nods to the gents, we ladies leave the board room toward the elevators. "So, how does it feel to be a millionaire?"

"The same. It hasn't really hit me yet." She glances at me. "I can't believe you were serious about this. What...I mean...are you sure? Truly? You're not just—"

"Drunk? Crazy? Not at this moment," I say with a smile. We step into the elevator. "I just want to focus on my charity work."

The doors close. "Is that why you're no longer wearing your engagement ring? You left Dr. Ambrose to focus on charity as well?" My mouth opens in surprise. "I noticed it on the flight to Independence. It was gone when you made your grand proclamation. You should know the press office has been contacted with questions about you two."

"What have they been saying?"

"No comment. But *I* have a vested interest in all of this. You could change your mind and—"

"I am not changing my mind," I insist. "The keys to the kingdom are yours, Shannon. They should have been in the first place. I just finally decided to let them go."

The doors open and we step out into the foyer. "Well, for what it's worth, I'm sorry for whatever happened that brought you to all this. And I'm honored you think I'm up to following in your footsteps."

"Oh Shannon, don't follow my footsteps. You'll end up in the Australian outback with no water. You kept me on track."

"Well, as my last act as your assistant—"

"*Lovely* assistant," I cut in.

"Lovely assistant, I am going to tell you Bennett Stone has phoned twice in as many days and three times before that. He was worried, and it seems he is now in town. He arrived this morning."

"Wonderful," I mutter.

"*And* Captain O'Hara called your line about an hour before you arrived. Something about a woman named Missy

Royal. He sounded concerned, especially when he couldn't reach you on your cell."

Shit. "Thank you. I promise from now on I'll keep my cell on. And if it's dire feel free to give out the apartment phone number. I'll probably be there a month or two."

"We should charge you rent," Shannon quips.

"Call it severance." We stop at the double doors to my office. "If you need anything let me know and I'll help any way I can." I hold out my hand for her to shake. "And take care of yourself. Take care of the company."

Shannon slips her thin hand into mine, giving it a firm shake. "I'll make you and Justin proud."

"Shannon...you don't owe us a damn thing." I pull away my hand and smile. "Give me twenty minutes and it's all yours."

"There's a box waiting inside."

"You think of everything."

With a reverent nod, I open the door and step inside. Like the mansion this space wasn't ever really mine. I didn't change a thing, not a painting, not the carpet or Persian rug, hell not even the photos on the desk. I did add two of my own: one of me and Pop as he blew out his birthday candles on his last birthday and the other a selfie of Jem and me on our boat *The Athena* making our best duck faces as the wind whipped around us. They sit right beside the photos of Justin's parents, of him and me at age fourteen playing video games in the living room, and one of Rebecca and Daisy at the playground on the swings. I take them all, along with the candy bars, deodorant, spare shirt, hairbrush, and cache of weapons. Fairly sure Shannon won't need to keep an arsenal in her desk "just in case."

I take one last look around this office and still feel fuck all. Life altering changes should elicit some emotion. Fear, regret, elation, relief. I got nothing. Maybe I've blown a gasket. "Good-bye, office." I shut the door and don't look back.

I am officially an unemployed bum. Now what?

I've kept my burner phone on since I left the bar, even taking it into the bathroom with me, but still no call. I check it again in the elevator. No joy. Something isn't right. Maybe it has something to do with why Harry called. The poor man isn't home a day from his honeymoon and he finds himself in a mess of my creation. Some things never change.

I wait until I'm in my car before I turn on my real cell. I cleared most of the voice mails—all seventy-five—from my lost week, but find five since last night. One from V thanking me for the dirt on Mayor Miracle, two from reporters, one from Harry sounding none too pleased, and the last from Bennett Stone sounding far *too* pleased. He's in town, wants to see me to pick my brain about a project, and is waiting with baited breath for my call. Jesus wept.

Only Harry receives a call back. He picks up on the forth ring.

"Captain O'Hara."

"It's Jo. How was Turks and Caicos?" I ask all sweetness and light.

"Hang on." I hear him walking then a door shutting. Privacy. This conversation's going to suck. "You need to tell me what the hell is going on *right now*. Your cousin left me two messages saying you've gone off the deep end that you're drinking again, and now someone in New Urbana PD researched your old undercover rap sheet. So I'll ask again, what the hell is going on?"

"Is the squad working the Gearhead case?"

"What? Yes. Why?"

"Have you compiled a list of what was missing or destroyed?"

"What does that have to do with—I'm not telling you a damn thing until you talk to me. Are you drinking again?"

"I fell off the wagon but got right back on. I swear on Pop's grave. I'm attending two meetings a day. I'm fine."

There's silence on his end. I can sense the disapproval wafting through the line. At least I don't have to see it on his face. "What happened?"

If anyone deserves the truth, it's him. The man had a front row seat to the fallout and was damaged by it as well. "The short version? Justin's alive. Jem knew."

"What? Are you—"

"Harry, I am many things but crazy isn't one of them. I saw the fucker. I spoke to him. I puked on him. He's alive and well and living in Independence."

"Jesus Christ, Jo. And Ambrose knew?"

"Yeah. So I had a mini-breakdown, but I'm over it. I'm good. I'm keeping busy. Which is good for both of us because I have a thread on Gearhead. It might be something, it might be nothing. I didn't want to bring it to the squad until I had something concrete. And I'm not in any danger because I know that's your next question. Just like all the other times Informant 794 helped before. Just me and my computer. Nothing's changed," I lie. "And short of arresting me, you can't stop me either. So there's no point in worrying about me. You have a new wife and baby on the way to concern yourself with. I shouldn't even be an afterthought. It's my mess, my stupidity. I'm handling it. Alone."

"I'm so sorry, Jo."

"It's my own fault for trusting men who consciously choose to lead double lives. Or hell, maybe it's karma. I betrayed you and damned if it hasn't come back to me three fold."

"Don't say that. You don't deserve this."

"Maybe."

"Well, I'm here for you if you need me. If you feel like taking a drink, if—"

"I will call my sponsor and go to a meeting. I swear it."

"And *I* swear if you're holding anything back on the Gearhead case or put yourself in danger, I will arrest you."

"I know. Just, you might want to compile that list I mentioned. Mr. Ross might be far less complex than we gave him credit for."

He's silent for a moment. "You think this is a robbery? He killed almost a dozen people yesterday. He destroyed half a building."

"As I said, early stages. I'll call when I have more. And say hello to the guys and Bella for me. Bye."

I hang up before he can rip into me further. I truly don't want him worrying about me. He's done it far more than I deserve. Another reason we never would have worked as a couple. He'd have a heart attack a year from the stress alone. He'll forget all the worry when I hand him the goods on Gearhead.

If Diamanda Roth's checking up on Missy Royal then I've made the first cut. Missy worked well for me when we were trying to track down a weapons supplier in the Giuliani syndicate. Missy Royal acted as a front for the 1-8-7 gang in New Urbana, at least per the rap sheet implanted in the databases. I resurrected her in the system before I left for the bar. Damn good thing too, it seems. But I'm tired of waiting. Through my investigation I tracked down Darryl Paul's home address. Quick pop home for a costume change. And—

My phone rings. A 138 area code. Independence. Hell no. Voice mail do your thing. I pull out of the parking garage onto the always hectic city streets. I need to hire my own car service now that privilege was signed away. I'll add it to the endless list. Which leads to the question, *how* exactly will I fill my days? There isn't always going to be an investigation in need of my skills. I *could* actually focus on charity. Form a few of my own. The Joanna Fallon Foundation for Children in Need or whatever. Give kids in the foster system counseling or something. And endowments, lots of endowments and grants, but in my own name. All the charities I help are in the Pendergast name. Nothing has my personal stamp on it. *I* want a legacy, not just to be a footnote in the Pendergasts'. I'll form one in Pop's name too. That way he'll never be forgotten either.

The cell phone beeps to inform me of a voice mail. Fuck. Just rip off the Band-Aid, Jo. I punch in my code and listen.

"Hello gorgeous," Bennett Stone says. I breathe a literal sigh of relief. "This is my, oh, fourth call and no reply. I'm beginning to think you're avoiding me, which is a shame because there's something I need to tell you." He takes a deep breath. "Okay. Here goes…Joanna, I'm pregnant." He says it so seriously I can't help but chuckle. "And it's yours. So you have to call me now." He's silent for a moment. "Seriously though, I would like to speak to you about something business related. I'm in town for a few days, and I'd love to take a meeting. Just a meeting. So please call. For the sake of our child," he says melodramatically before chuckling. "Bye."

Oh, what a dick. But a funny dick. With a big dick. Okay, Mr. Stone, you made me laugh. That deserves a response. He picks up on the third ring. "Well hello, Ms. Fallon."

"Mr. Stone."

"Screening your calls?"

"Always."

"Hopefully next time I make the cut. How are you?"

"Sitting in traffic behind a semi. Been better."

"And are the rumors true? You've officially given Pendergast Industries the finger and walked away?"

"Word travels fast."

"It does indeed. So how do you feel about it?"

"Relieved mostly. My dream of becoming an unemployed waste of space has finally come to fruition. I now have time to be a lady who lunches between plastic surgery visits and talking down to the help."

Bennett chuckles. "Living the dream, right?" His chuckles subside. "No. Really. What will you do with yourself now?"

"Focus on charity, I guess"

"Really?" Stone asks.

"Yeah. Why not?"

"Precisely what I hoped to hear," says Bennett. "*And* it sounds as if I've caught you before anyone else can scoop that luscious butt of yours up."

"Okay…"

"Are you available for dinner tonight?"

Oh, I knew it. "Bennett, I told you—"

"A business dinner. Nothing more. This will be worth your while, I promise. I'll even pay."

I consider the proposal for all of a second. Anything is better than sitting in that apartment waiting for a call that may never come. "Komodo's. Best sushi in town."

"Nine work for you?"

"Sounds good. But this is just a business dinner. What happened was a one off. I mean it. And keep the flirting to a minimum."

"No guarantees on that last one," he says, "but I will try my utmost. Until nine, gorgeous."

"Until nine. Bye." I end the call with a sigh. "You are playing with fire, Jo."

Damn good thing I've spent my whole life juggling that element. Maybe this time I won't get burned. Hope springs eternal.

*

Darryl Paul ain't doing too shabby for a lowly bartender. The man actually resides in my old neighborhood. I lived two blocks away before Ryder blew up my apartment. Like that building, hell like eighty percent of the buildings here, Paul lives in a building owned by Pendergast, one built before the Great War. Not cheap, but no doorman. Lucky me. I press all of three buttons before I'm buzzed in. The super should hold a building meeting about the importance of vigilance while living in a major metropolitan area. I just stroll in and up to Paul's third floor apartment. My bartender friend opens the door after the second round of knocks, obviously roused from bed judging from the boxers and Independence Eagles t-shirt. He can't place me at first, it was dark in that bar, but my grin sparks recognition.

"Greetings and salutations, Mr. Paul. Sorry if I woke you." I pause. "Okay, not really."

"How did you—"

He's left enough room for me to snake past him into his messy, modestly decorated apartment. "You think you and your boss are the only ones with people inside police departments? I handed you ten grand in diamonds. You really think I didn't know who I was handing them to? I don't represent some bushwhack gangbanger. We're talking millions here. Not to mention my employer needs his order expedited. He's not really into games. Well, not unless whips and stilettos are involved."

"Get the fuck out of my apartment," Darryl orders.

I flop on his cigarette reeking couch. "Yeah, not until I talk to Ms. Roth."

"Bitch, you are—" He slams the door shut to take a step toward me.

The snub nose .38 I whip out of my black hoodie's pouch stops the second step. I don't point it at him, I just keep it in my hand, which I rest on my thigh. "Have you ever met a supervillain, Mr. Paul? I mean, a real one? Alkaline? That Emperor guy? The Basher? The kind with a double or triple number body count?"

His bloodshot eyes don't leave the gun. "No."

"Well, I *work* for one. I see him almost every day. So, ask yourself, do you think *you* scare me? The only thing that scares me is going back to my boss empty handed. And Mr. Paul, I will do anything to make sure that doesn't happen. So I either start putting holes in strategic points of your body until you give me Ms. Roth's number, or you just pick up that fucking phone over there so she and I can have a little chat, and you never see my beautiful face again. I vote for option two. You?"

The bartender glares at me, studying my impassive face, I guess to gage the severity of my threat. I cock my head and smile. One upside of finding yourself often facing down psychopaths, you can learn to mimic their mannerisms. I must be doing a good job channeling my inner sociopath because his shoulders slump slightly and he begins moving toward an end table where the portable phone sits. "Thank you, Mr. Paul. And your kneecaps thank you as well."

His gaze stays on the gun as he dials. "Dee? It's Darryl." He listens for a second. "Not really. There's someone in my apartment who wants to talk to you. The chick from New Urbana." He listens again. "She said someone in the police department." He pauses then scowls. "I don't know, Dee. Just talk to the crazy bitch, okay?"

Holding out the phone, he bridges the small gap between us. I grip the pistol tighter, but he just hands me the phone. "Thank you." I press the phone to my ear. "Ms. Roth? Glad we could finally connect."

"This is not how I conduct business," snaps the woman on the other end. I'd place her late forties, early fifties and from Galilee.

"Nor me, but as I was telling your man here, time is of the essence. My employer *needs* the drone Mr. Ross stole the other day."

"Well, unfortunately that particular item was a commission and has already been delivered to its buyer. I *was* working on finding you a substitute from my list of contacts, but in light of this unprofessional behavior, I don't think I'll bother anymore. Do not contact me or mine again, Miss Royal. We're done here." She hangs up without another word.

That could have gone better, but it went well enough. Before I left my apartment, I set up a trap and trace on Darryl Paul's home phone and cell. The moment he dialed Doris began tracing the number. I now have her direct line and possibly her location. Gotta love the technological age. "Your boss is a bitch," I say as I stand. I toss him his phone back.

"You're one to talk."

I roll my eyes behind my fake glasses. "Sorry to have bothered you."

I slip my gun and hand into my pouch and walk toward the door. Darryl doesn't move I'm sure until I shut his door. With a satisfied grin, I meander down the almost empty hallway behind the man in the dark purple hoodie. Smooth as clockwork. I...my smile drops to the dirty ground when the man rounds the corner and I catch a glimpse of his profile. If the familiar cologne wasn't a tip off those damn lips and cheekbones would be. Motherfucker.

Suddenly filled with righteous anger, I pick up the pace. He's already a flight below me, hooded head bowed when I reach the staircase. "I know it's you, asshole!" I shout down. "I bought you that damn cologne and sweatshirt, remember?"

He slows his descent almost to a standstill and looks up at my scowling face. Jesus Christ. I haven't seen him since I moved out over a week ago and in that time I swear he's lost ten pounds and hasn't shaved once. With the hood, baggy blue jeans, and scruffy face no one would ever conceive that this is Galilee's premier neurologist and superhero. I'm sure I'm no model right now, but he looks almost sick. Dark circles, hollow cheeks, waxy skin. That could just be a disguise. I *hope* it's a disguise. But his present state does little to quell my anger. I hustle down the stairs, my scowl intensifying with each step. I do get some satisfaction when the man who regularly beats the crap out of the baddest bastards on the planet shrinks in on himself as I approach. He *should* be terrified. I grab his arm and yank him to the corner of the stairwell.

"What the fuck, Jem?" I hiss. "Have you been following me all this time? Are you stalking me now?"

"Of course not," he says.

"Then what the hell are you doing here? How did you know where I was?"

"Doris. Lizard, y-your hacker set-up another laptop for me to access her. I was working the case and noticed from the files you were as well. I know all about Missy Royal's re-emergence, but I grew especially concerned when Harry O'Hara phoned me. He told me you fell off the wagon. That he thought you'd lied to him about working the case. He's worried about you. So *I* grew worried about you." He pauses. "I traced the GPS on your cell."

"*What?*" I snap.

"We installed the program on both our phones, remember?"

"Stalker!" I turn on my heel and begin walking away before I punch him.

"I was concerned and with just cause!" he calls behind me. I'm about halfway to the next floor when he reaches my side. "What on earth were you thinking? You went into a known criminal's apartment without back-up. Without letting anyone know where you were. He could have raped you. He could have killed you, and we never would have found your body."

"Give me a little damn credit," I snap back. "I survived the ghetto, over a decade on the force, and two supervillains. One underling isn't going to take me down. I'm not stupid. I have on a flak jacket and arsenal hidden on me."

We walk out onto the sidewalk. "It was still reckless. And idiotic. And dangerous."

"*And* none of your goddamn business! Nothing I do now is your business anymore. You've lost the right to lecture, hell to even *speak* to me." He grabs my arm and spins me around. I yank my limb from his grip. "And you certainly lost the right to touch me!"

"I'm sorry," he says, holding up his hands in surrender. "I'm sorry. I didn't…" He groans in frustration. "You hate me now. Fine. I can take it. Perhaps I even deserve it. But don't you dare punish yourself for my crimes. Don't you dare needlessly endanger your life. Don't you *dare*."

"And don't you dare flatter yourself thinking I hate you, Ambrose," I fire back. "That implies I actually give a shit about you anymore. You mean *nothing* to me. You are nothing but a tainted memory not worth a second of my time." I smile cruelly. "Now, if you'll excuse me, it seems I have to go purchase a new cell phone before my date tonight. Bennett Stone's in town, you know. Flew all the way here just to see me. I have a *long* night ahead of me." I drop the smile. "So fuck off."

This time he doesn't stop me from turning my back on him and walking away. "And you claim you don't hate me," he calls behind me.

I don't look back. I don't dare.

CHAPTER SEVEN

PLAYING WITH FIRE

"Better late than never, I suppose."

The hostess at Komodo pulls out my chair across from the smirking playboy. I sit with an apologetic smile for my dinner companion. I'm only twenty minutes late, and I did text him to let him know I would be. Still rude of me. After the Jphone store, which took over a freaking hour, I became so immersed in tracking that bitch Diamanda I lost track of time. The trap and trace not only got me her phone number but the general location of where she took the call, near a cell tower in Greenwitch, a suburb of Galilee. I started culling through the property records of every warehouse or large building in that thirty mile radius. That's over a hundred buildings. I only got through two thirds when I noticed the clock. After emailing my findings to Harry, I had about ten minutes to get dressed and beautified, which took double the allotted time. The only dress not wrinkled from its time in a trash bag is so low-cut a stripper would feel immodest wearing it. Bennett's gaze glues itself to my overflowing rack the moment I step into view. Despite what I told Jem, I have no intention of letting this dinner veer into romantic territory. None.

"Sorry. It's been a hell of a day," I say.

"So I heard. You're the talk of the business world. The story went national."

"Oh, God," I groan. "What are they saying?"

"That you had a nervous breakdown. That you were forced out. That you're in rehab. That you quit to become a supervillain. I think a body switching machine was mentioned as well. Let them talk. It'll be forgotten in the next news cycle."

Our waitress comes over and leaves with my coffee order. "Forgive me if I pass out in my miso soup," I say.

"Well, at least you look great. I could see why someone would want to switch bodies with you."

"Please keep the flirting to a minimum, alright? I don't have the energy to play with you tonight."

"Well, I have no problem with you lying back as I do all the heavy lifting," he says, cocking his left eyebrow. "I'm in a giving mood."

I open the menu. "Good. Then you can pick up the check. I'm fucking starving." The waitress hustles back with my coffee and leaves with our orders. Great service here. "So, what brings you to my neck of the woods?"

"Just a bit of business. A pet project is finally getting off the ground. I'll be popping in and out a lot in the next few months."

"Does your project have to do with the proposition you mentioned on the phone?"

"Yes and no, but mostly no," Bennett says.

"Cryptic. So give me the pitch, playboy. The suspense is killing me."

He sips his martini. "Do you recall when you said you and I could be the poster children for super powered collateral damage?"

"That was a lifetime ago. No."

"Well, I do. And unlike you, it stuck with me. It even sparked something inside me. An idea. A vision if you will."

"Glad I could be of assistance."

"You're not off the hook yet, Fallon. *You* started it, you're going to help me finish it."

"What?"

"I want to start a global fund, maybe even an organization that provides aid to anyone affected by supers." He leans forward. "I did some research. Only about a third of the major population centers have *any* charitable organizations that focus on super violence. Galilee and Independence are two of the lucky ones, and I use the word loosely. And once the baseline organization or foundation is established, in the future we can branch out into lobbying for changes in the laws and—"

"Providing information and counseling, not only to those affected by the violence but those with powers," I cut in. "A lot of these people, when they discover they have an ability, the only resource available about how to behave is from mass media. They have no other examples of what to do save for the heroes and villains they see on TV."

"Which leads to more heroes and villains popping up and more collateral damage," adds Bennett.

"We can stop the problem before it even becomes a problem."

"I never thought of that possibility," he says, impressed. "I was thinking more along the lines of reconstruction and covering medical bills, but...I like it. It's a holistic approach to the issue. Did you just come up with that?"

"Not exactly," I say. "Jem had the idea awhile back. It was just talk though."

"Well, if you have to steal, steal from a genius, huh?" Bennett's cell phone rings, and he rolls his eyes. "Shit. Just when things were heating up. I am so, so sorry." He rises. "I have to take this."

"Go right ahead."

With an apologetic smile, he hustles away for some privacy. I chuckle to myself. I have to say I'm surprised. I really thought the only business we'd be discussing would be who would pay the cab fare when we went back to his hotel. Not that I planned to go to his hotel room. I made a promise to myself no matter how charming he was tonight, the man wasn't getting so much as a kiss. Until I get my head on completely straight, I'm gonna live like a nun. No more self-destruction for Joanna Fallon. Hell, if Bennett has his way I may be in the saving the world racket.

The waitress returns before Bennett with our edamame and miso. I don't care if it's rude I begin eating anyway. It's actually not a bad idea this foundation or fund of his. The medical bills alone after a concussion or just removing glass from an explosion can be in the thousands, forget it the person needs surgery. After Cain, my hospital bill was almost $100,000 even before the plastic surgery for my face. Two years ago that would have bankrupted me. Most people don't have a best friend who fakes his death then leaves you billions. Okay, I'm fairly sure I'm the only person ever that's happened to. Well, it's time to put my ill-gotten gains to better use.

Jem and I did discuss setting up something similar once or twice, we were just too fucking busy to go beyond talk. I've got nothing but time now. I find myself frowning. Another thing I wanted to build with him I have to do alone. Well, not alone.

Whoever called Bennett must have had complex news because my companion doesn't return for over ten minutes. I've finished all our hor'derves when he finally hustles back. "Thought maybe you abandoned me here," I say as he sits.

"Never."

"Everything alright?"

"Wonderful. Better than the projections."

"So what is this secret project?" I ask.

"If I told you, it wouldn't be a secret," he says with that butter wouldn't melt smile of his. "No, you'd just find it incredibly dull. I'd much rather return to our original discussion. As I said, early stages I know, but I have built an international charity from the ground up before. I know the right people to hire, the right people to bribe to speed up the process both in our country and many others. I already have my accountants crunching numbers. Consequently, just for the infrastructure, advertisements, office space, bribes, endowments, just getting started we're talking twenty-five mil, fifty if we set up counseling centers. Now I'm more than willing to split that cost. My issue is time. In that I have precious little to spare. This will be a full time plus endeavor. Lots of travel, lots of meetings, lots of press junkets. I do want us *both* to be the face of the charity, though. Any major events or interviews, I would want to be there as well."

"So I'd do all the work and you'd get all the limelight."

"Pretty much. But I do shine in the limelight. How I imagine it is I'm the fun-loving rapscallion who makes people feel good, whereas you are the strong, capable gal who makes them feel secure."

"Good cop, bad cop. I always did rock bad cop."

"So you're in?" he asks with excitement.

My eyes narrow. "I…you want an answer tonight? Right now? Bennett, this is a massive commitment, not just financially. You're asking me to become your partner, this minute, on an undertaking that will basically consume my every waking hour. I need more to go on. Time to think. Time to review this with my accountant, my lawyer. I—"

"Fallon, I'm not asking you to elope," I raise an eyebrow, "metaphorically of course. Think of it as engaged to be engaged. I brought the projections, a list of potential staff, a preliminary proposal, basically a road map to guide you. All I'm asking right now is that you take a look at those files. If you envision yourself partnering with me, trusting me on this journey." He leans forward. "Look, I know we've just met, I do, but for whatever reason I trust you. I feel…a kinship with you. I have never connected with someone so fast like this before. After one minute with you I just *knew* we were going to be friends. I did. We're cut from the same cloth. We get each other. Am I wrong?"

"No," I concede.

"See? And I also know there is no one on this earth that will put in more time, fight harder for the people we mean to help than you. You've been there. You know their pain. If in some way helping them helps you, more's the better."

"So this is pity? I'd prefer that you just wanted to bang me."

"Well, there is that too." And there goes the boyish grin. "But I swear, this offer comes not from my libido, not from pity, but from a place of respect. Let me prove it. Just take this first step, okay? Just say yes."

It is an intriguing proposal. I could do a lot of good. It'd be my chance to build something from the ground up, shaping it to fit my vision. It's definitely a prospect worth exploring. The only downside I see is the man sitting across from me. I don't entirely trust his motives, or him for that matter. I could just be gun-shy when it comes to friends. We'd be partners, though it sounds like he'd be closer to the silent variety save for when there are cameras around. It really couldn't hurt to just skim the proposal and documents.

"I'm not going to sleep with you."

"If you say so."

"And *I'd* be the captain of this ship. If we plan on me doing all the work, I get a greater say in how its run, personnel, policy, allocation of resources. Your input matters, but I'd have final veto power."

"Exactly how I imagined it as well. I'll even concede top billing in whatever we decide to call it."

"Okay." I hold out my hand across the table. "Consider us engaged to be engaged."

Bennett gives my hand a firm shake. "You won't regret this, gorgeous."

Yeah, like I don't regret my last engagement. I'm still culling through the damage from that crash and burn. And here I go again, playing with fire. At least this time the only thing on the line is my time, money, and reputation. There isn't a shred of heart or soul left to destroy.

*

"How about The Fallon/Stone Super Rescue Foundation?"

I crinkle my nose with distaste. "That sounds like we're a superhero rescue team."

Bennett laces his fingers behind his head and crosses his ankles on the bed. "Well, if you think about it, we kind of will be. Just minus the flying and laser beam eyes."

No, I am not in bed with him. I sit at the desk across the giant studio apartment-like hotel room surrounded by papers, a cup of coffee, and notepad where I've been scribbling thoughts for two hours since I agreed to return to his hotel. I have to get my financial advisor and lawyer to review everything, but so far it all appears on the up and up. For once Bennett Stone isn't trying to screw me, at least financially.

"I just think the word 'super' sounds ridiculous no matter what we put around it," I say.

"Then perhaps The Fallon/Stone Aberration Rescue Foundation? Inhuman? Freak? Mutant?"

"I still vote for the Fallon/Stone Shit Happens Foundation." I toss my pen down and rub my eyes. "Okay, maybe we take our egos out of the equation. One thing people can get behind besides a person is a symbol, right? A word, a concept. People hear it, see it, they know what we're about. So what are we? Throw out some words."

"Rescue," Bennett says, "angels, crisis, heroes, idol, champion, defender, protector—"

"Guardian," I add with a scoff.

Bennett's arms fall to his sides, and he sits up in bed. "The Fallon/Stone Guardian Society. Our volunteers would be called Stone Guardians. Our emblem…a shield with angel wings engraved on." He holds up a finger as he leaps from the bed. "No! Not just wings. Icarus. The god who flew too close to the sun. He flies on the shield."

I have to admit it's better than anything I've come up with in an hour. "Society not foundation?"

"Foundation sounds too stuffy and formal. Society implies it can go anywhere, is inclusive of all, that it can have many facets."

I write it down on the pad and circle it. "Then we have a winner. Hallelujah. I can go home." I glance at the clock. Jesus, it's past one AM. Even with three cups of coffee I'm bone tired. Excited but tired. Because I've been playing it cool, but I am so absolutely doing this. Even if he pulls out every cent of his, I'm going forward. I just don't want him to think I'm *too* easy. "Fuck, it's late."

"You're more than welcome to stay the night. I even promise to keep my hands to myself."

"I think I can make it home, thanks." I rise from the desk. "Just gonna use your bathroom before I go. Can you gather everything for me to take? I'll have my people review it tomorrow."

"I live to serve you, Miss Fallon."

With a smirk, I cross the room to the bathroom just as his cell phone begins buzzing on the nightstand again. The man's been getting calls all night long. I turned mine off before I got to the restaurant. It's just good manners, not that Bennett apparently ever learned that. He took two more calls at the restaurant then several more as I reviewed the files. He was gone half an hour at one point. It seems he might not have been lying about being too busy for our newly formed society. Good. This queen sure as hell doesn't need a king meddling in her realm. She's got this.

The coffee is just about out of my system when there's a knock on the door. "Um, Joanna?"

"Occupied!"

"Joanna, uh, phone call for you," he says, sounding almost confused.

Phone call? No one knows I'm here. "Who is it?"

"Your ex. He sounds…forceful."

Oh Jesus Fucking Christ you are shitting me. I wipe and flush before hustling out of the bathroom where Bennett stands at the door, phone in his hand. I snatch it. "How the hell did you get this number? Are you out of your fucking mind? I told you to stop—"

"Where are you?" Jem cuts in.

"None of your goddamn business! You are really starting to freak me—"

"Joanna, just stop talking," he orders through gritted teeth. "Stop! This is...Guardian, Code Pink. Repeat: Code Pink."

My mouth snaps shut as my stomach clenches. Fuck. *Fuck.* When Jem went back in the field we came up with a shorthand code system. Blue means call the police to his location, Green I'm needed at the scene, Purple is he's been unmasked and we need to enact the Houdini Protocol, and Pink meaning *I'm* in immediate danger and need to flee. Just...fuck. "You sure?"

"Yes. Just tell me where you are so Captain O'Hara can dispatch a squad car to collect you."

"You're with Harry? What happened? Is—"

"Joanna, just give me the address! Now!"

I glance at the confused Bennett. "Um, The Firebrand Hotel. The Executive Suite."

Jem repeats the information to someone, who responds, though the words are muffled. "O'Hara's sending a car now. Do not leave until they get you. Are you armed?"

"Um, no."

"Three minutes," I think I hear Harry say in the background. "Grovner and Parker."

"Did you hear him?" Jem asks.

"Yes. But what the hell is happening?"

"What's going on?" Bennett asks, now more concerned than confused.

"There, uh, was a prison break at Xavier," Jem says.

"Oh my God. Who escaped?"

There's a pregnant, bile inducing pause before he says, "Everyone. Every supervillain housed there has vanished. They're just…gone. Including him. He's free, Joanna. They all are."

Shit. Shit, shit, shit, shit, shit… "Fuck."

"The officers will escort you home. Then you know what to do, right? Pack, check into a hotel under an assumed na—"

"I remember the protocol. I'll call you when I get to the hotel."

"Good. I'll see you as soon as I can. I love you."

"I lo—" I stop myself. "See you soon." I end the call and close my eyes to better concentrate on quelling the rising panic about to overtake my much needed wits.

"Fallon, what the hell is going on?" Bennett asks.

This is bad. This is fucking apocalyptic. I can't go through this again. I can't—

Someone grips my shoulders. "Joanna!" Bennett's shake forces my eyes open. "Tell me what's happening. What protocol?"

"I…uh…Ja-James Ryder's escaped from prison again. They-They *all* escaped. I, uh, you-you should probably leave town. You should go. I-I…" Need to collect my shit because the police are coming for me. Because my life is in danger. Again. I move to the desk and begin gathering papers.

"You should come with me."

I spin around. "What?"

"We could go somewhere. Thailand, Australia. We could work on The Society. Do it on the beach. You'd be safe. We could even have separate bedrooms if you want. Or you can go alone."

It is an idea. A good idea. If I'd run the last time, or the time before that, I wouldn't have nightmares every week. I wouldn't have literal scars. But there is a reason I didn't run. Why I didn't hide. If I'm the target, my friends, my family, innocent people could be drawn into this mess. That is Ryder's M.O. after all. And I couldn't hide forever.

"That's nice of you, Bennett, but I'll be fine. This is all just a precaution."

"So what's this protocol you mentioned? You going to be tied to a stake in the town square covered in blood to lure them all to you?"

"No, I'll be in a hotel, which I'm not supposed to leave, under a false name."

"Will I be able to see you? Call you? What about—"

"I don't know!" I scream. "I don't know anything right now! Stop asking me questions! I don't—I—"

"Hey, hey," he says, striding toward me. My friend wraps his arms around me in what I think is supposed to be a comforting embrace. I'm too hyped up to appreciate the gesture, but find myself hugging him back anyway. "It's okay to be afraid. I'd be shitting myself. But it'll all be okay. You'll see. And I'm here for you. I mean it. Call and I'm there."

"Thank you." I remove myself from his grasp and half smile to reassure him. "You—"

The telephone rings by the bed. Guess my escort's here. Bennett walks over to answer it while I collect the last of the papers. "Hello?" Bennett asks. "Yes, I am."

"Ask their names," I say.

"What are the officer's names?" He listens. "Parker and Grovner." I nod. "Send them up. Thank you." Bennett hangs up and sighs. "Well, this night didn't turn out as I'd envisioned."

I slip on my shoes. "Sure you still want to partner with me?"

"Is it always like this?" he asks as he approaches.

"Sometimes it's much, *much* worse." I shrug on my coat and grab my purse and the box. "But if I do get kidnapped and tortured again just think of the publicity The Society will get."

Bennett stops a foot in front of me. "Is it terrible I was just thinking the same thing?" he asks with a smile.

I can't help but chuckle. Not even the knock on the door stops the black mirth. Gallows humor, my favorite kind. "Miss Fallon?" a man says on the other side of the door. "Captain O'Hara sent us."

"My squad car awaits," I say to Bennett.

"And my jet is fueled," he parries. "Frolicking, fun, fucking. Yours for the taking." His smile dims a little. "You *can* sit this one out, you know. You don't owe anyone a damn thing. You've done enough, Joanna. More than enough. Just come with me, gorgeous. *Please.*"

And here I thought he didn't have a serious bone in his body. The man's positively grim right now. Before I can stop myself, I kiss him. Our first. Quick and sweet. "It's never enough, playboy. But we gotta keep trying, right? Because if we don't, who will?" I kiss him again and smile. "I'll call when I can."

Smile still affixed, I pick up my box and walk toward the door. Through the peephole I see the officers. I recognize

Parker from the wedding. What a way to reconnect. I open the door. "Hey, Parker."

"Fallon," he says with a nod.

"Shall we?" I give Bennett one last smile for the road. "See you around, playboy."

"That a promise?"

"God willing." I pucker my lips to blow him a kiss before returning to my new friends. "Okay boys, take me away."

And once again I'm thrust into the freaking fray that threatens to consume Galilee Falls. It must be a day that ends in "Y."

CHAPTER EIGHT

AT YOUR PERIL

It is a damn good thing I recently spent a week in an alcohol coma because I don't think I'll be getting more than an hour of sleep here or there for the foreseeable future. Diamanda, the Society, life in general including trips to the Land of Nod will have to wait. First order of business is fleeing.

The officers escort me to my apartment where I quickly pack two large suitcases, a satchel full of weapons and disguises, my Society box, and Doris Jr. My bodyguards help me carry them back to the squad car then drive me to the nearest hotel, where I check in, quickly slap on my Missy disguise, gather by bags again, and double back to my apartment to get my Accura. Part of the Pink Protocol is no one but Jem knows my location. Joanna checked into the Intercontinental and Missy checks into the Extended Stay across town with a month paid up front in cash. Welcome home, Missy.

My body wants me to climb into the lumpy bed and sleep until noon, but my brain would never allow it. I switch on the TV as Doris Jr. boots up. Local news is on the story, cutting into early morning infomercials, but we haven't gone national yet. Looks like they've kept the press on the city side of the drawbridge but police and news helicopters circle the island. Skip Martin on Channel 6 appears to have little information, just that there was a major incident at Xavier Maximum Security Prison. The police and Feds are keeping mum about how many people are involved, if there are any fatalities, yeah they know nothing. I switch it off when the reporters begin rehashing the last major incident, the Alkaline/Justice nightmare. No doubt every news hound in Galilee is hoping for Round Two with yours truly in the ring this time. I pray they'll be shit out of luck.

I sit at the chipped, slightly sticky table in front of Doris and call up the Moonlight video and audio links. Judging from the white cinderblock walls and tiny bed, Jem's standing in a prison cell. "Guardian online," I say into the headset.

I must startle him because the camera on his head jolts. "Guardian? Are you okay?"

"I'm at the Extended Stay on Kirby, room seven under the name Missy Royal."

"Okay. Good. Thank you." He pauses. "And I'm sorry if I inconvenienced your boyfriend. Your old number was disconnected and I knew—"

"Just get me up to speed, Moonlight," I cut in. "It's past two am. I'm exhausted." And he's not my boyfriend. "What the hell happened?"

"A call came in just before midnight, around 12:30 to Warden Myers' and 911. The entire prison population, save for the guards in the watchtowers, were rendered unconscious for approximately two hours by a volatile anesthetic gas. I'm not sure what kind yet, the canisters have no labels, but whatever it was left everyone with headaches, nausea, and double vision. Those who weren't already asleep report muddled thinking, growing tired, and falling unconscious within a minute. This was across the board in all four cell blocks, each of which has its own heating unit therefore its own timed canister. The surveillance system wasn't tampered with. The recordings show that five minutes after the last guard passed out, a team of sixteen men, all wearing gas masks, black hooded sweatshirts, and black jeans exited a manhole leading to a storm drain they must have cut the bars on previously. The men came through the storm drain, out the manhole, into D block with a key and keycard, then entered the control room to open all the cells in the Hardcore Unit. Thirteen stayed to load the thirteen villains on the block into body bags which they then carried out, while the other three used two pilfered key cards and keys they took from the unconscious guards to access the lower level. Those three loaded Ryder and the other two, Jericho's Tombstone and Lake City's Magnus, into bags and like the rest were carried back to the manhole and presumably to an awaiting boat. In and out in fifteen minutes."

"And they only took those with powers?"

"Haquim Chaplain, the terrorist responsible for the DeConnick Street bombings a decade ago, remains in his cell right beside where Ryder was housed. All other prisoners are accounted for. All the guards and support staff on duty as well. No fatalities either. Yet. Who knows what long term effects the gas could have. I'll know more when their blood samples come back."

"Shouldn't people be wearing gasmasks?"

"GFPD Hazmat cleared the buildings. Besides elevated levels of nitrogen and carbon, the air is normal. Now. We're all experiencing headaches, some responders nausea as well, but nothing debilitating."

"Have you personally reviewed the footage?" I ask.

"Yes. It should be loaded into the GFPD database soon. They were professional. Precise. Fluid. I'd guess ex-military. They knew exactly where to go. What to do. No mis-steps."

"What about the canisters?"

"No fingerprints or distinguishing marks. The heater in C Block was repaired three days ago, and I assume they installed the gas then. GFPD is already onto the repair company, but they've had a contract with the prison for over a decade."

"So there's the heating company, the canisters, and the gas as leads," I say as I jot that down. "Plus the guards and staff. There's usually an inside man involved."

"Over 150 people work here. That's a lot of vetting."

"Well, lucky for you someone quit her job yesterday and can't leave her hotel room. But I think we can rule out Ryder's guards in Super Max. They're still on my payroll, which you should probably tell Harry in case he dives into their financials and finds the monthly payout."

"I will. When was the last time you spoke to Ryder?" Jem asks.

"Couple days ago."

"And how was he?"

"Helpful. Normal. Nothing out of the ordinary."

"You didn't tell him…about—"

"Of course not," I snap.

"I'm sorry. I simply…it-it would just explain why *now*."

"Moonlight, he's not the only prisoner missing," I point out. "Maybe Ryder had nothing to do with this. Any one of them could have orchestrated this. They were all supervillains, they all had henchmen and criminal networks before getting arrested. And besides those five guards *I'm* the only one Ryder had recent contact with."

"That you know of. His guards already accepted one payout, it certainly makes taking another that much easier," Jem says.

He has a point. "Fine. They're back in the suspect pool. But that still doesn't mean Ryder was the mastermind. If he were the only one missing, then hell yes, he did it, but I very much doubt he'd pay to have the others busted out too. He hates Chameleon almost as much as he hated Justice. In fact, none of these guys are exactly best friends. So why take all of them?"

"Misdirection? Someone on the outside needs them all?"

"You think some psycho is putting together an evil supervillain boy band? To what end?"

"World domination?" Jem suggests.

"I suppose Earth is due for another world domination plot. It's been almost fifteen years since Dr. Avatar's weather dominator."

"All we do know for a fact is right now over a dozen megalomaniacal murderous superpowered villains are loose in the world, one of whom has attempted to kidnap and murder *you*."

"Actually, if anything, he'll probably be gunning for you, Dr. Ambrose."

"Why?" Jem asks.

"You broke my heart. He didn't take too kindly to that. And he also figured out you were Lord Nightingale. And, though he didn't say it, he probably knows you're Moonlight too."

Jem just stares at the wall for a few seconds, not saying a word as the wheels in his mind revolve possibly faster than his usual million miles a minute. I'm surprised the earth isn't spinning off its axis right now. Yet all he says is, "Shit." He swore! Guess I've rubbed off on him.

"Do you still have everything in place for a Code Purple?" I ask.

"Yes." A pregnant, like its water just broke, pause. "And I assume you wouldn't be goin—"

"No."

"My enemies would still try to use you against me," he points out.

"Moonlight, I'm the damn supervillain pin-up girl. They don't need you as a reason to kidnap me. And it won't come to that. Ryder won't come after me. Grace Pickering, yeah. Me? I'm not worth his time. Any of theirs. If this was a prison break, running is the priority, not mindless mayhem."

"Still. We thought the same last time. If you have to go out—"

"I remember the protocol."

"Yes, but you have a problem following rules," he counters.

"Thought you love that about me," I say with a smile which immediately drops when I realize what I've just said. "I'll be careful. I promise. Just watch your back, okay? And don't forget to eat. You always forget to eat when things get busy. You're gonna need all your energy for this one. Even the world's most perfect man needs to fuel up on occasion."

"I'll do my best."

"Good. I'll be here if you need intel. Just radio. Guardian out." I cut the feed.

Okay. So…shit is bad. Very bad, but nowhere near the flaming pile I'd envisioned. No one died. Yet. There aren't currently over a dozen supervillains running down the streets in tanks shooting civilians with nuclear bombs ticking down to detonation. Of course that could be on tomorrow's agenda. What we have here is a weird ass situation. I thought someone opened all the prison doors or blew a hole in its side. The fact only the villains were taken was by design. They were targeted. But why? If one of the villains *was* responsible and wanted to cover up they were the mastermind, take one or two others, sure. But the more people abducted the more risk, not to mention cost. It doesn't make sense to grab them all.

Forget motive for now, Jo. Move to means. Who has the means to organize and fund this? I pull up the list of the escapees from Doris' database. Oh, I forgot to add Hardcore's newest guests, Hexen and Abbalam. Jem caught Hexen and New Urbana shipped Abbalam to Xavier last week. Add them to Virus, Chameleon, Boneshaker, Dr. Avatar, The Traveler, Warlord, Atomic Adam, Arch, Dragoon, Crimson Lilith, Black Pearl, Goblin, Professor Elven, and of course Alkaline. Okay who could fund this? Ryder for sure. Who else has the cash? Lilith's ex-husband is a millionaire, maybe she rekindled their romance. Dr. Avatar, Warlord, and Traveler all amassed fortunes and had their assets seized when they were arrested, but like Ryder they could have secret accounts. The rest were lower on the totem pole. A few robberies, a few bank heists, all trying to make a name for themselves. They all failed, hence prison. But Ryder is the only one of the group who's successfully broken out before. Dr. Avatar, Virus, and The Traveler attempted but were caught in hours. That places my old pal at the top of the suspect list. This is just his style too. Smart, quick, efficient with plenty of misdirection to throw us into confusion. But my gut rolls its eyes. It's possible, but I don't think it's probable. And even if he did, it wasn't done just so he can come after me. I'm in no more danger than any other citizen of Galilee. Which is still a shit ton.

Good thing I've got a big damn shovel.

"Doris…let's get to work."

*

I get in four hours of investigating before I can't fight back sleep a moment longer. I crawl into my lumpy bed with its scratchy, stiff sheets and pass out. My nerves or overexcited brain only allow me the bare minimum amount of sleep needed to function, two hours. Worse there's no food or coffee in my new prison, also no room service, so not even a few hours into Protocol Pink I break the rules and venture into the city. Or Missy, with her blonde wig and glasses, does. She even pays in cash. Thank God there's a Starbucks on every corner, including this one. Double shot of espresso and chocolate croissant and my brain tops off at fifty percent efficiency. Enough so when I return to the hotel I can make sense of my chicken scratches from last night. They'd barely loaded anything into the GFPD or Federal databases last night but have begun to catch up. Time to watch the security footage.

At exactly 10:38 the guards begin exhibiting symptoms of lethargy. Drooping eyelids, inability to walk straight, confusion. Thirty seconds later those still on their feet drop to the linoleum floor. Ouch. Every cell block shows the same scene. If only C Block was breached, why gas the others? It would be safer for the extraction team, I guess. No stragglers or people to go investigate. They'd have almost total control of the prison save for the men in the watchtowers. Those four could be on the take, paid to literally look the other way. I jot that down.

Three minutes pass before the men begin climbing out of the manhole cover on the ocean side of C Block like ants on the march. One more minute passes before all sixteen have surfaced, each wearing the same black hoodie, black jeans, black gloves, gas mask, and carrying an actual empty body bag over their shoulders. Creepy. By the time the last man pops out, the leader has the side door open, and the men begin hustling inside the cell block. That door opens with a key card, regular key, and code. Definitely an insider involved.

The leader uses the keys to unlock all three doors needed to gain access to the Hardcore Unit's guard station, where my old pal Garrett Leon drools in his chair inside the clear plastic enclosure. We met on the Alkaline case. The man was as dumb as a post with a ton of kids at home. Just because he didn't help Ryder then doesn't mean he's innocent this go-round. Wouldn't put money on it though. As Leon slumbers, the leader puts his key in, turns it, then presses a button. All the cells slide open. The henchmen each enter a cell. After pressing something to Leon's hand, the leader hustles out of the guard station and with the last two henchmen, they run down the block to another stairwell. To Super Max. To access it, not only are both keys and a code necessary, but also two fingerprints with only a dozen authorized. Narrows the suspect pool.

The leader and another man remove what look like cell phones and hold them up to the fingerprint readers. Whatever that is, it does the job. The bars and steel door both lift and the men sprint down to the Super Max. The two guards, Jaime Santiago and Edwin Kemp, are both on the floor when the men breach what is supposed to be the most secure prison block on the continent. Twenty feet underground, walls lined with an inch of steel, no windows, only one way in and out. These men just run in, push a few buttons, and open the cells, including Ryder's. Unlike the other villain cells, Super

Max's have cameras inside, so I can watch as the men glide inside the three cells. Like everyone else, Ryder, The Traveler, and Dr. Avatar appear unconscious. They don't stir, not even as the men remove something from their belts and press it against the villain's bare skin. Did they just drug them? That's weird. Of course picking them up and lowering them into an open body bag is far weirder. The men zip up the bags, toss them over their shoulders again, and exit the cells. They're strong. It's hard to tell with the hoodies, but if I had to guess, they're all fit. Tall and muscular. And Jem's right. From the way they move, how mechanical this whole event is, they're ex-military or professional mercenaries. Everyone knows their role and the plan, executing it without misstep.

Even without their leader, the men in Hardcore stick to their tasks. I watch as each man exits his appointed cell with his villain package and moves to the stairwell, opening doors with his own keys and cards, before returning to the manhole. One by one they lower their payload down the hole, I assume to someone waiting down there, before climbing down themselves until all sixteen are gone from sight. Time since this all began? Six minutes. Fine work, gents.

There are no cameras in the sewer but per the reports, investigators hypothesize the storm drain bars were cut earlier, as was unsealing the manhole cover. Only if someone were really examining each would they notice something amiss. That side of the island is only accessible by boat. The prison has patrol boats that circle the island, taking fifteen minutes to complete the circle. My hypothesis is a boat most likely dropped the men off at the storm drain, sped off, then returned at the appointed time. I write "check CCTV footage at docks." The only problem being Galilee has ten miles of docks.

The GFPD made some headway with the gas as well. I don't understand ninety-seven percent of the report, but do glean it's a widely bought aerosol anesthetic used in the majority of veterinary surgery centers and zoos, mostly used to knock out larger animals like horses and gorillas to keep them under. The good news is only ten companies in the world manufacture it, the bad there are tens of thousands of orders for it this year alone. So, hello dead end number one.

I don't—

The sudden knock on the door makes me gasp and leap an inch out of my chair. When I land, my hand instantly touches my pounding heart. I'm as skittish as a fucking cat in a house full of rabid dogs. Too much coffee.

"Jo-Missy?" a familiar voice says on the other side of the door.

Of course. Who else would it be, Fallon? I pad to the door and open it for the hooded Jem. "I-I brought you groceries," he says, holding up the bags.

"Uh, come in."

With his head hung, he steps inside toward the kitchenette where my own grocery bags still sit on the counter. He spots them and spins around. "You went out?"

"I needed coffee," I say as I shut the door.

Oh, I know that face. His Joanna's done something stupid face. His mouth flops open and head cocks to the left in annoyance. "You're not supposed to leave this hotel room, Joanna." He sets the bags on the carpet and removes his hoodie. His normally shiny black curls are all but plastered with grease. "One person. It only takes one person to recognize you. *One*. It-It-It-It's part of the protocol you approved to follow."

"I was in disguise. I kept my head down. I even used a New Urbana accent. I needed food, Jem. And the protocol isn't house arrest, its limit leaving the hotel."

"The more you leave, the probability if discoverability grows exponentially."

"Hey, same goes for you," I snap. "If you're out in the world someone just needs to tail Jem Ambrose or Captain Moonlight here. The more often you come here, the bigger the chance is that happens. So I'm fucked either way. There are uncontrollable variables in every plan, you've said so yourself."

"If we stick to the original—"

"I don't think that's a good idea."

The original plan was he'd come to me, we'd hole up together investigating, and Captain Moonlight would go out and kick ass. He'd change into a disguise, do the shopping on his way back. I'd only leave for emergencies. This morning's need for coffee was damn sure an emergency.

"I'm not even sure if we can work together. Yet. Besides, there might not even be a threat to me. I really think you're overreaching."

"A superpowered maniac with limitless resources who attempted to kidnap, vivisect, and murder you is walking the streets."

"Well, he's not walking them in search of me."

"Are you willing to bet your life on that assumption? Because I'm not." He shifts his weight and annoyance onto his right side. "At least promise me you haven't informed anyone else of you location."

"Only Bennett Stone. He's in the shower now. Care to say hello?" Jem actually glances over his shoulder toward the bedroom. He doesn't see me roll my eyes. He always chides me when I do. "I was kidding, genius." He turns back around, shock morphing back to annoyance by the end of the trip. "You didn't used to be so gullible, Ambrose."

I bridge the gap between us and begin picking up the grocery bags. Damn. Being so close, I can smell him, the stale sweat and his natural musk. Better than the most expensive perfume on the market. Or aphrodisiac. One whiff is enough to rev my motor, even now. Guess my body hasn't received the message we're supposed to hate him, not jump his bones. This too shall pass. With time. Today I merely collect the bags as fast as possible and walk into the kitchenette the same way. "I was just reviewing the security footage and reports. Have you read them yet?"

"Read? No. I-I just left the prison. I sat in on some of the interviews."

I hoist the bags onto the counter with the others. "Let me guess: know nothing, saw nothing, check please!"

"That was the gist."

"The mercs had keys and codes. They had to get them somewhere."

"The Warden provided GFPD and the Marshals with a list of those with access. The codes are changed weekly. If I recall, about twelve have clearance."

"Even to Super Max?"

"Yes."

"Still manageable." My stomach rumbles when I pull out the eggs he brought. "Pardon."

"When was the last time *you* ate?" Jem asks.

"Dinner last night. You?"

"I can't recall."

"Then you catch up on reports and I'll scramble us some eggs."

"Fine." He pauses and bows his head a little again. "Thank you."

He sits at my table, and I start on the eggs. This is the one food I somehow manage not to fuck up. Pop would usually just be getting in from his night shift as a cabbie when I got up for school. We'd take turns scrambling eggs and popping Eggos into the toaster. Jem and I fell into the same routine. He'd stop patrolling around five when I had to get up for work. I'd whip up some eggs as he told me stories of what I'd missed after I signed off Guardian duty. As I swish around the eggs I stare across at my ex hunched over the laptop. It's as if nothing's happened. There's no rage, no sadness, no tension. Yesterday I wanted to knee him in the balls, now I'm downright wistful. I'm probably just exhausted. Lucky for his balls.

When the eggs are done, I sit beside him at the dining room table. He smiles when I hand him the eggs. "Thank you."

"So, anything catch your fancy, yet?" I ask with a mouth full of eggs.

"Nothing I didn't already know. Have you fed the villains' photos into Doris' CCTV analysis program yet?"

"One of the first things I did," I say. "But these are seasoned criminals. They know to disguise themselves. I also had Doris cull all prior police reports to generate a list of past accomplices. It will save the police time and hassle. I sent it last night."

"So, as of right now, we have what?"

"A giant fucking mess?"

He flashes another smile. "Besides that."

"The guards," I suggest. "All the guys in Super Max are on my payroll. I know them. I can reach out."

"I spoke to the two on duty, Santiago and Kemp. When I pressed them about the payoffs, they did admit to accepting money from you. And I did believe them when they stressed they were not involved in the escape." He shovels his eggs into his mouth. "I overheard someone tell the Warden that the other eight with Max access were being pulled in for interviews by GFPD right now."

"I'm surprised you're not sitting in."

"I trust them to do their jobs. Besides, I thought you needed groceries. And I should put in an appearance at the hospital."

"You might add shower and shave to your To Do list there, Ambrose. As a member of the hospital board, I have to comment that having our star neurologist looking like a bum is bad for business."

"My apologies to the board," he says with an undercurrent of anger. "I've simply been…busy."

"You have to take care of yourself, Jem."

He sets the plate on the table. "And here I thought you didn't care. I do believe those very words left your mouth whilst you were screaming at me on the street before your *date.*"

Oh, for fuck's sake. "It wasn't a date, okay? He wants to partner on a worldwide foundation that helps people whose lives have been affected by supers. Rebuilding, medical expenses, even therapy for powered and civilians alike. We're calling it The Guardian Society."

His shoulders slump a little. That took the wind from his sails. "Oh."

Why the hell do I suddenly feel guilty? Shit. *Shit.* Looking at him, so dejected and weighed down by everything, including my perceived betrayal, I have the strongest urge to leap onto his lap and hug him until all the tension and pain evaporates. I want to lead him into the bathroom, climb into the shower, and wash all the grime away. Slip into bed and sleep for twelve hours in each other's arms. Because this pathetic, angry creature next to me is my creation. No matter how justified I may be, I'm the source of all his misery, the misery now twisting my insides and breaking my resolve not to follow my instincts. Fuck.

I fall back in my chair with a sigh. "Maybe we shouldn't do this."

"What?"

"Work together. At least in person. Hell, maybe at all. I look at you and I just want to..." Kiss you. "Slap you. Still. I don't know if we can divorce the personal bullshit from the mission. And his mission is too damn important for distractions."

His shoulders slump all the way to China. "Whatever you want." He rises from the chair. "I won't contact you in any form unless it's absolutely required. I trust that you'll share any pertinent information you uncover with me via Doris."

"Of course."

"Then I have things to attend to," he says, striding toward the door. His head may be held high but those shoulders and ice in his words give away the pain.

My stomach, hell my heart, clenches again. Fuck. "Jem..." Hand still on the door handle, he spins around, face tight as he struggles to hold in his emotions. "I...none of this is to hurt you. I don't...I don't want to hurt you. Truly. It's just...it hurts *me* to be around you."

"I know," he all but whispers. "And I'm not..." He gazes up at the ceiling as the cracks begin to form across his face's defenses. Ripples of torment move across his forehead, his eyes, his cheeks, finally to his open lips. "This isn't your fault. It's mine. What happened, all of it, is *my* fault. And I deserve every moment of the pain I'm experiencing. You don't. And I don't want to cause you another millisecond of anything but joy. But…" He pauses to reign in his emotions, and failing judging from the tremors across his face. "I don't know how not to have you in my life. Every cell, every single one, still craves you. I miss you every minute of every hour. So much so I almost wish I'd never met you, because then I'd never know what I'm missing. Because you showed me that existing isn't enough. And without you, that's all I'm doing. And will do. So though I don't want to hurt you…I don't know if I'm strong enough to not have you in my existence in whatever capacity I can get you. But I'll try. Because I love you. I love you, Joanna. And I know a part of you still loves me. Even if you won't admit it to yourself." His jaw clenches. "Contact me if you uncover anything in the investigation. And stick to the protocol. Because if anything happens to you…you're taking me with you." Somehow he manages a small, aching smile before gazing down at the floor. "I love you. Bye."

He opens the door and steps out. When it shuts I let out the breath I'd been holding since his proclamation in a ragged spurt. Goddamn it. Fuck. *Fuck.* Why do I get the sense I've managed to do what over a dozen supervillains have tried and failed to do. Defeat Jem Ambrose. Knocked him down so he hasn't the strength to get back up. Love. The strongest damn force in this universe, bar none. Embrace it at your own peril.

I don't think I'll ever escape its clutches. Maybe I don't want to.

CHAPTER NINE

THE RADIOACTIVE MAN

He's dead. I can't believe he's...dead.

I only met him once in person. The day after Ryder was sent to Super Max, we met at a coffee shop a block from the precinct back when I was still a cop. He was the second guard to accept my offer. My bribe. A payoff every month for the man to just do his job. To keep that psychopath in his cage with no way out. James Ryder used money, charm, and old connections to escape the first time. I did everything in my power to make sure there wouldn't be a second. I failed. He's out, David Garr is dead, and my best, once again, proves not to be enough. Nothing is ever enough.

The police found his body at his home in Lewiston just outside the city. He lived alone after his divorce, both kids in college, only a cat to keep him company. The cat is fine. Garr was tied to a dining room chair with both his kneecaps blown out, three fingers broken all before his assailant or assailants shot him in the head right in his own dining room. All very professional. The local ME puts the time of death from 2-4 AM the morning of the escape. They tortured him for the codes then stole his keys. He wasn't due into work or anywhere else for two days. Twenty-two years on the job. Three commendations. Poor bastard.

It's going to take all day to process his house for prints, fibers, trace evidence, but if this was the same group I doubt they left any. Ditto with the neighborhood canvass. The mercs attacked Garr in the middle of the night, so witnesses would be few and far between. One lead. The guards were our one fucking good lead and now it's gone. A man is dead and a shit ton of others will be close behind whenever these psycho fucks implement their grand master plan. And I don't have a damn clue what else I can do. Which is driving me fucking crazy. Stuck in a stuffy, grungy faux apartment like a prisoner staring at a computer screen for seven hours straight is driving me batty. The killers are free and I'm a prisoner. So fucking unfair.

I walk into the equally nasty bedroom and plop onto the bed. Maybe a nap will…fuck. When I close my eyes, it's as if I'm transported back seven hours with my ex declaring his eternal love as the weight of his words threaten to flatten him dead with me right along with him. Nope. My eyes fly open, but my second attempt garners the same trip back to hell. Same with the third, fourth, and fifth. Fuck. I grab a pillow and shriek, "Fuck!" into it. That's a little better. What I need is a damn drink. Why didn't I—

My cell phone rings in the living room. I picked up a GPS free pre-paid at the bodega and texted Jem, Harry, V, Shannon, and Bennett so they could reach me at this new number but to delete the text and tell no one else I'd been in contact. I debated adding Bennett to the list, but after last night's theatrics figured he'd want to know I was alright. Seems a text wasn't enough.

"Hello, Mr. Stone."

"Miss Daniels," he says back. "That's what you're called in my phone anyway. Miss Jackie Daniels in honor of what you were drinking the night you ravished me."

"How sentimental of you."

"I'm actually quite enjoying all this cloak and dagger business. Secret calls, aliases, it's fun."

"Trust me, it gets real old real fast. Especially when you're the one stuck inside a depressing hotel room with only crap TV and police reports to keep you company."

"Say the word and Miss Daniels can find herself on a sunny, sandy beach with a gorgeous billionaire providing her multiple orgasms."

"Does the billionaire have to be you?" I quip.

"You wound me, Miss Daniels," he says playfully. "To my very core."

I chuckle. It feels good to do that. "A thousand apologies."

"So truly, all kidding aside, how are you? I've been worried," he says, voice softening.

"I'm…safe. Or as safe as I can be."

"And how goes the investigation? I've been keeping current with the news coverage. Sounds as if there's been no progress."

"What makes you think I'm involved in the investigation?"

"I simply assumed. Why else would you stay, hell risk your life, if you didn't think you could help?"

"Aren't you the clever one?"

"Brains, looks, and I'm hung like a donkey. I'm damn near perfect if I do say so myself."

"We can add humble to your list of attributes as well."

"If you got it, flaunt it, gorgeous." He pauses. "You didn't answer my question though. How goes the investigation? The news made it sound like commandos stormed the prison."

"It wasn't as dramatic as that. It was actually very professional."

"So no leads?"

I raise my eyebrow. "Why are you so curious?"

"Just living vicariously through you, Miss Daniels. I'm a thrill junkie dying for a fix. You of all people should know how that is. Not to mention I am worried about my business partner and dare I say friend. Because I do consider you a friend, Miss Daniels."

"You sure you want to be my friend? The body count in that category is fairly high."

"You're worth the risk, gorgeous." He's silent again. "Please answer my question, okay? Are you in danger?"

"I'm being cautious. No one knows where I am. I'm not even allowed to go outside. Just me, these four walls, and my thoughts."

"That sounds like hell."

"Close. Plus I had this…fight with Jem that just…*I'm* the injured party here. I'm the wronged one. *He* betrayed *me.* But every time I talk to or see him, I just want to beg his forgiveness. And I'm stuck in this shitty apartment, already frustrated to fuck because there are no leads, and now I'm beating myself up for destroying the love of my life. I'm just…I need a damn drink."

"Don't you dare," he orders. "You're better than that. You're stronger than that. He's not worth it. He's a dishonest, passive aggressive fool who all but destroyed *you,* and it sounds as if he wants to finish the job with emotional blackmail. Don't let him. Go to a meeting. Go exercise. Go to a shooting range. Beat the hell out of a criminal. Channel your rage into something constructive. Make the misery count for something."

"What happened to 'I don't lecture?'?" I ask.

"That was before we were friends. Business partners."

"You just don't want to have to do all the work on the Society, you selfish bastard you," I say playfully.

"I may be a selfish bastard, but it doesn't make it any less true," he points out. "Oh. I'm sorry, Ms. Daniels, I have a call coming in I need to take. I'll call you later. Promise me you won't drink. *Promise*."

"I promise."

"Thank you. Talk to you later, gorgeous."

"Bye, playboy." I hang up with a sigh. He just had to make me promise.

Channel the misery. I've been doing that since childhood, one would think it'd be easy by now. The infrastructure should already be in place. It's just there's so much misery right now, a Biblical flood, its overwhelmed the channels. Justin, Jem, the dead ends, and poor David Garr, my well runneth over enough to cover the whole planet. I have to start rebuilding all over again. But not in here. I'll go to a meeting. Misery, company, horrors people have endured that put mine to shame here I come. Fucking promises.

After looking up meetings, I slap on my wig, glasses, and hoodie. Doesn't get more anonymous than this. The next meeting is five stops on the Metro. Bad choice of transport. Stuck in a metal tube with the threat of widespread violence hanging over everyone's heads, not fun. The tension's as strong as the usual B.O. I hate the city when it's like this. Paranoid. Uneasy. One wrong word, one quick motion, and it sparks the tinderbox that can burn down a whole city. I keep my head down and pretend to listen to my iPod. I—

My cell phone vibrates. I'm so goddamn popular all of a sudden. I check the display. Harry. I have the feeling I'm not going to enjoy this call. The subway doors open and I step into the almost empty DeConnick Street Station and sit on the bench. "Hello, Harry."

"Why didn't you tell me you were bribing Ryder's guards?" Harry whispers.

Knew it. This call's gonna suck. "Because it's a crime? Because it's none of your business? And I resent the word 'bribe.' That implies I was getting them to do something they weren't meant to. What I did was more…insurance."

"Well, it looks like a damn bribe," Harry hisses. "And you were communicating with Ryder. Weekly."

"How—"

"Moonlight. And it's a damn good thing he said something, otherwise we would be having this conversation at the station. But I can only protect you so damn much. The Feds are involved, and *they* are asking questions. A man is dead, Jo! One you were engaged in illegal activities with!"

Fuck. I can't do this with him. Not now. Only one way to get rid of a cop. "Then perhaps you should be speaking to my lawyer, Martin Ferdman. And if you accuse any of the guards of accepting an alleged bribe, then a swarm of attorneys will descend on the GFPD like the plague. We had nothing to do with the break-out, and I have nothing more to say on the subject. I'm hanging up, Harry. Bye."

I end the call. Fuck. Fuck! This is not good. At all. I could be in serious trouble. Harry'll shield me as much as he can, but the truth is I have committed a crime. The guards'll lose their jobs at the very least. I planned for that contingency though. Pendergast is always hiring loyal souls. Still. I might want to talk to Martin. I have to call information for his number just as a train comes and goes. I make an appointment with his assistant for tomorrow morning. If I get hauled in before that, he's on notice. The guards know his number too. If it gets bad, they'll call him. I hope. If it gets bad…fuck. I sigh. How the fuck can it get any worse? Maybe the guy in the hood standing by the stairwell plans to rape me. He has been hanging around since I got off. Too tall and wide to be Jem. Luckily the train screeches into the station, and I hurry on. So does the man, but he keeps his back to me. He doesn't turn around once. He also doesn't move to get off the train when I do. Jesus, I'm as paranoid as everyone else in this city. The two times I glance back on my way to Trinity Church, a two-story former store by the looks of it, now a house of God, the man's not there.

The meeting has already begun. A decent turn-out, about a dozen people from ages twenty to eighty, some in suits but most in hoodies and jeans like me. I take a seat toward the middle of the small space as the group leader pontificates on the steps about how brave we all are to be here. I can recite this speech verbatim by now. Yet I still come. I have no idea why this works, but it does. Maybe it's the visual proof I'm not the only one struggling. Maybe it's the fact I decide to attend that cements in my subconscious I'm dedicated to my sobriety. Maybe they just put something in the coffee. I don't care. All that matters is it works for me.

I'm not one for sharing though. It's hard to be anonymous when your face has been plastered on every newspaper around the world more than twice. I give mad props to everyone who has the guts to get up there and bare their soul, air their dirty laundry. The rapes, the abusive parents, their own crimes. Such damage. A vicious cycle we're all hoping to break. I—

Motherfucker.

The thing about paranoia is sometimes they *are* out to get you. In the giant mirrored cross at the front of the church, I see the hooded man from the subway take a seat off to the side in the back. He's added an Independence Eagles cap to his disguise and keeps his head down. Fuck. One of Ryder's goons? Just a garden variety nutto? Thank Christ I brought my gu—

My stalker glances up and my stomach, my lungs, hell my whole body locks up tighter than a boa constrictor's grip. Not from nerves but from pure goddamn rage. I stare straight ahead at the twentyish speaker but suddenly can't hear her words. All I can hear is my pounding heart and deep, ragged breaths. Motherfucking, cocksucking prick. I ball my hands into fists, digging my nails into my palms to quell the fury. To stop myself from giving into my overwhelming impulse to use those fists against his face. At this moment in time all I want to hear is the crack of his nose as I break it. To rake my fingernails down his cheeks. To watch as the blood gushes down his beautiful face. To spit on it. But because life is unfair, five minutes later he'd be fully healed and I'd be under arrest for assault. How the hell did he even find me? Only— Jem. Of course. Bosom buddies. Tag-team stalking brothers in arms. Bastards. This is supposed to be anonymous for a reason. A safe haven to share our worst without fear of judgement. Another violation of trust. What am I going to do? They cannot keep doing this to me. What the hell *can* I do?

The girl must finish because the people in front of me applaud, and after a nervous smile she steps away from the podium, replaced by the leader. "Would anyone else like to share?" he asks, voice far away.

"I would," someone with my voice says.

"Come on up," says the leader.

I rise from my seat before I realize I'm actually doing it. I don't look at anyone on the walk down the aisle. Not until I reach the podium. Then I only have eyes for one person. The coward in the back who bows his head and pretends to find the floor fascinating.

"Hello, my name is J-Missy, and I'm an alcoholic," I begin.

"Hello, Missy," says all but one.

"Until about a week and a half ago, I was 442 days sober. Not a single slip. And it wasn't until Day One that I thought I had a problem. My mother was an alcoholic. She could down a fifth of Jack in an hour, but she passed out in her own vomit. She finally burnt herself to death in her apartment. That wasn't me. I never broke my kid's arm for playing the TV too loud one morning. I never forgot my daughter's name or make her pay the bills when the utilities were cut off. I was top in my profession. The people closest to me could always rely on me, even when they didn't fucking deserve it," I say with a titanium edge. "I drank. Sure. Got into minor trouble when I did, sure. Slept with the wrong people. Went to work when I wasn't a hundred percent, but I wasn't hurting anyone. It dulled the pain. It dulled the anger. It made it possible to watch my best friend, the man I loved, flirt and fall in love with women who weren't me. Really *that* was my only problem. I just liked to drink. I had it under control. Until the man I loved, who I trusted, abandoned me. Left me alone to clean up his giant mess. Let me think I was responsible for his death. The man I loved. My supposed soul mate," I say, voice cracking.

Keep it together. Don't you dare fucking cry. I literally swallow my emotions as best I can. My audience of one bow his head lower. His leg twitches a mile a minute. Uncomfortable. Good.

"So, I lost it. I lost everything. My job, my boyfriend, my fucking mind and will to live. And I'm not blaming him. Not fully. I chose to drink. He didn't force it down my throat. But a person can only take so much. The alcohol felt like my only lifeline in the ocean of shit and pain and guilt he'd left in his wake. Thank God I still had people in my life, true friends who knocked sense into me. Got me into rehab. Supported me. Forgave me. And slowly but surely I found my feet. Got strong enough to help other lost people. Fell in love with a man who returned that gift. I was the happiest I'd ever been in my life.

"Until *he* came back. The Radioactive Man."

Justin finally looks up. Looks at *me*. His face is as stony as mine, as my words. He's breathing heavily, almost shuddering with each intake.

"Because that's what he is. Radioactive. He can power cities. Help people survive the worst. Stop wars. He's a goddamn marvel without question. But God forbid you get too close. Because he also infects everyone around him with poison. Mutating them into monsters. Riddling their lives with cancer until they're praying for death to ease the agony. Maybe he doesn't know he's doing it. I don't believe he sets out to hurt us. He doesn't set out to be purposely cruel, but that almost makes it worse. He justifies his actions and worse convinces others he's right. He convinced my fiancée to betray me. He opens a fucking door and my life explodes. Again. And I'm sure he's sorry. That he never meant to hurt me. But he has. He has hurt me more than anyone. More than my mother. More than the fucker who murdered my father. More than the psychos who have threatened my life. My best friend. My soul mate. My devil. The Radioactive Man. He's taken everything again. And I will *hate* him until the day I die."

I wish I were holding the microphone because if ever a moment was perfect for a mic drop, this is it. Instead, I finally break eye contact, curl my lip in a snarl, and step away from the podium, and stalk down the aisle with my trembling chin stuck out. They were right, sharing does unburden the soul. Only a hundred tons to go.

*

Of course he follows me out. I barely make it out the church door when a stiff hand clamps on my shoulder. I spin around, my snarl rivaling a lion's. "Touch me again and I'll chop your head off. Not even you could survive that." He jerks it away. "Now do what you do best. Fuck off."

I turn on my heel again and continue down the city sidewalk. The bastard didn't take the hint. In the storefronts reflections I see him tailing me about six feet behind. Fine. I warned him. I turn down the first ally with my shadow doing the same. Halfway down, I change course charging toward him. Justin puts up no resistance as I grab him by the lapel and shove him against the piss soaked brick wall. He even holds up his gloved hands in surrender. Jem did say he lost his hand. Must be a prosthetic. "Go back to the hole you crawled out of and leave. Me. Alone," I growl through gritted teeth.

"I can't do that."

I release him. "The fuck you can't. *That's* been proven."

"Ryder's loose. You're not safe."

I release him and take a step back. "*Now*? Now you're worried about my well-being?" I ask incredulously. "Where

- 148 -

the hell were you when I was drinking myself to death? When Jordan Ambrose was trying to kill me and half the city?" I shove him again. "Every fucking night when I cried myself to sleep?" I shove him again. "When the guilt was crushing me so hard I literally couldn't breathe? *Then*. Then I needed you. Justin. And you abandoned me."

"I had no choice."

"No. Bullshit. *No.* You had a choice. A phone call. An e-mail. A message through Lucy or Jem. Something. Anything. One word. But you let me go on thinking I was responsible for your death. You convinced my fiancée to lie to me. You ruined my life. James Ryder may be a monster, but I meant it. You're my fucking devil."

"I know," he says, hanging his head. "You think I don't know that? Marnie. Daisy. Rebecca. Aunt Lucy. You." He shakes his head. "You're right. I am radioactive. *Anyone* close to me gets hurt. I *knew* you'd be better off without me. And I was right. You flourished, Jo. You conquered the world. Saved millions of lives. You fell in love. You came back better. Stronger. I was holding you back. Making your life miserable. I could sense it. I could. I just didn't want to face it. Because I needed you. Jo, I needed you a hell of a lot more than you needed me." He takes a step toward me. "I did what I did to save you. From me."

"Just like you never told me about Justice. Just like you had Jem betray me. It was for my own good. Do I seem good, Justin? Do I?"

"No. And that's on me too."

"Then leave."

"I can't," he says quietly. "He's out there. Planning God knows what. Jem can't watch you. You're not safe, Jo."

"James Ryder has better things to do than terrorize me. And even if he didn't, he wouldn't touch a hair on my head. A lot's changed since you abandoned me. Ryder and I are...colleagues of sorts."

"What?" Justin snaps, finally getting angry.

"He helps me. On cases. Hell, just in general."

Justin's jaw drops in horror. "Yo-You're friends with him?"

"I wouldn't go that far. He's my informant. But unlike you, the great hero, *he's* never lied to me. Not once. He respects me. He has no reason to hurt me. Unless *you* give him reason to." I take the final step, bridging the small gap between us and catching his eyes with my hard ones. "Do us both a favor. Crawl back into your empty grave and pull the dirt back over yourself. Because you got one thing right: I don't need you. I don't *want* you in my life. I wish I'd never met you. And I'm not going to waste another minute of my life on you." I turn my back on him and start walking away. "You're not worth it."

If he follows, I don't know. I don't care. I don't look back. Nothing but agony there.

For us both.

CHAPTER TEN

THIRD DEGREE BURNS

Jesus, it's been awhile since I've set foot in here. Nothing's changed. Same bullpen with overworked cops in either rumpled suits with coffee stains or barely out of puberty uniformed officers answering phones or running around. Priority Homicide: my home away from home for almost two amazing years. I closed almost fifty cases, had a seventy percent clearance rate, and made lifelong friends within these walls. I always got a tiny thrill walking in here. Guess it's different when you enter as a potential perp. Now I feel like throwing up.

A hush comes over the room when Martin and I stroll in. A few mouths even drop in nervous surprise. The joy of infamy. I spot Kowalski reviewing the whiteboard with Cam in the corner, and the momentary lull in conversation draws their attention my way. Their faces aren't as friendly as I'd like. Both quickly smile at me before returning to the board. This must be awkward for them as it is for me. Of course, they don't run the chance of leaving in handcuffs.

Harry steps out of his office with two suited men holding files behind him. Feds. I can always tell. Same dark blue three-piece-suits, same stiff posture, same scowl. I'd swear they're all clones save for the one of the left has red hair and the other is African American. "Joanna," Harry says without a hint of pleasantry. "These are Marshalls Devitt and Jackson. They'll be conducting your interview."

"Wish I could say it was a pleasure, gentlemen. This is my attorney Martin Ferdman. Shall we get this over with?"

"You're in Interview Two," Harry says.

"I remember the way," I say with a smile.

With my head high and shoulders straight, I start toward the back of the office. People try not to stare but most can't help themselves. I catch more than a few gawkers before they gaze back to their desks. I wonder what they're thinking. I do look formidable. Martin made me change from my jeans and hoodie to a black suit with white button down shirt. I even took time to do my hair and make-up. If my mugshot is going to be distributed worldwide, I want to look good.

When I enter Interview Two I almost sit on the interviewer's side, the one without the ring used to handcuff the bad guys. Force of habit. The small white concrete room, barely the size of a bathroom and just this side of cold, does its job. The door hasn't even closed and I want out. Not that I'll allow these men to glean that, not even the ones behind the mirror. Head and shoulders locked, back straight, and legs crossed. This is just an interview. I'm innocent. I've done nothing wrong. Perhaps if I keep telling myself that we'll all soon believe it.

"For the record," begins the red headed Fed Devitt, "this is the interview of Joanna Fallon in regards to Federal Case 15-5436A9. Marshalls Matthew Devitt and Griffin Jackson conducting, and we are joined by Ms. Fallon's attorney Martin Ferdman. Ms. Fallon is here voluntarily and at this time has not been read her rights." Devitt opens his file then smiles at me. "Let me just start by saying it is an honor to meet you, ma'am. My wife was on Pendergast Bridge the day

Emperor Cain blew it up. She wasn't hurt but five seconds either way and she could have been. This city owes you several debts of gratitude."

Hello, Good Cop. "And yet here I am having to defend myself against claims against my good character."

"You have to understand, ma'am," the African American Jackson says, "we need to pursue every lead. A name comes up, we follow the thread. You of all people can appreciate that."

Oh, so we're going with the "One of Us" tactic. Oldie but goodie. "So please tell me about the thread with my name on it. You can't possibly think I had anything to do with the prison break considering how hard I worked, and how much I sacrificed, to get some of those men in there in the first place."

"Well, while conducting our investigation, you know its customary to review the financial records of anyone suspected of having involvement in the crime. In this case that included the prison guards assigned to the Hardcore and Super-Max Units. During that review we uncovered monthly payments being made, beginning approximately a year and a half ago, to all guards in Super-Max. We traced the funds to a bank account linked directly to you."

"Linked?" Martin asks. "Is it her personal account?"

I'm not that much of a moron. "The payments come from a charitable organization, the Lock-Up Foundation, and when we examined their financials we found nothing beyond a bank account and basic documents with the city," Jackson says. "Your name appears all over those documents. And you're the sole contributor to the fund Ms. Fallon."

"My client lends her name, time, and money to multiple charitable organizations," Martin says.

"Sixty million last year alone," I add with pride.

"We also have a sworn statement from Guard Kemp who claims you had been in direct contact with him and the others," Devitt says. "First a year and a half ago to offer them bribes, then again six months ago to set-up a weekly video chat with James Ryder."

"Do you have any other proof of these allegations beyond this man's word?" Martin asks.

"How about the word of two other guards?" Jackson asks with a half grin.

Dicks. I manage to maintain my poker face but inside my stomach flips. Prison orange is not a good color on me.

"My client fiercely denies any allegations of wrongdoing," Martin answers for me.

"What I don't understand," Jackson continues, looking directly at me, "is why you'd want to talk to the man who tried to kill you and did kill your best friend. All we could come up with was phone sex. He is a handsome man."

"I'd fuck him," Devitt adds.

"Or maybe you're actually grateful to the man. He killed the bastard who screwed with your emotions for twenty years. Maybe your way of thanking him was to break him out."

"Don't be ridiculous," I snap.

"Joanna—" Martin says.

"Or maybe love and gratitude had nothing to do with it," Jackson continues. "Maybe you saw a chance to wash away all the scum in one stroke. Abduct and kill the very kind who've made your life hell?"

"What else are we supposed to think, Ms. Fallon?" Devitt asks. "Regardless of the motive, the mastermind of this break would have needed massive funds, a way inside the infrastructure of the prison, and underworld connections. Does that sound like anyone in this room?"

"You've also recently undergone some drastic personal changes. Gave up your empire, dropped your boyfriend. Gives you plenty of time to focus on a new project. Perhaps that's the kidnapping and torturing of over a dozen men."

"If I wanted them dead, and if I had men inside the prison, why would I take all the trouble, not to mention money, to abduct them when I could just have them shot in the head in their cells?" I counter. "And how dare you bring my personal life into this? People break up all the time, and they don't take it out on the prisoners either." I turn to Devitt. "As for my empire, it wasn't mine. I never wanted it. And I left it in more than capable hands to build something of my own. Which is precisely what I was doing while those men were sieging the prison. Bennett Stone and I were out to dinner at Komodo before retiring to his hotel room to begin work on our new foundation, The Guardian Society. The press release just went out this morning." By design. "I was with him from nine until I received a call about the prison break when two GFPD officers escorted me home."

"When you promptly gave them the slip and haven't been seen since that morning," Jackson adds.

"If the man who kidnaped, maimed, and tried to kill you suddenly was walking the streets with fifteen other madmen, you'd keep a low profile as well."

"Ms. Fallon there's at least one man dead," Devitt says. "Tortured. A man with direct ties to you. A man who died so the psychopath who killed your best friend could go free. I would think you, of all people, would want to be helpful."

"With the corroborating stories of the guards, the paper trail, bank accounts, we have enough to charge you with bribery, fraud, and possibly even accessory to murder and kidnapping," Jackson says.

"And I'm sure we'll be adding tampering with investigations, data theft, hacking Federal Databases and vigilantism when we execute our search warrants and impound your computers."

"I can't wait to get my hands on the infamous Justice computer," Jackson adds.

Fuck, fuck, fuck, fuck, fuck. "I—"

There's a knock on the door, and a moment later a familiar masked man steps in, much to everyone in the room's surprise. As if this day could get any worse. Of course he's here. I just cannot shake superheroes. Justin never halted his guard duty. I refused to look back, but I could sense him all the way to the hotel. To my lawyer's office. To the apartment. Here. I don't think he came inside here but can't be sure. For all I know he's behind the glass with Harry and the others. Doesn't he have a new city of his own to protect? It needs him a hell of a lot more than I do.

Jem, in full dark blue and yellow Captain Moonlight regalia, commands the room's attention without a single word needed. He does seem to become a totally different person when he dons the costume. Strong. Capable. Intimidating. Even I have the urge to shrink in my chair when he closes the door. Martin glances at me, but I shrug like I don't know why he's here. Devitt and Jackson seem equally surprised though their reaction's real.

"Um, for the record, Captain Moonlight has entered the interview room," Devitt says. "He has been deputized as a Marshall in this case."

"I apologize for the disruption, but I can shed some light on Ms. Fallon's actions," Moonlight says. My eyes narrow at my ex. He ignores me. "She speaks to James Ryder at my behest."

"What?" Jackson asks.

"The man has been instrumental in helping me close several cases. He's my informant, but will only speak to Ms. Fallon. She has been gracious enough to ask him a list of questions I prepare and email to her. It was the only way he would cooperate. As for data theft, hacking, tampering, and vigilantism those are my quote, unquote crimes alone. When I arrived in the city from New Urbana, I wanted to hit the ground running. I approached Ms. Fallon about using the database and computer Justin Pendergast built. Ms. Fallon has not been using it since the death of the Triumvirate and Emperor Cain, according to her for personal reasons. Since then I have seen no activity but my own on the system beyond the video chats with Ryder of which she records and I review. In fact, beyond those interviews and use of the computer, Ms. Fallon has refused my many requests for her assistance. Her boyfriend even once threatened to call the police to have me removed from their domicile."

"Yeah, sorry about that," I say.

"No, I apologize. And please extend that apology to Dr. Ambrose as well," he says, smooth as wet ice.

"If I ever see him again, I'll do it right after I slap his face," I say with a huge smile.

"Very well." Jem returns his attention to the Marshalls. "Gentlemen, I do not claim to know Ms. Fallon well, but like you, I can gage the measure of a person better than most. It is the blessing and curse of those of us in law enforcement. And you and I both know Ms. Fallon had nothing to do with the release of these fugitives. Like us, Ms. Fallon has made it her life's mission to stop the agents of evil from walking the streets. And if she was providing money to the guards I am more than sure it was done with that good in sight. Many prisoners have escaped by bribing guards, men who can barely afford to make ends meet on the paltry salary they make. *If* she is guilty, I would wager she enacted the payments as a form of insurance or incentive for them to do their jobs and not give into temptation as many have before. Isn't that right, Ms. Fallon?"

"No comment," I say with a smile before rising from the table, "save for I have committed no crimes, have no involvement in these events at Xavier Prison, and as a taxpayer I am sickened to see my money wasted on wild goose chases such as this. Martin?" My lawyer pulls out a piece of paper and slides it across to the men. "Those are a list of my movements the night Mr. Garr was killed to the morning after the prison break. I've also included the names and phone numbers of those with me who can verify said activities and my state of mind. If you require anything else, speak to my lawyer or arrest me. But I think we all have better things to do, no?" I turn my gaze to the superhero. "Good to see you again, Captain. Good hunting. Martin?"

My attorney rises as well. I nod at the Marshalls then begin toward the door. As I pass Moonlight, he whispers. "Doris," but I don't look at or acknowledge him. I don't acknowledge anyone as I stalk out of the squad room or precinct. When I step outside into the snowy, gray day, I let out the breath I held. I really thought I wouldn't be walking out of there a free woman. But I'm free. For the moment.

"Thank God he showed up when he did," Martin says as we descend the steps.

"How bad is it?"

"They pretty much have you dead to rights on bribery, possibly tax fraud if you declared the Lock-Up money as a charitable contribution."

"I didn't."

"But I think this was a fishing expedition. They're hunting sharks and you're just a guppy. A high profile guppy who can make them all look even worse which is the last thing they want right now. On the flip side, if they really have nothing else, which is looking to be the case, you do make a good suspect. And they can always bring charges after this has all blown over. If you have any favors piled up, I'd call them in now. And stay out of trouble. Stay away from this case. Don't give them any more ammunition."

"I'll do my damndest."

"Do better than that."

On that ominous note, I flag down a cab to go do the very thing I was just warned against. Interfere with the case. The taxi takes me back to the hotel where I collect my Acura and start toward Galilee Gardens just over the bridge. Pendergast Bridge is still a month from re-opening, so as always Dini Bridge is gridlocked, but it gives me time to make an uncomfortable yet necessary phone call. Bennett picks up on the forth ring.

"Miss Daniels. You saved me the trouble of phoning you. My press office has been fielding calls about my new international foundation. Care to comment?"

"I did try to call you last night and left a message. The announcement just couldn't wait. I'm sorry. I've found myself in a bit of trouble, and I may have dragged you into it."

"This should be interesting."

"You may or may not be getting a call from some Federal Marshalls about my whereabouts on the night of the prison break, my general demeanor, if I disappeared for long periods of time, took phone calls, things like that. Just tell the truth. Except for how I found out about the break. With that, if you could just say an unknown man called you, that he didn't ID himself, I'd really owe you."

"Why? Do they think you had a part in the break? That's ridiculous."

"I know. It's just…complicated."

"Happens to you a lot. Complications." He pauses. "You didn't, did you? Have anything to do with the escape?"

"Of course not."

"I wouldn't care. I'm sure you would have had your reasons. It's not as if the world's better with them in it," he says nonchalantly. "You know I'm right."

"Right, wrong, it's got fuck all to do with me. That shit's above my pay grade. Just tell the cops the truth, alright?"

"Save for the one omission," he says. "And what will be my reward for my compliance?"

"Eternal gratitude?"

"Think I can come up with something a little more…fun than that next time we meet. Which should be sooner rather than later. You've sped up our timetable with the announcement. We now need to get lawyers, advisors, accountants, legislators, and the Holy Spirit involved. This needs to be a priority, Joanna. Both our reputations are on the line."

"I know. I just need to put out this fire and I'm all yours."

"Call me tonight at eight. We'll powwow then."

"Okay. And thank you."

"What are friends for? Talk to you later, gorgeous. Bye."

I hang up. Crap. Just what I need, more shit on my To Do list. He's right, my life is just one giant complication after another. Knots tied to knots until the only choice is to accept defeat and walk away. That would be the smart, sane thing to do, but here I am driving to meet the biggest, twistiest, most aggravating knot of all.

Pendergast Manor remains on its desolate cliffside exactly where has sat for over a century. What's under the house is a hell of a lot more interesting than this architectural marvel. We have a fully stocked lab in the Chamber with DNA sequencers, an electron microscope, even a mass-spec machine. That's more Jem's domain than mine, and a good thing too because I hate coming here. I closed up most of the rooms, a giant weeklong undertaking, so not only is it stuffy and freezing as a tomb, but has its own ghosts in most rooms. Every painting, every antique is covered in plastic or white sheets to preserve them until I decide what the hell to do with it all. Burn it down seems the best option at present. One more knot, one more headache.

I hustle through the manor, my footsteps echoing with each step, until I reach the living room. Goddamn, it's cold in here. The snow's getting worse outside. This meeting better be short because I'll be damned if I'm spending the night here. I reach into the fireplace and open the secret door to the Chamber of Justice. A gust of cold air whooshes up from inside the cave. I clutch my coat tighter. A *really* short meeting.

Jem's waiting by Doris, phone pressed to his ear, as I descend the ramp. He hasn't changed out of his costume save for removing the cowl. Stray curls are plastered to his sweaty forehead. Oh, how I loved to twirl those soft tendrils, often on the nearby leather couch, which led to other intimate moments. The man became a tiger every time he returned from patrolling. Goddamn I miss those nights. I could use a good roll in the hay. Best release of tension out there.

"...no, she's already on Doxy," he says into the phone. "Just keep an eye on her vitals. I should be there within the hour." He hangs up.

"You don't have to stay on my account," I say.

"I think he does," a familiar man's voice echoes from the beach entrance. My shadow arrives. He's dressed in a black parka and black leather pants to combat the water. I hope he's gotten frostbite following me today. Doesn't seem like that's the case. As always, even with his brown hair tousled from the parka's hood, he looks like he's stepped out of an ad. Bastard.

"Fuck off. This has nothing to do with you."

"Your safety has everything to do with me."

"Did you not hear a goddamn word I said?" My gaze spins to Jem. "And why the fuck did you even bring him into this? Do you have that little respect for me?"

"Someone needed to watch your back. I couldn't."

"I would prefer James Ryder watching my back than him."

"Now you're simply being cruel," Jem chides. He looks at Justin. "She doesn't mean it."

"Hello, I can speak for myself," I snap. "Hell, do I even need to be here? You two have been plotting my life behind my back for years now. I mean," I whip my gaze to Justin, "did you tell him exactly what to say and do to get me into bed so he could be your spy?"

"Of course not. I simply asked him to keep an eye on you. Be there in case you needed anything."

"Like an orgasm."

"Like a friend."

"Well, he obviously took friendship lessons from you. 'How to fuck up a friend's life by simply existing.'"

"Enough," Jem snaps. "You're furious. We understand. You have every reason to be. But now we need to come together to pull you out of the quagmire you've fallen into. If Harry hadn't phoned me about the interview, you could be under arrest right now. That is still a possibility, Joanna. They have you dead to rights on bribery."

Fear shuts down the anger. "Are they going to pursue it?" I ask.

"There was a discussion about sending the evidence to the DA, yes" Jem says. "I'll attempt to convince them sullying the name of the city's champion would be a PR and political disaster, but I do not know if they will listen. I know you're friendly with the Commissioner and DA. In a day or two you should reach out to them, though it being a Federal prison, you may have to go higher. Senators. I can speak to the Vice President. I treated his wife for her Parkinson's."

"Okay. What about the prison break and hacking thing? Think they believed you?"

"I do. As far as they know, I have no cause to lie. However I do think you should exercise caution from here on. You'll have to give Doris Jr to me. If they do execute a search warrant and they find her, end game."

"Then how am I supposed to investigate the break?"

"You aren't," Jem says.

"Fuck that! They accused me of orchestrating the whole thing. I have to shove that accusation down their throats when I catch the real culprit."

"You cannot give them any more ammunition, Jo," Justin chimes in.

"And as of right now there is nothing to investigate," Jem says. "We have no fingerprints, no fibers, and no paper trails beyond yours. The men who perpetrated this, even the prisoners, are nothing but phantoms. They've interviewed three dozen people: accomplices, victims, staff, and *nothing*. There is nothing to be done except…" His mouth shuts.

"Wait," Justin finishes for him. "Wait until they crawl out of their holes and blow up the city."

"We don't know that's going to happen," Jem says.

"Bullshit," Justin shoots back. "Those men—"

"No, Jem's right," I cut in. Both men do a small double take as they hear those words. The corners of Jem's mouth perk up in a momentary smile. I pretend to ignore it. "There are only two reasons for this crime. One, it was an actual prison break. That one of the missing prisoners went to considerable trouble and spent a wad of cash breaking out every supervillain out of the kindness of his or her heart. We all know these people are lunatics but that, to me, is just batshit crazy. Not to mention not a single villain has surfaced. Not a single rumble or sighting? If we were talking one or even three, maybe. But over a dozen? Come on."

"So if not a prison break than what?" Justin asks.

"I'm leaning toward option two: abduction. For whatever reason—revenge being most likely—someone targeted these people. Supervillains. Maybe we shouldn't be looking inward but out."

"I had the same thought," Jem says. "Of course that means we have thousands if not millions of suspects instead of sixteen. You being in the top five with means, motive, and opportunity."

"At least we can cancel Protocol Pink," I say before turning to Justin. "And you can fuck off."

"No," Justin states plainly.

"Justin remains your shadow in case we're wrong," Jem says.

"Then fuck you both."

"It's really not up to you, Jo," Justin says.

"Hey, assholes, don't forget who has the leverage here. One word from me and you're both exposed for the lying pricks you are. I don't owe either of you a damn thing, certainly not loyalty."

Jem's face remains neutral as he steps toward me. "You're right. You don't owe us anything. You may even hate us. But everyone in this room knows you will never, ever expose us. Not out of hate, not under torture, and certainly not out of annoyance. Justin stays. You protect us, and we are going to protect you right back. He will stay out of your way. You won't even know he's there. But *should* you need him, he will be there. Because that's what we do. That's who we are. All of us."

Fuck. I glance at Justin who remains as neutral as the other hero. They both know me too well. Bluff called. "Fine."

"Good," Jem says with a nod.

"You need to act as if everything is business as usual," Justin suggests. "Word will spread the police brought you in for questioning. You've been acting suspicious lately. Quitting. Disappearing. The break-up with no explanation given. It's dug you into a deeper hole. People will start filling that hole with wild conjecture. Jem discovered your plot, broke up with you, and you quit to oversee the break. You need to show that you have nothing to hide. Be seen in public. If you have any scheduled appearances, attend. If anyone asks about the break, why you quit, be honest. Don't evade. And—"

"I cheated on you," Jem cuts in.

"What?" I ask.

"That's what we tell people. On my last trip to Independence, I slept with another woman. On your business trip you uncovered my betrayal and ended our engagement. We were both embarrassed and as usual decided to keep mum regarding our personal lives. But not anymore. We leak the story. We also spread the story that you'd been talking of leaving Pendergast to do what you are now, focusing on charity. *We* were going to start a foundation ourselves, but that thought ended when our relationship did. How far along are you with The Guardian Society?"

"Very early stages. All we have is a vison and name. Bennett's pissed I announced. We have to plow ahead now."

"Perhaps you should go to Independence," Justin suggests. "Might be safer."

"Not sure I'm allowed to leave town," I point out.

"If you let them know, and Stone confirms the meetings, it shouldn't be a problem," Jem says. "If anything develops, I'll keep you informed. You'll be a phone call and plane ride away."

"No way. I'm not running away. That's—"

"You're no good to anyone in prison, Jo," Justin snaps. "And there's nothing left for you to do. You're benched. You're going to look out for yourself for once."

My gaze whips to Jem. "And you agree with this? You want me to run off to Bennett Stone?"

"Of course I don't want you to-to be around th-that priapismic dilettante," Jem spews, showing emotion for the first time. "I never liked the man to begin with and positively loathe him now. I wouldn't trust him to feed my fish let alone look after the woman I love. But I trust *you*. And quite frankly we have no other option. So go to Independence, build the charity, be seen around town, and cozy up to as many senators and people in the justice department in case you're arrested. I will handle everything here."

Shit. Fuck. Shit. He's right. They're both right. Motherfucking fuck. That's the part that really pisses me off. "Fine. *Fine*," I growl through gritted teeth. Fuck. "Guess I have some phone calls and packing to do. Fuck you both very much."

"You're welcome," Justin says with a small smile. "736-555-3456. My phone number. When you know your flight and—"

"I'll call. I promise."

"And carry a panic button," Jem says.

"Okay."

"And the tracer from…Jordan. It should still have three hours battery life left," Jem says.

"I know. This isn't my first rodeo."

"Of course," Jem says sheepishly.

"Okay then. Class dismissed." The homework's going to be a bitch. I start out of the cave.

Halfway up the ramp Jem calls, "Joanna?"

"What?"

"I…" His mouth twitches and his shoulders slump as he re-thinks his next statement. "Please take care of yourself."

Be it the worry in his eyes, that damn defeated posture, or just my general exhaustion, I smile down at him. "*You* take care of *yourself*. And my city."

He presses his fist to his heart. "I'll guard it with my life," he says with a smile too.

"Don't go too far there, Ambrose. You've already died once for this city."

"I didn't do that for the city."

Goddamn it. My whole body lights up with warmth and I have to hustle out of the room before they see me blush or I say something I'll regret.

Running away. Backing down. I swore I'd never do either. That's not who I am. Of course lately I barely recognize myself. And I'm not sure I like the person I've become. Merely good enough. That's me now. Miss Good Enough. It'll have to do. But once a person recognizes there's something better than good enough, going back into the shade feels like you've entered perpetual darkness. Because good enough really isn't.

CHAPTER ELEVEN

MISS GOOD ENOUGH

"My eyes are up here, playboy."

If I had a dollar for every time I've caught Bennett glancing at my chest or ass this past week, The Guardian Society wouldn't need my millions for funding. I'm beginning to think he can't help it, like it's a nervous tick or Tourette's. My tits are decent but tastefully concealed tonight. Even a gal from Diablo's Ward knows you don't meet the President with your boobs spilling out.

Bennett talked me into tonight. The Selena Weiss Parkinson's Foundation is one of the most influential charities in Independence. All the glitterati and power players will be at the President's Mansion for the event, including heads of other charities and politicians we need to befriend. What he meant is suck up to them. I've been attending these events for over a decade, first as Justin's plus one of last resort, then as the head of Pendergast. Never got to meet the President though. I'm actually nervous. Not that I voted for him.

I'd completely forgotten Jem and I were supposed to attend this together until I was getting ready tonight. As part of Selena's medical team, he was meant to be an honored guest. He's not coming. He hates these things even more than I do. Any excuse to miss one. Not that he didn't have cause this time. Besides an appearance by the villain Eclipse, all's been quiet on the Galilee front. At least he finally got that bastard.

Alex Nunn is now the only supervillain inhabiting Xavier's Hardcore Unit awaiting trial. No luck finding his brethren. This case is in serious danger of growing cold. I'm still on the suspect list but firmly in the middle. Same nothing news on the bribery charges. The case against me is still open but hasn't moved ahead. Yet.

The one light in my otherwise dark gray world is The Guardian Society. It's moving ahead like an express train fueled by plutonium. I've been pulling sixteen hour days this whole week, tonight's ass kissing included, but the infrastructure is almost erected. We have a preliminary board of directors with me at the head, we have filed with the tax office and been incorporated, and hired the last of the dream team. The trunk of the tree is established and we even have a few branches sprouting. All thanks to me. Bennett's been in and out, an hour or two here and there, when he's not running his empire or side projects. He still found time to bring and eat dinner with us most nights and even dragged me out to a movie when I began screaming at our marketing guy over a missing file.

Tonight I spent an hour at the salon, have no circulation in my feet thanks to three inch heels, and am more dress than woman. Normally my personal shopper Isolde just tosses a designer dress at me, but Bennett's designer friend brought over a black and gold beaded satin kimono gown that covers my scars and has a tasteful V-neck, hence my companion's downright staring at my chest. I pray the tape holds. I think Bennett's hoping for the opposite.

"What?" my friend asks innocently. "Truly beautiful sights should be admired. And often. But I promise to change things up and stare at your ass when we get out of the limo."

And cue that damn smile of his. It never fails to draw one to my face. I manage to keep this grin relatively quick. "Seriously though. Keep the flirting to a minimum tonight. This is not a date. It's business. We need to appear professional. Capable. The kind of people they can trust to give money or put their reputations on the line to help cut through red tape."

"Then maybe we should have a quickie in the limo. It'd help me focus," he says with that smile.

Damn it. There goes mine. I do whack him with my clutch bag. "I'm serious," I chuckle.

"I know," he chuckles back. "There's no need for violence, Fallon. I'll be on my best behavior. I promise."

The limo pulls up to the first security checkpoint. The dogs sniff as the President's First Guardsman check our IDs. We're flying solo tonight. Bennett was very accommodating when I flew into town. There were a car and two bodyguards waiting for me at the airfield. His one stipulation for our partnership: round the clock protection, not just for my own safety. I couldn't argue with the logic. He and the team aren't used to having looming threats surrounding them. It seems to put the others at ease. And maybe my new guards were enough for Justin to stop his stalking. I've only caught sight of him twice, once in street clothes and the other in his new White Knight uniform. I liked the Justice costume better. But tonight what with half the IDP, Feds, and the First Guardsmen detailed to the party, my guards get the night off. I do wish I could have brought a gun. I feel naked without one.

A Guardsman helps me out of the limo, and after a few more hoops and metal detectors, Bennett loops his arm with mine and we advance to the step and repeat, my least favorite part of these events. Dozens of flashing lights, people shouting questions, then the next day you're plastered all over the newspapers and tabloids getting judged. Too fat, too thin, still drinking, mind controlled by aliens, I've been called them all. Normally I bypass the gauntlet, but Bennett vetoed that action. The more people talk about us, the more press the Society receives. So I stand like a mannequin with a fake smile as I'm blinded and rendered almost deaf by their questions.

"*Did you leave Jonathan Ambrose for Bennett Stone?*"

"*Who are you wearing?*"

"*Did you kidnap James Ryder?*"

Those are just the ones I can make out. Bennett waves to the masses with his best boyish grin affixed. The three people in this country who don't think we're a couple will by tomorrow. It hasn't gone beyond flirting, though there is that open invitation to stop by his penthouse day or night wearing nothing but a smile. Even if I wanted to take him up on the offer I've been too exhausted after work to do anything but sleep. Which is what I wish I were doing right now.

At least he doesn't make me answer questions. The journalists get their photos and Bennett ushers us toward the final security checkpoint. Our publicist is setting up real interviews for next week when we officially become a foundation. First I need to return to Galilee and rent offices, begin hiring there, ugh just stop, Jo. Baby steps. Just get through the night without offending anyone.

The President's Mansion is a lot smaller than I'd envisioned and a lot more modern, probably because this is the third incarnation. It was blown up the first time forty years ago by the villain General Chaos then again fifteen years ago by Left Hand. Jordan Ambrose tried too, but Jem defused the bomb in time. Hopefully tonight we can smooze unmolested by nutcases trying to make a name for themselves. *God* I wish I had a gun.

As always I seem to be the resident curiosity. This event is $5,000 an invite. I've found rich people often have the worst manners. A glance, look away, then whispers. Almost every person, hell even the paintings of past presidents we pass down the hall to the ballroom. Even my companion notices, his eyes narrowing at one such guilty party. Then the next. "Wow," he whispers.

"That's what you get for bringing a girl with a reputation to the ball."

We enter the packed ballroom where easily four hundred people chat, dance to big band classics, sit at tables surveying the dance floor, or line the walls bidding on the silent auction items. Beyond the odd movie star, I don't recognize anyone save for one. I thought she was in Milan. My stomach knots a little. Alexia "Lexie" Darby is hard to miss. The supermodel and secret former superhero holds court with three other socialites, no doubt gabbing about fashion and gossip. One woman glances over at me, eyes growing before turning to her clique to announce my arrival. Lexie gazes over and nods. I stare straight ahead. Okay, now I wish I had my gun *and* a drink.

"Bennett!" a man says to our right.

"Graham!" my companion says with a grin as the man and his pretty, petite blonde wife approach. The men hug and the blonde stares at me, a serene smile filling her elfin face. I nervously smile back. "I didn't know you two were coming."

"We needed a night out after everything," Graham says. He turns to me as well. "And we heard you'd be here."

"Joanna Fallon, may I present my cousin Graham Stone and his wife CeCe. They're my goddaughter Nathalie's parents. You remember—"

"Right," I say, my brain finally booting up. "I'm so sorry. How is she doing?"

"So much better," CeCe replies almost breathlessly. "All the advice you gave, the facility you recommended, is working wonders. It's saved her life. Truly."

"I just told the truth. It was all of you who really saved her. And will continue to. Just love her and do what's best for her, no matter how hard or harsh it may have to be."

"We will," Graham says.

"Can I...hug you?" CeCe asks with tears in her eyes.

"Uh, okay."

The tiny woman wraps her arms around me, and I give the stranger a squeeze back. CeCe breaks apart first. "Thank you." She turns to Bennett. "Don't you dare let this one get away from you, Bennett Stone. She's a keeper."

"Oh, we're not—"

"I'm doing my utmost to convince her of that," Bennett cuts in. "But do save me a dance, CeCe. Now, if you'll excuse us, there are several senators whose asses we need to kiss. We'll find you when the business portion of the evening is done. Have fun."

"Nice to meet you," I say before stepping away. PDA. Not my thing.

We manage face time with two senators, leaving both men dazzled, and one with my autograph. Five more targets to go, including our next mark, the Director of the Justice Department. We're halfway to our destination when I spot two faces I hoped I wouldn't have to see. Justin, like Bennett, was born to wear a tuxedo. I remember the first time I ever saw him in one. My breath literally stopped. Every time after that, for twenty years, I'd get butterflies. Even now as a brunette with a beard, and wearing black gloves, he turns heads. Lucy stands a head shorter than him. I swear she only owns three dresses. Tonight it's the black and silver satin with lame jacket. Matronly is an understatement. They move toward us like cruise missiles. I sigh before plastering a smile on my face. Nice, sweet, professional Joanna Fallon doesn't spit in people's faces no matter how much she may want to.

"Joanna," Lucy says, as always with a hint of disapproval.

"Lucy. Bennett, have you met Lucy Helms and...I'm sorry. I know we've met, but I guess you never made an impression."

"This is my cousin Charles' son, Joe Proctor."

"Right. Right, you were one of the few of Justin's cousins who *didn't* sue me," I say. "Boy that was a nightmare when I was already in the middle of another one. I should have just turned the company to the hyenas."

"Justin knew you were the best person to continue his legacy," Lucy says. "And now you've turned it over to strangers."

"Shannon is hardly a stranger. And I was tired of living for other people."

"And Pendergast's loss is the world's gain," Bennett adds.

"Yes, we were just talking about this new organization of yours," Justin/Joe says. "A very worthwhile endeavor. If there's anything we can do to help..."

"How kind of you," Bennett says. "We can use all the help we can get."

Justin nods at my date before turning my way. "Well, it will cost Ms. Fallon a dance." He holds out his arm. "May I?"

Fuck. With a fake smile, I take his arm. "Anything for the cause."

Justin leads me to the dance floor. "You look very pretty tonight."

"Flattery will get you nowhere, Mr. Proctor. That ship sailed two years ago after waiting at the dock for twenty."

The corners of his mouth twitch with displeasure. Good.

When we reach the floor, he takes my hand and wraps the other around my waist. He must have a top of the line prosthetic because not only do the fingers close around my palm, but it feels almost soft. Almost real. Cold but real. "I always knew you were pretty, Jo. Even when *you* didn't."

I roll my eyes right before we begin waltzing. "So, is Joe Proctor a fixture on the social scene? Kind of dangerous, especially if the real Charles and Joe Proctor get wind."

"They died in a car accident decades ago and were black sheep. Heard of but never met. But I still keep a low profile."

"You here to continue your stalking duties? Risking exposure for little old me. I should be honored."

"That's part of it. I heard a rumor The Nothing Man might attempt something."

"He your new arch-nemesis?"

"Not exactly. Just an annoyance. If he does crash—"

"Run and hide. I know the drill. I'm too exhausted to fight tonight."

"Could have fooled me," he says without a hint of humor.

"You just bring it out of me....*Joe*."

We dance in silence for a few seconds. "Do you remember the last time we danced together? My engagement party. Do you remember that night?"

"Of course."

More oppressive silence, then, "I miss her. I miss them both. That little precious girl..."

Shit. I cringe at the memory, not just of finding their corpses. No, worse is the thought of the three of them playing on the beach, Daisy giggling as she ran into the water where Justin waited for her. He spun her around as Rebecca beamed. I hated her then. For taking him away from me. He was blissful, and I was miserable. Not my finest moment. "I, uh, found some pictures Daisy drew. I can send them to you or...whatever. If you want them."

"I would. Thank you." He pauses. "And I haven't, uh, had a chance to thank you for going ahead with the Thornton Wing."

"You're welcome."

"And thank you for everything else. Taking over the company. Taking care of Dobbs. The manor. I know it was a lot to ask. You did an amazing job. Just like I know you'll do an amazing job with your new venture. Even with him as a partner."

"What have you got against Bennett?"

"Nothing. We were friendly. He's a sharp businessman. He's also a shrewd, shallow, selfish cad. You deserve better."

"In a business partner?"

"You know what I mean. He's not good enough for you."

"Why? Because he doesn't lie to me? Doesn't drag me into life and death situations? Save the speech, okay? I'm not *with* Bennett. And even if I was, it's none of your business. Your opinion means less than a stranger's. We have only just met, *Joe*."

"Just don't do anything you'll regret. That you can't take back. Will you at least concede I'm an expert on *that*?" I keep my mouth shut, as close as he'll get to an agreement. "I know what you're doing, Jo. So do you even if you won't admit it to me or yourself. Jem's a good man. One of the best people I've ever met. Behind you. Just don't take too long forgiving him, okay? Or punishing yourself. You and I both know from experience how quickly life can change. How easy it is to lose people we love. That every moment is precious in this fragile world. He made one mistake for the right reasons. You forgave me for Justice."

"Then not a week later you were back lying to me," I point out. "Fool me once, shame on you. Twice? That's on me. I've learned that lesson. Never again."

"Jem's not me. Don't penalize him for my transgressions. Or yourself."

The song ends, and I pull away to clap. "Thank you for the dance. And good hunting. Hope you do that better than your therapy sessions." With a fake smile, I walk away.

Oh I do so love our chats. They're so uplifting.

Just to piss him off, I zoom straight to Bennett, who talks to an elderly gentleman, and snake my arm around his waist, much to his surprise judging from the narrowed eyes. "Sorry about that, playboy. Hope I didn't make you too jealous."

"Maddeningly so," Bennett quips back before turning his attention back to the man.

We hit up targets three and four before I have to excuse myself to the ladies' room. I need a break from smiling and false compliments. I—

When I step out of the stall, another blast from the past waits by the sinks, giving me one of her million dollar smiles. Really. She can get a million dollars just to hold a perfume bottle and smile. Perhaps I'm just too tired, but feel only minor irritation when I set eyes on her again. "Seriously? You too?"

"Nice to see you too, Jo. You look…tired."

I roll my eyes. "What the fuck are you doing here?"

"I've supported the charity for years." She smiles and shifts her weight to her right hip. "So. Should we give them the catfight they want?" Lexie asks. "Of course everyone thinks I'll be instigating since you got my husband killed." She lifts her chin up. "Come on. I'll let you take the first punch."

"You're not worth ruining my manicure." I walk past her to the sinks to wash my hands. "Or my time."

"Well, you can try to throw me out but we both know I can take you." She opens her purse and removes lipstick. "So, the rumors are true. You and Bennett Stone. He is good in bed. I remember our night fondly. He—"

"Really? You want to talk about this? You don't have anything to say about, oh I don't know, your betrayal? Lying to me?"

"No. You're mad. I understand. I have no real defense except a promise is a promise. That and it's over. It's done with. If I could go back in time, I would do it all over again. There isn't anything I wouldn't do for my friends. You included."

"So you're here to plead his case too? You, who won't even speak to him?"

"Perhaps I'm not here for *him*," she says with a smirk. "You're being a moron, Joanna."

I roll my eyes. "Jesus."

"Do you have any idea how lucky you are? You have a wonderful man who loves you. He's out there. He's alive. And even with you acting the fool with the town ride, he still wants you. I had a firsthand view of you two falling in love. How deep that love runs. How you brought out the best in one another. I would give my soul to have that back. And you're throwing it away like it was nothing. Like it didn't matter. And we both know that isn't the case. It's the *only* thing that matters.

"Life is so fleeting, Jo. So goddamn precious. I have so many regrets. I should have told Brendan I loved him more. I should have taken more time off to spend with him. I should have...had our child when he first asked. That's what I'm left with, Jo. Nights full of regrets. I want to spare you that. He is a good man. If *I* can forgive him for misleading us, you sure as hell can too. And I have forgiven him. We are speaking and what he's told me..." She shakes her head. "Whatever pain you're experiencing, that man feels it ten-fold. If you still love him, and I know you do, then stop being a damn stubborn fool. Or your nights will be as haunted as mine until you draw your last breath."

Lexie smiles sympathetically at me before sauntering out. Guess some good has come out of this. Jem and Lexie are speaking again. For months I'd been trying to get them to reconcile. All it took was our world explodes. He forgave her for killing his brother, she forgave him for lying about seeing his brother die years before. Maybe they're just better people than I.

I plaster on a smile before I leave as well. Lexie is chatting with Justin and Lucy when I reach the ballroom again. Of course. They're all conspiring together. I shake my head, and scan the crowd for the one person truly on my side. Bennett stands near the dance floor speaking to an elderly man.

"There you are," Bennett says.

"Thought I'd ditched you? Never."

"Good to know." He turns back to the man. "Dr. Kurt Martinson, may I present Joanna Fallon, my new partner on The Guardian Society."

"Oh, I've heard of you," I say to Martinson. "My fia-ex-fiancée spoke of you often."

"Fondly, I hope," the man chuckles. "I am surprised he mentioned me. Not the biggest talker, is our Dr. Ambrose. Hated to see him leave the hospital, though. One of the finest researchers and doctors I've ever worked with."

"Our Lady Hospital is lucky to have him," I say.

"Though I hear you may be losing him as well," Dr. Martinson says.

My arm drops from Bennett's waist. "I'm sorry?"

"Dynamic Biotech in Beijing phoned me a few days ago. Dr. Ambrose listed me as a reference. Seems he applied for a positon in their virology department. I recalled he had an interest in that discipline but never dreamed he'd switch focus from neurology."

"I…"

I have no idea what to say. I don't know I could physically say it if I did. It's as if I've been punched in the gut with an iron bar. The world morphs into nothing but a pinpoint for a moment. When it refocuses both men stare with concern.

I somehow maintained a blank expression, but something must give the shock away. "I...didn't know."

"China's research laws are far laxer than ours," Dr. Martinson explains. "He'd gain years."

"Oh," I say.

"Joanna, I could use some water. You?" Bennett asks, sliding his arm around my waist this time. "Please excuse us, Dr. Martinson. It was good to see you again." Bennett ushers me away from the messenger before I shoot him. "Are you okay?"

"I'm fine," I lie. "Who's next on the hit list?"

After getting our drinks, Scotch for him and Ginger Ale for me, we play nice with two more targets or really Bennett does. I become nothing but a decoration, smiling and agreeing with everything the men say. My brain went into autopilot mode and won't disengage. Not that I want it to. It's keeping the swirl of emotions at bay like an iced over lake with the drowning pounding to surface. If they're kept underwater long enough perhaps they'll just die and sink to the bottom. The pounding's distracting enough. I can't even enjoy meeting the President and First Wife, even when she asks for an autograph for her son and he thanks me for taking care of Emperor Cain. Me, little Joanna Fallon from Diablo's Ward. The girl who barely passed high school, who almost every teacher said I wouldn't amount to much, who used to collect used needles for pocket change, made the leader of our county *proud* and I don't feel a fucking thing.

He's leaving.

After schmoozing target five, "Moon River" begins playing. "I love this song," Bennett says.

"Me too," I say quietly.

- 182 -

Bennett leads me to the dance floor. "Almost a full sentence. That's an improvement of the last hour," he says with a smile.

For the first time I don't have the involuntary reaction of reciprocating. "Sorry."

"They seemed enamored with you regardless. The President included."

"That's nice."

"And I fear the Proctor fellow wants to break my arm every time I touch you. Look." Bennett spins me around, and there's Justin at the edge of the dance floor watching us with a scowl. I gaze down. "He's been shadowing us all night, acting the jealous husband. Another contender for the hand of the fair maiden?"

I scoff. "Hardly."

"Oh, there he goes," Bennett says. I glance back at Justin, who now stares at his watch and hustles through the crowd. "Late for something, I guess. Good. Now I can do this." Bennett draws me in closer against his body. It actually feels nice, the weight and warmth pressed against me. I have the strongest urge to rest my head on his shoulder like I used to with Jem. He loves to dance. I'd be sitting on the couch working and he'd just randomly turn on the radio, present his hand to me, and we'd sashay around the penthouse or hold one another like this. I close my eyes now, hoping it'll bring the same peace, but no. He doesn't smell like Jem. He's not as warm. It's good. Nice. But not the same.

I open my wary eyes. "Can we please get the hell out of here? I don't think I can do this anymore. Can we just go? Please?"

With a comforting smile, Bennett nods. "Okay." His smile grows. "We'll go. And I know just the place."

*

I expected to find myself at his penthouse or some loud club, but my new friend continues to surprise me. The limo drives us to the edge of the city with bodegas, boutiques, a tiny movie theater, and apartments above the shops. As close to middle class as a city can get. We pull up to an old fashioned diner, Irma's Diner, judging from the blue neon sign in the window. My kind of place. Inside is all red and white vinyl and chrome, right down to the stools at the counter and booths. The two middle-aged waitresses wear red polyester dresses and paper hats. We stick out like nails in old floorboards decked out in our formal wear. The wino at the counter nursing coffee and the taxi drivers in a booth all do a double take as we enter, but the waitresses just smile at Bennett, who returns the gesture. "Hey Carla. Hey Lola."

"Benny!" the Latina one behind the counter says. "Twice in one week!"

"You know I can't stay away from you, Lola," he replies with a wink. "Booth for two, please."

Carla hurries over to us, grabs two menus, and leads us to a back booth. "So, where were you guys tonight? Prom?" Carla asks.

"An intolerably dull fundraiser. My lips are numb from all the butt kissing."

After hanging our coats on the hooks, we slide into the booth on opposite sides. Carla grins at me as she hands me the menu. "Can I get you something to start with?"

"Coffee. You know how I take it."

"Same. Black," I reply.

"And we don't need menus. Bring us your biggest platter of your greasiest fries and a hot fudge banana split. Extra whip. That okay with you, gorgeous?"

"Sounds perfect."

"Coming right up," Carla says before walking away.

Bennett undoes his bowtie and the top two buttons. "Oh, that's better."

"Looks it, *Benny*."

He chuckles. "Don't you start. Only Carla, my mother, and my sister were allowed to call me that. You have not earned the right yet, Ms. Fallon."

"So how come the waitress does?"

"Because I've known her all my life. Three generations of Stones have frequented these hallowed booths. My grandparents actually met here. She, the socialite who came in to escape the rain. He, the busboy with a heart of gold. Dad even escorted Mom here on their second date, and then they brought Molly and me here for celebrations. A treat."

"Let me guess. Fries and banana split?"

He nods. "I still come when I'm stressed or just need to disappear. They have the best fries I've ever tasted, and I am a French fry connoisseur. You know what they say: starve a cold, feed heartbreak."

Carla returns with our coffee before departing with a smile. "That obvious, huh?" I ask as I sip my coffee.

"When Martinson mentioned China you turned white as snow. I didn't want to say anything until we were out of there." He adds more sugar. "I thought you two were over."

"We are. I just…it was a shock. It's all been a fucking shock. And I haven't exactly processed everything well. Or at all. One minute you're planning your wedding, the next he's not the man you knew. The man you knew is gone. That wonderful life you had planned is gone. Your head knows it, but your idiot heart, the one that got you into trouble in the first place, just won't catch on. It won't…let go. And everyone keeps making it worse. They keep telling me I'm making a huge mistake. That I'm hurting us both out of spite." I fall back in my seat. "Hell, maybe they're right. Maybe I am just a cold, vindictive, hateful, heartless bitch." I scoff. "Not like I don't have just cause after everything."

Bennett leans forward across the table, folding his arms on the linoleum. "Look, I know we've only known each other a short time, but I call absolute, utter bullshit on that. You do have just cause. Anyone in your shoes would have gone nuts. But you haven't. You saw a problem in your life and dealt with it the way you saw fit. You took care of yourself for once. That's not cold or heartless, that's survival. If a few people don't like it or got hurt in the process, then that's their problem. Sometimes you have to be cold and heartless in this life. That doesn't make you bad. It makes you human. And maybe it'll be easier if he's across the world," Bennett suggests. "Unless you don't *want* to let him go. You wouldn't be the first woman to take back a cheating man. He made a mistake. No one's perfect."

"You're on his side too?"

"Hell no," he scoffs. "Fuck him. You can do better. I just don't want to see you in pain."

"I—"

Police sirens stop my words. Three squad cars zoom down the street. "Just another night in the big city," Bennett quips. "The things we human beings do to one another, no?"

"It's The Nothing Man," Carla says, sundae in hand. "Heard it on the radio. White Knight's after him now."

"Just in case you were homesick," Bennett says with a wink. "I'm shocked we made it through the gala unmolested."

I pick up a spoon. "Come on. A party's not a party without a supervillain crashing it." I spoon out some ice cream. "And here I thought you were a thrill seeker."

He scoops some ice cream too. "Thrill seeker, yes. Death wish, no." He eats his food. "God, that's good."

"Very good. You were right. I needed this."

"Nothing junk food can't cure. Besides high cholesterol." I chuckle for the first time in hours. "See? It even brought a smile to your sour face. Hell, you might even be up for some...*fun* after the fries come."

"You don't give up, do you? Surely there's easier prey out there for you than—"

"A woman going through an identity crisis who's still in love with her ex-fiancée?" he finishes for me. "Maybe I think you're worth it."

"Or maybe you're chasing me because I keep running, and you just can't help yourself," I suggest.

"Or maybe...I know how rare it is to find a kindred spirit in this fucked-up, God forsaken planet. To find a person who sees the world the way I do. Believes in the same tenants and principals." He scoops in more ice cream. "And who can fuck like a stallion."

I chuckle. "You are good for my ego, Mr. Stone, that is for damn sure."

"Hope that's not all I'm good for, Ms. Fallon. We—"

Tires squeal outside, drawing our attention outside. Through the window we watch as a car veers onto the sidewalk across the street, narrowly missing a strolling couple before crashing into a building. "Jesus!" I gasp before rising and taking a step.

Bennett leaps up to block me. "Wait!"

"Wh—"

"Everyone get away from the windows!" Bennett orders.

"What?" Carla asks.

"The Nothing Man," Bennett says, nodding outside.

I don't see anyone at first, not until a second car quickly jerks toward us. A figure all in black stands in the middle of the road, trench coat flapping in the wind. "What the hell is he waiting—"

A flash of white zooms down the street like a charging bull, connecting with the villain. A tackle worthy of a football star. The black clad man falls to the asphalt with the white blur on top of him, leaving a crater in the road. The man in white rises first. My stomach knots when my brain puts it all together. White Knight. Justin. *Shit*. I—

The Nothing Man vanishes. I blink and he's no longer on the ground. Teleporter. Justin's barely upright when The Man appears behind the hero. I move to bang on the glass, but don't get my arm up before The Nothing Man shoves something into Justin's back. The hero wails in agony but at the same time whacks the back of his head against his assailant's face. It must stun the villain because he staggers a pace back, knife still dripping blood, before teleporting away again. I'm moving toward the door before I realize I'm doing it. "Jo!" Bennett calls behind me. But just as I make it past the second booth, Justin speeds away again. I keep running too.

"Call the police!" I say before stepping out into the freezing night.

I glance left. The car accident survivors are being aided by other bystanders. They're—

Another bout of skidding tires to my right, the way Justin ran. My gaze whips that direction. Oh, thank Christ. A block down, in front of the old movie theater, the hero and villain stand in the center of the road, oblivious to the oncoming out of control car. The Nothing Man stabs Justin again as a car drives straight into the front of the theater. "Jesus Christ."

I kick off my heels, pick them up, and bolt toward the madness. But I'm not fast enough. The Nothing Man stabs the hero again. That's all he can take. Knight doubles over, falling to his knees and hands. Fuck. *Fuck!* The Man looms over the hero, head tilting to the side, studying his prey. He raises the blade again. No! No, no, no, no...

The blade comes down. It doesn't connect. Justin's hand rises to catch the villain's arm. There's a crack as bones break before the hero lets out a war cry and grabs the villain's leg. Then they're gone. *Poof!* What...? Up. Movement in the sky. I glance up a moment after the men appear above the movie theater. Falling. I stop to gasp. Falling. They crash through the roof, White first. Jesus.

Bennett passes me on the sidewalk, running toward the demolished theater. I didn't know he was following me. This time I trail after him, though he's faster than me. Traumatized people begin filtering out of the theater, most bleeding or crying. The entire front is gone, the glass doors nothing but shards from the car crash. I have to waste seconds putting my heels back on. Bennett simply charges inside.

Bedlam. That's what I walk into. Popcorn and glass everywhere from the demolished concession stand. A teenager in an orange vest aiding the driver of the smoking car out of the wrecked vehicle with Bennett's help. Screams of pain and terror echoing from the theater even as people run through the doors to safety. Most appear intact with only a few cuts on them. Over the screams there's the screech of twisting metal as lights flicker in the lobby. That can't be good.

"Get him outside," Bennett orders the teen.

"Everyone outside," I shout. "Watch out for the glass! Clear the building!"

No one's listening. The crowd's so crazed one man falls in the doorway and people ignore him, even trampling the poor guy. I reach him a second before Bennett does. My friend knocks a person aside as I bend down to help the man to his feet. "You're okay," I say to the now bleeding man. He yowls in agony as he rises. Probably broken ribs. He leans on me as I help him hobble outside and deposit him on the curb. "Try not to move. An ambulance is on its way."

"Thank you," he sobs.

"Peter!" a woman shrieks. I turn around, and she's running over to us. He'll be fine.

I push and shove my way through the maddening crowd back inside to the lobby. The flickering lights have gotten worse, where it's more dark than not. I scan the crowd but don't see Bennett. Shit. I slip through the small opening of people into the theater. Oh, fuck me. The hole in the celling gapes open, far bigger than the man who created it and still crumbling. Metal girders hang by cables still swinging like a pendulum in a Poe story. Some have already collapsed, crushing rows of seats I fear with people under them. The white screen's ripped as well with another hole in the far wall. Justin. Where's—

"Help!" I hear a familiar man shout.

My attention whips toward the center of the theater directly under the hole. Bennett's head peaks above the seats, glancing around wildly for aid, as a bloody teenaged girl sobs beside him. I maneuver through the stragglers toward them. The hyperventilating teenager notices me, her face is a mix of blood and what must be dirt or soot. I think she's attempting to form words but can only tremble. Bennett is too busy with something on the floor to look up, even as more of the roof collapses not ten feet away from him or as I run closer. Oh, fuck me. A girl, or I think it's a girl judging from the torn yellow tights and silver sneakers now splattered with blood, lies on the ground, one leg pinned by a huge hunk of concrete and a metal girder in her abdomen. "Fuck," I gasp.

"You're okay, Ariana," Bennett says to the girl. He kisses the hand he's holding. "You're okay."

His voice snaps me from my momentary stupor. I hustle down the aisle toward them. It's worse up close. Like her friend, she was once a beautiful girl. Blonde hair now becoming red from the bleeding gashes in her head. One blue eye swollen shut and the other staring up at Bennett with tears flowing. They both glance at me as I toss a broken seat aside so I can kneel beside her too. I learned first-aid at the police academy, but with one look at the position of the wound, the black blood seeping from it, and the tiny blood bubbles she breaths out, I know not even a trained doctor could save her now.

"I-I-Sh-Should y-you re-remove the metal?" the friend asks. "It-It-She—"

I gaze up at the girl. "Go outside," I order, voice titanium. "Wait for the ambulance and bring them back here the moment they arrive. Go! *Now!*"

The command breaks through the shock. The teenager nods and sprints the opposite way down the aisle. She doesn't need to be here. She doesn't need to see this. Bennett gives me a little nod of approval before returning his attention to the girl. "It's okay, Ariana," he whispers, voice trembling right along with the rest of him. "She's gone to get help. You're okay. You're going to be fine." He pets her hair. "You're gonna be just fine. I'm here. I'm right here with you. I'm here, sweetheart."

The girl tries to smile but only groans in pain, clutching onto Bennett's hand as tight as she can. "Hey. Hey," he says. She opens her eye again. "You're doing so well. You're being so brave. You just have to be brave a little while longer. You have to be strong. Can you be strong for us?"

She opens her mouth, trying to speak, and succeeds the second time. "Mo-Mommy," she croaks. "I-I w-want Mommy. Mommy," she sobs through the blood bubbles.

Jesus. *Jesus.*

Bennett kisses her hand again. "She's coming. She's on her way. Just be strong, sweetheart. Be strong for me. Be strong for her."

"Mommy. Mommy. Mo—"

She coughs up blood as her body convulses. Oh, God.

"No. No," Bennett whispers, holding onto her hand tighter even as her body grows limp. "No. No. No. No."

"Bennett…" I touch his shoulder. His body jolts, I think in surprise. He'd forgotten I was here. I meet his tear-filled eyes. "She's gone," I whisper.

"No. She'll be fine. She's…" He looks down at the still girl. "We-We can do something. CPR. We-We—"

"She's gone, Bennett. She's gone. There was nothing you could do. She—"

"*No!*" he roars, rage filled gaze whipping my way. It cuts short my breath as if any movement could cause him to lash out at me. The moment passes. Anguish overtakes the madness. "There is," he croaks out. "There was. I-I-I…" He stares down at her. "Too late. I'm sorry. I'm sorry, sweetheart. Never again. I promise. Never again." He kisses her hand. "Never again. *Never*. I'm sorry. I'm so sorry," he sobs.

He sobs until he cannot breathe. Until his eyes sting. I've been there. I know exactly what he needs. I wrap my arms around my friend and hold on tight until there are no tears left. Until the world fades away and returns. I let him know he's not alone, no matter how much he may believe he is.

Sometimes that's all you can do. And sometimes that has to be good enough.

*

When the night began I promised myself I wouldn't end it in Bennett Stone's penthouse. My word is gonna be worth less than a politician's at this rate.

It took emergency services forever to arrive at the theater, almost twenty minutes. Not that I blame them. They had their hands full. The battle spanned almost ten blocks, not a single one of those blocks left unmolested. We heard on the radio the fight continued on after the theater until White Knight finally apprehended the villain. I did breathe a literal sigh of relief upon hearing Justin was alive. Cold comfort when you literally have a dead teenager's blood on your hands. Bennett and I stayed with Tina, Ariana's friend, until EMTs got around to her, keeping her warm, still, and feet elevated. Shock. She should be fine though. At least physically.

It was nice to see how everyone in the surrounding restaurants and apartments came out with water and blankets for the injured. Even Carla and Lola popped by with our coats and trays of water for the people. Bennett barely spoke. He just rubbed Tina's feet as I asked her questions until she was carted off. Since there was little else we could do after that, and I was shaking from both the temperature and adrenaline withdrawal, I called the limo driver from Bennett's phone and got him out of there. Even alone he didn't speak, didn't do anything but stare out the window, face an unreadable mask. There was no way in hell I was leaving him alone after all that. There was no way in hell *I* wanted to be alone after all that. I told the driver to take us to his penthouse and got out after him. Still not a peep, even as we ride up the elevator.

His place isn't as I'd imagined. I'd anticipated chrome and modern simplicity not deep, plush burgundy carpeting, wood paneling, polished antiques, oil paintings and ancient maps framing the walls. Reminds me of an English manor house. Warm. Classy. Homey even. Bennett drops his keys, wallet, and cell phone on the end table by the front door then just stares at the specks of blood on his white shirt and cuff. "I still have blood on me," he whispers, shocked.

I take a step to his side and slip my hand in his. "Then lets get cleaned up, huh? Come on."

I lead him down the hallway, past family photos on the end tables, to his bedroom. Not as I'd imagined either. A king size four poster bed fills most of the space with an ornately carved armoire in the corner, dresser with TV on top, and more oil paintings of serene men and women on the walls. I sit him down on his bed, and he stares up as if he sees right through me. I smile anyway before going into the bathroom. Jesus. My make-up has held up fairly well but my hair's half fallen out of its side bun and tiny red dots mar my cheek and chest. I grab a wash cloth and scrub the blood away. I still feel dirty down to my bones. I close my eyes, take a deep breath, and force the revulsion, the sadness down. Not now, Jo. You're needed.

Bennett hasn't moved. He *doesn't* move as I kneel in front of him to remove his shoes. His cummerbund. As I unbutton and remove his bloody shirt and wipe the fluids from his neck and face. At least he sees me this time. His eyes follow my every movement, a small, sad smile growing with each act until the corners of his mouth begin to tremble and tears well in his brown eyes. "Shit," he whispers. "Shit."

"You did everything you could," I whisper back. "I mean it. You gave that girl comfort. You kept her calm. You let her know she wasn't alone when she needed it the most. That was all you could do. And you did it to perfection. *Good job.*"

Bennett lets out a choked laugh as tears fall from his eyes. He wipes them away and shakes his head. "I-I just…" He swallows. "Why? Why did…? She was so young. She just wanted to see a movie with her friend. If she'd just sat somewhere else. If those…fuckers had chosen to go down another street. If they'd just done us all a favor and killed each other. If I moved up—" His mouth suddenly snaps shut. He closes his eyes and lets out a puff of breath before opening them again. He doesn't look at me this time. "Do you believe in God?"

"I-I don't know."

"I wish I still did. I used to. When I was a child. We went to church every week. Mom made us say grace at every meal, thank God in our prayers every night. I even considered becoming a priest." I raise an eyebrow and Bennett smiles. "I know. Never would have happened, but I was young and I…think I just wanted to help people. Seemed the best way all around." He gazes up at the heavens again. "We were actually on our way to a church fundraiser when it happened. One minute we were driving, talking about riding the Ferris wheel they'd rented, then just…bang. I blinked and the roof crushed in my parents' heads. They just vanished in a spurt of blood, metal, and rock.

"Molly and I must have been knocked to the floor. That metal and rock slid farther, pinning my baby sister underneath it." He shakes his head and wipes away the tears before looking at me once more. "I tried to move the rock. I tried and I tried, even as her blood curling screams begged me not to. For half an hour as I prayed to God, as I tortured my little sister with my stubbornness and ineptitude, *I tried*. I swore I'd become a priest. I'd donate organs. I'd give away every penny in my trust if He would just help me move the boulder and save my Molly. This little girl who still believed in Santa Claus and loved butterflies. But it wouldn't move," he says, voice cracking. "And the moment my arms gave out, the moment I lost my strength, was the moment I lost my faith. It was the moment I realized that if God ever did exist, he didn't give a shit about us. I realized that we were on our own. That there is no karma, no plan, no divine retribution or punishment for the wicked. If we wanted it, we'd have to dole it our ourselves. It's on us, and only us. *We* change the world for better or worse."

"Hopefully for the better," I whisper. "That's all any of us can hope for. Strive for. That the good we give and receive outweighs the bad. That there are more good people out in the world than evil. That even the evil are redeemable. That love will always be a far greater force than hate and apathy. That good intentions can be enough. That we always at least *try*. Like you did tonight."

He actually smiles, which brings one to my face too. Hesitantly, he reaches up, hand lingering a centimeter above my cheek a second before he touches me. I place my hand over his. "I *have* to kiss you right now, okay?" he whispers. "It doesn't have to go beyond—"

I silence his words with the needed kiss. Sweet and tender quickly growing savage. Primal. The type of kiss that only a nightmare night can spur. When you've gone to hell and back and need to remind yourself that pleasure is still possible. We fuck the pain, the loneliness, the rage at life away until when we come crashing back to earth we can continue on another day. And as I fall asleep in my friend's arms, I don't dread the sun rising or the fresh hell the new day will bring. For tonight good enough might actually be enough.

At least until the dawn comes.

CHAPTER TWELVE

BECAUSE IT MATTERS

Oh, there is nothing like waking up well and truly fucked.

Sore in the right places, limp in all others. Scorched earth where no tension can take root. I don't even care that the clock reads 11:12. I'm beyond late for work on a day I haven't that luxury. My give a damn's busted. I stretch like a cat and sigh contentedly. Boy, I needed that. But now I need to pee and brush the cat box out of my mouth. Fuck you reality. I throw off the covers, snatch a shirt from Bennett's dresser, and pad to the bathroom. Coffee right after.

"No, goddamn it, you're not listening," Bennett says behind a closed door down the hall. "Doc, I don't care about the cost. After all I've put into this, two hundred million is pocket change. I am just asking if it's medically possible to move the timetable up. *If* we're ready for roll out."

Shop talk. Coffee's more important than eavesdropping right now. He's left me half a pot waiting in the small kitchen. Taking in the shiny counters and appliances he is definitely the type who has never turned on the oven in the corner. Okay, now I have my coffee, it's time to snoop. Bennett's muffled voice continues as I meander through his penthouse, starting at the entrance hallway, specifically the photos on the table. Bennett, wearing a ski suit holding up a pole as a blizzard storms around him. Bennett in church cradling a baby in a christening gown as Graham and CeCe flank him. Bennett waving on a wall cliff, suspended by ropes probably a thousand feet off the ground. Shaking hands with the President. Him as a teenager with a younger girl in his arms. Has to be Molly. Same smile, same large brown eyes. She would have been a beauty. Goddamn waste.

The living room's next. Like my penthouse, shit *former* penthouse, an entire wall is glass and for good reason. The expanse of Independence is laid out before me. The National Monument's gray arch, the Great Garden Park, President Huddleston's memorial coliseum, all there. Must be breathtaking at night.

The wall behind me proves no less interesting. Books, books, and more books, some leather-bound and others the more modern paper. You can tell a lot about a person by their choice of entertainment. The old tomes are standard classics that appear never opened. The paperbacks are far more eclectic. Seems Bennett and Jem have similar taste in reading material. Spy novels, biographies, non-fiction about the Black Plague, Spanish flu, several on the uber-gene. Hell, he even has one written my Jem's "father," the psycho fucking fuck Dr. Christian Ambrose. Dr. Frankenstein more like. His monster turned on his maker too.

I pluck that book from the shelf and flip through it. All medical mumbo jumbo. I turn it over to the author photo and find myself staring at an older version of Jem straight down to the horn-rimmed glasses. So. This is the madman who genetically engineered then tortured the love of my life. There were nine failures: Adam and Aaron, Benjamin and Bernard all the way until Jonathan and Jordan came into the world, perfect in every way medically possible. Maybe if old Christian had let them be boys instead of lab rats their minds could have been perfect too. If he'd given them love. Support. Kindness. Not lab tests and vivisection. It's a damn miracle Jem turned out as wonderful as he did. Kind, caring, strong, a man who strives to always do the right thing. Who devotes his life to helping others, usually to his detriment. Who...shit. My eyes are suddenly wet. Guess last night's ice thawed.

China. He's going to China. They do have better facilities. Probably more funding. Greater freedom. Work. All that matters is the work. Changing the world for the better. That's why we made such good partners. We understood and fueled that part of each other. But I'm never going to see him again. Never. He's moving halfway around the world. He...*shit*. I close my eyes and force the tears down. I'm not crying over him again. *I'm not.* He—

I sense his body heat a moment before one hand snakes down over my hip while the other glides under the shirt to my bare breast. I gasp as his fingers begin toying with me, playing my body like a guitar. I don't open my eyes. I just let the sensations overwhelm the negativity. He does what he wants, and I let him. Anything to push Jem out of my mind. I don't open my eyes again until my breathing regulates. Bennett smiles down at me, playing with my hair. I manage a smile back. "Thank you. I needed that."

"Thank you right back. I did too," he replies, grin growing. "So...?"

"So...?" I chuckle. "Everything okay at work? I heard you reaming someone a new one on the phone. Problems with the Society or—"

"No. Just a speed bump on another project."

"Anything I can do to help?" I ask.

"Believe me, Miss Fallon," he says, hand sliding up my thigh again, "you have helped enough."

I stop his advance. "Enough of that, playboy." I extract myself from his sweaty body and snatch up my shirt beside that damn book. "I am already late for work." Bennett flips on his side as I stand. "I have a trillion loose ends to tie up before I leave."

"Still plan on going back to Galilee tomorrow?"

"I have an appointment with my realtor to look at office space tomorrow, and my cousin's birthday party at night, so I kind of have to. Can I borrow some clothes?"

"Take whatever you want."

"Thanks," I say as I walk to the hallway.

I think he was gearing up for a serious conversation which I am in no mood for. I find a set of sweatpants and hoodie in his dresser. My beautiful dress lies on the ground torn along with my pantyhose. At least my panties remain intact. Bennett, wearing nothing but jeans and a smile, walks in as I dress. "You know, I'll probably be in Galilee in the next few days."

"Oh. Good. Hopefully I'll have a space to show you. We might even be to the local hiring phase."

"Fantastic," he says with little enthusiasm.

Okay, I am seriously out of practice with the whole getting away clean the morning after thing. I'm not sure what to say or do except leave. I slip on my heels. "I'll e-mail you photos of the offices I like."

"That's okay. I trust your judgement. I'll be busy with other things anyway."

"The pet project? Care to share?"

"A guy's gotta have his secrets to keep the mystery alive," he says with that boyish smile.

Cue mine. "Well, you have my number if you need help. Or a sounding board. Or—"

"A blowjob?" he asks, eyebrow raised. "You do owe me one after the living room, us being equal partners and all."

That's better. Banter I can handle. With a sly grin, I saunter over to him. "I am all about equality." I kiss him. Twice. "See you in a few days, playboy."

"I'm counting the moments already."

He swats my ass as I walk past. Getaway complete.

It's still freezing but sunny as I begin my walk of shame. The doorman leaves his seat to hail me a cab. I need to get back to the hotel, shower, and change. I'll be up all night with my loose ends so I can make the flight and appointments tomorrow. A cab pulls up before I begin shivering. I thank the doorman and climb in. The stop and go of city traffic does nothing to help my sense of urgency. So damn much to do. I'd walk but in these heels—

We barely get around the corner when the taxi door opens. My eyes whip right just as Justin slides in. "Jesus, it's cold," he mutters.

"The fuck?"

The driver starts talking in a foreign language, but I hold up my hands, smile and say, "It's okay. It's okay." Justin smiles at the man as well. Shaking his head, the driver turns back around, placated. I'm not. "What the hell? How did you know where I was?"

"GPS on your cell. Why the hell weren't your bodyguards there?"

"No one knew where I was. I was perfectly safe."

"*I* found you," he points out.

"Then you win," I say, rolling my eyes. We stop and go in silence for a few seconds. Out of the corner of my eye, I assess him. No bruises, cuts, weeping knife wounds, or any evidence of last night's epic beat down. Un-fucking fair. "Are you okay? After last night? I heard you caught him."

"I did. Thank God." Justin pauses, his jaw clenching. "He's only nineteen years old. *Nineteen*, Jo. Just some kid from the suburbs who thought it'd be cool to become a supervillain instead of going to college."

"Jesus," I say.

"They went to his house, well his parents' house, and found a file on his tablet filled with stories about Emperor Cain, Alkaline, Dr. Avatar with notes on what they did right and wrong. He even posted something called fan-fic about how he was Cain's son and about them taking over the world. Another about him raping Lady Liberty. And there are millions of stories like that on these sites."

"Well at least you got one pervert off the streets. How are you physically?"

"A little stiff and sore." His lips purse in disapproval. "Waiting outside for you in sub-zero temps while you were literally screwing up your life didn't help matters."

"Excuse me?"

"You spent the night with Bennett Stone, didn't you?"

"Yeah. So?"

"And you intend to continue the relationship with him?" he asks, close to sneering at the prospect.

"I...don't know. Maybe."

"What about Jem?"

"What about him? We're broken up. He-He's moving to fucking *China*."

"You don't..." Justin groans in frustration and looks away out of his window. "I see you walking off a cliff *you* don't even want to walk off, but damned if you don't keep taking those steps. To spite yourself. To spite him. And you're so close to falling, to reaching the point of no return, and losing everything."

"Excuse me. I already lost everything because of you, and because of a choice *he* made."

"Like you've never made a mistake," he spits out. "Like you've never made a hard, morally gray choice for the right reasons. Look, I don't know if what we did was right or wrong, but the choice was made with the best of intentions. To save your ungrateful life. Even after all this, I would make the same choice. Because look at what's happened since I came back. You're lost. You're cruel. You're pushing away the best damn thing that ever happened to you. A man who has proven he will fight to the death for you. Would Bennett Stone do that?"

"Jesus Christ, I'm not marrying the fucking guy! We're friends. We had a shitty night and had sex. Nothing more."

"It'll mean something more to Jem," Justin says, voice hard. "You keep this up, you keep pushing and pushing, and he *will* go. And you'll be alone with the knowledge *that* one, that one you can only blame on yourself."

The truth of those words drops a rock in my stomach, but I'll be damned if I'll let him know that. He's not winning this battle. "You know I find it really fucking hypocritical *you* of all people are lecturing me on acting without thinking of others' well-being. Do you know the real reason I spent last night with Bennett Stone? Because neither of us wanted to be alone after we watched a teenage girl *you* left to die bleed out in front of us."

His face falls. "What?"

"The movie theater you demolished last night. We were there. You left a crumbling building, one of many, to capture a single man. Dozens are in the hospital. One died that I'm aware of because *I* was there. Bennett and I watched her take her last breath. We stayed with her, a sixteen-year-old girl named Ariana, buried in the rubble you helped create. *We* were there for her while you were acting the supposed damn hero. So don't you fucking dare lecture me on right and wrong. On hurting people. *Your* decisions killed a little girl last night. Say what you want about Bennett Stone, but he was there. He's been there for me. It's easy with him. Simple. And I can use some simple in my life. Complicated hasn't served me very well. I'm tired of living on a damn rollercoaster. I could use a break on a merry-go-round."

"If you were anyone else, I'd agree. But you're not. You don't do half measures. And shallow will kill your fucking soul." He leans in so we're nose to nose. "It hurts because it matters, Jo. Never forget that. *Never*."

"Get out of my fucking cab," I growl, "before I scream."

He stares into my sub-zero eyes, trying to keep his the same temperature, but can't even come close. He looks away first and climbs out of the taxi where it's a hell of a lot warmer than in here. Good. I gaze out my window and sigh. Goddamn it. I sigh again in an attempt to expel the rage. But not at the rage for him. No, I'm pissed because he's right. When it matters, when it's important…all or nothing. That's me. It used to be what I loved about myself. My loyalty. My fierceness. Now it just makes me sad. Exhausted. Angry I can't coast through with blinders on. Worse, I *know* I can't. Fuck you, Justin, for that. Fuck you for knowing me so well even now. My goddamn soul mate.

Makes me wish I was born without a soul.

CHAPTER THIRTEEN

WHEN IT RAINS

Party time. *I'm* certainly in the mood. Okay, I'd so much rather be at my depressing apartment lying in bed watching TV or just sleeping as my new bodyguards stand vigil for a threat that's never coming. They were waiting for me at the airfield when I landed early this morning, and the poor men haven't had a break since. Driving me to my apartment, then all around town looking at offices, picking up V's present, more office properties, and finally ending the day at V's favorite pub for her surprise party. We rented the whole place out, well my Uncle Ray and Aunt Leslie did. I'm just the bankroll. They did an excellent job. Several of V's friends from college, from the paper, from the neighborhood are here along with my three handsome cousins R.J., Bobby, and Eamon. Each gave me a bear hug when they saw me. I am a shitty, shitty niece and cousin. I haven't seen my family in three months when Jem and I went over for Sunday supper. They adored him. The moment I introduced them all it was as if he'd been in the family forever. He just fit. Hell, I think they liked him more than they do me. Not without cause.

Tonight I'm the interloper or at least that's how I feel. I'm too tired to disengage from wallflower mode. I stand off to the side in the corner nursing my coffee, listening to the bluesy music, V's favorite genre, and watching the others mingle and laugh, that is when they aren't stealing glances at me. The most infamous woman in Galilee in a room filled with reporters, their excitement is palpable. Pretty sure the only thing keeping them at bay are Maser and Zuker, my new hulking best friends packing heat. I left a message for Justin telling him his stalking services were no longer required. I don't know if he listened, but I haven't seen him which will have to be good enough. If being conspicuous and having no privacy is the price I pay to get that bastard gone, it is well worth it.

"She's coming!" V's best friend Cassie shouts to the crowd. "One minute!"

My phone buzzes. Shit. A text from Bennett. Jesus, that's the fifth in two hours. *"Hey gorgeous how ru?" "Call me." "Getting worried. RU alright?" "Plz call me." "Whats the matter? Rlly worried now."* Fuck.

I quickly text him back: *"@party. Am fine. TTYL."*

The man is as needy as a teenage girl with her first boyfriend. It's not like I haven't spoken to him today. I half expect him to walk through the door and glue himself to my hip all night. The man's hundreds of miles away, and he's still suffocating me. Until I get my shit sorted, until I can think about Jem leaving without having a minor panic attack, I don't even want to talk to him. When I think of him I just feel…shame. Guilt. Even at my lowest I wasn't a user, not of someone who wasn't already in on it. Fucking Justin. It's like I've created a bomb without meaning to and the only people about to get hurt are those I care about. I'll lose them all if I let it detonate. I'm just too chicken shit to clip the damn wire. I—

"Surprise!" everyone shouts.

Oh, shit. V walks in, blushing and laughing as everyone crowds her. Another of my victims. She hugs and kisses her way through the throng until spotting me. I hold up my coffee mug in salute and nod. I haven't seen her since she kicked my ass, so I was hesitant about tonight. The information on Mayor Miracle I sent must have smoothed our rumpled feathers because she grins and nods back. My birthday gift should take us the rest of the way. One thing. I can fix one damn thing in my life. I can. I will.

I remain in my self-imposed exile until the birthday girl finishes the rounds, ending with me in my corner. "Fancy seeing you here," V says with a smirk. "The nerve is strong in this one."

"You still mad at me?"

"Shouldn't I be? You haven't apologized."

"I thought I'd let that email I sent and my gift do the talking for me. You know how much trouble my mouth gets me into."

"Understatement of the century." She smiles. "So, what'd you get me? A diamond tiara?"

"Better." I pick up the bag from the floor, giving it to her. We move over to a table for two where she begins unwrapping the package. "You lose that and I *will* have to kill you."

When she sees the laptop, her eyebrow rises. "A laptop? Wh—"

"Meet Doris IV."

"What? I don't...you-you mean this is—"

"Linked to the Justice databases, all its search engines, and research capabilities. Why, yes it is. I really will have to kill you if you lose her."

"Holy shit, Jo," V whispers.

"Now you can do your crusading on your own. I trust you to use the power wisely," I say mock serious. "So, am I forgiven *now*?"

She stands up, slides into my side of the booth, and gives me a bear hug. "Hell yes!"

I hug her back just as tightly. "And I am sorry. Truly."

"I know." We break apart. "And you're okay now?"

"Relatively. I haven't had a drink since you last saw me."

"Awesome. Good. And...everything else?"

"Like..."

"Well, there's Tweedledee and Tweedledum over there giving me the evil eye, who I assume are here to protect you from serious danger. I've heard rumors you're under investigation for bribery, possibly aiding and abetting murderers, and that you're halfway down the aisle with Bennett Stone. You've had a busy few weeks."

"Oh, you mean all of *that*, right?" I ask jokingly. "Yeah."

"So how much is true?"

"Uh...about seventy-five percent? Eighty?"

"Fuck, Jo."

"It's all under control. Well, seventy-five, eighty percent of it anyway," I quip. She doesn't smile. "I'm fine. I can handle the Feds and the guards are just a precaution."

"And Bennett Stone? In the pictures you two looked pretty damn cozy. Should I be picking out a bridesmaid dress or is it just a rebound?"

"I..." I sigh. "I don't fucking know. I like him. He's easy to be around. We have similar interests. He's...great. For the most part." I scoff. "Hell, maybe I should marry him. We can work on the charity together. We'd have to have an open marriage though since he'd probably bang a waitress at the reception, but at least I know that about him."

"Yeah, that would last all of a day before you ripped off his balls. Not to mention the biggest obstacle…he's not Jem."

I gaze down at the table. "Who is moving to China."

"What?"

I look back up at her. "Jem's moving to China. Work. I got the news the other night from a total stranger. He's leaving."

"Well. Shit. What are you going to do?"

"I don't know. What *can* I do?"

V chuckles and shakes her head. "Oh, my God. Seriously? Don't give me that. Don't act like you don't have any agency in this situation." She leans forward. "Look, I know what he did. And you have every right to write him off. He fucked up. Normally, I'd tell you to keep going and never look back. But I know you, Jo. I've known you all your life. You were a better person with him. You lit up when you just thought of him. You were calmer. Nicer. Goddamn serene almost. You were *happy*. And you can be happy again. He didn't kill anyone. He didn't cheat on you. He kept a promise to a friend. A promise he made before he even got involved with you, I might add. You love him. Even now you love him, and he loves you. What you two had was rare. It's true. Pure. I would give my eyes for it. Don't throw it away for pride. Don't throw it away for other people's sins. Forgive him or lose him. It's that simple. Black and white. But if you chose black, cuz, that's gonna be the color of your life from now on. You will spend the rest of your life pining for him. Aching for him. And you'll only have yourself to blame for your lifetime of misery."

"You sound just like Justin," I scoff.

"Well, if everyone's telling you it's raining outside," she says, rising from her chair, "it's your own damn fault if you don't bring an umbrella." She kisses the top of my head. "It's raining, cuz. It's raining like a motherfucker. Don't you dare get wet." She ruffles my hair like she did when we were kids, grabs Doris III, and saunters off in time to the bluesy music playing over to a group of laughing friends.

Fuck me. Come for the party, stay for the therapy session. She doesn't understand. She'd been with the same guy since college, and they just grew apart. They're even still friends. She's never been betrayed. She...fuck. Why do I always feel so damn guilty after these talks? *He* lied. *He's* the bad guy here, not me. I didn't sleep with Bennett Stone to hurt him. Okay, well not the second time. There's too much damage. Right? Why...fuck. *Fuck!* It doesn't matter. It doesn't. He's leaving, I have a sort-of boyfriend, and in a year Jem Ambrose will be just another mistake.

Right. Yeah. Right.

My phone buzzes again. Another text. Nope, it keeps buzzing. A call. Goddamn it. Bennett'll just continue calling until I answer. I remove the phone, but the display triggers another almost heart attack. Jem. Fuck. Do I answer it? Do I want to answer it? We haven't really spoken since I left for Independence. God, what if he knows about Bennett? What if...*fuck.* Stop it. It doesn't matter, remember? Stop it. Prove here, now, it doesn't matter. I take a second, suppress my emotions, and accept the call. It doesn't matter. "Joanna Fallon," I say nonchalantly.

"Joanna, it's Jem."

"Oh, hello. How are you?"

"Fine. Fine." He pauses. "Fine. Uh, I-I-I'm so-sorry to bother you. I just, I-I received a strange message earlier at the hospital. I was in the lab and just picked it up now. Miranda's gone home for the night, but the slip says Diamanda Roth phoned regarding Doris."

"What?"

"It just reads 'From Diamanda Roth, Re: Doris.' I thought perhaps this was you or—"

"No. No it…shit. Maybe Roth worked out who I was."

"How?"

"She's into tech. Maybe she hacked Doris or something. Shit!"

"I'm almost to my car. I'll pop by the mansion and—"

I stand up. "Well, I'm at Friar Tuck's Pub right now. It's only a few blocks from the hospital. Swing by and pick me up."

"Is that a good idea? This could be a trap or—"

"Then two is better than one, no? And I'm carrying. Besides if she did do something to Doris, it'll take us both to check all her systems. It's my computer, Jem. Come get me."

"Fine. I'll be there in a few minutes."

"Bye." I end the call. "For fuck's sake," I mutter. Just what I need.

With a sigh, I slip on my coat and gather my purse. First things first. I walk over to my hired thugs and dismiss them for the night. Only a handful of people know where Doris is and these mercenaries aren't allowed inside the circle of trust. Since I'm the boss they barely utter a word of protest. Probably glad to spend the night in their own beds. I'll call them back when I'm done with Doris. Next stop is the giggling birthday girl at the bar with her family.

"Hey cuz," Eamon says with a smile. "Come to join the party?"

"Actually, no. I have to go. Something came up."

"Seriously? You're bailing already?" Bobby asks.

"Is everything alright, dear?" Aunt Leslie asks.

"You're not in danger again, are you?" Uncle Ray asks.

Lord, the Spanish Inquisition had nothing on my family. "No, nothing like that. Just work stuff." I go around hugging and kissing my family, ending with the skeptical birthday girl. "Don't use Doris until you hear from me," I whisper as I embrace her. I let go with a smile for them all. "I'm so sorry, guys. Happy Birthday, V."

"Take care of yourself," V shouts as I hustle toward the door. "Oh, and I heard there might be rain!"

"When isn't there?" I shout back before blowing her a kiss.

Actually tonight it's snowing. There's already an inch with another coming. The streets are fairly clear at least. Of course Jem's Porsche Speedster isn't the best choice of automobile in weather like this. He pulls up to the curb, and I hustle out of the pub to the passenger side. My heart skips a beat when I see him inside but keep my expression neutral. He seems a little better since I last saw him. Still gaunt, hair still wild as if he forgot to brush it, hollow cheeks and dark circles, but he's shaved at least. His mouth twitches up into a nervous smile. I flash him a quick one back. "Hi," I say.

He pulls away from the curb and we drive toward Dini Bridge. "W-Were you at a party?" he asks.

"Yeah. It's V's birthday."

"Oh, right. I-I'm sorry to have dragged you away."

"I'm not. Wasn't in much of a party mood." I turn up the heat. "Just a miserable night all around."

"W-We're su-supposed to get two inches by tomorrow," Jem offers.

Oh God we're talking about the weather like perfect strangers. Has it really come to this? "So, the message. That was all it said on the slip: 'Diamanda Roth, Re: Doris?'"

"I just got off the phone with Miranda. She told me the caller was a man, a sick man who kept coughing. She thought it was about a patient."

"But this caller definitely said 'Doris?' Because only a couple people know we call her that. How the fuck would Roth know it?" I gaze out the window at the passing city and shake my head. "And why call you and not me?"

"Your new number is unlisted. Anyone can reach me at the hospital," he points out.

"If Doris is compromised, I don't know what the hell I'm going to do."

"We'll figure it out. We-We'll rebuild her if necessary. We talked about it before. Moving her and the lab from the mansion someplace safer. The apartment directly below us is still vacant. We—"

"For fuck's sake, will you please stop saying 'we?'" I snap. A knot twisted in my stomach every time he did and now I can barely breathe.

"I-I-I'm so-sorry," he all but whispers before hanging his head as his mouth twists into a frown. Great now I've hurt his feelings. Again. "I-I just—"

"No, I'm sorry I snapped at you. It was uncalled for. It's been a really long day after a really long month."

"I understand. You're forgiven."

We drive in silence for a full minute but every passing second that knot tightens until the tension brewing inside me must be palpable because Jem keeps glancing at me. We're in crisis mode. Focus on Doris, Jo. This isn't the time to bring up anything but work. I—

"Jo, are you—" Jem begins.

My gaze whips in his direction so fast I'll probably get whiplash. "China? You're moving to fucking *China*? How long have you been planning this? Why the hell didn't you tell me?"

His mouth opens and closes like a moored fish as he attempts to find the right words. "I-I-you knew about the offer. We talked about it."

"Not seriously. We also talked about taking a year to sail around the world. Hell, we talked about changing our names and moving to the damn suburbs, but it was just that. Talk."

"I'm not...I'm simply exploring my options."

"*Seriously* exploring?" I ask, voice brittle.

His silence speaks volumes and acts like a punch to my already tender gut. "It's a fantastic offer. My own lab."

"You have a lab. Here."

"The drug study's almost complete. *There* I could focus on research without the politics and patients. The laws and regulations are far more permissive." He glances at me. "And it's not as if there's anything keeping me here. Anymore."

I just stare straight ahead. I'm not taking the bait. I let those horrid words hang between us for a few agonizing seconds. "You'll hate Beijing. It's crowded. And you'll never find a decent Italian restaurant. I know you, you can't go a week without chicken parmesan. And what about the case? You're just going to leave without finding the villains? Leave this city unprotected?"

"The case has gone cold. If they were planning something it would have happened already."

"You can't know that. You'd be abandoning…the city. That's not like you."

"Well, I haven't felt much like me lately." He pauses. "Nothing is set in stone." He pauses again. "And speaking of stones…" Oh, fuck. "I understand the Society is coming along well. I've heard a lot about what you intend to do. Rebuilding. Counseling. Lobbying. You're going to do a lot of good for a great number of people, Joanna. You should be proud of yourself." He pauses again. "*I'm* proud of you."

I keep my expression flat and eyes forward, but inside I swell with pride. "I'm kind of proud of me too. I've never done anything like this before. Built something from the ground up. Something that'll endure even after I'm gone."

"And I haven't a doubt you'll succeed. None." He pauses again, and I can sense it coming. The question he doesn't want to ask but has to. My stomach knots again. "And has Stone been…helpful?"

"He's barely been around. Him being hands off is part of the deal."

"But you went to the gala together."

"Because he has connections I don't. It was work."

The tension from his side of the car lowers to a tolerable level. "So you're not…in love with him?"

"What? No! I've barely known him a month!"

"You fell in love with me in less than a month," he points out.

"We're different," I say offended without thinking.

Crap. I snap my mouth shut and keep my eyes forward so I don't have to see his expression. I *can't* look at him or I'll lose it again. He's moving to China. Maybe. No good can come from me looking at him. *Be strong.* Be…fuck.

I glance at my companion at the same exact moment he glances at me. Our eyes connect and *bang*. I'm back to the night he drove me home in this very car. The first night we'd spent the night talking and laughing and dancing for hours. I wanted the night to last forever. Would have sold my soul for it. He made every moment happy. Peaceful. Perfect. That was the night I began to fall in love with him. Even after everything, even now, if I could rewind the clock, talk to my past self, would I warn myself? Would I have walked away from him?

No. *Hell* no.

This man gave me the best months of my life. He showed me I was worthy of love. That I could give it in return. He made me a better person. I liked who I was with him. I will never love anyone the way I love him. What we have is pure, true, God anointed love that should last a million nights and a million more. Even now. Even after what we've done to each other.

Forever.

I break the gaze first, staring straight ahead and willing my heart to stop pounding. Goddamn it. Why can't I hate him? It'd be so much easier to live with the hate. I hate what he did. I hate he made a fool of me. And I hate that I'm not sure if I can forgive him. I hate that it still hurts to look at him. I don't know if I can let go. I don't know if I'm strong enough to trust again.

"Please tell me I'm not crazy," Jem whispers desperately, drawing me out of my own head. "Please tell me I'm not imagining this." I want to look over, but I won't. I can't. "Please...tell me you still feel this too. *Please.*"

Fuck. "I want to," I whisper. "I want to more than almost anything. I just...don't know if I have it in me."

"Well, that makes one of us." I finally look over at him this time, to that sympathetic, sad, heartbroken, imperfect face I adore. "I believe in you. I trust you with my life. I trust you with my heart. And I trust you with this. Because the one truth I know for sure of in this universe is you never underestimate Joanna Fallon. *Never.*"

His sincerity, his utter belief in those words makes me swell with pride again. A large smile fills my face at the same time I take his hand in mine. We ride the rest of the way to the mansion that way, smiling and fingers entwined. More than good enough. He doesn't let go until we pull up to the mansion gate when he punches in the code. The gate rolls open.

All the lights are off inside the mansion, and there are no other signs of life. So far so—

Just as the gate closes behind us, headlights flip on behind us from the wooded area and the roar of a car engine echoes through the night. There's barely time to look back before the Sedan guns it across the two lane road straight toward us. As it clears the gate, my hand intuitively goes for the gun in my purse. Jem jerks the wheel right, veering us out of the crazy's path. The madman skids to a stop right at the top of the driveway. We slow as well, stopping fifty feet from the interloper. Both our pants fill the silence. Ten seconds pass. Twenty. No one exits the other car. He's waiting. For us. He can wait. Thirty seconds.

The car door opens. I clutch the gun tighter, but there's no need. The driver literally collapses out of the car onto the snow. "Wait here," Jem says.

I open my door. "No way."

He knows better than to protest. I do let him take the lead but stay close behind, gun trained on the crazy in case he's playing possum. But as I hear the wet, hacking coughs while we approach, I realize he's not. Oh, dear God. The gun nearly drops out of my hand and I literally swallow back bile at the sight of the poor man. What the...?

Recent, raw blistering burns cover every inch of his visible skin, weeping blood and clear liquid from the cracks. His nose is nothing but a welt with bloody nostrils and lips pulled back showing of his bloody teeth. "Call 911!" Jem says as he sprints the rest of the way to the coughing burn.

911. 911.

I whip out my cell phone from my purse as Jem reaches the man, kneeling beside him. "Hello, I need an ambulance at 67625 Timm Lane right fucking now. Th-There's a man, he's severely burnt and coughing up blood." I step beside them. Jesus fucking Christ if possible he's worse up close. He reeks of seared flesh, coppery blood, and something metallic I can't place. "He-He's in critical condition." The man stares up at me, bloodshot eyes pleading for deliverance. His mouth opens and closes as he tries to speak. Jem begins taking his pulse. "He—"

"Joanna," the man croaks. "Help me."

"Oh, God," Jem gasps.

"What?"

Jem moves the man's palm up, revealing the bone-line tube peeking out of the man's wrist dripping pink liquid searing the man's skin even now. My eyes dart back to the man's eyes for confirmation. Oh, dear God in heaven.

"Hello?" the 911 operator asks, snapping me out of my shock. "Ma'am?"

"Y-You need to c-contact Captain Harold O'Hara at Priority Homicide and Agents Jackson and Devitt with the Marshall Service with emergency priority and have officers escort the ambulance." I stare into those brown pools and feel mine tearing up.

"And tell them…I've found James Ryder."

CHAPTER FOURTEEN

WITH A WHIMPER

Jem carries Ryder inside the mansion as I switch off the alarm and flip on the lights. It's as cold in here as outside, but with my pumping adrenaline, the temperature barely registers. At least Ryder's out of the snow, though he might be better off there. His skin is hot enough to fry an egg. Jem gently sets him on the foyer hardwood floor before shrugging his jacket off and setting it over his patient. Wherever Ryder came from he forgot shoes. All the supervillain wears is a set of green scrubs and parka, the former caked in blood. His blood, or someone else's, I don't know. All that matters now is keeping him alive. Me keeping James Ryder alive. How times have changed.

"Stay here with him," Jem says. "I'll get the med kit from downstairs. I suppose I could fly him to the hospital. He—"

"How would you explain that? The ambo's on its way. Get the pack. Now."

Jem nods and begins flying down the hall toward the Chamber of Justice. But there's nothing I can do for Ryder except hold his hand. Let him know he's not alone. He squeezes mine with the strength of a dying kitten. "It's okay," I whisper. "You'll be okay."

It takes him two tries before he can whisper back, "Liar," before coughing again, this time bringing up blood from his lungs.

Jesus fuck. "Who did this to you?" I ask, voice as brittle as he is.

"Do-Doctors," he whispers before groaning in pain and coughing again.

"Were you at a hospital? Were the others there?"

"Lab," he gasps. "In…lab. Strapped. Tests. Shots. Made…breathe something. Days maybe then this. Started." He coughs again, this time for almost thirty seconds, as he squeezes my hand. "Don't know…about others. Killed a nurse. Ran. Escaped."

"Where's the lab?"

He gasps and begins coughing, this time digging his fingers into the palm of my hand so hard I wince. If he still had fingernails, he'd draw blood. He needs water. I extract my hand and the skin of his index finger comes with me, clear liquid pouring on my hands. That's it. I dry heave. Oh, fuck me. "I-I-I'm going to get you some water. Ju-Just rest. Be right back." I leap up and run toward the kitchen. Oh fuck. *Fuck.* I wash the blood and fluid off my hands before getting a glass. I've seen some gruesome shit in my life, but what's become of him ties with the sight of Rebecca and her mother after the man in there murdered them. Poetic justice or not, I still wouldn't wish what he's enduring on anyone. What the hell did they do to him?

Jem's returned before me and a damn good thing too because Ryder lies on his side coughing up blood and what looks like sticky coffee grounds. The slurry sizzles on the floor. Acid. Jem holds Ryder's head until everything's out, at least for the moment. But Ryder's spent. A man, even a supervillain, can only take so much. He collapses onto his back, eyes firmly closed. Fuck. Jem checks his patient's pulse and after a second, his face falls. "I need your help. His heart's stopped." I drop to the floor. Jem hands me scissors. "Cut off his shirt." As I perform the task, revealing more burns and gore, Jem removes the portable defibulator and turns it on. Shirt off, I begin chest compressions. There's no way in hell I'm giving him mouth-to-mouth. Jem places the pads on his chest. Ten more seconds pass before the defibulator's ready. "Clear!"

I pull away, and Jem presses the button. Ryder's body jerks as electricity passes through him. Nothing. I begin compressions again as the machine recharges, and Jem prepares a shot. Thirty seconds later the machine's ready. "Clear!" Another jerk but nothing. Fuck. One last option. Jem raises the needle and plunges it straight into Ryder's heart. Before it's even out, Ryder's eyes open and he takes a gasping breath, only to fall back into oblivion. Jem feels for a pulse and breathes a sigh of relief when he finds it this time. The villain's breathing is shallow but present. He's alive. For now. "Keep your fingers on his pulse point and tell me if it stops," Jem orders and I obey.

Jem begins looking the comatose man up and down for a place to start treatment. The finger skin I ripped off wins the prize. Jem removes gauze and topical cream from his bag. "Did he say anything?"

"He woke up in a lab. They tested him, gave him shots, he said something about an inhalant, then this started. I assume he meant the burns."

"So this isn't from fire or chemicals?"

"I don't think so. And Jem, he has the same healing factor you do. He survived a subway station collapse. Now he's coughing up blood and has a fever?"

"I think whatever made it so his own alkaloid rich blood and organs were resistant to the heightened pH in his system has been shut off," Jem says. "I think his body's in essence eating itself."

"Fuck me."

"Did he say anything else? Where this lab is?"

"No, he started coughing and wouldn't stop. I went to get water. He did say he killed a nurse. I assume he stole a car after. He's the one who called you, isn't he? He is the one who told me about Diamanda. He knew I called the computer Doris. He wanted you here. Maybe me. Why?"

"I'm a doctor? He knew I'd bring you? Both?"

He wanted us to save him. Save the others. He trusted me. Jesus Christ.

"What the hell could have done this, Jem?"

"I don't know. Could be auto-immune. The body thinks something normal inside you isn't normal and begins attacking it."

"What causes it?"

"Genetics, external environmental factors, viruses, bacteria, but those are merely hypothesis. We don't really know."

"Brilliant."

"We need him to wake up to narrow the potential inciting act down."

"And to locate the others," I remind him. "Whatever they did to him, they probably did to them all. But why? Why the fuck would anyone do this?"

"God knows, Joanna. I don't...I've never seen anything like this. If it is autoimmune, it's extremely fast acting. These diseases are gradual. Years not weeks."

"Is there a treatment for autoimmune?"

"Steroids can help but it depends. There's no cure. And," Jem inserts an IV into Ryder's arm, "it might not be an autoimmune disease."

I take the IV and hold it up. Where the hell is the ambulance? "He's going to die, isn't he?"

Jem simply remains silent as he continues patching up the worst of the seeping burns. He's really going to die. I wished for his death, almost killed him myself, then why do I feel sad? Angry even? He's dying and there's precious little I can do. Except this. I lean down to his ear and whisper, "I'll tell Grace you love her. That your last words were about her. And we'll find who did this to you. On my life, I promise I will."

That must have been what he was waiting for. He lets out one rattled breath but no others follow. His pulse disappears. "Shit! Jem!"

The defibulator only has three charges left. Not a one works, nor CPR or more drugs. I keep pressing on his chest. "Come on," I whisper.

"Joanna..."

"Nope. We need him to find the others. We need him. We need him."

"Joanna..." Jem places his hand over my pumping fists. "He's gone. Stop. Just stop."

I gaze into Jem's sympathetic sapphire eyes, and the fight goes out of me. He's right. He usually is. My boogeyman. The only man who never lied to me. The world's

- 225 -

a better place without him in it, but my heart literally hurts staring at him. I'm gonna miss him.

Some villains go out with a bang. They take whole buildings, whole cities with them. But not the worst Galilee Falls has ever seen. He meets his demise without even a whimper. Perhaps that's the death he deserved. Perhaps that's justice. I don't know. It's not for me to judge. All I do know is I'll do all in my power to make sure no one else meets this fate. I owe him that.

"Good-bye, Ryder. Give the devil a run for this money. If anyone can…"

And they say there's no rest for the wicked.

*

One minute.

The paramedics arrived one minute too late. They performed the same acts as Jem with their defibulator and drugs, but his soul is already gone. James Ryder was dead the moment he was kidnapped from his prison cell, it just took two weeks for the journey to end.

Now ours begins.

As the paramedics clean up and radio for the coroner, and the patrol officers who escorted them in begin to search the house, Jem sneaks off with blood and tissue samples to our lab as I prepare for the army of guests on their way. This house is an icebox, and we'll need heat and coffee.

My new best friends Agents Devitt and Jackson storm in as the coffee drips. Judging by their scowls and narrowed eyes, I've just gone from host and traumatized witness to suspect. I lead the men to the library for my interrogation. I stick as close to the truth as possible, that the name Diamanda

Roth came up during our last conversation for Captain Moonlight and Doris was Justin's name for the computer. We came here to check it, and everything stays the same after that. Agent Devitt goes off in search of my missing ex, leaving me with bad cop.

"Why call Dr. Ambrose?" Jackson asks.

"I assume Ryder didn't know how else to reach me. He knew Jem worked at the hospital and would contact me."

"And why would he want to reach *you*?" Jackson asks, eyes hard as diamonds in an attempt to intimidate me.

As if. "He obviously thought I could help him. Or maybe it wasn't me he wanted. Jem *is* a doctor. I didn't get a chance to ask him."

"You have to admit it's suspicious he contacted *you*, someone under investigation for his abduction," he says.

"If I did abduct him, I would have gotten rid of the body, I certainly wouldn't have called an ambulance or you." I fold my arms across my chest. "Look, you and I both know I had fuck all to do with this. I was a straw in your grasping hand. I don't blame you. I probably would have investigated me too. But now there's a dead man melting on my floor. One who said he and fifteen others were part of some Dr. Frankenstein experiment to God knows what end. And the clock's ticking. Now you can either treat me as a suspect or you can treat me as what I truly am, a resource. A resource who has a supercomputer in this house that can get us instant answers, the same computer that helped stop Emperor Cain and dozens of others."

"You're talking obstruction and tampering with evidence."

"The Marshall service deputizes superheroes all the time. You can call me 'Guardian' on the paperwork. Just let me do what I do best: find the bad guys and bring them to justice. Behind the scenes of course. Whatever I uncover, you'll get the credit. Just let me walk out of this room, work my magic, and you'll become a big damn hero, Agent Jackson. What do you say? Have some guts and get some glory."

He stares at me, black eyes studying me up, down, sideways, as if he wants to see into my soul. I must pass muster because the tension in his face wanes. "I go with you."

"Harry O'Hara and Terrance Cameron go with me. Just them. They already know where Doris is."

"You expect me to trust you when you don't trust me?"

"Only seven people on this planet know its location. And you threatened me with jail time for using it once. I'm not leading you straight to any evidence. You've trusted Captain O'Hara and Detective Cameron this far, and they trust me."

His eyes narrow almost to pinpoints. "I'm leaving the room now. Perhaps you're feeling ill as you claim Dr. Ambrose is. If you see him, tell him I need to speak to him."

"I will."

"Then consider yourself deputized. Unofficially unless necessary." Jackson rises from his chair, turns his back on me, and walks out. Easier than I thought it'd be. I manage to wait thirty seconds before leaping up and hustling out toward the back living room. Our new guests haven't made it this far yet, so I can open the fireplace and sneak into The Chamber. Jem must be in the lab because I hear machines whirring, and the door is shut. He spent a few million dollars on new equipment like electron microscopes, the newest DNA sequencer, and a bunch of other stuff I don't know how to use. I'm on computer duty.

As Doris boots up, I watch the security feed of the mansion. Agent Devitt kneels beside the stolen car in my driveway, poking around in the glove box. I jot down the plate number. Best place to start. Okay, what have we got? Best lead is the car and the contents inside. Fingerprints, papers, any cell phones or GPS systems inside. We also have the scrubs Ryder wore. I didn't see any writing or distinguishing symbols on his clothes but wasn't really looking. Finally, there's the body. I'm fairly sure Jem's on that last one so I'll work on options one and two. A familiar Sedan pulls up the driveway. I drove a similar one for years. Harry and Kowalski climb out. *Now* I can get to work.

Doris seems fine. Even if she's not I have to risk it. Plate search first. Easy enough. Or not. The number isn't in the system. How the fuck is it not in the system? I try it again. Not found. Okay, that's odd. I pick up the phone and dial Harry's cell. Over the security feed, I see him examining the car with Devitt.

"O'Hara."

"It's Jo. I'm on Doris. The license plate isn't valid. It's not in the DMV database. At all. Are there any documents inside the glove box?"

"Uh…" he says, glancing at Devitt.

"I've been deputized. Just check and get me the VIN."

After only a second's hesitation, Harry complies, sliding into the passenger side. "Uh, it's registered to United Fleet Company. The VIN is GH762FH987SH. There's nothing else in the glove box but tissues, cigarettes, and a tin of cigarette butts we'll check for DNA. Bag and tag those," he tells Devitt.

United Fleet is the largest fleet company on the continent. Every police department, every car rental firm, hell Pendergast uses them. That's like a hundred thousand cars.

"We have a call into them already," Devitt says over the line.

"I'll see what I can do with the VIN. Call you back." I hang up.

Come on VIN. Don't let me...shit. Doesn't exist either. I groan in frustration. Maybe I can hack into the fleet's system. Lizard programed some algorithms that I just have to activate to get me past low level firewalls. But what are the chances it'll be in the fleet system when it's not in the DMV or tax records? I could erase them myself after hacking in. A few keystrokes and it's like the car never was. Shit.

I pick up the phone again and call Harry, who has moved inside to examine the body with Jackson. "Yes?" Harry asks.

"VIN came up negative as well," I say. "I think someone wiped all traces of it from every system. Probably the fleet's as well."

Harry informs the agents and Kowalski the bad news. Shaking his head, Jackson grabs Harry's phone. "Are you sure?"

"License plate and VIN do not exist," I say. "Not in the DMV or tax databases. If I had to guess someone erased them either when Ryder escaped or hell, when they started this whole plan of theirs. Talk to the fleet and I'm sure they'll say the same thing. The car doesn't exist. Fingerprints are our last best hope. I can run them here if you want. We have a—"

The door to the lab swings open so hard it smashes against the rocky wall. Jem, sporting an expression I've only seen a handful of times—absolute, utter terror—rockets toward me. Before I can ask what's wrong, he snatches the phone from my hand. "You need to recall the paramedics who were here *immediately*."

"What? Who is this?" Jackson asks.

"This is Dr. Jonathan Ambrose. I need you to listen to me and follow my instructions. You must order the paramedics who worked on James Ryder back this moment before they come into contact with anyone else. I need you to have the officers outside shut the car's doors and come inside the house immediately. Only, and I repeat *only* the paramedics are allowed to enter this house once those doors close."

"Why—"

"You also need to contact the Health Department and inform them we have a potential Code Eight of unknown origin and it needs to be treated with Level Four precautions. They'll need to call the Infectious Disease Control Agency. Have you got all that?"

"Are you sure? How—"

"Do it. *Now*." He slams the phone down.

I've been holding my breath since he uttered "Code Eight." Every police officer had to learn the health department codes at training. An eight is one of the worst. An outbreak of a potentially fatal substance ranging from toxic waste, nerve gas, or disease. "Jem…"

"His blood, the slurry he coughed up, even the blisters, they're teeming with a virus. A virus that was still active and multiplying in the tissue. Which means contagious. Which means…"

"Whatever they gave him, whatever they did to him, could happen to us."

"To anyone he came in contact with," Jem says gravely. "And then anyone they came in contact with. And so on and so on until… 'This is how the world ends, not with a bang but a whimper.'"

It's a damn good thing I'm sitting or I don't think my legs would support me. I was wrong. James Ryder would be the death of me. The death of us all.

I'm sure he's laughing his ass off in hell right now.

CHAPTER FIFTEEN

THE HOT ZONE

If you have to go into quarantine, a stately manor is a great place to do it. I thought we'd be whisked to the hospital by men in spacesuits, but since no one shows symptoms—yet—after a decon shower we're given antivirals and told to stay in the house. With conditions. Since they shut off the water we can only use chemical toilets and clean up in their showers, or as I think of them: the hose of hell. First time I've showered in a driveway. As we began that torture, the Health Department set-up their mobile lab in my driveway and placed giant HEPA filters over the heater and air conditioner that apparently creates a vacuum to keep the bad air in and filter out the good. At least the quarantine zone has cable.

I got the spacesuits right though. The virus astronauts come in through the front door, which now has a plastic, airtight portal attached to a lab where all ten of us spend several hours getting poked and prodded. The same astronauts bring us food and bottled water since there's none in the house. Had I known I'd be hosting a quarantine for several days I would have at least bought more coffee.

At least we're not sharing the house with a corpse anymore. The spacesuits loaded him in a biohazard body bag and wheeled him through the portal to be dissected then burned to nothing, not even ashes. The only evidence he was ever there is the now bleached white wood where his blood corroded the floor.

I'm exhausted. I was exhausted before this crap started, but of course sleep ain't happening soon. If this thing is contagious, fuck if it's airborne, the entire city could be infected within days. I'm trying not to panic, but I'm woman enough to admit I'm scared. Shit scared. For me, for the city, for every person inside this house. Harry has a baby on the way. Gates and Hernandez, the paramedics, are barely in their twenties. Jackson has three kids. Devitt two. Kowalski's wife has MS. The patrol officers Abrams and Scott just got out of the academy. And now they might all start boiling in their own juices just for answering my emergency call. For doing their jobs.

Well, if we're all stuck here in my house it's up to me to make my guests comfortable. There are enough guest rooms for double our current capacity. The beds are made but all the furniture is covered in plastic and sheets. No one's used them in years so even with the precautions the dust swirls around the stuffy enclosures. Every time we sneeze, a little jolt of terror radiates through my body. We know it's the dust, or at least the logical parts of our brains do, but fear is attempting to take over the whole show. I'll have a good freak out later when I'm alone.

Harry's beating the dust out of his pillows when I go check on him. Like the others he's still wearing the sweat suits the astronauts gave us when we surrendered our clothes. "Hey," I say as I walk in. "Just wanted to see if you need anything."

"Some Ativan would be nice."

"Might actually be able to help you there. We've got a pharmacy in The Chamber."

"The doctors said not to take anything," he reminds me.

I wave him off. "What do they know?" I quip.

"I wish they knew more right about now."

"Amen to that." I smile to lighten the mood. "So, how'd Bella take the news you're stuck in a house with your ex?"

"About as well as could be expected. She was…" He shakes his head. "I know the chances are miniscule we're infected, but—"

"But you still want to peel off your skin and stop breathing just in case," I finish.

"Exactly. What happened to Ryder…I'd rather die right here, right now."

"Jem thinks the virus triggered an autoimmune response. Unless your body runs on acid too, you won't cook like a ham as your body eats itself."

"At least there's that," he says with an awkward smile. He pauses again. "I thought for sure they'd escaped. I certainly never thought anything like this was going on. Who could have? Who would want to hurt people like that?"

"Besides me?"

He frowns. "You know we never considered you a serious suspect."

"Did I?" I ask with a raised eyebrow. After a second, I smile again. "It's okay. I forgive you."

"Thank you."

I nod. "So, were there any serious suspects? Anyone who sticks out now in light of recent events?"

"No. Someone with a lot of money. Connections. But this doesn't feel personal, does it? It's more—"

"Organized. Surgical."

"Exactly. If what Ryder told you is true, the villains were nothing but lab rats. But why go to such trouble? Kidnapping? Murder? Millions if not billions of dollars?"

He's going to make me say it. I don't want to. That always makes it real. I have to gather my strength before saying, "They all have the uber-gene, Harry. Xavier had the highest concentration in the country. Maybe…the fact they're criminals had nothing to do with it."

"Jesus," Harry whispers. "You think—"

"I *know* we need to track Ryder's movements. That's where our focus needs to be. I'll be on Doris if you feel up to helping."

"Give me a couple minutes."

"Just like old times," I say as I leave. "See you soon."

The moment I'm out of sight, I let out a ragged sigh. Keep busy. Don't think, just do.

I sneak downstairs to The Chamber. The lab door is closed but I know he's in there, trying to find out all he can about the little bugger. I barely passed Biology so I'm useless in there. Jem can handle the virus, I'll take the carrier.

So far the car is a bust. I access the GFPD and Marshall Service systems to see what they have so far. Since the car's a hot zone, specialists will have to examine it and even what they gather will go to a Level 4 Biohazard lab. More protocols, more procedures, more care. We probably won't have any results on fingerprints or anything else until tomorrow at the earliest. More bad news, the fleet has no record of the car. Not in their system and not in the insurance database. The plates and insurance card could both be fakes, but I doubt it. What's more probable, the user getting pulled over for speeding or a patient stealing the car? No it was all legit and official. They just wiped the systems when he escaped. Maybe there's a paper trail. The Feds will have to track that down now I'm stuck in this house like Typhoid Joanna.

Car trail's cold for now. Phone call to Jem, you're on deck. A photo of the message slip is in the Fed's file. Miranda took the message at 6:10 pm. Okay, Ryder wouldn't have known Jem's direct number which means he went through the main menu. Which provider does the hospital use? I should have paid more attention in those board meetings. I waste three minutes uncovering that they use Independence Bell like half the city. I walk into their system through Doris' backdoor. Assuming he may have had to wander through the phone menu to Jem's, I put the window of the call between 6:05-6:10. In that time there were, fuck, fifty calls from the outside. Cut out those from a non-Galilee area code, we're down to forty. Since we didn't find a cell phone on him chances are he used a payphone. They're few and far between but still out there. And every one in a high traffic public area.

"How's it going?" Harry asks as he descends the ramp. I didn't hear the door open.

"Slowly. Just working on tracing the call now."

"How can I help?"

"There's an extra terminal where the chair is. We can split the numbers." I waste a few minutes setting him up and showing him how to search, but he'll buy it back with the search split.

"Jesus, Jo. I had no idea it was this…capable."

"Justin knew what he was doing, I'll give him that."

"This is so illegal, Jo," Harry says.

"Arrest me later when we're not trying to save the world."

First five, all cell phones. Ryder could have thrown the cell out after he used it or something in case they were tracking the GPS. That's actually the better scenario. No breathing plague on innocent people. Of course if that's the case then the other area codes come back into play. This lab could be a hundred miles away or just around the corner.

"Jo," Harry says, once again snapping me out of my head. "Got a payphone. 805-555-7865."

"Okay, keep going. I'll see where it is and pull up the CCTV feed from the area," I say, already beginning.

"It does that too?"

"Harry, the only thing Doris can't do is your taxes."

Corner of Simone and 17th. 6:09. It takes a few minutes for Doris to cull through the footage to find the exact place and time, in which Harry finds another payphone number, as do I. Simone is a bust. Woman making the call. Gaiman and Wilson, gangbanger surrounded by his posse. 47th and Dini…motherfucker. Same car parked on the curb, same parka with the hood up. "Got him."

Harry stands and moves beside me. "Jesus. How many people would you say are on the sidewalk?"

"This feed's from right outside the Metro station." A surge of people walk out of the station as Ryder hangs up, body wracked with coughs. "That ain't good."

Harry grabs the phone and dials. "Cam, it's O'Hara." He listens for a moment. "Fine, just, we know where Ryder made the call. Payphone at 47th and Dini. He exited the car at 6:07, used the phone between 6:07-6:09, then left the area at 6:10. He was coughing on the feed. You need to find out which trains departed and arrived around that time. We'll work on tracking the car through CCTV in case he made more stops." He's quiet for several seconds. "I don't know, think of something. Anonymous tip. The number here is—"

"555-1981."

"They cut the house line and took our cells. This is the only way to reach us." He glances at me. "I already spoke to her, but can you give Bella this number too? But only her." He listens. "Call with updates and we'll do the same. Bye." He hangs up. "Hope that's okay."

"It's fine. Just no phone sex."

"No promises," he says with a smile. He sits back at his terminal and pushes up his glasses. "So, how *do* we track him?"

"Very dully. Check the footage at every intersection for his car. He probably took the most direct route here, Dini to Mignola to 76th to Kane Bridge. You're on that. I'll begin backtracking his movements." With any luck he'll lead us right to that lab.

Yeah. No.

After two hours of reviewing footage, the good news is as far as we know he only left the car the once. The bad news is we can't be sure because I lose him four miles from the payphone. Both Harry and I search every camera for the car but those are few and far between the further from downtown he gets.

"Fuck," I shout after fifteen minutes of nothing.

"Maybe we should stop for a while," Harry says, rubbing his eyes. "Get an hour or two of sleep. I have to use the bathroom anyway. We're no good when we're like this."

He's right. I passed running on fumes half an hour ago. But I don't have the luxury of sleep. I do have the luxury of coffee. It damn well better be on the approved quarantine diet. "I'll be up in a minute. I should check on Jem."

"Okay. See you in a few hours."

"Sleep well if you can," I shout as he walks up the ramp.

"You too," he calls.

I wait until he's out of sight before rising. Jesus, my body's so stiff. I stretch but it does little good. Oh fuck, what if body aches are a symptom? What if...okay, stop. *Stop.* I'm doing it again. Maybe my gummy eyes are a symptom or maybe I've been staring at a computer screen for hours. Yeah, so time for a break.

I knock on the lab door, but only get a response the second time. "Step away from the door."

I obey. "Okay."

He quickly opens and closes the door. "What?"

"Just checking in. It's really late. I haven't seen you since the trailer."

"I'm fine. Working. The others?"

"Mostly asleep. Or trying to be. How's it going in there?"

"Not as well as I would like. I'm limited in the types of tests I can conduct. Without live cultures, animals to test, more samples from the body, all I can do is cursory tests. We need an antibody test, serology reports, genetic testing, and DNA/RNA mapping. I can't do any of those in there."

"Luckily there's an entire team camped out on our front lawn who can. Have you found *anything*?"

"It could be an adenovirus. Possibly a retrovirus like HIV or orthomyxovirus like influenza. It has characteristics of all. I've never seen anything like it."

"Is it airborne?" I ask, the words sticking in my throat.

"I don't know."

"Well, I have good and bad news. Which would you like first?"

"Good please."

"We traced the call Ryder made to the hospital."

"Which I assume leads to the bad."

"He made the call at a public payphone, the one in front of the 47th Street Metro station. During rush hour."

Jem's shoulders slump. "You should have said I had neutral and cataclysmic news. If it is an aerosolized virus, we have a potential epidemic, possibly a pandemic by the month's end."

"Okay, you said it yourself, you don't know anything right now. There's no point planning for the apocalypse just yet. Let's review what we *do* know. Hang on." I go grab my pad and pen before plopping on the black leather couch. Jem, somewhat reluctantly, sits on the opposite end. The last time we were together on this couch we were naked, not preparing for end times. "Here are the puzzle pieces. A group of sixteen commandos drugged an entire prison and abducted every supervillain."

"Every person known to have the uber-gene," Jem corrects, the sides of his mouth twitching as he does.

"Right. They're brought to a lab, tested, injected, forced to inhale something, then days later they get sick. Which should be impossible because some have regeneration capabilities. Ryder's immune system and cellular creation capabilities were on super-steroids. He probably never even had a cold. So is it possible for a virus to override genetics?"

"Yes. It's what I've been studying, remember?"

"I sort of zoned out when you started using seven syllable medical jargon. Sorry. I'm paying attention now."

"What I've been studying is a way to do precisely that, overriding genetics. Parkinson's, Alzheimer's, cancer, all have a strong genetic component. What all viruses do, basically, is inject their own DNA or RNA into a cell, infecting and/or changing the cell's genetics like a cuckoo bird replacing its own egg in a bird's nest. Our immune systems begin to recognize the difference, create antibodies, and kill the infected cells so the body can create new, healthy ones. With adenoviruses, *we* create the virus' DNA and RNA to do what we want. Gene therapy. The virus helps, in theory, and can even eradicate the unhealthy genes. But it's a new science and our government has strict regulations on testing, especially regarding stem cells which are the greatest tool in this research. We're years behind where we should be and very few companies are throwing money behind the research."

"Which is why you're moving to China," I add.

"I'm not…" His mouth snaps shut. "The good news is there are only a handful of companies worldwide capable of creating adenoviruses, especially one this sophisticated. A contagious adenovirus is unheard of, and this one is more flu than adenovirus. My hypothesis is they mean for the flu to act as a flea."

"I'm sorry?"

"With the Black Death, the rats carried the disease, the fleas bit the rats, then bit humans who then contracted the plague."

"So you think whoever designed this, their ultimate goal is to infect people who have the uber-gene with this adenovirus."

"Taken in context with the prison break, that is a fair assumption."

"I guess it's possible, but it's still just a theory, yes? I mean, just to play devil's advocate, you're basing this on one dead body, conjecture, and the fact it *might* be an adenovirus. Maybe the virus and what happened are two separate events. They injected Ryder with something that-that made his body go haywire and injected the virus to *save* him. We don't know. We don't really know anything for sure right now."

Jem stares across the couch, searching my face for something, and whatever he finds garners a sympathetic smile. "You're right."

The knot in my stomach loosens a little. "Look we're both scared, frustrated, and run ragged. Harry's right. We need a few hours' sleep to process everything. The world won't fall apart in two hours, right?"

He smiles again. "I suppose. I'm exhausted."

I rise and hold out my hand. "Bedtime then."

He glances at my outstretched hand, but stands and puts his own hands in his pockets. My arm drops, along with my smile. Jem keeps his eyes down as he passes me and begins up the ramp. In fact he doesn't raise his head all the way to the second story bedrooms. He acts as if I'm not there, a mere phantom at his side. Oh fuck, what have I done now? How did I piss him off this time? I probably shouldn't have brought up China. I didn't mean anything by it. And now he's...and I thought—

"Which is my room?" Jem asks.

His voice snaps me out of my self-flagellation. "Uh...I don't..." I count the doors. Fuck. "I forgot to prepare one for you."

"Oh. Then where..."

"I, uh..." *Oh, just say it, Jo.* "you-you can bunk with me or—"

"No, that's not a good idea," he cuts in.

"Right. Yeah. Right." Oh God, if I could only turn invisible right now. Please, God? Please? No such luck. Jem stares at me, mouth opening and closing as he struggles to find words. "I-I-I don't know why I even suggested—"

"No, I-I-I-I would-would love nothing more than-than to...*bunk* with you. It-It's just truly not a good idea. Medically. I-I had the most contact with Ryder. I had his blood and fluids covering me. It's almost guaranteed he...transmitted the virus to me. I really shouldn't even be in the same room as you. We need to limit contact."

"Right," I chuckle nervously.

"I'll, uh, just...end of the hall."

"Okay," I say with a smile.

"Okay," he says with a smile back. He turns down the hall and starts toward his room again.

God, it's like we've gone back in time, back to the beginning. Feeling each other out, questioning every expression and word, awkward everything. Like we've never spent a dozen nights talking until dawn about nothing and everything. Like we've never seen each other cry or break down in fear. Like we haven't kissed every millimeter of each other's bodies. I hate this. I hate myself for my part in it. Especially now. Especially with him...no. Do it, Jo. You can. Be brave. Be strong.

Just do it.

"Jem?"

He spins around. "Yes?"

Say it. *Say it.* "Don't go to China."

The sides of his mouth twitches into a brief smile. "W-What?"

"Don't go to China. Don't go. *Please.*"

We stare at one another, our smiles growing in unison. "Really?" he asks breathlessly.

"Really," I say, voice brittle. "Don't go. Don't leave me. Never. Ever. *Please.*"

"Oh, Joanna."

He strides toward me and the moment he reaches me, he wraps one arm around my waist, pulls me against him, and places the back of his hand against my lips, kissing his own palm, before releasing me. Almost as sweet as a real kiss. He searches my eyes for my reaction but my smile says it all. He returns the gesture. "I'm not going anywhere. Never. *Ever.*" He kisses his palm again before beaming down at me. "I told you you had it in you. Never had a doubt, my love. Never." His smile grows. "Good night."

"Good night," I whisper.

He starts down the hall again, stealing coy glances over his shoulder the entire way until he disappears into his bedroom. My smile drops the moment the door shuts. I manage to hold in my tears until I shut the bedroom door and curl into a ball in my old bed. I muffle the sobs with the pillow, purging the horror, the terror, the anger, the sadness for Ryder, for us, into the soft fabric. I'm scared, I am *so* damn scared. And how the fuck am I supposed to fight something I don't even understand? All my money. All my power. All my connections. All my good intentions. What do they mean if I can't save the man I love? And I do. I love him more than life itself. I never stopped. He's in my blood. My heart. I can't lose him. I can't. I won't. *I won't.* Because he's right.

Never underestimate Joanna Fucking Fallon.

*

In our twelfth hour of quarantine we're all brought into the Health Department lab for new tests and bloodwork. The spacesuits barely answer any questions. Not the best way to stop people from panicking. It's getting damn tense in the house already. Devitt and the paramedic Gates almost came to blows over who got the last jelly donut. If this virus feeds off tension and terror, the fucker will be unstoppable. After breakfast, everyone went to their rooms and didn't come out until it was test time. At least they let us have access to our phones when we're not being poked and prodded. I have ten voice messages and twelve texts, more than half of those from Bennett. The rest are from V and The Guardian Society team. I text V back she can use her computer, and that I'm fine. Bennett's going to take more than a text. I wait until the lab tech leaves the tiny room with my samples before calling. He must have been waiting by his damn phone because he picks up on the first ring.

"Jo? Are you okay?"

"Hi. Uh, yeah. Relatively."

"What the hell is going on? I heard a rumor you were under quarantine after a supervillain attacked you?"

"Where'd you hear that?"

"I have friends in the Federal Health Department. Jo, is it true?"

"I'm not allowed to say much. Sorry."

His end is silent for several seconds. "Jesus Christ, Jo. Jesus Christ."

"It's okay. It's fine. Really."

"Bullshit! You-You're…I-I…I'm so sorry, gorgeous."

"Thank you."

"Is-Is there anything I can do?"

"Yeah, actually, I don't, uh, know how long they'll keep us here. Days, weeks, who the hell can say. They're not telling us a thing. I won't be able to handle any calls from the Society team. And—"

"No, I got it. I'll tell everyone to call me with questions and whatnot. Don't worry about a thing."

"Just what I wanted to hear. Thank you. And try not to worry about me, okay?"

"I won't because you are going to be fine," he says with utter certainty.

I wish *that* was catching. "Just don't let it all go to hell."

"Of course not. I'll take care of everything. I just…can't believe this is happening. I'll bet you wish you'd taken me up on my deserted island offer, huh? Well, the moment you're given a clean bill of health we're on a plane there. I won't take no for an answer this time."

I'm glad he isn't here to see me cringe. This is certainly not the time for a conversation about us. "I'll talk to you when I can. I have to go."

"Take care of yourself, gorgeous."

"I will. Bye."

I hang up and sigh. I *do* wish I were on a deserted island right now instead of inside this freezing cold, antiseptic reeking closet of a lab room. The assistant releases me, sans cell phone, after a breathalyzer test, and its back to the bigger cage. At least they've made us more coffee. I only slept two hours. I grab a full cup and the last donut before slinking off to The Chamber again. Jem's been conscripted by the Health Department, advising and aiding in their adenovirus research, but he did compile a list of doctors and companies worldwide he knows are working on adenoviruses. Having given up on tracking Ryder after several more frustrating hours, this is my new task. The list is longer than I thought and it's not comprehensive.

I lost an hour with the testing so begin by reviewing the updated reports. The Feds and police are on the virus angle. Any facility or lab capable of holding, experimenting, or creating this bugger within fifty miles are being investigated and searched. All forty of them. And those are the ones they know about. If I were this mastermind, the whole operation would be off the grid. No official channels. No government oversight. There are ways. God knows how much the man or group of people have spent just developing the virus itself. Billions. One would think the money factor would dramatically reduce the suspect pool, but I can't cross off a single name or company from Jem's list. Every biotech and pharmaceutical company is worth tens of billions, right along with the CEOs and owners. Judging from the reports filtering in, all the Feds investigating keep running up against stonewalls from these people and organizations. Lawyers demanding subpoenas and warrants while the owners call in favors with judges and politicians to quash them. It'll be months before they get access to a single record. Good thing I don't need to stay within the confines of the law and bureaucracy.

The autopsy report might help narrow things down. Cause of death: muti-system organ failure by reasons unknown. Blood, fluid, and tissue lining filled twenty-five percent of his lung capacity. The muscles in his heart, kidneys, liver, stomach and intestines, along with seventy-five percent of his skin was covered with chemical burns of unknown origin. Blood tests were inconclusive due to the high pH level being twenty times the norm. There were indications of a high

T-cell count consistent with fighting off a massive infection. The rest is about as useful, the crap I can understand. More tests required. In other words, his body went haywire. They have no idea what the fuck happened. Could be months before they know for sure. If ever.

Yeah, tracking the bug it is. First up, linking the scientists and doctors to the companies, followed by tracing the companies to their parent companies. Most of these, hell most of the companies on the planet, are owned by about ten corporations, Pendergast being low on that list. If memory serves we owned at least three biotechs, down to two when we sold Blackwater to Goliath. I couldn't tell you the other biotech's names let alone anything about the day-to-day running of the companies or their projects. Micro to macro, Jo. First focus on who could do this then onto who could give them the tools to. Another problem is just because this happened in our backyard doesn't mean the mastermind isn't from another country. Jem scribbled notes in the margin of his list. Typical doctor. I can barely make out the words even with months of practice. Something about not publishing and public appearances and patients for the past five years. I suppose if you're working on a super-secret/illegal project you won't be telling people about it. Should narrow the list. This is still going to take for-fucking-ever. Fifty items and nowhere near them all. That's another two hours gone, adding to Jem preliminary fifty. A hundred twenty now. Ugh.

I fall back in the chair and sigh. Twice. No help. The weight of this task, the weight of our unknown fate, probably the antivirals they made us take again, it's all making me want to crawl into a ball and sleep until this is over. I—

The tinkling noise from Doris stops my heart. My head whips up to her screen where the video chat window has popped up. What the fuck? Who has this…? My thinking *is* slow today. I accept the request, and Justin's handsome face fills the screen. "Hello? I can't see or hear you," he says.

I plug in the microphone. "I don't have a camera set-up," I tell him. "How did you know how to contact us?"

"It's my system, Jo," he says. "I still have access. I saw you were on. Are you okay? Ryder's name came up in an alert last night."

"How much do you know?"

"I've read the reports. He's dead? Really?"

Justin can't hide his excitement. His hope. The man's actually trying and failing to contain a smile. I understand it, I do, but I still want to reach through the screen and slap it off. "Yes," I snap. "His body burned from the inside out for days like a roast pig and he drowned in his own blood and mucous after being tortured for weeks and injected with a virus that's probably slowly killing us all. Time to party, no?"

The mirth drains from his face. "The bastard deserved it, Jo. You can't deny the fact the world's a better place without him wasting its oxygen."

"Well, his oxygen left a parting gift. I'm saving the celebration for when we're given a clean bill of health. Can we agree on that at least?" He nods. "You're not in Galilee, are you?"

"I am. I'm at Jem's. I followed you here. I—"

"Fuck," I mutter. "Okay, look. There is a very, *very* good chance this virus was engineered to attack the uber-gene. You are not immune. There is also a chance Ryder infected a lot more people than just us. You need to leave town or at the very least avoid people and wear a damn HEPA mask."

"Wait, targeting the…that wasn't in the reports."

"Because right now it's speculation, but why else kidnap supers? Jem thinks the virus caused an autoimmune response in Ryder. His body attacked itself. And these adeno things have to be engineered. Someone did this deliberately."

Justin lets this information sink in, his shoulders slumping as it does, until he's all but slumping in his chair. "Shit. And Jem's in there? Is he okay?"

"Fuck if I know. We don't know *anything*, Justin. We don't know what this is. If we can stop it. If there's a cure. If we're even infected. But Harry's in here. Kowalski. Jem's..." I shake my head. "This bug acts like a flu. It could have spread through the city, other countries by now."

"But why go to all this trouble?"

"Because they can? Because it was a fluke like penicillin? We know *nothing,* and we're running out of time. Hell, if this shit is airborne and already infected others, we didn't have time to begin with. And I have no idea what I'm doing. I don't understand any of this medical crap. Jem gave me pages of people and companies to investigate. Over a hundred names. And I can't even pay attention to any of it because I can't stop imagining holding Jem's hand as he literally melts in front of me, and there's nothing I can do about it. *Nothing.*"

"We are not going to let that happen," Justin says with utter certainty. "Not to him, not to any of you. You are not alone in this, Jo. I-I'll reach out to some people. You should have Jem do the same."

"People?"

"Other supers. We all have connections. We're all investigators or have access to people who are. Email me what you have now and have Jem send me anything else he can. We can have it all done in a day or two if we all pitch in."

"That's…a great idea. Okay. I'll talk to him."

Justin stares through the screen as if he can actually see me. "I know you're scared. For them, for yourself. But you are going to be fine. So are they. *You will be fine.*"

When he says it, sure as spring will come, I believe him. "What does Lucy always say? 'Pray to God but swim to shore?'"

"Well, you're going to have the entire army and navy coming for you, Jo. Put up the list and I'll start reaching out."

"Thank you," I whisper.

"Of course. *Of course,*" he says desperately.

I gaze at him on the screen, trying so hard to hide his own terror, it almost breaks my heart. He means it. Every word. My best friend, even after all we've been through. All the damage, all the anger I've directed and inflicted upon him, and here he is. He will do anything within his power to save me. It actually brings a smile to my face. "Glad to have you on the team. I'll be in touch. Bye." I end the chat.

An army. We have an army. It damn well better be enough.

It *has* to be.

CHAPTER SIXTEEN

ALL OR NOTHING

"You're all infected."

I knew it before Dr. Vaugh said it. If the fact he and his assistant entered the house wearing the Hazmat suits, or that they made us all gather in the library and wouldn't start talking until butts were in the seats, was. Yet the color drains from all our faces and the paramedic Gates bursts into tears. Her partner Hernandez wraps his arm around her. Kowalski begins taking deep breaths, and Devitt shakes his head. I glance at Jem, who stands near the doctors. He nods at me. Fuck. No. Him too.

"A-Are you sure?" Jackson asks.

"Yes," Jem answers. "We developed an antibody test using a genetically similar virus, and we all tested positive."

"Bu-But that could just mean we were exposed to the similar virus," Hernandez says.

"We also examined your blood and lung secretions," Dr. Vaugh says. "Our tests indicate the virus is aerosolized and can sustain in the air for an hour."

"Jesus Christ," Harry says.

"Now, I know this news may be frightening, but there really is no cause to panic yet," Dr. Vaugh says.

"Yeah fucking right," the patrol officer Handler says.

"As best we can glean, this virus is simply a highly virulent form of the flu," the doctor continues.

"Tell that to Alkaline," Kowalski says.

"There is absolutely no evidence that his reaction will be yours'," Jem pipes up. "His body chemistry was abnormal. And just because you carry the virus does not mean you will exhibit *any* symptoms."

"Or we'll all melt on the floor," Handler snaps.

This is getting us nowhere. "Alright, so what happens now?" I ask.

"You all remain in quarantine and we continue our tests," the doctor says. "If necessary we move you to the Infectious Disease Unit at Our Lady Hospital for treatment."

"What about the people Ryder exposed when he made the call?" I ask.

"That's for us to worry about," Dr. Vaugh says. "All you need to worry about is getting rest, drinking your fluids, and complying with all our tests."

"Just generally be good guinea pigs. Got it," I say with a shit eating grin.

"Really, it is far too early to panic," the doctor continues, ignoring me. "Now, we're going to bring you all in to the lab in groups for more tests and treatment. We were lucky to gain access to an experimental serum we wish to administer to you. Initial tests have shown it's effective in fighting this type of flu virus, but it's still experimental."

"But it could cure us?" Gates sniffles.

"Possibly."

Gates leaps off the loveseat. "Then let's go!"

Hernandez, Gates, and the two patrol officers follow the spacesuits out, leaving the adults to talk. "What *are* they doing about the people at the Metro station?" I ask Jem.

"Monitoring mostly. It's all they can do at this stage. It's flu season. They don't want to cause a panic without more information. Alerts have been sent out to hospitals and GPs, and there are posters up at the Metro station for people to call if they begin exhibiting symptoms, but Dr. Vaugh's right. We still don't have enough information about the virus or its effects yet."

"So the people at the Metro station go home, infect others, who infect others," Jackson says. "Great plan."

"We have the best people on this," Jem says. "Hundreds. Two government agencies. The greatest virologists and geneticists on the planet."

"Not to mention I reached out to some of Captain Moonlight and Justice's masked colleagues," I say. "They've already spoke to some of their friends. They're running down the virus and lab."

"That's great, but not to be a selfish bastard," Kowalski says, "what good does that do us? We're already infected. It could take weeks to locate the lab, and even if we do, we could be too far gone. Or there could be no cure."

"He's got a point," Harry says.

"Whoever engineered this may have also engineered a serum," Jem says. "I would in case I lost control of the virus. And even if they didn't, with our research and knowing the steps they took, *we* could engineer a vaccine."

"Which means we have to find the fuckers," I say. "Everyone just keep doing what you're doing. We are going to be *fine*."

"Please just stay calm. Now please excuse me," Jem says. "I need to return to the lab. Just wait here for the doctors to come get you. *All* of you," he says to me.

He nods at us all before departing. I want to chase after him, ask a million questions, but instead begin to ask everyone else questions to get a conversation going otherwise we'd all go crazy waiting in here for our turns. Ten minutes later the next group is called in, myself included. More needles. Can't wait.

And that is precisely what waits for us in the freezing cold, sterile, antiseptic airtight metal tube they call an exam room: needles. At least I'm getting a tan walking in and out of the lab what with the UV lights that kill the bug on our skin. The spacesuit draws three more vials of blood, swabs my tongue and throat, and makes me cough into a bag again. I get a few minutes of alone time before she returns with an IV stand and bag of what resembles orange juice in her hands.

"What the hell's that?" I ask.

"The serum. As Dr. Vaugh said, it's still experimental but Biodyne has conducted a preliminary study on its use against the N1F2 virus. The results were encouraging. There were some side effects including vertigo, upset stomach, nose bleeds, lethargy, and headaches. Knowing that do you consent it its use?"

"Sure. Yeah." I hold out my arm. "Hook a girl up."

I think she smiles, but I can't tell with the thick plastic of her helmet in the way. "Lie back." I obey, reclining on the exam table. At least they provided a pillow. The IV slides in like a painful dream. "This should take about ten minutes."

"Do you think this stuff will work?"

"As I said, the results were encouraging," she says, writing something down.

"And if it doesn't work? What's our next option?"

"We're looking into other avenues," she assures me.

"This is kind of a time sensitive matter," I point out.

"This serum is the best option. We have faith in it."

"Then thank you Biodyne."

The spacesuit finishes her notes and shuts off the computer. "If you need anything please use the call button. I'll be back."

"Can you get Dr. Ambrose for me?"

"I—"

"*Now*," I order with a hard glare.

"I'll see if he's available."

I settle on the table as she leaves me in my cell. Biodyne. That name's familiar. It has to be on the list, but isn't one of the companies I researched. I'll write to Justin about it when the juice runs out. I pull the blanket around my shoulders, but it does little to help the chill.

That's how Jem finds me, wrapped up like a bug in a rug. "Hey."

"Hello," he says with a sad smile.

"How—" we both say in unison before chuckling.

"Me first," I say. "I'm fine. How are you?"

"Fine."

"So…you tested positive? Are you sure?"

"I looked at the results myself."

"And do they know about…you?"

"Yes. I disclosed it when I tested positive."

"Can you trust them?"

"I know Dr. Vaugh. I've worked with him. He's promised to keep my name out of reports but…we'll cross that bridge when we come to it. A crisis for later," he says with a lopsided, nervous smile.

I hold out my hand to him. He steps toward me, taking it, and I yank him against me, into my arms and squeezing tight. Without hesitation, he hugs me back. Oh, I've missed this. The sensation of him against my body. His scent. His steady heartbeat against mine. "We're gonna be okay. I know it," I whisper.

"Right," he whispers, hugging tighter. "Right." We just stay wrapped in one another's arms for a few seconds before he chuckles. "If I knew it'd take a virus to get you back into my arms, I should of infected myself with the plague weeks ago. I—oh."

He sways a little and pulls away, closing his eyes as if he were about to faint but uses the table to steady himself. My heart leaps into my throat nonetheless. "What is it? What's the matter?"

"I-I'm fine. Just a bit lightheaded. I-I haven't eaten and—"

"Bullshit." I climb off the table and grab his upper arms. "Sit down. Sit," I order as I help him do that very thing. He pinches the bridge of his nose. "Talk to me. Should I get—"

"No. No, if they know I've become symptomatic they'll send me to the hospital and I can't continue my research. It just began. But it's almost impossible to…fly. I think that's what caused the vertigo. My attempt. I'm fine when I'm sitting. I just need to conserve my strength." I stare at him, my lower lip quivering as I try to hold back the tears. He smiles to reassure me and touches my traitor lip. "I'm fine. Truly."

"Stop it," I hiss. "Stop it. This is me, okay? *Me*. Fuck the brave face. Stop lying. Stop trying to be so goddamn selfless. You will take care of yourself first. Promise me you will. *Promise*."

"I-I can't Joanna," he hisses back. "You're in here too. Whatever happened to him can happen to you. I-I-I-I-As long as I draw breath, I will do *all* in my power to make sure it doesn't." Be it the exhaustion, my general emotional state, or just the absurdity of the situation, I burst into laughter. Jem's eyes narrow at me. "What?"

"It-It's just…you're in your little room doing all this to save me when I'm in here thinking the exact same about you. How there is nothing—not murder, death, prison, not giving away billions of dollars—*nothing* I wouldn't do to save *you*." He finally smiles back. "So I guess we'll just…save each other, huh? Old habits die hard."

He cradles my cheek in his hand, caressing it with his thumb as I press my own hand to his face. "There's so much I want to say to you. So much I—"

I stop his words with a kiss. I'm barely holding myself together now, and there's so much still to do. I break apart first with a smile. "Not here, okay? Not now. We have all the time in the world, no? A million nights and a million more."

He smiles back. "I better get back to work then."

"My hero." I give him another quick peck. "You damn well better take care of yourself or I'll kill you before the bug gets a chance."

"I will." I raise an eyebrow. "I promise." I raise it higher. "I promise!" he chuckles.

That gets him another kiss. "I'll hold you to that. Now go save the world."

"Yes, my love." He slips off the table and after another brilliant smile my way, he leaves the room. I sit on the very spot he was, the only warmth in this place. The only comfort.

I'm going to save him. I am. Because if I can't save him there's no point in saving myself. If he goes, he's taking me with him. All or nothing. That's how I am. How he is. How we always will be. No half measures. No excuses.

It's the only way *to* be.

*

Since this is my circus, all the monkeys send me their reports on their targets. The supers do fast work. Two thirds of the doctors have published papers on their breakthroughs so they fall down the list, not totally eliminated but not a priority. My minions are getting there, just not fast enough for my liking. Me, when I'm not skimming their reports, I'm investigating vaccines and other viruses to counteract the one in Jem. A person would think it'd be simple, just whip up the opposite of whatever shut the gene off, put it in a new adenovirus, and spark the gene back to life. But from what little I understand of this medical crap without knowing everything, right down to the atoms of the original, it would take years to create. By then Jem, Justin, Lexie, even those who just carry the uber-gene would be dead if not the whole damn world. Maybe it's just easier for me to concentrate and do what needs doing if I keep the fact *I* may be dying from this as well in the background. That serum made me lightheaded and nauseous, but otherwise I feel great. God knows what'll happen tomorrow so I need to use every damn moment now to discover a way to save him. I'm just so glad I have people helping me.

"Jo, look at this," Harry says beside me. He clicks the mouse and his own screen pops up on the main screen. He's been on the very helpful Biodyne Sciences. I've always looked gift horses in their mouths. "I cross-referenced the doctor's names with the company. One on our list works there, but he's published last year."

"Anything on that serum they gave us?"

"Yeah, they've been developing it for two years, three years after the N1F2 virus was discovered in the Virunga. The

International Disease Organization classified it as one of if not the most virulent flu they've ever seen. Ninety percent of those exposed become infected. The good news is there were only two deaths, both elderly and in poor health already."

"So this thing appears five years ago in Africa and just now appears in a dying supervillain?"

"It's not the same virus though," Harry points out. "At least not per the reports I've read. The Health Department calls it a chimera, a combination virus."

"A Trojan horse," I say. "This mastermind or minds chose a virus they knew would infect the most people just to infect ubers with the adenovirus. Us mere mortals just get the flu, the ubers get a death sentence."

"That's insane," Harry says. "Why would anyone do that? Go to such trouble?"

"Why does anyone commit genocide? Fear. Power. Just being painfully fucking evil. We'll ask when we find the psycho. What else is there on Biodyne?"

"They're owned by the Motoneslly Group, and makes only about two billion a year. That's as far as I got."

"Maybe we should go back. See if any doctors on our list have since left Biodyne. If I were this mastermind I'd keep everything about this project off the books."

"But that would rule out Biodyne, right? Since they're working on a serum," he points out.

"Not necessarily. I'd want a back-up plan in case my virus mutated or affected people outside supers. And if this thing creates a panic I could re-coup some of my billions of dollars I've spent on my genocidal virus by curing the virus I created."

The chimes of the video chat begin tinkling. I accept the chat. Justin's face fills the main screen. I've set-up the microphone and webcam so my pale, ratty haired head fills a smaller box. "I was just about to call you," I say.

"Jesus Christ," Harry mutters as he stares at Justin's face. Guess knowing he's alive and actually seeing him are two different things. At least Harry doesn't throw up like I did.

"Is someone—"

"Harry's here."

"Oh. Hello, Captain O'Hara. Glad to have you...on board. How are you all feeling?"

"*We're* fine. Jem's losing his ability to fly and obviously his regen capabilities has failed. It hasn't even been twenty-four hours."

"We may have a lead though," Harry adds.

"You were in the billionaire business world a hell of a lot longer than me. Have you ever heard of Biodyne Sciences or The Motoneslly Group?"

"Biodyne, yeah. I used to play golf with their CEO Randall Fujicawa. He wouldn't take part in this. He's a money man. No vison for something like this."

"And The Motoneslly Group?"

"Vaguely familiar. Can't place it though," Justin says.

"Says here they bought Biodyne three years ago," Harry says.

"About the same time Biodyne began the serum," I point out.

"Sounds promising," Justin says.

"We also need to get in touch with any doctor who can reverse this adenovirus. That should be our top priority. Antiviral drugs, gene therapy, vaccines, all of the above."

"A priority, yes," Justin says. "A top priority, no. Locating the culprits of this nightmare is priorities one to ten. We need to find them before they release this thing worldwide.

We find them, we probably find the information needed to beat this thing."

"Jem's going downhill fast. As soon as they realize he's symptomatic, they're shipping him off to isolation."

"Jo, maybe that's for the best. They can treat him or at least his symptoms," Justin says. "Ryder went into full organ failure. Dialysis can keep his kidneys going, a respirator his lungs."

"It's not going to come to that," I snap. "He's going to be *fine*, just like the rest of us."

"Of course he is," Harry says.

"I already have calls and emails into seven doctors, the ones at the forefront of research about the uber-gene, about rebuilding the gene."

"Are our doctors on the list?" Justin asks.

"Yeah. Of course. They are the—"

"Joanna, they're suspects. You're asking our suspects for help?" Justin snaps.

When he puts it like that…I somehow maintain my poker face. "I'm not."

"You do realize you're tipping our hat? Letting them know we're onto them? Potentially supplying them with information about our investigation?"

"Chances are they already know," I point out. "If the people can erase an entire car from government systems, they're bound to have their tentacles in the Health Department like we do."

"It's an unnecessary risk, Jo. We—"

"It is not an unnecessary risk. *We need a cure*."

"Not if it means jeopardizing the case as a whole," Justin says. "You're losing your objectivity and—"

"Fuck you!"

"I know you're worried about Jem, I am too, but—"

"Of course I'm worried about him! I'm not a fucking mindless automaton like you've become, asshole. You forget your soul when you came back from the fucking dead? Do you feel anything anymore?"

"Of course I do!" he roars. "I'm trying not to lose my goddamn mind here! *He's* not the only one infected, Jo. *You're* not the only one who has to stand by helpless as someone they love faces a slow, painful death. You do not have a monopoly on abject terror and love. So don't you dare say I don't care or I don't have feelings. *Don't you fucking dare.* There is *nothing* I won't do to protect and save you, including kicking your ass when you're being a moron. And quite frankly I'm getting tired of having to prove myself over and over again. You are going to have to trust me, Joanna. We need all our resources, all of them including you, on finding the people who crafted this virus because not only is it our best chance at finding a cure, but God knows what their next step is, when they plan to implement it. If they haven't already." He brushes aside a tear. "So if I can put aside my personal feelings for the greater good, you damn well can too. Because where the hell do you think I learned it from?"

I stare at Justin's face, his wet eyes, suddenly I feel like the biggest, most selfish asshole in the world. I have to look away, but get no comfort from Harry. His mouth is set straight, trying and failing to hide his disapproval. Fuck. "He's right," Harry says.

I know. I know he's right, I just really, *really* don't want to accept it. "Fine. So." I square my shoulders to regain some dignity. "The Motoneslly Group. We'll let the others continue on the doctor list, but we'll run down the group."

"Agreed," Harry says.

Justin sniffles. "Agreed." He turns away from me and the camera. "I'll take their other subsidiaries. See if any have any connections to creating and spreading a virus. Harry, stay on Biodyne. The executives, the doctors past and present."

"I'll look into who owns and runs the group," I say. "Stand-by the computer in case we need to talk."

"Fine. Good luck."

Justin ends the chat and I can breathe again.

"You okay?" Harry asks me.

"I'm fine," I say.

"He—"

"I don't want to talk about it," I snap.

"Tough. That bastard steamrolled through my life too, remember? I've watched someone I cared about disintegrate twice because of him. When you felt compelled to take over his vigilante duties, I covered for you to the point I could lose my job. So I'm going to say this and you are damn well going to listen." He pauses. "I hate what he did to you. I do. He could have handled the entire mess a lot better. But watching him, listening to him just now, there is not a doubt what he did, he did from the farthest reaches of his heart. He didn't know he would survive that fall but he took the chance regardless. His life, his friends, his work, he gave up everything for you, Jo. *For you.*" He looks away from me. "I know how hard it is to forgive a betrayal. It took…strength I didn't think I had to forgive you and move on from what you did to me. But I did, and I did for one reason: me. I learned to separate the betrayal from the person. Because I wanted you in my life.

"The one wrong doesn't wipe away the rest. That man you just spoke to is still the man who talked you off that bridge. Who looked out for you, who protected you, who loved you when no one else did. And he's still doing it." Harry looks back at me, eyes cold as icicles. "I forgave you, Jo, and I've never regretted it. I'm asking you to do the same. Not for him. Not for me. But for yourself."

"Why does everyone keep lecturing me?"

"Because for a smart woman...you're acting like a fool. It's hard to watch." He turns back to the terminal. "Plus, I'm going to be a father. Need to get some practice in."

"You're gonna be an amazing father, Harry," I whisper.

"Let's hope I get a chance to prove you right. Get to work, Fallon."

With a nod, I turn back to my terminal. The Motoneslly Group. You better be behind this. You better be easy to find. You better have a fucking serum or antivirus ready and waiting. For once, just once, let something be easy. Uncomplicated. Black and white. Let the path be clear in both vision and of obstacle. I need it. I damn well deserve it. Everything else is so damn tangled. One moment I think the path on the left is best only to discover I should have followed my instinct to go right. My pigheadedness could actually allow me the turnaround back this time. I just need strength and time.

I begin with a simple Noogle search since I know fuck all about where else to start. Their web site pops up first. All very generic with words like "excellence," "synergy," and "innovation" in every blurb. They've been around about fifteen years. Nothing about their board, holdings, or executives. They appear to be just a finance company. Oh, now based in the Cayman Islands. Imagine that. Based out of the one country that refuses to acknowledge all warrants and investigations. The Group has shell corporation written over them. The next few searches provide about as much information. A mention in *Fortune* as part of a list of the rise of investment firms ten years ago, an article about the buying and selling of Arcadia Motors by the group, and the group donating computers to schools in New Urbana, Independence, and Jericho seven years ago. Noogle claims there are only fifty entries in the whole of the internet related to the Group and none of those besides the website are from the past seven years. That's almost impossible if they're still conducting business. Unless they hired a hacker to erase all traces. I have heard that's possible. Costly and complicated but possible. So much for easy.

Okay, there must have been some government oversight when they bought Biodyne. When Goliath purchased Blackwater they—*Blackwater*. Wait. I think…they were working on a genetic something and close to a breakthrough. It was the one division that showed any progress. Maybe…okay, all of ten minutes in and I'm breaking our agreement. Fuck it. I Noogle Blackwater. The website is as generic as Motoneslly's. Nothing on the specifics of the research or how close they were to completion, but I jot down the name of the lead researcher, Dr. Vikander Sharpesh. I scroll to the other search results, most about the Goliath purchase and society gossip about Bennett and I. I click to the second page and the top result catches my eyes. An article about Goliath shutting down Blackwater dated two weeks ago. Surprising but not shocking. Conglomerates often buy struggling companies for relatively cheap—five hundred million dollars for a biotech is damn cheap—only to break it apart and sell the patents and offices to other companies like junking a car. Pendergast tries not to be so cold-blooded but that's why I'm only worth seven billion and Bennett's worth forty-five. I still take a few minutes to write Dr. Sharpesh an email about the gene therapy project. No one ever refuses Captain Moonlight.

Back to work. I access the FDIC and Tax Services databases. Finally. The FDIC have a file on Motoneslly. Offices in New Urbana and Independence. I write down those addresses so the super away team can check them out. Hopefully they'll get the CEO Peter Miller and CFO Victoria Lancaster to break down and confess everything within five minutes. There are several other names of employees in the reports, and all the companies they've bought and sold, in this country at least. There aren't many companies, only six in fifteen years. Per the current tax records the only other holdings besides Biodyne are Boar's Head Airline, a small fleet specializing in crop dusters and private planes based out of Jericho purchased two months ago, and something called Health Medical Inc. headquartered in India but with distribution centers all over the country. Justin's on those. I've got Peter Miller and Victoria Lancaster, and the seven other people who received W-2s from Motoneslly. Nine people to run a billion dollar investment fund. No way. I send both Justin and the Federal Health Department emails, asking the latter to investigate both offices.

Miller and Lancaster are mine.

Of course after an hour of searching, I uncover about as much about them as Noogle did on the Group. Peter Miller is a sixty-year-old resident of Independence, born and I assume raised. Victoria has the same address, though she's a decade younger than him. Their work history begins before I was born. I write down every company they're linked to, all five, but there's a gap of ten years from when they worked at Schafer Technology to forming the Group. No job, no taxes paid, then they have billions to start buying and selling companies? On paper they're model citizens: quietly donating to charities, no arrests, no investigations, not even parking tickets. Probably because I can't find a car registered to either of them. Even stranger for people with worldwide investments, and being based in the Caymans, neither has a passport. Yeah, these people only exist in databanks. That's the trouble with modern technology, we trust computers too much. If the computer says it's true or exists we just accept it and move on. "Motherfucking fuck," I mutter as I toss my pen down.

"Take it you're having as much luck as I am," Harry says.

"We're chasing ghosts. A mirage. A damn well built mirage I can't find my way out of. I wasted…" I shut my mouth to stop the litany of bile I want to spew out in frustration. "I'm fucking useless."

"I think we should take a breather," Harry suggests as he rises. "We should put up an appearance upstairs anyway. See if there's any news."

"I'll just send the new information to Justin and be right up."

He squeezes my knotted shoulder as he passes to the ramp. I open the email and quickly type up all I learned, and send it to Justin. My minions can bust down doors and scare the shit out of the seven underlings in the offices. Hopefully *they* exist.

My personal email proves far more interesting. Two from Bennett, both with pleas to call and let him know what's happening, but none from the Blackwater doctor yet. Bastard. Maybe Bennett can help. Apply some pressure. Technically *he* owns the research now. I pick up the phone and dial. A large part of me hopes he doesn't answer. No such luck.

"Bennett Stone," my friend says.

"Hi. It's Jo."

"Oh, thank Christ," he says after breathing a literal sigh of relief. "I've been sitting here worried fucking sick all day. Every time my damn phone rang my heart leapt into my throat thinking it was news about you. Ar-Are you okay? How do you feel?"

"Well, the only sickness I have right now is cabin fever. I am infected, but they keep telling us their tests indicate we're just in for the flu. Those of us without the uber-gene anyway. That's why I'm calling."

"Here I was hoping for phone sex," he quips.

"I'm sure you can find someone in town to scratch that particular itch."

"But you have the best claws, kitten. I still have the welts to prove it."

And *this* is why I dreaded talking to him. Because I have to lead him on. Life and death makes a person throw out all their scruples. "Well, with your help maybe I can get out of here and add to your collection."

"Believe me, gorgeous, I haven't been idle. Every favor, every string at my fingertips has been plucked and called in. *You* are going to be fine. I can all but guarantee it."

Wish I had his confidence. "Mind going the extra mile?"

"For you I'll to Tibet."

"I heard you closed down Blackwater."

"That was always the plan. Projections show we'll net fifty million. Why?"

"I've been trying to get in touch with the lead researcher on the gene therapy project. Dr. Sharpesh."

"Why?"

"This virus targets a specific gene. He's a genetic bioengineer working on adenoviruses. If I remember correctly

- 270 -

from the Pendergast reports, he was close to a breakthrough. We thought that's why you wanted Blackwater."

"Jo, we reviewed his research through back channels during the deal. He was a decade away from anything viable. I'm hardly going to junk a company potentially worth billions."

Damn it. "I'd still like to talk to him. Maybe have him send what he has to the health department. We are running seriously low on time here."

"What's your telephone number there?" I give it to him. "I'll see what I can do. Anything else? Are you close to tracking down the kidnappers?"

"Maybe. Have you ever heard of The Motoneslly Group or Peter Miller and Victoria Lancaster?"

"The company name rings a tiny bell. A charity of some kind, no?"

"Investment firm. They're based in the Caymans but have an office in Independence and the so called executives claim to have an apartment just around the corner from you."

"So called?"

"If those two exist outside of a computer I'm the Queen of Sheba. It's a shell company."

"Why do you think this shell's involved?"

"They own Biodyne who just *happened* to have a serum for this specific flu. A flu only before known of in a small African village."

"Sounds like a tenuous link at best, Jo."

"Maybe, but my gut tells me this is them. Just have to crack the shell, and we've got 'em."

"I'll ask around. See if I can find you a hammer, but now I have to go. I'm already late for a meeting."

"Okay. Call me if you find anything useful. And I know I haven't said it, but words can't express how much I appreciate all you're doing for me."

"You'd do it for me."

"Damn straight, playboy. Talk to you later."

"Bye, gorgeous." He hangs up.

Worth a shot, even if I do feel like I need a shower now. If leading him on leads me to a cure, I can live with that. And thinking of showers…and food, and coffee. If I intend to pull an all-nighter, all of the above will be required. Sadly the price for those necessities proves to be blood, saliva, urine, and more tests. The showers have hot water today at least, I get clean sweats and underwear, and there's a ham and cheese sandwich left. No coffee though. "We're making a fresh pot," the lab assistant informs me as she escorts me out of the lab. "We'll bring it out to you all soon."

"Thanks. And can you please remind Dr. Ambrose to eat? He forgets," I say.

"I think he did eat before he went upstairs."

"Upstairs?"

"He said he needed a nap. I assume that's where he went."

As usual I have to wait a full minute at the threshold with a rock in my stomach as the UV lights zap any stray virus from my skin before I can run two steps at a time upstairs. He *could* just be tired. Even he needs at least two hours of sleep a night to recharge. But he got four last night. Yeah, I fucking sprint down the hall to his bedroom and knock harder than needed. "Who is it?" Jem asks.

"Jo. Can I come in?"

"Of course." The rock in my stomach expands to my chest when I lay eyes on him. He can try to hide it behind that smile, but be it how pale he is or the fact that smile momentarily falters when he moves his head to look at me from the bed, I know something's wrong. Still, he says, "Hi," as that smile grows.

I shut the door and rush over to him. "What's the matter?" He doesn't get up, doesn't even lift his head from the pillow. I feel his forehead. Not hot but definitely cold and clammy. "Has the vertigo gotten worse?"

"I'm fine," he assures me.

"Don't you dare lie to me, Jem Ambrose. Not to me."

His smile slowly fades even becoming a frown. "Come lie down." He pats the bed. "It's difficult to keep my head at this angle. You're making the world tilt on its axis. Although you always were good at that."

"Not so bad at it yourself," I say as I climb into bed. I rest my head on the pillow so we're staring at one another like we have so many precious nights and days. For a moment, as I gaze into those sapphire pools rimmed with thick coal black lashes, it's as if we're back in our penthouse after a long day finally able to relax. Finally safe with the one person who understands. The most perfect moments of my life. But the moment passes when I notice how red the whites of his eyes are. "How bad is it?"

"The vertigo is progressing with more frequent bouts that last longer. Half an hour this time. My strength…I'm not sure I could lift you now. I cut my finger two hours ago and it's just now healing. I'm exhausted. My body, my mind. I can't focus. I don't know how much longer I can hide this from them."

"Maybe you shouldn't. There are drugs that help with vertigo and—"

"The moment I tell them I'm symptomatic they'll drag me to the hospital where I'm under twenty-four hour surveillance hooked up to machines with no communication outside."

"And where they can manage your symptoms," I stress. "Maybe they can slow the progression. Buy time."

"Joanna…" He tries to find the right words, but judging from the sad smile he affixes, there are none. "My body is attacking itself. Every organ, every cell. By tomorrow I won't be able to hide it. At this rate of progression I have two days—"

"*No.*"

"…until I am in full systemic organ failure."

"No," I say. I'm surprised I can talk my heart's pounding so hard and the weight of that boulder in my gut makes it seem like I weigh a literal ton.

"They can keep me on life support for perhaps a week, but…unless my regen can be fully restored, the damage will be irreparable. Even with it, I'm not sure that much damage can be reversed. You still hold my power of attorney. It will fall to you to—"

"Pull the plug? Kill you?" I ask, voice brittle.

"End my suffering."

I shake my head on the pillow. "You can't ask that of me."

He reaches across to caress my cheek with his thumb. "I know. But I am. And I trust you to make the right decision." He wipes my tear away.

Goddamn it. I'm crying again. Sniffling like a weakling. "This is a pointless conversation. We-We're close to finding them. The Motoneslly Group. It's a shell corporation. They-They own controlling interest in Biodyne, a medical supply company, an airline, and those are just the ones we know of right now. By tomorrow we'll have them."

"Joanna…"

"You are *not* going to die," I say with utter certainty.

The love of my life smiles again. As if he actually believes me. Guess I'll have to keep the faith for us both. It is my turn after all. *His* faith got us *here*. He cups my face in his palm which I kiss. "There's so much I want to say to you," he whispers. "So much…" He closes his eyes and shakes his head. "Ho-How difficult is it to hang up a towel?"

I do a literal double take. "What?"

He opens his eyes again. "Or put the cap back on the toothpaste? Or wipe the counters when they're dirty? I *hate* how much of a slob you are. It drives me mad."

"I-I'm sorry," I chuckle.

"I hate how you snore and steal the covers. It's a miracle if I get a few hours of sleep."

"Wait, is that why you bought the earplugs? You told me it was because you could hear the neighbors when they got up in the morning."

"I lied to spare your feelings." He pauses. "Just like I lied when I said I enjoy those action and horror films you drag me to on date night. I loathe them. Just as I loathe when we're out at a business or formal function and you spew vulgarities. You swear more than is necessary in any situation. It embarrasses me. And I hate…" He pauses for a second, the sides of his mouth twitching, "I *hate* that you slept with Bennett Stone. *I hate it*. It was cruel. Vindictive. And I didn't deserve that."

"No. You didn't. And I'm sorry. I'm so sorry."

"I know. And I forgive you." He smiles. "With all my heart and soul, I forgive you."

"Thank you," I whisper as another tear falls. "And I'm sorry…for all the cruel things I said. How I behaved."

"*That* I deserved. I should have told you about Justin."

"Yes, you should have," I whisper before slowly smiling. "But I forgive you."

Jem lets out a tiny sob as tears spring from his eyes too. "You do?"

My turn to wipe his tears away. "Yes. I forgive you because…I don't have a choice. The only other option is not having you in my life, and that's not a goddamn option. I've tried to hate you. To not feel a damn thing about you, but…seems the only thing I can do is love you. Because in spite of being an anal retentive, awkward, know-it-all, you're also the sweetest, kindest, most brilliant, best man I have or will ever meet. You showed me I was worthy of love. That I'm just not some coarse, bitchy, pigheaded, damaged thing. You made me *believe* it."

"How could you have ever doubted that?" he asks desperately. "How can you not see what I do? Joanna, you…are *beautiful*. Not only on the outside. Whenever I look at you, whenever I watch you talking to people, fighting for what you believe in, fighting to make this world just a fraction better, I swell with such pride. That this astonishingly, clever, fierce warrior is mine. That *she* deigned to cast her lot with mine. That she thought me worthwhile enough to piece me back together. To bring me back to life with her love. How could that woman *not* be worthy of love?" he asks as if he cannot fathom it. "You are a miracle, Joanna Fallon. Don't you *dare* think otherwise. Not for a single solitary moment."

I stare at this man. This god among men who accepts me as is. The love of my otherwise dark, cold, cruel world and feel as if I'm going to burst with light. With pure happiness.

How did I think for a minute I could live without him? "Marry me."

The corners of his mouth twitch into a smile. "What?"

"Not this again," I chuckle. "You heard me, Ambrose. Marry me."

His smile wanes. "If this is merely because I'm dying—"

"Excuse me, you're the one here who thinks you're dying," I point out. "I *know* you're not. I'm asking because…I love you. Because I know we're going to get our million nights and there isn't a single one of those where I don't want to be by your side." I shrug. "It's as simple as that, genius."

"Then I guess I better marry you, huh?" he chuckles.

"Damn straight."

He breaks into happy tears, as do I, before I bridge the now miniscule space between us until it's gone forever. We kiss and caress the sins of the past away. I'm sweet and gentle, something only he draws out of me. I never want to make love to another man again. I never will. Only him. Afterward is just as perfect, lying in each other's arms, my head resting over his heart.

"I missed you," he whispers as he strokes my hair. "I missed you so much. Your smell. Your laugh."

"My snoring?" I quip.

"Even that."

I rest my chin on his chest and gaze up at my fiancée. "Well, unless you have any more life altering secrets hidden away, you're stuck with me now." He stares down but doesn't smile. I can read his face better than a book. "Do you trust me?"

"More than anyone on this earth."

"Then why won't you trust me now? Trust me on this? If you think I'm going to let a little microscopic bug take you from me, you are not as smart as you pretend to be. This isn't over. We're just beginning. I refuse to become a damn widow before we're even married, and we *are* getting married. We are going to stand before our friends, our family, God and whoever the hell else is listening and pledge our love and fidelity to one another. We are gonna let the world know what we already do: we're friends. Lovers. Partners. You're not standing me up, Ambrose."

"Never," he says, finally smiling.

"Then you just lie back and let me save *you* this time."

He caresses my cheek, the smile growing. "You already have."

And I'm damn well going to again. He's all I have. All I want. I need him. And nothing will stop me from getting my million nights and a million more with him.

Nothing.

CHAPTER SEVENTEEN

DOWN AND OUT

For the first time since we last slept in the same bed, I wake feeling like an actual human person. Rested. Coherent. The only problem is I wake alone and slept five hours longer than I'd wanted. I can still smell him on the pillow and take a few more seconds to savor that. To remember his touch, his taste, his kisses and laughs. How could I have thought I wanted to go through life without them? That bleak thought spurs me out of the warm, comfy bed to quickly dress into my sweats and hustle downstairs. I can't save him from bed.

Unfortunately, I'm not the only one up at four AM. I pay the price of needing to use their toilets with more blood, urine, and lung secretion tests. At least I get cereal with real milk out of the bargain. Jem's in their lab, working away already. My lab rat duty done, it's my turn to get to work. I find Doris all by her lonesome in The Chamber. Harry must be sleeping. Smart man. First I check Harry's notes on Biodyne. Seems while I was getting laid, he was working. That's why he's the best.

Per his investigation, he found no evidence of Biodyne researching adenoviruses. None of the doctors on our list, save for one, has ever worked there, and that one doctor has since moved to India to work on stem cell research. Shit. Of course this doesn't mean Biodyne's clean, but its disconcerting. They could have kept the research off the books, secretly funded by

Motoneslly through back channels. A forensic accountant could suss that out but it'd take months. We—

The video chat rings over the speakers. I put on my headphones and mic before accepting the call. Justin sits on a familiar couch scowling over the monitor. I miss my couch. "Where the hell have you been? I've been trying to hail someone for over an hour."

"It's the middle of the night. We were...sleeping."

"It's gone," he says.

"What's gone?"

"Motoneslly. The tax records, what little there was on Noogle, the offices, their website, *everything*. It's gone."

"What?" I pull up Noogle and sure enough no links appear. Nothing on the whole of the internet matches my search.

"It's the same in every database, Jo. The few records we found have been deleted."

"What about Biodyne and the others?"

"Their records do still have Motoneslly listed as their owner, but unless we know precisely which companies to search for, we won't find any more links. No one will. They've effectively cut off our intelligence gathering. The government's as well. What we have is all we're probably going to get. And in further bad news, Lexie went to the Motoneslly apartment and office in Independence. No surprise the apartment was empty, however the office wasn't. Three men in ski masks were there, wiping the computers and literally torching the place."

"Is Lexie okay?" I ask.

"She barely got out of there before the roof collapsed. They're still trying to put out the fire. Same with the office New Urbana. And when I tried to check the telephone number at those addresses, there were no files found. They deleted all records on incoming and outgoing calls to those offices. Just like the fleet car Ryder drove."

"Who the fuck are these people?"

"Trying to uncover that fundamental question just became twenty times harder. The question we really need to ask now is how did they know we were investigating them?"

"If they can break the internet then I'm sure they have programs that let them know when someone's searching for them. I've sent emails to the Health Department and feds with my findings."

"I thought that too, but the offices went up in flames half an hour before the feds began investigating them."

I shrug. "There has to be an informant then. I'm sure they have one in every country's government they operate in. Several."

"Maybe."

"So what the fuck do we do now? Harry spent hours on Biodyne and got nowhere. All we have left are the airline and medical supply company."

"Already done. Like Biodyne, both check out clean. The only connection to the case is that Health Medical Inc. manufactures the same gas used at the prison, but so does every other supply company. They're based in India but have distribution hubs in Jericho, Starling, Carsten, and seven others."

"Carsten's only thirty miles from here."

"The hubs are outside every major city. Geronimo offered to take a look. He just reported back. Found absolutely nothing out of the ordinary. He downloaded their shipping manifests for the past year, but it'll take days to review. There are thousands of entries. We're concentrating on any within twenty minutes west of the city, the way you tracked Ryder. We have the list Jem sent of what would be needed to equip a full lab to house sixteen patients. Maybe we'll get lucky."

"Because our track record with luck is so wonderful." I pause. "This is bad."

"This is bad," he concedes.

"Jem's getting worse. Fast. Last night he had vertigo for almost an hour. He thinks they'll send him to the hospital today, and that he'll…we-we don't have time for this bullshit."

"I'm sorry."

"Don't be sorry," I snap. "Don't bring me more problems. Bring me goddamn solutions!"

"We have the government, top scientists, and half the superhero population working around the clock, Jo. We have a suspect now. Even the press has mobilized. I called Veronica and she's getting in touch with major networks worldwide to plaster The Motoneslly Group name everywhere. Someone will come forward with information and we'll nail the bastards."

"That was…smart," I say.

"And the government is taking Motoneslly seriously now. The airline and supply company are top priorities. Warrants are already issued. And Lexie suggested we search social media sites for mentions, which I was just about to do. If they didn't hack those yet, we may find people who list Motoneslly as their place of employment. We were knocked down, sure, but we're not out yet. Nowhere near."

Damned if I don't feel a little better. "Okay." I pause. "Sorry about snapping."

"I've been your best friend for over two decades. I'm used to it," he says with a smile. I find myself smiling back.

"Catch up on everyone's reports then help me search for a needle in a field of haystacks."

"Okay. Jo, out." I cut the call.

Down but not out. Story of my damn life.

I've missed so much while I slept. The majority of our suspected doctors have been cleared and more than a few have even offered their services in helping with research. Only seven remain, all out of the country. Guess no one has contact with the supers in India, China, and Malaysia who can go knock on their doors. And thinking of India, Dr. Sharpesh formerly of Blackwater, finally wrote back offering to chat and help anyway he can. Even if he was only at early stages, it can't hurt.

Next I review my chicken scratch from last night about the phantomous Peter Miller and Victoria Lancaster: their alleged previous employers, the now useless home address, and random thoughts. This is it. This one piece of paper is all we have and will get on them. Why didn't I write down their Federal ID numbers? Print out their W2s? All lost now. I shouldn't have slept so long. I should have been down here, nose to the fucking grindstone. Well, not again. No breaks, no sleep beyond naps, until this is over.

Okay, think. I need to think. There is usually one piece of evidence, one person, an offhand comment, one mistake that solves the case. I brought a serial killer to justice after finding a pizza receipt. We're got Motoneslly running scared now. They're desperate, and the desperate make mistakes.

Okay, I'm the mastermind. I've spent billions and years, decades, on this project. I've created a shell company, bought a biotech, medical supply company, and airline and those are probably the tip of the iceberg. I use all three, funneling funds to my secret projects using Biodyne's facilities and infrastructure. The medical supply company provides the equipment, once again off the books, including the lab where the villains were taken. Equipment gets lost all the time. When the virus is ready, I use the airline to disperse the virus worldwide. Spray close enough to major airports or trade winds, and it's around the globe in weeks. But if it was Biodyne then why create a serum against the virus? Maybe there's another biotech company we haven't found yet owned by Motoneslly. And our government wouldn't let them release the serum until multiple tests were conducted. That would take months and by then it's too late for supers. It would have worked, all of it, if James Ryder hadn't broken out. Now they have to move or all of this was for nothing. Which means…they have to be planning to release the virus sooner rather than later. We need to ground that airline or at least keep it under surveillance.

I re-read all my notes, all the other's notes, trying to assemble the puzzle. Find the key. The one. The facility where Ryder escaped from. Find that, find it all. It's nearby. The mastermind bought Health Medical Inc. to supply it and his other research facility. The supplies could have gotten "lost" in their computers, but if they used an outside transport company and we get *their* records, and we may get our location. I type that up and email it to both the feds and Justin. Geronimo hasn't sent the records yet. That reminder goes in the email as well. Can't do fuck all until I get a copy. The doctors will pass the time.

India keeps popping up. It's where the supply company's based, and it seems Dr. Andrew Mendelson, Dr. Sergi Lermantov, and Dr. Kelvin Tan all live there. After a forty year career, most notably on the team that discovered the uber-gene, Mendelson's been retired for over a decade. India's not the place I'd retire to. Drs. Lermantov and Tan last worked at Synergy Tech, the former specializing in adenoviruses and the latter in the recombinant DNA structuring. All that's missing from Jem's proposed list is a virologist. Dr. Sabine DeRue, who last worked in Malaysia for B.N. Sciences Industrial, transferred to their Malaysian facility before abruptly quitting to "focus on family" six years ago. Except her husband died two years before in the supervillain Bastille's second bombing. She's vanished since. She's a French citizen but one of the supers in France couldn't find an address on her. Missing scientist with a grudge against supers? We need to find the bitch. Of course *how* to find her eludes me at the moment. That goes in the email too.

A second after I press "send," on the house surveillance cameras, I see three lab assistants coming out of the front door. Shit. I rush upstairs before they come looking. I join the other prisoners as the lab techs escort down Jackson and the paramedic Hernandez. Though I just gave over an hour ago, my tech draws more blood, saliva, and air samples before hustling out again. They keep me waiting in this freezer almost half an hour, and when someone finally returns, I leap off the gurney. "What the fuck—"

"Ms. Fallon, Dr. Ambrose just collapsed. He's asking for you."

I practically body slam past her after the word "collapsed." She nods to the room down the narrow hallway. Jem's on a gurney as two spacesuits adjust the monitors and take his temperature. "What's going on? What's happening?" I take his icy hand. "You collapsed?"

"Doctor, his temp is 96.4," the assistant says.

"I'm fi—" Jem says before coughing. Hard, wet, wracking coughs just like…my stomach seizes. One tech gets him water while the doctor listens to his chest. All I can do is hold his hand until the fit passes.

"How long have you been ill? When did this begin?" Dr. Vaugh asks Jem.

"Yesterday afternoon," I reply. "He said it began as vertigo which grew worse and led to headaches and muscle fatigue."

"Why didn't you tell us?" the doctor asks him.

"He's telling you now," I cut in.

Dr. Vaugh turns to the assistant. "Nurse, prep the chamber for transport to Our Lady Hospital. Contact them that we have an incoming patient to the Infectious Disease Ward with Level 4 precautions required. Have Dr. Strong return post haste. I'll escort Dr. Ambrose myself."

The nurse nods before walking out.

"Is all this necessary? Can't you treat him here?" I ask.

"The hospital is far better equipped than we are here to manage his symptoms," the doctor says.

"I understand," Jem says quietly. He squeezes my hand. "John, can you give my fiancée and I a minute alone?"

"Of course, but someone will be just outside the door if a problem arises."

"I'll be fine," Jem assures him.

With a nod, the doctor leaves as well.

"Is there any way to stop this?" I ask.

"No. We knew this was coming, Joanna." He coughs and tries to clear his throat. "God."

"Are you okay?" I ask almost breathlessly.

"This just began. It's manageable. I just…" he squeezes my hand. "There is some good news. Your blood tests are clean. You've fought back the virus. We even think you're no longer contagious."

"That's wonderful. I-I can come with you to the hospital. I—"

"It hasn't been verified yet. Besides, there are no visitors in the infectious ward."

"So you're saying…"

He squeezes his hand tighter. "I'm saying…I love you."

"No. You think…you think this is it, don't you?"

"Joanna…"

I snatch my hand away. "No. *No.* This isn't goodbye, you idiot. You—"

"Joanna, shut up," he snaps. I'm taken aback. This is a man who can face down seven men with assault rifles and never lose his temper. "*I* need to talk, okay? Please let me say this. I need to." My mouth snaps shut, and I give a little nod. "If, *if* the worst occurs…you will need someone. Your first instinct will be to push people away. Lash out. Because even though I am telling you right now *none* of this is your fault, you will blame and want to punish yourself regardless. I know you will. So I'm going to ask you to promise me you will fight that instinct. I am asking you to promise that you will allow people to take care of you until you're strong enough to care of yourself. That you will lean on them. Let them in. Especially Justin."

"Jem—"

"You forgave me, my love, now I am asking you to forgive him. Twenty years, Joanna. Twenty years of love and laughter and acceptance. You know one another better than anyone, present company included. You can beat him bloody, call him every name in the dictionary, spit on him, and he will always be a phone call away. What you have together is rare, so rare. He loves you, and deep down you still love him. You always will. It's too ingrained in you both. It's weaved into your very fabric. There is no…Joanna Fallon without Justin Pendergast. So, if this is the end…please honor my request. Let it go. Let the anger go and try to celebrate the fact he's alive. Celebrate you have the other half of your soul returned to you. Promise me you will at least try. Promise me or I'll torture myself with worry about you. If you love me, Joanna, you'll spare me that. Promise me?"

I take a deep breath. "I promise."

He kisses my hand. "Thank you."

I rest my head on our entwined hands and stare into his bloodshot eyes. "I am going to save you," I say with utter certainty. "I am going to save you, Jem. I am going to fight until I don't have the strength to lift a pinky finger or take a breath."

"You wouldn't be you if you didn't."

I kiss his hand again. "Don't you dare leave me alone in this world, Jem Ambrose. Don't you *dare*."

He manages another smile. "I don't know if there's a heaven or hell, but I do believe we leave something behind after we're gone. So know…you're never alone, Joanna. You think of me, and I will be there. Watching over you. Cheering you on as you fight and claw and do all the wondrous things you do until this universe exists no more. You gave me the greatest moments of my life. You are everything I never knew I needed. I love you so much. More than I knew I was capable of. Thank you. Thank you for casting your lot with mine."

"It's my pleasure," I whisper. "It's my *honor*."

The door opens again and two spacesuits come in with a plastic casket with a HEPA filter on top. Oh, God. Not yet. There's still so much to say. They have to physically pull me from his side so he can climb into that fucking box. As they seal the lid, it's as if I'm the one who cannot breathe. Somehow Jem maintains a small smile for us all. A brave face. I want to scream, punch, cry all at once. This is it. It could be. No. Please. I all but float outside my body as they wheel his clear coffin out of the room. It's the only way I can handle this. The only way. The only way to keep from losing my fucking mind. His smile never wavers. His eyes never leave my stricken face. I want to touch him. Crawl in there with him. "I love you," he mouths before coughing again.

"I love you too. For a million nights and a million more."

He presses his hand to the plastic, and I place mine over his all the way to where Dr. Vaugh reviews papers on a clipboard. That's all Jem is to him, paperwork and a disease. Who is going to be in his corner? Keep the nurses in line and doctors attentive? Hold his hand and make him laugh when he's in pain or terrified? I'm stuck in here while he...

"I need to go with him," I tell the spacesuits.

"Ms. Fallon," a nurse says.

"My tests are clean, right? I'm not contagious anymore? Then you have no right to keep me prisoner anymore. I want to go with him. *Now.*"

"Ms. Fallon, we require further testing before clearing you—"

"Joanna," Jem tries.

"I want to go with him."

"And that is not possible, Ms. Fallon," Vaugh snaps before looking at his assistants. "Nurses, let's get the case through decon. The ambulance is standing by."

"Yes, doc—"

"I'm going with him!" I shout. "I-I'm—"

Ignoring me, they wheel him to the next room. The moment he's out of sight, my lungs seize up along with every muscle in my body and fold of my mind. I try to draw in air but the tall roadblock of terror and panic won't allow any to pass, which increases the strength of both those bastards. My legs won't support myself much longer. The spots will begin soon. After another attempt at air with no success, the tidal wave of fear crashes into me. One of the nurses rushes over to me, getting right in my face, hers still behind the helmet but I wouldn't be able to hear her words anyway. Jem's the only one who can help me now. He presses my hand to his heart and stares into my eyes, ordering me to break the block. I can't. I can't. He's gone. He may never return. I can't breathe. I can't do this anymore. I can't. I—

Oblivion tags me out.

*

Oh, why couldn't it have been a dream?

I open my eyes to find myself back in an exam room. At least there's a friendly face by my side reading the newspaper. "What happened?" I ask Harry or really croak at him.

He sets down the paper and smiles. "Hi. Welcome back. How do you feel?"

I manage to sit up. "Embarrassed. I haven't had an episode that bad since Cain."

"I think this whole situation ranks up there, don't you? I'm shocked we're all not dropping like flies from panic attacks."

"I guess. It's still fucking embarrassing. How long was I out for?"

"Two hours. Jem told them to wake me so I could watch over you right before they took him to the hospital."

"The man's dying and he's still the one taking care of me."

"The nurse just came in a few minutes ago. She told me he's resting comfortably at the hospital."

"I have to get out of here, Harry. I need to be there with him. He might not—" I snap my mouth shut. I'm not putting that out into the universe.

Harry takes my hand. "He'll be okay. He's strong." Harry squeezes my hand. "And he has everything to live for." My ex releases my hand and sits back in the chair. "Plus, you may be sprung sooner rather than later. There's been an update on our progress. Seems like whatever was in that Biodyne serum worked on you, Jackson, and Hernandez. You're no longer contagious, and your viral load is almost nil. You should be released in a few hours."

"What about everyone else? What about you?"

"The rest of us are running low grade fevers, have headaches, muscle aches, and Kowalski's been coughing since he woke up."

"You're sick?" I ask, my still tender stomach and lungs seizing again.

"They've assured us there's a seventy percent chance we'll only experience a standard flu."

"Seventy percent?"

"I'll take those odds, Jo."

Another one putting on a brave face for the broken woman. "Guess it's a good thing the people who did this don't hate all of humanity, just supers."

"Good for some," Harry says solemnly.

Time for more bad news. "They knocked us out, Harry. They found out we were getting close and wiped away every record, every search of Motoneslly. Blew up their offices too. We're fucked."

"When the hell did this happen?"

"After we went to bed. What we have is pretty much all we're getting which means we've got fuck all. Even with the doctors. I think I know who they are, but there's nothing more on them that we can find. And Jem's..." Fuck, I'm crying again. I swat away the tears. "*Millions* could die. Hell, they've probably already released the virus by now, and we're no closer to finding them then when this whole shit show began almost a month ago."

"We do. We have suspects, we have evidence, we have dozens of avenues to walk down now. Biodyne. The airline. The doctors. They can't all be dead ends. Don't lose hope, Jo. I'm not."

Staring at my friend, my mentor with a thin layer of sweat on his fevered brow, trying to keep on a brave face, my stomach twists, this time from guilt. He's the sick one, the newlywed with a thirty percent chance of never seeing his wife again. Never holding his son or daughter. I know I can be selfish, but this is beyond the fucking pale. I force the misery, the hopelessness behind my mask once more. "You're right. We'll get them and make them pay for this."

"Damn right," he says with a nod. I nod back. "Now, if you'll excuse me," he says, rising from the chair, "I'm going to let them know you're up. They have more tests."

"They can remove my liver if it helps you all get better."

"*Your* liver?"

"You have a point there," I say, even managing a smile.

He smiles back before departing. I drop the front and fall back on the gurney. Two more hours stolen. God knows how many more while I'm stuck in here getting tested again. At least I get to leave this prison soon. Three out of nine. Only one third of us helped by the serum. Not great. Not enough to pass federal regulations for wide use. If they release the virus now it won't do any good. Non-supers could die too. The elderly and children. The weak. Maybe that'll keep the genocidal sociopaths from jumping the gun on spreading it. God, I hope so.

More painful tests follow. Tubes stuck down my throat, a spleen and lymph nodes biopsied, the worst of all bone marrow. I have to scream into a pillow for that last one. They're going to use it all to try and develop a serum and vaccine. Work fast assholes. I have to lie on the gurney in horrendous pain despite the pain meds—there go weeks of sobriety—before they finally come in with good news instead of needles and agony. They have officially verified I am no longer contagious and have no legal right to keep me here anymore. I just need someone to come get me and keep an eye on me for the rest of the day after the biopsies. V doesn't answer her phone. I could call my aunt and uncle, but they'll follow the instructions to a T and I'd go from one prison to another. Which leaves...

"They're letting you out?" Justin asks over the phone.

"Yeah. You have a car, right? You can come get me? It's perfectly safe to come to the gate. You won't even have to leave the car."

"Okay. I'm on my way. See you soon." He hangs up.

Since all my old clothes are contaminated both old and current, they help me undress before forcing me into another decon shower after which I'm blasted by UV lights for a few minutes, wheeled into another clean room where I put on a new set of sweats and socks, and wait for my ride. This is how I leave my own house, pushed in a wheelchair in borrowed clothes. They won't even give me back my purse. More oncoming hell. A trip to the DMV.

A police cruiser blocks the end of the driveway down at the gate. I'm surprised the press hasn't arrived. There's a tarp across the driveway to hide the huge lab from the street view, but there are a half dozen cars lined up to the tarp. People must think I'm having a party. One of the officers in the squad car climbs out and runs up to me and my wheelchair chauffer, taking over the duty. She has better things to do then push me. A gold Sedan waits on the other side of the gate which opens for us when we reach the squad car. Justin leaps out of the Sedan, a sight for these beyond fucking sore eyes. Both men help me into the warm car. Justin gets in and a second later, without a glance back at his former home, drives us away.

"What happened? Why were you in a wheelchair?"

"Bone marrow biopsy. Lymph node and spleen too. They might need me to do it again. We need to stop by a pharmacy. They gave me prescriptions for Percocet, an immune booster, and Ativan."

"No problem. I've been staying at Jem's penthouse. I'll take you home first."

Home. It isn't home without him there. "I don't have clothes there."

"Then I'll pop over to your hotel and get some while I'm out."

"First, take me to Our Lady Hospital. Jem—"

"I know. He called me. He sounded good. But there are no visitors allowed."

"Well, good thing I'm on the board. Think they'll make an exception. I'll make some calls."

"Just take it easy. You've been through hell. You need to rest."

I turn up the heat. "The wicked aren't resting so neither will I. What did I miss?"

"Not much. They're still processing the burnt offices and empty apartment. We did locate two employees through social media. IPD are bringing them in for questioning. And those remaining doctors on our list, three friends are traveling to India to investigate as I speak. More are on stand-by if the three need them. The Feds are also about to execute warrants for Biodyne's financial records."

"What about the medical supply company? Anything on the shipping forms?"

"GFPD is running them down. I've been trying to cull the list."

"So we have nothing."

"The press is getting interested, so we should be getting more leads. Biodyne and Motoneslly are firmly on everyone's radar. And you're healthy. I'd say we're doing pretty damn good."

"Tell that to Jem. And Harry. And all the others still in that damn house worried they're about to die."

"You always were a ray of sunshine, Jo."

"My fiancée's dying in the hospital. A virus that can kill millions is about to be released, if it hasn't been already. And I have a hole in my hip that aches like a motherfucker. Point me to light, rich boy." A small smile flashes across his face for some reason when I utter those last two words. "What?"

"Nothing," he says, smile returning again for another moment. "Wait, did you say 'fiancée?'"

"Yeah. We…yeah. Last night."

"Oh, my God. Shit, Jo. Congratulations," he says with a huge, wide grin.

"Don't plan the bachelorette party yet. That altar is a thousand miles away and growing farther by the moment."

"But I am in charge of the bachelorette party? Good to know," he says with a smirk. "I'll start looking around for male strippers right away."

"Ha ha ha," I say sarcastically.

"Joanna Fallon. Getting married." He shakes his head. "They must be having a run on ice skates in hell right now."

"Shut up."

We ride in silence, save for the radio, the rest of the way home. Traffic, weather, local news about shootings and proposed tax hikes. All so inconsequential. No one has any idea what's coming. Billions sick. Millions dying. I say a silent prayer to whoever's listening that it's not already too late.

"Don't think about it," Justin says as my apartment building comes into view.

"What?"

"How much is on the line. How many lives hang in the balance. It'll paralyze you. We're doing this for *him*. For the people in that mansion. We're fighting for them. All else is incidental."

How did he know? It always amazes me when he does that. Reading my mind. Knowing what to say to make it better. I could always do the same with him. I'm just shocked that connection's still there.

That's the only time he speaks until we reach the building. We park in the underground garage, and Justin helps me shamble to the elevator, my hip throbbing with every step. He could carry me but knows I'd never agree. I bear it the elevator ride up, the walk down the hall, and into the penthouse. Home. It's all the same. The couch we bought together. The skylight we'd lie under and stare out at the stars. The happiest place on earth. Now it's just a cold shell. A house not a home. Not without him here.

"I need to catch up," I say as I hobble in. "Where's Doris Jr?"

"Let's set you up in the bedroom, yeah? Better for your hip. I'll get everything sorted before I leave."

"Thanks."

Justin follows me to the master bedroom and helps me into bed before retrieving water, aspirin, a telephone, pen, pad, and Doris Jr. Quite the nest. After asking me three times if I was okay, Justin finally leaves. He is such a mother hen. When I got pneumonia a few years back he took off work to watch over me. Warming up soup, renting us movies, making sure I took all my meds. When he had to attend a meeting he sent over Dobbs to take over nursing duty. He must have been going out of his fucking mind with me in quarantine. And I was such a bitch to him. Neither of us does helpless well.

First things first. I put calls into Danforth Mills and Dr. Westfield, Head of Attending, to beg them for access to the Infectious Ward. Neither answers so I leave desperate messages for both. Threatening comes later. Next I'm transferred to Jem's ward where a nurse informs me my fiancée's being examined, and he'll call me later. Now back to work. I review the new reports, making a few notes, but nothing inspires much confidence. Halfway through the phone rings. "Hello?"

"Joanna?" Jem asks.

Oh, a half ton of bricks lifts off my spirit when I hear his voice. Only another thousand to go. "Yeah. Hi."

"Hi. Are you okay?"

"I'm good. I'm home. I'm sorry if I scared you earlier. It was panic attack."

"I know. You're okay now?"

"Yeah. Justin's taking good care of me. They took some bone marrow. That shit hurt. Who knew my polluted, black Irish blood could ever help people, huh? How are *you*?"

"Still a human pin cushion. The meds are helping but making me tired."

"You sound better. How's the cough?"

"Better. I'm fine, Joanna. I'm in the best of hands."

"Well, mine are included. I'm working on getting in to see you as soon as possible. Do you want me to bring you anything? Books? A cake with a file so you can bust out?"

"That last one's tempting, but—" He begins coughing again. "Sorry."

"Are you fine? Don't lie to me."

"I am. I'm exactly where I need to be."

"Okay then." I pause. "There is some good news. We narrowed down the list of doctors to four. Dr. Sabine DeRue, Dr. Sergi Lermentov, Dr. Kelvin Tan, and Dr. Andrew Mendelson. We think they're—"

"Did you say Dr. Andrew Mendelson?"

"Yeah. Do you know him?"

Jem's silent for a few moments. "He was one of my...engineers. You can cross him off the list."

"Why?"

"Because Jordan hunted down all the doctors linked to the experiment and murdered them. He called it his pet project. I'd receive photos. He flayed Mendelson alive then slit his throat four years ago."

"Jesus."

"The other names," he coughs, "are vaguely familiar."

"We think they're in India. Operatives are already on their way."

"Sounds as if you're on the gun." He pauses. "I love you."

"I love you too. So much," I say.

"Get back to work. Love you."

"Say it again."

"I love you," he says.

"Once more with feeling," I say with a smile on my face.

I can all but hear his smile too. "I love you with all my heart, and all my soul Joanna Fallon. For a million nights—"

"And a million more," I finish. "Call me if you're up for some phone sex."

He chuckles. "I love you, Joanna. Bye." He hangs up.

He sounded good. Better than before. I'll take it, at least until I can get in to see him. I can think now. Concentrate on the task at hand. I fire off a quick email to everyone, including the state department and Indian ambassador, about Dr. Mendelson, including the manner of his death. Maybe he was on the project before Jordan found him. The man hasn't been reported missing. I suggest they check for any unidentified corpses with those types of wounds. It'd give us an approximate location of where Mendelson was at the time. Where the research facility could be now. Of course Mendelson could be a dead end, but my gut tells me no. If he was evil enough to create then torture two small boys in the name of science, he's sure as shit evil enough to help develop a virus to obliterate a race of people just to see if he can.

Next order of business. I continue to catch up, but nothing piques my interest. Shipping forms it is. But before I begin that mind-numbing task, I call Dr. Sharpesh. I almost forgot about him. Glad I didn't delete his email. We need any help we can get.

"He-He-Hello?" the man asks nervously.

"Um, Dr. Sharpesh?"

"Y-Yes. Who-Who is this?"

"You can call me Guardian. I work with Captain Moonlight in Galilee Falls. I'm the one who sent you the email about your work and—"

He hangs up. Uh…okay. I dial again, and he picks up on the sixth ring. "Hello?"

"Dr. Sharpesh, I think we got disconnected. I just—"

"I can't help you. I'm sorry. Please don't call here again." He hangs up.

Curiouser and curioser. Someone's been threatened. I've had a dozen informants say the same exact words with the exact same tone. Shit scared. I dial again and when he doesn't pick up, I hang up only to try again. And again. And again. After nine tries, he finally picks up. "Leave me alone!"

"I can't do that, Dr. Sharpesh. And quite frankly I'm sensing you can't afford to let me do it. Sir, I work with Captain Moonlight in Galilee Falls, White Knight in Independence, and Lionheart in Jericho. If you are in danger you must tell me right now so I can dispatch someone to your location to protect you. Lionheart can be there in fifteen minutes." Where'd you put his contact information, Justin?

"I-I don't…they threatened my family," he whispers. "They threatened my medical license if I talk about my research. I don't have a legal right to talk about it anyway. It belongs to Goliath now."

"Doctor, they threatened you for a reason, and these are not the type of people to leave a loose end hanging for long. I have the sense these are the same group that have kidnaped, killed, and are planning the genocide of all humans with the uber-gene. You are in mortal danger whether you talk to me or not." Got it. I pull up Lionheart's email and begin typing Dr. Sharpesh's home address and telephone number. "We're going to get you and your family someplace safe, okay? Lionheart is on his way over. Do not let anyone in unless they give the password, 'Guardian.'"

"O-Okay," he says. "H-Helen! P-Pack bags for us and the kids," he shouts. "Fo-For how long—"

"Pack for a week. It really depends on what you can tell me."

"A week, Helen!" I hear a door shut. "I've been so afraid, ma'am. Th-The phone rang at three this morning. I-I got it and a person with an electronic voice t-told me that I must not speak to anyone about my research, must not share it, or they'll kill my wife and children. They knew where the boys go to school, where my wife works. Then, when I went out this morning…my cat was dead. Lying on my doorstep with a bullet in her head."

Fucking hell. "I'm so sorry. You must be terrified. But we've been consulting with dozens of doctors and researchers worldwide, and none have reported being threatened. So why you? Why now?"

"Ma'am, I've asked myself that question all morning. I don't know. I didn't tell anyone you contacted me, not even my wife. Co-Could they have my email under surveillance? This phone?" he asks, voice now trembling.

"I don't know."

"H-How do I know th-this isn't a trick? You're not with them? This isn't a test?"

A fair question. This is big. I can sense it. I can't lose him. "Because I'm going to trust *you*. You can't tell a living soul, not your wife or anyone, otherwise my life and the lives of the people I love could be in danger. Trust for trust, okay?" I pause. "I'm Joanna Fallon."

The other end remains silent for several seconds. "You ruined my career."

"What?"

"When you sold Blackwater. Goliath shut us down. They stole my research!"

"I know. I just learned about it yesterday. I-I had no idea that was their plan. I swear on my own life I would have stopped the deal had I. But I'm friends with Bennett Stone. I'll convince him to turn all rights back to you. I'll personally pay for a facility for as many years as needed. You must be onto something for these people to threaten you. What precisely were you working on?"

He's silent for a few moments again. Moment of truth. "An adenovirus that degrades other adenoviruses." If I wasn't sitting down I'd probably collapse from relief. "It is such a new area of science, we figured mistakes would be made along the way. Our hypothesis is if we knew which adenovirus and which genes were targeted, we could input all that data into our virus and have our virus attack."

"C-Could a person make a full recovery? I ask, voice brittle.

"In theory. With the rogue virus dead, the patient would certainly have a better chance. With no virus, there'd be no autoimmune response attacking the body. But there are a million factors at play. I-I'd need as much information about the original virus. How it was developed, the exact sequencing, all the raw data otherwise our virus loses its efficacy and can potentially cause an autoimmune response as well. I reviewed what you sent last night. I need more information and a lab, but can begin—"

"Wait. I-I thought you were years away from producing a viable result."

"Miss Fallon, we were about to request permission to enter the human testing phase. Our previous tests on chimps produced a eighty-three percent success rate."

My stomach seizes. "But…th-that's not what I was told. H-He said…"

"Who said?" the doctor prompts.

Oh, my God.

Oh, my God.

I begin to see spots again and bile rises into my mouth. I swallow it down and take several ragged breaths to calm myself. Fuck. Fuck.

"I, uh…" I all but float out of my body. I can't stand to be inside anywhere he's touched. "Y-You need to gather all your research, anything you've still got. Lionheart will be there in a few minutes. Have your bags and family ready, but we'll need you to connect with the task force and get to work immediately. He could release the virus worldwide soon, if he hasn't already. There's a man dying in the hospital. M-My fiancée."

"I'm sorry," he says. "I'll do what I can, but as I said, I need all data on the original virus for full efficacy."

"You'll get it. I-I just…I have to hang up. I have to go. Lionheart will be there soon. Goodbye."

I hang up and despite the absolute agony rippling through my hip, I race to the bathroom just in time to collapse to the floor and throw up in the toilet. Not good enough. I whack my forehead against the rim several times, I guess hoping to render myself unconscious to escape the deeper circle of hell I've just plummeted into. "Stupid, stupid," I keep saying with each whack. "Stup—"

I burst into tears. Hard, from the bottom of my soul, wracking sobs. I curl into the fetal position, sobbing and sobbing until I can't breathe. I don't know how long I stay here, losing my fucking mind again, before I hear, "Jo? Joanna?" I can't move. I can't stop crying. "Jesus Christ! Jo? *Jo?*" I sense him fall to his knees beside me. Touch my back. I still can't stop crying, not even when he collects me into his arms, hugging tight. As tight as I do him. "It's okay," he whispers, stroking my hair. "It's okay, Jo. I'm here. I'm here."

I hold onto my best friend as if he were the only thing keeping me from falling off the face of the earth. "I-I-I-I-I…"

"I'm here. I'm here, Jo. Just let it out. I'm here. I'm not going anywhere. I've got you. Let it out."

I begin to calm down with every stroke, with every word until after another minute I can finally say it out loud. "It-It…Bennett Stone," I whisper.

"What?"

I sit back and look into his frightened blue eyes. "It's Bennett Stone. He's killed my Jem."

*

- 304 -

As I take a scalding hot shower in an attempt to burn off the skin I allowed that monster to touch, Justin coordinates with Lionheart to help the Sharpesh family get to safety. To save them from the danger I placed them in. Because of my stupidity. My blindness. He was so close, and I just couldn't see him for what he was. He stepped right into my blind spot. I trusted him. My friend. Another betrayal. I'll never be clean again. He's still in there. Under my skin. Like a virus.

Justin waits in the living room, phone pressed to his ear and typing away on Doris Jr. when I come out, my skin as raw as my nerves. "…reimburse you, Lionheart. It can't be in her name." He listens for a moment. "It just can't, but he needs to get here. *Now.* I'll transfer you the money but charter it in the name Joe Proctor." He listens again. "We can use any help offered, but with the outbreak, it's not safe here. It's your call." Justin looks up at me and give me a sad smile. "He's fighting. If anyone can beat this, it's Moonlight. Just get that doctor and his research here. I'll be in touch." He hangs up. "Feeling better?"

"Are they safe?"

"They're on their way here."

I flop into the easy chair. "Good. If anything happens to them, I'll slit his goddamn throat myself."

Justin stares at me, lips pursed. "Are you sure— "

"He's the only one I told about Sharpesh. I-I asked him about Motoneslly and hours later they're wiped off the face of the earth? He's been asking me about the prison break and virus every chance he got. He was here, in Galilee, excusing himself to use the phone at the precise time of the prison break. He has books on plagues. It fits. It all fucking fits. He has the means, the motive, all the opportunity in the fucking world. And I…"

"Jo, I've known Bennett Stone for over a decade. I've had lunches, we've partied, we—"

"And I fucked him. Twice. I'm business partners with him. I-I knew he disliked supers, but this…?"

"Who the hell could have seen this coming? How many years, how many billions, how many lies and plans have gone into this? Who could have that much hate in their heart? And the man came to you with the idea for The Guardian Society. To *help* supers. Why do that if you plan to wipe them off the planet?"

"So, if the worst happened, and he was found out, everyone would ask that very question? To entice me into becoming partners because he knew I'd be a good source of information? Because the demonic voices in his head told him to? It doesn't matter. *All* that matters is finding information Dr. Sharpesh needs to create a cure. Bennett Stone is the key. So, how do we approach this? Do we tell the feds or—"

"No. The man's friends with the fucking President. And he's probably already on edge with the Motoneslly leak. No, we keep this in-house. Just us and the other supers. Eventually he'll find out about Sharpesh but—"

"We could just kidnap and torture him for the information," I cut in.

"No," Justin states plainly. "Not unless we have no other option. No, we'll analyze his phone records, travel records, business dealings for the past year and—"

"That'll take too long." I pause. "There is another way."

"What?" I stare at him blank faced, but he still reads me like a fucking book. "*No*."

"I get in, I knock him out, download the information from his phones, his computers, make copies of his files, sneak out, and he's none the wiser."

"You are never going near that psychopath again, Jo," Justin declares. "He's liable to slit your throat the moment he sees you."

"You've got that reversed there, rich boy, but I will find a way to control myself. My way is the best way, and you know it. If the roles were reversed—"

"Don't play the misogyny card with me," he snaps. "If the roles were reversed, you'd be blocking the door or shooting me in the leg to stop me too."

He's got a point. "One life. One life against millions. We need to use every weapon in our arsenal. Including my female wiles." I pause. "He likes me, Justin. I think he genuinely likes me. As much as someone like him can. If I approach it right, he'll never suspect a thing until it's too late. I can do this, Justin. I'm *going* to do this." I pause again. "With you at my back."

He smiles. "Really?"

"Figured you'd just follow me anyway. Now give me the damn phone before I lose my nerve," I say, hand out. He gazes at my outstretched hand, hesitates for a moment, but does pass me the phone. "Get the Sharpesh family here. Quietly."

"Yes, ma'am," he says with a nod.

Okay. *Okay*. I can do this. It's just a phone call to a friend. My trembling finger somehow punches in the telephone number. My stomach seizes when he picks up. "Bennett Stone," he says.

At the sound of his voice, I lose the ability to speak. So much's riding on this. On *me*. All those lives. All—one life.

Just one life, Jo. This is for *him*. God give me strength. "Guess who got a clean bill of health?" I ask cheerfully.

"I was just thinking about you," he says seductively. I'll bet you were. "So you're out?"

"Resting comfortably at home. Seems not even a virus is a match for me."

"*I* could have told you that."

"And here I thought you were worried about me."

"Oh, I was." The way he says it, I actually believe him. *He* must have arranged for us to get the serum. At least for me to. Maybe the others got a placebo. "But you're okay? Really?"

"Physically. Finally got a moment of peace, and the survivor's guilt just kicked in. My friends are still sick. Jem's in the hospital. He might not..." I can't say it. Not even now. "It just feels wrong, you know?"

"I could give a three day seminar on survivor's guilt, gorgeous."

"I'm trying to work, but I can't focus. It's just all going to hell. One step forward, seven back."

"Then take a break. I could use one too."

"Shocking though it may be, I am not one for phone sex." Justin narrows his eyes at me, and I roll mine. "I-I'll be fine. This is helping already."

"Well, I am in your neck of the woods," he purrs.

I figured he would be with everything going to shit here. "What? Why? Do you want to catch the fucking plague?"

"Believe me, I would not be in town if it wasn't absolutely necessary. A deal's proving more complicated then I'd like. Put out one fire only to discover there are two more about to spring up. I'm exhausted. If you help with my little problem, I'll distract you from yours, at least until the next fire crops up."

"Where are you staying?"

"The Firebrand. My usual room."

"Give me an hour to shower and assemble myself into a human woman."

"I'm counting the minutes, gorgeous."

"See you soon, playboy." I hang up. "God, I really need another shower now."

"Well done. Now what?"

"Now…I get ready for my date with the devil."

CHAPTER EIGHTEEN

HEART OF STONE

How far are you willing to go for someone you love?

We all think we'd walk to the ends of the earth. Storm a castle. Throw ourselves off a cliff if it meant they would live. Most people never have to face this trial. They've never been pushed to that edge. If they were, would they flounder? Stare at the castle but never enter? Hold onto the edge of the cliff and let him fall? I failed this test once. I held on and he fell. I won't fail again. I'd rather die than live with the guilt. If I have to give my body to the monster, if I have to strangle him with my bare hands, I will. I am not leaving without the information I need.

I will not fail.

"You are a sight for sore eyes, gorgeous."

I cannot.

I plaster on my smile and even bite my lower lip seductively. "And I come bearing gifts," I say, holding up two hot chocolates. I hand him the one with whip cream. And roofies. "Mr. Sweet Tooth."

"You remembered," he says, taking my offering. He steps aside to let me in. I hobble through the door. "What? What's the matter? Why are you limping?"

"Ever have a bone marrow biopsy? I don't recommend it."

He shuts the door. "Bone marrow?"

"Seems I not only have a killer rack, but my immune system ain't no slouch either. They think my marrow might help with a vaccine or cure." I lower myself onto the couch. "They better work fast."

Bennett sits on the couch beside me, close enough I sense his body heat. "I'm so sorry this happened to you." He reaches across and brushes a stray strand of hair from my forehead. I suppress a cringe. "I've been so fucking worried about you. I haven't been able to concentrate on anything when I desperately need to."

Yeah. Right. I plaster on a sweet smile. "It's so surreal, you know," I say before taking a sip of my cocoa. "Ryder dying like that. The virus…" I shake my head and take another sip. "Jem's…dying and all that goes along with it. Guilt. Regret. Grief. Even after all he put me through, I did love him once upon a time. And he was only at that house because of me."

"It's not your fault," Bennett says sincerely. "You *know* it's not your fault."

"Ugh." I take another sip of cocoa. This time he does too. Keep drinking, asshole. "I haven't slept in three days, which isn't helping matters. Oh, and let's not forget we have next to fucking nothing on whoever did this." Another sip for us both. "Those Motoneslly bastards got wind of our investigation and cleaned house. What we do have is gonna take weeks to investigate, which won't save Jem or anyone if they've already released this virus worldwide." I drink again. He does as well. "You know I thought Jem was a genius, but whoever planned this…" Another sip. "I almost admire them."

"Why?" he asks before another gulp of cocoa.

"I don't know. The dedication? The patience? The intelligence involved? We have the top minds on this, several world governments, and they're still ten steps ahead of us." Another sip for us both. "The only mistake they made was letting Ryder escape. If he hadn't, we never would have known about any of this until it was too late. Hell, it still may be too late."

He's about to open his mouth to spew lies, when his phone buzzes. Instead, he sighs. "I'm sorry."

"No, you're busy. Take it. Go."

He rises from the couch, drink in hand. "Just give me a minute, and I'm all yours, gorgeous. I swear." He begins walking to the door, pressing the phone to his ear. "Bennett Stone."

The moment the door shuts after he steps into the hallway, I leap up to follow. I press my ear against the closed door. Shit, he must have walked down the hall. I can't make out the words. Asshole. Fine. I hobble back to the sofa. "He's on the phone," I say into my watch/communicator to Justin who waits a floor below. "The computer's on the desk. I've seen him with another laptop model, so I'll have to find it too. Stand-by."

I don't dare start snooping now. Good decision too because Bennett returns a few seconds shy of a minute, all smiles. "I'm sorry. I'm so sorry. I'm shutting it off now."

"You don't have to. You're busy. I understand."

"I know you do, but I'm gonna shut it off anyway," he says with that smile of his.

I force one to my face. "I'm honored."

"Besides, this is far more interesting than a real estate deal." The monster sits beside me again. "I'm only sorry I couldn't help you more." He takes a sip. "Did you ever get in touch with Dr. Sharpesh? I have a call into him, but he hasn't responded."

"Yeah, after I spoke to you, he sent me an email. I have a call into him too, but we have a few dozen other doctors already on this, we don't really need him."

"Well, I'll try again anyway."

I touch his hand. "Thank you." I squeeze it. "And thank you for listening. There's…no one else. And it's just so goddamn much, you know? I thought I was dying. Harry…Jem…the whole fucking world…I…" Okay, I'm genuinely getting emotional now. I shake my head to clear it. "I don't want to talk about this anymore. I don't want to *think* about it anymore. Take my mind off things, playboy." I take a sip. "Give me good news. How is Nathalie?"

A sip. "Still doing well. Attending meetings. Focusing on her fashion. I have real hope this time." Another sip. "Thanks in part to you."

"A very small part." Another sip. "And *our* little girl? Our society hasn't toppled since I've been neglecting her?"

"I'm sorry, but between work and worrying about you, I've been an absent parent as well. I get the odd update, but as far as I'm aware, everything's on schedule."

"Let's just pray there will be a need for the Society by the time it's set up." He chuckles and gulps his drink. "What?"

"A need for charity. In a perfect world, there would be none."

"This situation might be the exception to the rule," I point out.

"You got me there." He takes and squeezes my hand again. "You have such a good heart, Joanna Fallon. I adore that about you. Your heart…everything about that general area," he says with a smirk. Here we go. Moment of truth. He reaches up to cradle my face, caressing my cheek with his thumb. "I was terrified when you were in there." I believe him.

"You've come to mean a lot to me. More than I knew until all this happened."

"I'm sure you say that to all the girls just coming out of quarantine," I say with a smirk.

"Got me," he says with the same smile before it slowly drops. "But it's true in this case."

"Ben—"

He leans across and presses his lips to mine. Thank God. I was worried I'd vomit in his mouth or bite his tongue clean off, but I don't feel a damn thing. It helps when I close my eyes. Now he's nothing but a stranger. A random man massages my tongue. Runs his hand through my hair. Squeezes my breast. Lowers me down on the couch. Presses his erection against my thigh. I can do this. I can—

I let out a cry of pain when his hip presses against my wound. The hands and mouth lift off my body, and I open my eyes, greeted by confusion and concern in his brown eyes. "Did I hurt you?"

"I…I don't think we should…I still feel dirty. Infected. And my hip…"

He strokes my hair. "I understand."

"You do?"

"Of course," he says before kissing me again.

"Can you just…hold me? I never thought I'd miss just having arms wrapped around me. Just for a little while?"

"Okay," he says, still stroking and smiling. "Gladly."

Thank God.

We move to the bed, and with the gentlest of care, he removes my shoes and helps me lie down. He climbs in beside me, wrapping his arms around me and nestling against my back. At least I don't have to look at him now. "I'm exhausted," I whisper.

He tenderly kisses the back of my neck. "I'll bet. Saving humanity really takes it out of you."

"Just hold me until I fall asleep," I whisper. Or you do.

He kisses my hair. "You got it, gorgeous."

The drug takes anywhere from fifteen minutes to half an hour to take effect. It takes him twenty-five minutes before I sense him fully relax and begin breathing heavily. Feels like a damn hour. "Bennett?" I ask loudly. No response. "About fucking time." I gently peel his tentacles off me. "He's out. Stand-by."

As quietly and gently as possible, I rise from the bed and tip-toe back to my purse for my tools. His cell phone is easy to clone, just a simple download of every number, website, and GPS coordinates on there. He might have another phone or at least another SIM card, so as the download continues of the phone and computer on the desk, I begin my search of the hotel room. Okay, I'm looking for another computer, another phone, and any papers that might prove useful. He probably hid the incriminating good stuff before I arrived. There's nothing on the desk and the files in his briefcase seem useless. I take a picture of them on my phone anyway.

Okay so, if I needed to hide my nefarious evidence, where would be the best spot? I check the drawers, the dresser, even under the corners of the mattress. Where—

Bennett moans, damn near making my heart leap out of my mouth, and turns over onto his back. I stand still for ten tense seconds before even blinking. He remains asleep. He should be out for hours with no memory of anything, but I'm not going to bet my life on it. Just every super in the world's life.

The one place I haven't checked is the room safe. Most five star hotels don't place safes in the closet, so I check behind every painting. I find it behind the Galilee cityscape. Fuck. Guess my luck just ran out. I grab my purse and put in the earwig. "Guardian to Knight, come in," I whisper.

"Knight here," Justin says.

"We have a safe. Keypad. Remington A2. Thoughts?"

"Let me see if I can find the override code."

Think, Jo. Think. What would he— "I need Molly Stone's birth and death dates."

"Stand-by."

Gives me time to secure the cell phone information. The download's done, but I've been around scumbags long enough to know their tricks. He must switch out the SIM cards. We only get one shot at this, I have to be through. I move to the bed. Here comes the real test of luck. I gently reach into his pants pockets. He doesn't stir. Jesus, he really has the face of an angel. Soft. Serene. Handsome. I want to scratch it to pieces. Bite his nose off. Instead I look away and get the SIM card. He's nothing but a common criminal after all.

As I switch the cards and prep to download again, Justin says, "Found the dates. Still working on the override."

"Give me the dates then stand by."

With the new SIM card downloading, I return to the safe. Please let this work. Her birthday? Nope. Birthday in reverse? No. Death date? No. Fuck. Death day in reverse? The light turns green. Goddamn, I'm good. And my reward is a thick stack of papers and another laptop. Jackpot.

As the second computer downloads, I snap pictures of all the papers with my cell phone. A lot of it's medical and business crap I don't take time to comprehend. There are so many pages it takes ten minutes to finish. The second laptop download takes the same amount of time. The monster doesn't move. I may actually get away clean. All that remains is to bug his room phone, the room itself, put a tracer/wire in his cell, and pat myself on the back. One hour and I have all his secrets. Mata Hari had nothing on me.

I pack up my purloined Intel and gadgets before scribbling a note for my slumbering psychopath. "*Thanks. XOXO Jo.*" I place it on the nightstand and slip the SIM card back in his pocket. Like nothing happened. Not wanting to press my suddenly amazing luck, I tip toe out of the room, gently shutting the door. God willing that's the last time I'll ever see that fucker until the trial. "Knight, I'm clear. Meet me in the lobby."

"Copy."

When the elevator doors close, I finally let out the breath I've been holding the past hour and a half. I love the rare times a plan goes off without a hitch. They are few and too fucking far between. When the elevator door opens, Justin stands in front of me, sighing himself when he sets eyes on me. "Mission accomplished, rich boy."

We both smile at one another. "Excellent work, Guardian. Never doubted you."

"Liar," I say as I start walking to the lobby. "But onto Phase Two, which hopefully requires a lot less saliva."

"Phase Two?"

"The phase where you drop me off at the hospital to cash in some brownie points before sending this data to our minions to analyze. Top priority. I have the distinct sense things are about to go downhill from here, rich boy. I'm taking advantage of the eye of the shit storm."

"Always the pessimist, Jo."

"If you aren't a pessimist in this world, my friend, then you haven't been paying attention."

He chuckles. "Then why fight at all?"

"For those rare moments when I'm wrong."

*

Thank God the HEPA mask and plastic glasses hide most of my face because I can't fully contain my horror when I set eyes on my once mighty fiancée. It could be the overhead UV lights or all the tubes and machines attached to him, but though it's only been a little over half a day since I last saw him, Jem's deterioration terrifies me. He's always been thin but now he's almost emaciated. His skin has a yellowish tint and the dark circles under his eyes and in the hollows of his cheeks are black as coal. Hours. It's only been *hours*.

"Jem?"

"Joanna?" he croaks before coughing. That wet hack he endures almost brings tears to my eyes. I shut them down. I shut all emotion down and close an iron door on it. He needs me strong. Fierce. Capable. I rush over to the water pitcher beside him and pour. He takes the water which thank God helps. "Th-Thank you."

I pull up a chair to his bedside. "Are they treating you for that?"

He nods yes. "I'm going for a procedure to aspirate my lungs in an hour. It will drain the fluid and mucous that keeps building up."

My fear momentarily crashes against the iron. "I'm sorry."

"I'll be able to breathe, that's all that matters." He reaches for my gloved hand, and we lock our fingers together. God I wish I could touch him. "I'm so glad you're here."

"Danforth and Dr. Westfield took my threat about pulling funding seriously. Cut some red tape for me."

"Bullied your way in, huh?"

"I'd burn this place down if that's what it took."

"No, you wouldn't," he says, squeezing my hand again with the strength of a newborn.

"They don't know that. I'm only a puppy dog around you, my love." I pause. "Besides, you won't be in here much longer."

"What do you mean?"

I wish he could see me smile behind the mask. "We got him."

"Him?"

"The mastermind. Better, we're zeroing in on a cure. A Dr. Sharpesh has developed an adenovirus that kills adenoviruses. He just landed in town. He's on his way to the command center now to kill this fucker."

"That's...amazing. Who-Who—"

"Bennett Stone."

Jem stares at me, bloody eyes zeroing in on my own. "Really?"

"Really. You were right about him. He's..." I shiver. "He's gonna pay for what he's done to you. To us."

"Just be careful. Don't do anything crazy."

"Me? Crazy? Perish the thought," I quip. I press our hands to the only part of me exposed, my cheekbone. "What about Austen Castle?"

"What about it?" he rasps.

"Where we'll get married. We didn't talk about it the first time around, but I know you. You want a big to-do. White gown, flowers, chocolate fountain. After this I think you've earned a damn chocolate fountain, no?"

"I do love chocolate," he whispers.

"Then I think Austen Castle is perfect, no? We had our first semi-date there. Remember? The labyrinth?"

"How could I forget? I fell in love with you in that labyrinth," he whispers.

"'No matter how many twists, how many turns, as long as you solider through as long as you don't give into despair, you'll always reach your destination.' You taught me that."

"I think the Castle is perfect," he whispers. "I can't wait to—" he coughs.

And coughs. And coughs until he cannot breathe. Until his face becomes red. He can't breathe. Shit. I pour more water but now he's doubled over, hacking out green then red tinged mucous on the floor. Oh, God. The nurses and doctor are stuck in the UV compartment for a minute, a minute where all I can do is pat his back and tell him everything will be all right even though he's not getting air. For every ten seconds he takes one shallow breath, only to expel that hard won gasp with more agony. Oh, God. Oh, God. I don't think I've ever felt so helpless in my life. When the staff finally hurry into the room, he hasn't taken a breath in thirty seconds and the blood he's coughing up spreads like ink spots on the sheets. I back away in horror as the doctor and nurses take over, lowering the gurney while a nurse wheels over a machine. "Ms. Fallon, leave now!" the doctor orders. Jem grips the bed as they stick a tube down his throat and vacuum out his lungs. I have to turn away before the iron inside shatters, and I lose my fucking mind. "Now, Miss Fallon!"

I'm walking away without realizing it. I'm ripping off my mask as the UV lights kill the virus on me so I can breathe after this deed is done. He'll be fine. They'll fix him. This is the best hospital in the country. He'll be fine. *He'll be fine.* When the airtight door finally opens onto the next room, I rip off all my protective gear and step into the hallway. I have to sit down and put my head between my legs to stave off another panic attack. He was fine hours ago. "He'll be fine, he'll be fine," I keep repeating in time to my jittering leg. I can't sit for too long. When I'm sure I'm not going to pass out, I begin pacing the hall. He'll be fine. He will. When I hear the door swish open about five minutes later and the doctors and nurse step out, I run toward them. "Is he okay? Is he—"

"We drained the fluid, but we're pushing up the surgery."

"Okay. Good. Great."

"Ms. Fallon, this surgery is merely a stop-gap. Dr. Ambrose's lung, kidney, and liver functions are deteriorating at an alarming rate. Dialysis may be required and—"

"Listen, I'm going to assume you know what he is and what his body is normally capable of. Right now there is a team working on an experimental cure, a virus that will attack and destroy the one inside him. We just need *time*. Do you understand, doctor? I have his power of attorney. You have my permission to do anything, and I mean *anything* to keep him alive. And you will do just that or I will make it my life's mission to have your license to practice revoked. You won't be able to sell tongue depressors."

"There's no need for threats," the doctor snaps.

"I'm not threatening, I'm *promising*. Now, can I see him?"

"No. He's getting prepped for transport to surgery. He shouldn't be talking anyway. You never should have gone in there in the first place. We have rules for a reason. Now, if you'll excuse me, I have a patient to attend to."

The doctor spins around and starts back to the ward. Okay, that was stupid of me. I shouldn't have lost my temper and threatened him. Now he may never let me in again. Hell, maybe I shouldn't go in. I made everything worse. What can I do? I have to…I fall back into a chair and use all my willpower to stop the tears. The iron trap's cracked. Some tears stream out, and I wipe them away. I will not crumble. I will not shatter. So I get up and walk away. I'm no good here. I'll fall apart again if I stay. I locate a nurse, tell him to call me the moment Jem's out of surgery, and run out of this wretched hospital as if it were about to explode. Again.

To clear my head and work off the tension, I walk the ten blocks back to the penthouse. A bad idea. Every other person coughs. I cringe each time. From now on Justin isn't leaving the penthouse again without a HEPA mask on. None of them should. I'm not even sure I should return home in case my clothes or something infect my friend. Hell, a large part of me just wants to run away. Hop on a plane and ride out the apocalypse on a beach alone with a bottle of Jack. I don't want this responsibility. Because if we fail…I'll never be able to live with myself. I won't want to live period.

The walk does bring my tension level down enough I'm no longer trembling, at least from the adrenaline. I am frozen to the core. Justin sits in the living room, phone to his ear when I enter. Hard at work. "…someone's breaking the encryptions now. When he's done, I'll parse sections out.

There's so much data already. You just handle what I sent. We're looking for a facility west of Galilee and any medical data on the virus itself. That's the priority. Contact us if you find anything. Bye." He turns to me. "Hi. How is he?"

"Coughing up blood and in surgery."

"Fuck."

I join him on the couch. "Tell me you have good news."

"The second SIM card and laptop are both encrypted. We have people on it, but it may take a few hours. I'm organizing packets of data for the others to review of what we do have. Good news is Lionheart checked in. The Sharpesh family is settling into the safe house and the doctor has joined the research team at Our Lady. Olympia's guarding him."

"Bennett's gonna hear about that soon. When he wakes."

"Still asleep. His hotel phone rang a few times and he didn't answer."

"Did you gain access to the hotel's phone system?"

"I did. And I've already checked both incoming and outgoing. Two numbers, both unlisted, but one is local. That number's billing address is the Motoneslly office in New Urbana."

"So a dead end."

"Not entirely," Justin says with a grin. "I did find the cell tower the second call came from." He pulls up a map of Poplarville, the suburb west of Galilee, with a gray circle covering a ten mile radius. "I'd bet my life our lab is somewhere in that circle."

We kind of are. "We can't narrow it down?"

"No. Sorry."

"No, this is good. We cross-reference this area with the shipping forms and what we got from the unencrypted Stone files."

"Judging from this map, half the area is residential with strip malls, a quarter warehouses, and a quarter undeveloped."

"They'd want privacy so residential, even a shutdown strip mall, is out. Cuts it in half."

"I could run that in an hour. I'll suit up"

As he rises from the couch, I say, "Wear the HEPA mask. Don't take any chances."

"Yes, Aunt Lucy."

"Bite me, rich boy."

His chuckle carries on as he walks to the hallway. And I'll be here with the paperwork. He absolutely has the better job. I barely have time to retrieve the printed photos from my phone from the printer when he returns in gray sweats that cover the majority of his white and black costume. "I've linked my comms to the computer. The list of emails is up already and the packets assembled. There's only a few more to send."

"I can handle it."

He picks up the HEPA mask on the coffee table. "No doubt about that. Be back in an hour and a half."

"Be careful," I call as he leaves.

I fall back on the couch and sigh. We've gone from the whole world to five square miles. Almost worth having that asshole's tongue down my throat. First, I send out the remainder of the packets to the supers before digging into the data myself. Anything with medical jargon I forward to Dr. Sharpesh. I'm not smart enough to know what's important. The rest mostly consists of spread sheets. I quit my job to avoid having to stare at these things and here I am being bored to death again. At least now I'm suffering for something more important than a bottom line.

So far he's spent thirty billion on this project yet recouped half that with Motoneslly and Goliath selling the companies they no longer needed. Blackwater alone netted fifty million. That'll buy a lot of mercenaries. The prison break mercs probably came from another company bought and sold, Red Reaver Enterprises, an elite mercenary company in England. Sold six months ago. Probably at least sixteen employees short. Motoneslly loved buying and selling biotechs as well. Seven in total. My guess they'd buy up the company for their research, and when they got the needed information, they sold. You build one part here, another somewhere else, soon enough you've got yourself an atomic bomb with no one the wiser.

"Guardian, copy," Justin says over my headset.

"Guardian here."

"One possible. 17654 Feige Ave. Seeing a lot of security."

"Stand by." I plug in the address. "Owned by Carl Slater Holdings. Name's not familiar. Stand by." A few minutes later, "Not on the spreadsheets. Slater is a developer in Poplarville. I'm staring at a pic of him winning an award from the Chamber of Commerce. Stone wouldn't rent."

"Something's going on here."

"What kind of cars do you see?"

"Uh, SUVs, Escalades, a Hummer."

"Probably drugs then. Ryder stole a fleet car. It follows all the people at the lab are driving them. And guess who owns the fleet service?"

"Goliath."

"A subsidiary, yep." I hear a phone faintly ring in my other ear. "Stand by. Stone's getting another call." I pull up the tracer program. "Same number as before, but...not the same cell tower." It's from the one near his hotel. Shit.

Over the bug, I hear a knock on the hotel door. Then a few seconds, another pound. Bennett groans. Another pound. "C-Coming," Bennett says. A few more seconds I hear him say, "W-What? What are you doing here?" he asks groggily.

"We've been trying to reach you for two hours, sir," a British man says.

"I-I must have fallen asleep. I—"

"Sir," the Brit exclaims, scared.

"I-I need to sit down."

Shit. Shit, shit, shit, shit, shit. The drug hasn't had time to wear off. "Knight, Stone woke up. I think we've been compromised."

"Wh-Where's...her? Uh...Joanna. Fallon?" Stone asks.

"Sir, I think you need a doctor."

Shit. "Yeah, we've been compromised."

"Guardian, pack up and get out of there," Justin commands.

Yeah. I unplug Doris Jr. and hurry to the bedroom for my suitcase. "Sir, I'm calling a doctor. I think you've been drugged," the Brit says over my computer.

"N-No," Stone says. "H-Help me...safe."

I throw what little I've unpacked back inside the suitcase. "Guardian?" Justin asks.

"He's checking the safe. Where should we meet?" I hustle into Jem's office for the secret stash.

"It's all here," Bennett says over my headset. "I..."

"Sir!" the Brit shouts.

Guns, Taser, code breakers, everything I returned to him before I left for Independence. I grab as much as I can fit into the satchel. "I'm fine," Bennett says. "I don't need a doctor. Why are you here? What happened?"

"Dr. Sharpesh has gone off the grid," the Brit says. "Vanished. We had someone on his house, but they snuck past him."

"Joanna," Bennett says before chuckling. Damn straight asshole. I close the satchel. "Duncan, we've been compromised."

"Then why haven't the authorities—"

"I don't know," he snaps. "She's up to something. Maybe she just suspects...we're leaving. Don't say another word. Come with me."

Fuck. "Knight, he's ditching the hotel. The cell will be next. We need to find that facility right fucking now before he burns it down or something." I throw our cell phones, the papers, all our evidence into the satchel. "You keep searching. I'm on my way to Poplarville."

"I'm parked at Maple Park," Justin says. "Meet you there in half an hour. Be safe."

"Guardian out." I unplug the headset and power down Doris. We need to—

My cell phone rings, and I jerk in shock. My trembling hands remove it from my purse. Bennett. I don't know what to do. Pretend? No. I throw the phone back in my purse. I need a plan before we talk.

Suitcase, satchel, purse, and computer bag secured, I flee yet another apartment. I am getting so goddamn sick of being on the defense. I get into the elevator. We probably now have all of an hour before all the evidence, the facility, the cure is gone. Once again all we have is what we've got now. If we don't get those files unencrypted, we're fucked.

The elevator door opens, and I hurry through the lobby past Paul, one of the doormen. "I need a taxi."

He takes some bags and follows me outside. "Leaving again, ma'am?"

"Yeah. To the airport," I lie.

A taxi waiting down the street pulls up. We throw my bags in the trunk before I climb in. "Maple Park in Poplarville."

The taxi drives off. Okay, I need a plan. I need—

The taxi turns the corner before coming to a full stop. "Excuse—"

I barely have time to register it as a man climbs into the back with me. One word screams out: DANGER. Shit. I reach into my purse for my gun, but not fast enough. The moment I look away, something sharp pierces my skin. There isn't even time to cry out before the world turns black.

Gotta give the devil his due. He got me.

CHAPTER NINETEEN

GODS + MONSTERS

A sharp stab against the crook of my arm suddenly brings me back to the land of the living. Whatever they pump inside me this time makes my whole body jolt as if stuck by a live wire. My eyes fly open, and my legs kick, but the rest of me tries to move with no luck. It takes a second for me to realize I'm zip-tied to a chair and another to remeber this fact should frighten me. As should the huge man, easily 6"4' and two hundred fifty pounds in front of me holding a needle. "She's awake, sir," says the man with a familiar British accent.

My tormenter steps aside, and without the need for my addled brain to process his largess, I can take in my surroundings. Just a boring, ordinary medium sized office. The last time I was held hostage it was in a shipping boat miles from land strapped to a giant bomb. There may be no ship and no bomb this time but my kidnapper is no less dangerous. Bennett Stone stands a few feet away at the cheap desk, staring over the shoulders of two men tapping away at their respective computers, one of which looks familiar. Doris Jr. Fuck.

"Get her some water, Duncan," Bennett says, never taking his eyes off Doris' monitor.

The henchmen obeys, walking over to the water pitcher by the bank of surveillance monitors. Over the screens I see people hustling down hallways in Hazmat suits pushing boxes. More in labs packing up equipment or at computers. A warehouse with huge metal tanks and more people in Hazmat suits packing up smaller cylinders. Screens and screens with empty gurneys. Swiveling views of an empty field surrounded by a barbed wire fence, and a parking lot with sedans and vans getting loaded with boxes and equipment. I'm here. The facility. Not how I wanted to find it. I—shit. I press down on my ring finger, activating the tracer under my skin before Duncan returns with my water. Please God, still work. He pours it into my mouth with such little grace I choke. Bennett gazes up from Doris, mouth opening a little in concern. "Easy, Duncan. Don't drown her."

I keep hacking until I can breathe again. "W-Where am I?"

"Don't play dumb, gorgeous," Bennett chides. "It doesn't suit you."

"How long have I been unconscious?"

"About two hours. Same as I was."

"So this was revenge? I drug you, you drug me?"

"I know how important equality and fairness are to you," he says with that goddamn smile of his. He pats the two men at the desk on their shoulders. "Guys, why don't you continue that in the next room? My lover and I need privacy." The men unplug their computers and rise. Duncan doesn't move. "You as well, Duncan."

"Sir, should you—"

"She's tied to a chair. Just wait outside the door. If you hear screaming—well, *my* screaming—then come in. But only then."

Duncan glares at me, but begins toward the door. "Yes, sir."

Bennett's smirking eyes never leave me as the men depart. Duncan slams the door behind me and the loud noise makes me jump. With whatever they injected in me, and the normal adrenaline boost I tend to get when in mortal danger, I'm trembling and my heart beats double time. Bennett grabs a chair from the desk and begins dragging it toward me. "You know…when I fantasized about tying you up, and having you at my mercy, this is not what I had in mind." He sits about three feet away, just out of range of my legs if I choose to kick him.

"How long did you have people following me?"

"Since you left the mansion. For this very contingency. In case you hadn't noticed, I place great importance on contingency plans." He folds his arms across his chest. "So, I have questions for you, and I am positive you have many for me. Since I too find equality and fairness paramount, we will take turns. I'll begin if you don't mind. We've found no evidence the government is aware of my involvement with the virus. All we have found in your computer are emails to private accounts. So who knows about me, gorgeous?"

"It's been two hours. My people could have sent all the intel to anyone by now. Especially if I've gone missing. Everyone at the end of those private accounts know who you are and what you've done. You're fucked."

He twitches. "What precisely *do* you have?"

"You have my computer. You know. *Everything.* I made copies of all the files in your safe and downloaded both SIM cards and laptops. Every company, every transaction, every dirty deed, over a dozen people now have access to it. All your planning, all your contingencies, its all gone down the tubes because of one errant supervillain and your need to get laid."

The sides of his mouth twitch. "And Dr. Sharpesh. Where is he?"

"In a lab somewhere under heavy guard creating a cure. I don't know what lab if that's your next question. I didn't ask. My allies are big on compartmentalizing. There'll be a cure in days. It's over, Bennett. You're about to become the planet's most wanted man. If you were half as intelligent as I thought you were, you'd be halfway to Brazil starting life under a new identity."

"Obviously I have planned my disappearance—I would be a fool not to—but some things supersede the life of one man. In the grand scheme, what is my existence versus the millions my actions will save?" He scoffs. "*You* of all people should understand that, Jo. How many times have you risked your life for that very tenant?"

"Don't you dare fucking compare us, asshole. What you've done is-is…monstrous. It's genocide, Bennett."

"No, it's simple arithmetic. Kill one million to save ten. You're a pragmatist. Can you really discount those numbers?" He leans in closer to me. "You were there that night at the theater. That girl, that innocent girl, died in our arms for the simple crime of going to a film. White Knight didn't give her a single thought when the supposed hero was allegedly trying to save the city. All he saved was his pride for not letting his opponent best him. He's a murderer lauded as a hero. Th-There's no accountability. No one puts them in check and innocents suffer. *No*. I say no. Not on my watch."

"By your logic, Bennett, I should want all men dead on the off chance they'll commit rape. Maybe we should kill all the poor because they commit the most crimes. Where does it fucking end, Stone? What right do you have to play God?"

"The job was vacant," he says before shaking his head. "You know, as a victim of their crimes, I really thought you could at least open your mind a little and see where I'm coming from. Justin Pendergast and Jem Ambrose both dragged you into their hells. You were beaten, broken, betrayed because of their little power games. Can you honestly tell me your life has been enriched by your involvement with these men?"

"*Yes,*" I say, leaning forward. "Abso-fucking-lutly. You know why? Because they showed me what sacrifice is. What love is. They helped me realize you can either overcome the shit hand you got dealt or let it corrupt you. Your family died, Bennett. And I'm sorry, I truly am, but I lost my family too. I lost my father, my mother, my best friend, hell my whole fucking life more than once. But you don't see me using my wealth and power to punish innocent people, innocent *children* who had no choice in being born different just to avenge something they had nothing to do with."

"Vengeance doesn't factor into this, Jo," he insists.

"Bullshit. If your sister died in a terrorist bombing you wouldn't have created a virus to go after Arabs? If the mafia put out a hit on them it wouldn't be Italians facing extinction? You may need to dress it up as altruism to get through the day, but from where I'm sitting this is just a damaged, sad, angry little boy lashing out. And *I* would know. More than once in my life I was you." I catch his weary eyes. "And that's how I also know you can come back from this, Bennett. There is still good in you. I've seen it. You were a friend when I truly needed one. I've seen how you are with your friends. How wonderful you were with that girl in her final moments. You've just let hate corrupt you. I've been there, but if I could fight it back, you can too. Right here. Right now. There's still time to call this off and just go. Run. You can just…let it go. Let the hate go and live your life."

"Are you trying to save me, Joanna? Or are you trying to save them? Him? Your *fiancée*?" He breaks eye contact and shakes his head again. "Ten years. This has been my life's mission, my life's work for ten years. And what brings it almost crashing down? The one time I put myself before the project. When I heard you were infected, I made sure you had the serum. Because I couldn't bear for you to suffer even a little because of my actions. Because I care about you. Even now. And I even believe you still care about me. So I am *really* trying to get you to see the light on this."

"What do you think I'm trying to do, Bennett? I do care about you. And I do know why you think you have to do this. But you *don't*. This will not bring your family back. It will not bring Molly or Ariana back. All this will do is turn you into the biggest monster the world has ever seen. Your family, your legacy will be mired in hatred and cursed forever. And while you watch children cough up blood, while you listen to your victim's sobs and pleas to God for deliverance, you will realize just how wrong you were." I pause and close my eyes. "I don't believe this is who you truly are. I don't. And I know, I *know* the man I laughed with, cried with, who comforted a scared girl, my *friend* is in there begging you to stop this. Listen to us, playboy. Trust us." I open my eyes again. "This is it, Bennett. The moment. The moment when you decide: darkness or light. Hate or forgiveness. Rise above…or fall."

My friend's eye twitches, and I think I've gotten through. That the man I hoped he was is inside there. That even the greatest sinner can be redeemed. But the corners of his mouth fall with disappointment, I know I'm wrong. My heart breaks a little inside my chest. Damn it. Some people are just too far gone. "There is no talking to you, is there? Stubborn as hell even now. I admire that about you. I do. Holding strong to your convictions. But you can only see black and white, Jo. The world is gray, gorgeous. Always has been and always will be." He rises from the chair. "I don't know if what I'm doing is right or wrong. I can only trust my instincts. 'The only way for evil to win is for good men to do nothing.' I *will not* do nothing anymore." His handsome face falls. "My only regret is what I have to do now. Please know I didn't want this. I did all in my power to make sure it didn't. What has to happen now...*you* will haunt me until my dying day, Jo," he says, voice brittle. "You're a hell of a woman. A good friend. We could have..." He sadly smiles as his face almost crumbles from regret. "But this is bigger than you and I. *This* is the right thing. This is how it has to be." He starts toward the door. "I don't believe you about Dr. Sharpesh. Maybe Duncan and his bag of tricks will have better luck. I'm sorry, Jo. From the depths of my soul, I am sorry. I'll miss the hell out of you. Good-bye, gorgeous. Bye."

He walks out of the office, shutting the door behind himself. Shit. *Shit.* God knows how long it'll take someone to get here, if they even remember I have the tracker. Hell, who knows if the damn thing still works. Fuck. Think. I attempt to pull against the zip ties, but they're so tight I can barely feel my fingers. I damn sure feel the rope burns as I struggle against my binds. Double fuck. No go. Hands are out for the moment. Legs, you're up. I rock back and forth in the chair until the momentum helps me to my feet. Yes! Alright, I—

The door handle jangles and the door begins opening again. Shit. I'm still more or less helpless, even on my feet. On instinct I sit back down just as Duncan enters, carrying a black satchel. The bald, dour hulk barely glances at me as he makes his way to the desk.

"We have limited time, Miss Fallon," the Brit says. He sets the satchel on the desk, unrolling it to reveal syringes, scalpels, knives, pliers, everything a torturer could need. It's here. Bile rises into my throat. Okay, here comes the terror. It's been creeping forward and is almost here. "We've rigged the facility to vaporize and the boss fears your friends are closing in." He removes the pliers and a knife from the collection. I saw the pictures of what happened to the prison guard Garr to get the codes and key. Flayed, cut, lost fingernails, broken limbs. My breath catches. "So I'm afraid the psychological dance I normally perform is cancelled."

"Please. Don't," I gasp.

The veins in his neck bulge as his jaw tightens with disapproval. And a flash of inspiration from the lizard, Neanderthal part of my brain fills my terrified mind. Okay. Okay. Yeah. I can do it. I already did once. No choice then, no choice now. I start breathing heavily, almost panting as he stops a few feet in front of me. He holds up the pliers and knife. "Fingernails or flaying? The choice is yours."

I can do it. *I can do it.*

Still panting as if I've climbed a mountain twice in a row, I gaze down and mumble to myself. I can do this. "I-I'm sorry?" Duncan asks. I mumble again, softer this time. He moves closer, but I don't look up. "Say that again." I mutter in a whisper this time. He's right by my face now, so close I can feel his hot breath on my cheek. He presses the knife's tip against my chin. "I said speak up—"

Now!

As fast as possible, before I lose my nerve, I bite into his neck like an alligator leaping out of the water to catch its prey. I bite. *Hard*. Hot blood fills my mouth, spilling down my chin as the man howls in agony. He pulls away, leaving a large chunk of flesh in my mouth as blood spews all over him down to the floor. He only makes it one step before, with all my might, I kick him in the balls. Once. Twice. Three times until the motherfucker falls to his knees in his own blood. I take all of a moment to spit out the hunk of meat before rocking forward to my feet. The henchman barely has time to register I'm mobile before I twist at my hip and swing the chair right into his face. He finally falls to his back, dazed. I stare at him, my breath still coming out in pants as the adrenaline courses through my every cell. "I said, this is for Garr asshole."

He reaches for his side arm. Fine. Without hesitation, I position the side of the chair right above his already ravaged throat and bring the fucker down on his windpipe with the full force of my weight. Bones, tendons, cartilage all crack. Nothing. I'm beyond feelings. His hands seize several seconds, trying to move the chair, to claw my legs until they cease moving completely. Until he's dead. I throw up all over the floor a second later.

I only grant my body and mind ten seconds to recover before the Neanderthal gains control again. I hurry over to the desk and fumble to retrieve a knife. Thirty seconds and many bleeding cuts later, the first zip tie comes off with the second a moment later. "Okay, okay," I pant to myself. Second order of business. I rinse out my mouth and wash off the blood from my chin. Okay, a plan. I need a plan. I pick up the phone on the desk but there's no dial tone. Fuck. I need to get out of here. The place is set to blow. That's why they're packing up. I need—

Fuck. Shit. It'll all be gone. The data for the cure. Where they intend to send the virus. And Bennett. If he leaves here, he'll never be seen again. Even if I get the data out and Dr. Sharpesh develops a cure, if he's out there in the world, he can start again. Ten years from now we could be right back here with no warning this time. No. This has to end. Tonight.

As I clean off the blood, I watch the surveillance monitors. Things are slowing down in the warehouse. No more canisters moving around, no more vans outside. People in lab coats and Hazmat suits still filter up and down the halls. Where are you asshole? Where…there. In camera 113 Bennett, a woman in a lab coat, and the two computer nerds from before stand in another office. One of the nerds hands something small from the computer to Bennett, who pats the man on the back, before walking out with the lab coat. A moment later I see Bennett step into the hallway and hurry down it, chatting with the woman. Two huge men in black join the walking duo, flanking them. Okay.

A spare white lab coat is draped over the desk chair. I slip it on. It covers some of the wet blood on my shirt but everyone seems too busy to pay each other much attention. It'll have to do. It also covers the knives I put in each pocket and the dead man's gun I clip to the waist of my pants. God willing I won't need them. I'm so into ransacking the corpse I don't notice the cell phone in his pocket until I've already stood. Thank you, Jesus. I dial Justin's cell first but it switches to voice mail. "Justin, it's Jo. I-I'm in the facility. I don't know where exactly. I-I've turned on my tracker. Follow it. I…They're-They're-It's going to blow up. I need to find Bennett. I…just get here, okay? Bye." I hang up and dial 911 this time.

"911 what is your emergency?" the dispatcher asks.

"He-Hello, this is Joanna Fallon. I-I've been kidnapped. I-I'm…I don't know where I am. Somewhere in

Poplarville, I think. A man's been killed. And th-there's some sort of bioterrorism event about to occur."

"Ma'am, slow down," the woman says.

I take a breath to calm myself. "Listen, you need to contact whoever is in charge of the Xavier Prison break and Dr. Robert Vaugh at the Health Department. Tell them the virus is shipping right now. One or two white panel vans are loaded with live virus. Level 4 biohazard. We also need the bomb squad. This facility is rigged to blow once the personnel have cleared. Could be five minutes or an hour, I don't know. Responders need to remain out of sight or they could detonate this place prematurely. Bennett Stone. This was all Bennett Stone of Independence. He's behind it all. He attempted to kill me. Contact all airports, helipads, private airfields, train stations and see if he's filed a flight plan."

"Miss Fallon, can you help us find your exact location? Do you see a piece of mail or—"

"No. I need to move from this room. I'm putting the phone in my pocket. Trace it."

I slip the phone into my pocket with the knife, take a deep breath, and step into the hallway. It's relatively empty, only about three people, but I keep my head down and walk with purpose past them. Look like you belong, act like you belong, nine times out of ten no one will question you. The problem is I have no idea where I'm going inside this generic office building with my hip aching with every step. I have to turn around twice before I find room 113. Unholstering the gun, I turn the handle and step inside. The two computer nerds glance behind them to me, or really at the raised gun pointed at them. The man with his paws on Doris Jr. raises them up in surrender.

"Holy shit," the other says.

"Put your hands up too," I order.

The trembling man obeys. "D-Don't—"

"I need access to the facility's records. Everything on the virus, dispersal plans, projections, shipping records, and destinations."

"I-I can't—"

I cock the hammer back and press the gun against his forehead. He closes his eyes and whimpers. "This is not a request, asshole."

"No, h-he really *can't*," the other says. "Mr. Motoneslly had him purge the system. Ev-Everything is being deleted right now."

"Then stop it."

"I-I-I-I *can't*," the nerd says. "O-Once the program st-starts, it can't be shut off. It's mostly deleted now anyway."

Shit. Shit, shit, shit, shit...I take a step back. "Was it sent to another server somewhere? Is there a back-up?" The nerds exchange a worried glance. Fine. I press the barrel against his head again. "Asshole, do not test my patience right now."

"Just tell her!"

"He'll kill us!"

"*I'll* kill you for sure if you don't talk. *Now!*" I roar.

"Mr. Motoneslly!" the other says. "He-He-He has two flash drives Kent made him before the purge."

"And where is he going next?"

"We-We don't know," the other whimpers.

I believe him. I take a step back. The reek of urine is a bit much. "Okay. Both of you move to the corner of the room. Now!" Both rise from their chairs and hustle to the corner. Gun still trained on them, I sit in front of Doris. "What were you doing to my computer?"

"Se-Sending a virus to all the people on your email list t-to crash their computers so they'd lose what you stole from Mr. Motoneslly."

Fuck. "What the hell is the address here?"

"H-here? 7643 Shadowbrooke Rd. Poplarville."

As Doris' comms boot up, I pull out the cell phone. "I'm at 7643 Shadowbrooke Rd, Poplarville." I turn to my hostages. "How long until this place blows?"

"W-We don't know," the pee soaked one answers. "When everyone's clear. Only Mr. Motoneslly and Dr. DeRue can activate the Code Red."

All these people putting their lives in the hands of maniacs. Books and street smarts don't always go hand in hand. "What about the test subjects? Where are they?"

The duo exchange another scared glance. "I-I heard the la-last one died last night."

May God have mercy on their souls. The link to Justin finally boots up on Doris. "White Knight, this is—"

The door opens behind me. By the time I swivel around, and find a woman in a lab coat stepping in, the hostages are shouting, "Get help! Help!"

The woman leaps back into the hallway saying, "Guard! Help! Guard!" Fuck! I leap up from the chair after the woman. "Guard! Guard!"

She rounds the corner out of sight. When I enter the hallway my body stops itself from chasing after her. The bad guys will come from that direction. I quickly spin around and dash the way I came toward the security room. Of course I can't remember exactly where it is. Most doors are locked and the rest are only offices. I have to backtrack until I find a vaguely familiar hall. I always go left when I should go right. I—

The moment I reach the T-junction again two men dressed in black, guns in their hands, zero in on me. Shit. I dash down the hall just as four gunshots ring out. Fuck. Heavy footsteps grow close. This hall's a dead end. What—? Fourth on the left. I remember now. I don't dare look back. I just run to the security room and shut the door. Of course now I'm trapped. Wonderful. There's no lock on the door. Double fuck. Stepping over the dead Duncan, I grab my old chair and jam it under the handle. That'll keep them out for ten seconds. Taking a deep breath, I back away. What, what…think! I hide behind the side of the desk out of sight. It's nothing but plywood. Bullets will rip right through. I've got one chance at this. Three against one. I have only one clip. I—

The door handle jiggles.

Fuck. My heart leaps into my throat. Someone bangs against the door. Fuck. I peek over the top of the desk. The chair shimmies and moves a little. I get on my knees and place my hands and gun level on the desk. "You can do thi—"

Bang! The door and chair fly inward. The henchman's leg is still up from his kick. He doesn't get the opportunity to lower it before I shoot him between the eyes, brains splattering backwards onto his friend. I fire twice more, but the other henchmen's quick reflexes save them. I barely got the second shot out when they duck to either side of the door. My bullets end up in the far wall. Fuck.

I hide behind the desk the moment their guns appear on either side of the door. I cover my head as they fire inside. Nowhere near me. This time. "Cover!" one of them says. Three shots my way, and I don't break cover. I don't need to see to know his partner enters the room. I fire around the desk but no screams of pain. Fuck! What—

One shot rings out at the same time a man howls in pain. I barely have a moment to try to wrap my mind around a scenario when two men's groans begin. I blink and both men zoom past me. Sideways. Into the wall, leaving a crater in the drywall. One lands on top of the other. Another blink, and a tall man in a lab coat and HEPA mask brings his fist down on the top henchman's face then the other. They're out.

My savior turns to me. Of course. Thank God. Thank you, God. "You okay?" I leap up and hug my best friend as tight as I can. He hugs me back. "Take that as a yes," Justin chuckles.

"How did you find me?"

"I stayed in the area. V's been watching the comms on her computer and radioed when the tracer popped up. From there I just followed the gunfire."

I release him and take a step back. "We have to find Stone."

"No, we have to get the hell out of here. This place is set to blow."

I move to the TV bank. "Not yet. Bennett Stone is the only one with the data to save Jem. And if he gets away...we'll just be delaying the inevitable. I think he's already shipped the virus too." I turn back to my friend, eyes hard. "We are *not* leaving without him."

"Okay," Justin concedes. I return to the screens. Where are you, asshole? "Guardian has been found," Justin says. "All agents move in on our position. The target Stone is active and in possession of vital Intel. Note, building is rigged to detonate and a dozen armed guards are active inside and outside the property." He listens for a second. "Good to know. Stand-by." He walks over to me. "The police are five minutes out. What about the virus?"

"I think I saw two white panel vans outside the warehouse. I can't be sure but I think the canisters are in them."

"Put out a BOLO for two white panel vans," he says into his comms. "There might be volatile biohazardous material in them."

"That's him. Monitor twelve."

Definitely Bennett. Three henchmen with guns hustle down a hall with a shorter man in the center.

"We've got incoming," Justin says, pointing to a monitor in the corner. Three more men sprint down a hallway, I assume toward us. "We have to go. Here." He removes his HEPA mask before I can protest. He could have just signed his death warrant. "They know what you look like. Put it on."

As I comply, Justin removes the guns and comms units from the unconscious men, bringing them back to me. He slips one gun into his pants waist and gives me the comms and spare clip. I put in the Bluetooth and follow my partner out of this slaughterhouse. The henchmen chatter over the radio. Number sixteen is almost done in the warehouse. Four, eight, and twelve are proceeding down corridor-C to the overseer office. Eleven reports the helicopter is three minutes out. Six, nine, and two are en route with Motoneslly. "We need to reach the helipad," I say.

The three guards round the corner, and I lower my gaze. "...shame we'll never be able to put this on the resume," I say, using my New Urbana accent. "I don't know about you but I've been saving every penny."

"Very smart of you," Justin says. "We should go out for drinks after this."

The guards walk past us with only a cursory glance.

"Only if you're buying, handsome," I say. "Need it after a day like—"

We turn the corner and cut the chatter. They don't follow, so I assume it worked. "I didn't see a helipad," Justin says. "The roofs are arched with vents and HEPA filters. It could be landing in a field. We're surrounded by one."

"Well, I am more than ready to leave this building. Let's get the fucker."

Head up, looking straight ahead, no one even pays us a second glance as we join the hurrying throng down the hall and through the lobby. Gunfire in a building set to explode has gotta make anyone run for the nearest exit. Despite the fact it's snowing again, with half an inch down already, people mill around the front parking lot, not sure what to do next. The intelligent ones climb into their identical cars, the same model Ryder stole, and begin driving down the only road to the open gate. "This is bullshit," one of the workers says. "Let's just go."

"Are we allowed?"

Justin and I break away from the crowd toward the side of the large building. Three stories high, gray as the sky, and if not for the lack of windows and giant smokestack looking cylinders with familiar HEPA filters on top, it could pass for a very long, regular office building. Not that anyone would even have cause to come out here. We're flanked by dense forest on all four sides after about a football field length of field on every side. More than enough space to land a helicopter. I scan the gray and white sky but don't see one. Shit, I should have grabbed a jacket during our escape. Not even rubbing my arms as we run along the building's perimeter helps much.

"Agents, ETA?" Justin asks to our cavalry.

Four, eight, twelve have no luck finding me, proceeding outside. Eleven reports helicopter one minute out.

"Where the fuck is it?" I ask myself, scanning the skies again.

We continue walking the perimeter and a thirty second later I hear it, the whirl of the helicopter blades. The metal bird begins descending from the gray clouds. On the other side of the building. "Shit," Justin says.

We won't make it in time. He glances at me, and I him. We read each other's minds. "We *need* the flash drives. No. Matter. What."

He quickly kisses my forehead. "Get out of here. I won't let you down."

I hand him the mask. A superhero isn't one without a mask. "I know. Go."

My friend zooms away off to stop the villain. Bennett doesn't stand a chance.

I give myself a whole second to take a deep breath and release it. Feels like I haven't had the opportunity to do that in months. But I only get the one. I run as fast as I can, my overtaxed hip aching with every step, back to the parking lot in case Justin needs ground support. I'll shadow the helicopter by car just in case. I pull out the cell phone. "Stone is attempting to leave by helicopter," I tell the 911 dispatcher. "Inform air traffic control—"

Gunshots overshadow the chop of the helicopter and my own words. My first instinct is to change course again and run after my friend. To help. But he can more than handle a few henchmen and gunshots. I won't reach him in time anyway. So though it goes against my instinct, I continue toward the parking lot. The helicopter disappears as it lands.

The gunfire continues in short bursts, I think as Justin fires back. Nothing I can do. He'll be fine. *He'll be fine.*

I finally reach the parking lot, panting like a dog, as the gunshots continue. Worse, as the helicopter rises. Just keep going, Jo. I—

Oh, fuck.

It's him. Motherfucker.

Fifty yards away. Talking to another hulking henchman. Opening the SUV's driver side door.

"He's not in the helicopter," I whisper.

Who-Who-I-I don't have comms to Justin. What...? Bennett climbs into the SUV. I'm walking his way, pressing the cell phone to my ear before his second leg gets inside. "Stone is not in the helicopter. Repeat, not in the helicopter. He's in a black Range Rover about to depart down Shadowbrooke Rd. I am in pursuit." I sprint through the parking lot toward the nearest worker getting into her car. "Excuse me." The redhead looks up at me, her eyes bugging out behind her glasses when she notices the gun in my hand. "I need your car." She whimpers as I snatch the keys from her hand. "Thank you."

The SUV begins out of the parking lot as I get in and start the car. Before I even put it into gear, the woman runs screaming toward the henchman. Nothing I can do now. *Nothing* matters but catching the bastard. He continues driving down the road at a normal, cautious speed with snow on the ground until the gunshots begin again, this time directed at us. He—

The back window explodes, and I can't help but shriek. As I lose a precious second focusing on the fact I'm under fire, the SUV speeds up. Shit. More gunfire and I lose another second. The front window cracks as the bullet passes through. Fuck this.

Pedal to the metal.

Bennett's got a small lead growing by the moment. Not for long, asshole. By the time we reach the gate, he's only a hundred feet ahead. Ninety. Eighty. You are not getting away. *You're not.* You're—

We round a turn, and my car hydroplanes. I turn the wheel to gain control, losing precious time. Back to ninety feet. Fucking snow. I roll down the window and fire at him. Not even close. He must switch gears because ninety feet becomes hundred. One ten. Shit. I haven't been in a car chase since Ryder escaped. If only I'd caught him that night. If I hasn't failed. Rebecca. Daisy. Justin. Me. I *will not* fail now. Not tonight.

Bennett takes the corner and luck finally finds me. His back tire veers left and right, almost driving off the road. I take the turn with care as he attempts to gain control. Eighty. Seventy. Turn cleared, I floor it again. Sixty. Fifty. Bennett's hand comes out his window holding a gun. He fires, twice, missing me. I grip the steering wheel hard enough it hurts. My heart, my mind, the whole of me runs on adrenaline. I barely exist inside myself. I am nothing but that righteous purpose. I will not fail.

Another curve in the road ahead. As if God himself speaks to me, I know what must be done. The exact degree of the curve. The precise speed needed. The slight incline of the ground right before the curve. My mind crunches the numbers. The physics and machinations of an SUV vs. a small Sedan. All laid out before me. I grip the wheel with the strength of Hercules. I will not fail.

Bennett decelerates at the curve only ten miles per hour, but that's all I require. The second he reaches it, I gun this beast for every mph she can muster. *Now*. The moment I hit that off-road incline the natural order of the universe takes the wheel. A vague notion of fear enters my brain as I lift off the ground, but I don't *feel* it. My brain enters a protective cocoon to shield me from the trauma of what occurs the next moment. As my car smashes into his with the force of a meteor impact. As I'm flung forward and backward at almost the same second, metal and glass shattering and tearing around me. I'm aware of my arms shielding my face and head from the airbag and debris then the pure torture in my left arm and forehead. Of the car landing back on the asphalt and this broken machine skidding left, right, in a circle. Of my lizard brain forcing my arm to grab the wild wheel and press on the breaks. Of Bennett's SUV flipping before zooming toward the forest. My car skids to a stop for what seems like three hours but can only be three seconds later. I'm stopped. I'm—

Fuck!

Pain. Arm. Head. Neck. Chest. Hip. Cheeks. That cuts through the fog first. What…? Something hot running down my forehead from the source of the pain. I move my left arm to touch the hot, but pure agony radiates from that appendage. I think I scream. Fuck. *Fuck*. More seconds pass, just me and the pain, before I can focus again. The mission. Keep going, Jo. I will not fail.

Using my good arm, I unbuckle my seatbelt and open the door. Keep going, Jo. My whole body protests as I climb out of the demolished car. My legs won't support me at first. My knees buckle and I fall to the snow. Fuck. I close my eyes and take a painful, deep breath. "Get up, bitch. *Get up*."

Gritting my teeth, I use my good arm and the car to help me rise. "Don't do that again. *Don't*."

Okay. Okay. I wipe the blood from my eye and begin to survey the site. Tire marks to the trees. Broken limbs. Smoke billowing into the gray sky. Bennett. "One foot in front of the other, Jo. One step at a time. You can do this. You will not fail. *Go*." The first step is the hardest. My ribs, my head, even my shredded legs and hip protest the movement so much I fear I'll throw up again. The second isn't much better. "Keep going, Jo. Just keep going." Third. Fourth.

Keep going.

I somehow make it to the tree line, over the shattered branches, and seven steps in I see it down the slight hill. The SUV. The front is a smoking accordion with a large branch staked through the windshield. He must have hit at top speed. That's what happens when an unstoppable force meets an immovable object. You can't fight the natural order. I can't see Bennett through his shattered side window. He has to be in there. He *has* to.

I limp to the wreck, leaving drips of blood like bread crumbs the whole way. The reek of gasoline assails my nose. It's gonna blow. "Pick up the pace. Go." I use my last bit of adrenaline and drive to make the rest of the trek to the SUV. "Please, please, please…"

I open the door and my prayers are answered. He's here.

Bennett sits upright, face and head a bleeding mess, but the worst is the downward branch impaling his right abdomen. Smoke wafts through the almost disintegrated windshield but he doesn't move or stir. For a moment, a flash of regret and sadness echoes through me. Not for this man, but the Bennett Stone I laughed with. Who helped me through the most difficult time in my life. Who gave my life new purpose and a path, even if it was built on lies. He was my friend. He was. And I'll miss him. But the moment passes. That man's dead, and this monster is still alive. For now.

Flash drives. Get the flash drives. I reach into his left hand pockets but nothing. He still doesn't wake. I'm going to have to do this. I get in so close I could kiss him. He's still alive. Still breathing right on my head. They're not in the right cardigan pocket. Not in his right overcoat. Oh, please. Please…I feel them. Right pants pocket. His blood pours out over my hands as I reach in and remove them. Thank—

"Joanna."

His voice startles me. I gasp and look up. He stares down at me, nose dripping blood on my head. I meet his pained, teary eyes. That's when I feel it. Something hard pointed against my chest. I glance down. A gun. I look back up to find a sad smile on his face.

"I really did have the best of intentions, you know," he whispers. "The suffering…if I could save one person from enduring what I did…worth it. It *is* the right thing, Jo. The way it *should* be. Why can't you see that? Why? If anyone should…"

"Bennett…" I whimper.

"It's not too late, gorgeous," he whispers, tears falling. Eyes pleading. "Don't make me do this, Jo. I don't want to do this. Not to you. Just let it go. Leave it. Walk away from this one. It's not your fight. You don't owe them anything. You've given enough. *They* are not worth it. Just…let go. Please, gorgeous. *Please.*"

I stare into his agonized, tear filled, heartbroken eyes and just shake my head. "If you truly think I would ever, *ever* do that…you never knew me at all."

Flash drives clutched in my fist, I move away from my friend.

Bang!

I hear the shot before I feel a thing. It isn't until I'm standing that the pressure begins. The pain. Before I gaze down and see the growing red bloom in my chest. Huh. I stagger backwards as the realization I've been shot finally dawns on me.

"Goddamn you, Joanna Fallon," Bennett cries disappointedly. He raises the gun again. "Goddamn—"

The explosion sends me literally flying backwards several feet. I register the heat, the light, the force, my airless state, then the fall. I land on my back, the air knocking out of me. I stare up at the gray sky as the snowflakes dance down and melt on my face for seconds. Hours? I don't know. Nothing and everything hurts. Pressure on my chest like the weight of the world. I'm so cold. I think this is shock. Maybe I've been in shock this whole time. The human body's a marvel. Did Pop feel like this when he was shot? He must have. Oh, Pop. I hope I've made you proud.

"Joanna!"

That's my name. That's my best friend standing over me. Falling to his knees. My Justin. He's here. Thank you God for this man. "Hi," I whisper.

Justin surveys me, beautiful blue eyes growing in horror as he studies me. "Lexie! G-Go flag down the ambulance! Now!" he roars. "Hurry!"

Lexie's here. I can't move to look at her, but she's here. My friend. She better forgive Jem. He's gonna need her now.

My own best friend rips off his mask and stupid lab coat, draping it over me. "You're going to be okay, Jo. You're gonna be okay."

"Y-You always were a good liar," I whisper. Ow. The pressure's becoming pain. My chest hurts. I-I have to…I force my hand open. I didn't lose them. "W-We're even now."

"What?"

"I-I…did it. I saved you. I saved you, rich boy," I begin to cry.

Justin takes my hand, lifting it to his lips to kiss. "Oh, Jo."

Oh, not yet. The spots begin. The light. The darkness. So much still to say. "I-I love you, you know. Always have. Always will. I-I'm so sorry—"

He squeezes my hand so tight I almost forget all the other pain. "No. *No.* Don't you *dare* say good-bye. You are *not* giving up on me. That's not who you are. You are Joanna Fucking Fallon. You are the bravest, strongest person I've ever met. You are a fighter."

The darkness. Oblivion. It's coming. "I love you, Justin."

"*Fight*," Justin says suddenly far away. "Keep fighting. For me. For Jem. For *you*. Fight, Jo." Farther away. "You've never let me down before, don't start now. Fight." Farther. "Fight." Blacker. "Don't give up." Going. "Don't leave me, Jo. I love you."

Fight…

I don't have any left in me.

Gone.

*

I've always liked this bridge. Even when the sun isn't shining, when the sky isn't blue as the ocean like it is now, it draws me in like a beacon. To this day I have no idea why. Perhaps because I enjoy duality. Extremes. Look left and behold the wonder of nature. Forest. River. Sea. The Falls of Galilee roaring like a tempest until the end of the universe. Turn right and see all man has accomplished. Buildings touching the sky. Commerce. Community. Progress. And here I stand in the middle of both worlds. Inside and outside them both. Grounded yet up in the air. And I stand at its precipice. On the edge.

The water below calls to me. One step. A leap. Part of me knows it's not safe here. That I should know better than to stand here and take the leap. But the water, the calm dark water is so peaceful. Comforting. And I'm so tired. *So* tired. I don't even think if I have the strength to stay on my feet. I don't know if I even want to anymore. I can just…let go.

Joanna…

"Hello."

Oh, I thought I was the only one drawn to this specific point in the universe. I'm glad I'm not. I don't want to be alone. I've been alone so long.

A girl steps beside me. My God, she can't be more than twelve. Nowhere near beautiful but pretty. Large blue eyes. Pale white skin. A crown of black mops in desperate need of brushing. Everything about her cries out in need. Of loss. Of abandonment. Of anger. Of determination.

"Hey," she says again.

"Wh-What are you doing here?" I ask.

"I'm here for you," she replies.

"No. Y-You shouldn't be here. It's not safe. You can fall."

Joanna…

She slips her hand in mine. "You fall…I fall."

This isn't right. I can't… "No. I don't…" I stare down at the water. "I don't think I can hold on much longer. You need to go, sweetheart."

"No."

Joanna…

"Wh-Who is that?"

"Justin."

Joanna…

"Jem."

Joanna…

"Harry."

Joanna…

"V."

Joanna…

"They're there. Waiting for you. You just have to make a choice. You can let go."

The water's so close now. So inviting. Easy. I've done enough.

"You can give up. No more pain. No more sadness. No more fighting."

Joanna…please. I need you, my love. Please.

"Or you can be the fighter. The survivor. The hero I know you are."

"Because we're alike," a man says. I look up and find *him*. Not the girl anymore, but my soul mate. Holding my hand. Smiling at me as he has a million times before. "Because as long as I have you, I can survive anything. And if that's true for me, then it's true for you. Because we're the same. I trust you, and I love you." He raises his free hand to cup my cheek. "And shame on you if you throw that away."

"*Joanna.*"

I glance back and they're all there against the gray sky. V. Lucy. Dobbs. Cam. Lexie. Harry. Jem. The love of my life stands in the center with a huge grin on his face and tears of joy in his eyes. My Jem.

"I don't think I have the strength," I whisper.

Justin squeezes my hand tighter. "Then I'll help you. That's what I'm here for. Forever and always."

He takes a step toward them. "The first step is the hardest," he says.

The water calls to me again. So inviting. So freeing.

"What if everything is horrible again? I step forward and there will be pain. Fear. Betrayal. Hate. Insecurity."

"Yes, but also joy. Beauty. Goodness. Laughter. And above all...love."

Jem extends his hand to me.

I glance over at Justin who grins. "*Worth it.*"

I look straight ahead at Jem. "A million nights..." he says.

"And a million more," I finish in a whisper.

"A promise is a promise," Jem says. "Come back to me and keep yours. Because that's who you are. My fierce warrior. My hero."

"One step," Justin says. "Fight. For him. For me. *Fight.*"

I close my eyes. Fight. Fight.

Fight.

I take the step away from the abyss.

CHAPTER TWENTY

WHO WE ARE

I cannot believe I'm late for my own damn wedding. Everyone's gonna kill me. And dying once this year was more than enough, thank you very much.

Justin and I hustle through the garden of Austen Castle toward the labyrinth, not easy in heels and wedding gown. The sacrifices I make for the love of my life. This is what I get for marrying a romantic traditionalist. Heels, an hour in make-up and hair, satin and lace dress, flowing veil. And white. We've been living together over a year. We're not fooling anyone.

"I called Lucy when you were in the bathroom," Justin says. "She'll tell everyone. And nobody expects a wedding to start on time anyway."

We reach the labyrinth's arched opening and of course my ankle chooses now to almost give out on me. I totter but Justin grabs my arm to steady me. "Okay, we're slowing down now. Don't want you limping down the aisle."

"Fucking heels. Fucking...veil!" That stupid thing keeps blowing in my face. I swat it into submission.

Justin chuckles. "You know, most brides are actually happy on their wedding day."

"I'm happy," I snap. "I'd just be happier at a Justice of the Peace."

Justin holds out his arm. "Too late now. Shall we?"

I lock my arm in his. He nods at the wedding planner. She's done an amazing job today. I hired her after she proved herself with The Guardian Society gala two months ago. We raised a million dollars that night alone. Enough to fund the counseling center in Independence. My baby's growing strong. Hope she'll be okay for the next two weeks when I'm on my honeymoon.

As the planner radios to the party, Justin leads me into the labyrinth. Wedding. Focus on the wedding. We walk down the rows in silence for a few seconds before he starts shaking his head. "What?"

"Nothing. Just…Joanna Fallon, getting married. Never thought I'd live to see the day."

The scar on my chest suddenly throbs. "We almost didn't."

To think, seven months ago, I died. Really. When I was in surgery, I coded. For two minutes I was legally dead. Turns out it was Bennett Stone who finally broke my heart. They had to crack my chest and manually massage my heart back to life. I was in a coma after the surgery for two days and doped out of my mind on painkillers for a week after that. I now have a new scar running down the length of my abdomen. The dress covers it. I was stuck in the hospital for three weeks, but at least I had a cute roommate for the second week. It took Dr. Sharpesh almost a week to create the adenovirus, and by then Jem was on life support. Good thing I was doped up or I probably would have given up again. But a day after he received the cure, his body began healing itself. By day three the only indication anything happened were dark circles under his eyes. I've actually taken steps to ensure Dr. Sharpesh is up for a Nobel Prize.

The others got away intact too. Harry, Devitt, all the rest all made full recoveries. And were the only cases. While I was dying in surgery my army located the canisters before they shipped. There've been over a hundred arrests worldwide, including Dr. Frankenstein DeRue and Goliath is all but bankrupt. Stopped a plague, brought down an evil corporation, and saved my fiancée. Not bad for a kid from Diablo's Ward.

"But we did," I continue.

"And now you're getting married." He shakes his head. "Did you ever think you'd be the one to do it first?"

"Honestly, I thought we'd be getting married at the same time."

Justin hangs his head. "We never…really talked about that, did we?"

"We got busy. You died, came back, then *I* died. Now I'm marrying the sweetest, dorkiest, most brilliant man on the planet. This is how it was meant to be. The rest just got us here. The road was long, it was usually dark as night, but no matter how many twists and turns, as long as we never gave up, the path would take us right where we're supposed to go. Right here."

We smile at one another, as brightly as the sun shining above. "And there's nobody I'm prouder to walk this path with than you, Joanna Fallon," Justin says.

"Well, as the smartest man alive reminded me, there is no Joanna Fallon without Justin Pendergast."

He lifts up my hand to his lips. "You got that the wrong way around, my friend."

We smile at one another again, the pure joy radiating from that mystical place we're joined forever. And we continue down our path to the very heart where all our loved ones wait to celebrate love. Where V stands with her parents and brothers, all smiling. Where Lucy and Dobbs dab tears. Where Harry stands beside his wife holding his newborn son and making funny faces at him. Where Lexie stands in a tuxedo winking at me from her spot as best man. And where the man who taught me about the greatest force in the universe, true love, meets my smiling eyes with his tear filled ones, gazing at me as if I were a miracle. As if I were the only person in the universe.

Yes, it was worth it. Every stumble. Every fall. Because it shows us we can rise. That we *will* rise.

Because that's just who we are. Each and every one of us.

THE END

ACKNOWLEDGMENTS

First, to all of you who write, Tweet, review, even send me presents. I have the best fans ever. Thank you.

Thanks to my Betas: Susan Dowis, Ginny Dowis, and Jill Kardell for their corrections. Any mistakes are mine and mine alone.

Thanks to the Peachtree City library for being a wonderful place to write and edit.

Finally to all the wonderful comic book writers who came before and currently write in the medium. You have inspired me more than I can say. Keep up the excellent, fantastic work.

ABOUT THE AUTHOR

Jennifer Harlow spent her restless childhood fighting with her three brothers and scaring the heck out of herself with horror movies and books. She grew up to earn a degree at the University of Virginia which she put to use as a radio DJ, crisis hotline volunteer, bookseller, lab assistant, wedding coordinator, and government investigator. Currently she calls Atlanta home but that restless itch is ever present. In her free time, she continues to scare the beejepers out of herself watching scary movies and opening her credit card bills. She is the author of the Amazon best-selling F.R.E.A.K.S. Squad, Midnight Magic Mystery series, The Galilee Falls Trilogy, and the steampunk romance *Verity Hart Vs The Vampyres*.

For the soundtrack to her books and other goodies visit her at www.jenniferharlowbooks.com